The Listener

by

Frances Gaudiano

For Carol, who always believed in my dreams.

ARGUS

When wise Ulysses, from his native coast
Long kept by wars, and long by tempest tost,
Arrived at last – poor, old, disguised, alone,
To all his friends and ev'n his queen unknown,
Changed as he was, with age, and toils, and cares,
Furrowed his rev'rend face, and white his hairs,
In his own palace forced to ask his bread,
Scorned by slaves his former bounty fed,
Forgot of all his own domestic crew,
His faithful dog his rightful master knew!
Unfed, unhoused, neglected, on the clay,
Like an old servant, now cashiered, he lay.
And though ev'n then expiring on the plain,
Touched with resentment of ungrateful man,
And longing to behold his ancient lord again.
Him when he saw, he rose, and crawled to meet,
('Twas all he could), and fawned, and kissed his feet,
Seized with dumb joy; then falling by his side,
Owned his returning lord, looked up, and died.

Alexander Pope

GLOSSARY OF GAELIC*, IRISH SLANG, TOWNS, AND A BIT OF FARMING TERMINOLOGY

*Irish Gaelic words appear in italics.

Acushla – darling (literally, 'pulse of my heart')
Airmid – an Irish mythological figure that gathered herbs from the dead body of her brother. These were all the herbs of the world that could be used for healing.
Anamachara – soul mate
Arse – derogatory term for one's behind, also an insult.
Ardara – a market town in Donegal, Ireland.
Asthóre – treasure (an endearment)
Babby – baby
Bad cess – a curse of bad luck upon a person
Ballybofey – a town in County Donegal, Ireland
Bán – white
Brawn – strong
Cailín – girl
Conall Cearnach – a heroic warrior of Ulster in Irish mythology
Capall – horse
Céilidh – traditional Irish gathering involving music and dancing
Cottier – the term for tenant farmers that lived in basic cabins and worked small parcels of land.
Craic – good fun
Culchie – derogatory term for a country person
Da – father
Dagging – removing the soiled wool around a sheep's backside. This prevents flies laying eggs in faeces encrusted in the wool.
Divil – country dialect for 'devil'
Eala – swan
Eejit – fool/idiot (Buck eejit – an even worse fool)

Firbolg – an ancient race of wise giants who were believed to inhabit Ireland in the old days.
Git – ridiculously stupid person
Girseach - girl
Gob - mouth
Glenties – a town in Donegal, Ireland
Goal – jail
Gombeen – man of shady character
Grá mo chroí – love of my heart
Whist – Silence!
Jaysus- a common oath, derivative of 'Jesus.'
Leanbh- child (*a leanbh* – my child)
Letterkenny - a large town in Donegal, Ireland
Maghera – a beach and caves in Donegal, Ireland
Mo mhuirín di lis – my one true love
Morrigan – a Celtic goddess often associated with death.
Mavoureen/ mo mhuirín – darling
Peelers – derogatory term for police
Póg mo thóin – Kiss my arse.
Quare – a bit odd or unusual
Selkie – a woman who takes on the shape of a seal (Scottish mythology)
Skirtle – the action of a dog crawling forward on its belly
Smoor - a Celtic term for arranging the coals from a night-time fire so that the fire could be easily relit in the morning.
Stocious – very drunk
Storeen/ mo stoirín – darling
Strabane – a town in Northern Ireland (Ulster)
Stramash – an upheaval with much shouting and disturbance
Tuatha Dé Danann – a mythical race with great magical abilities. They were believed to have settled in Ireland, overthrowing the Firbolgs.
Wean – child.

Contents

Part One: Fire

Part Two: Air

Contents

INTRODUCTION

I believe everyone who loves animals wishes they could communicate with them. How wonderful it would be to place your hand on an animal and know its feelings and concerns. Working in the veterinary profession, this wish becomes almost overwhelming. If only they could tell us what is wrong!

And yet, there have been times when I have sat quietly with an animal and have felt it speaking to me. There was a very, tired old cat who clearly told me it was time for him to go and a dog who was sick of the pain and indignity and made clear her wishes. If only we listen carefully, sometimes we can hear them.

Fiona, the protagonist of this story has the gift of listening and can use that gift for good or evil. Unfortunately, it places her with one foot in the world of animals and one in the world of man. That is not an easy place to be. Coupling that with her time in history, the late 19th century in Ireland, her journey is not a smooth one. Women had little power in that period and poor women even less. The tumult of 'the Anglo-Irish troubles' was brewing but that was not the concern of the most deprived citizens. They were just hoping for a dry place to live and enough food to make it through the winter. In many ways, their needs were not much different from the needs of their livestock.

Not that long ago we were happy to rely on the plants of the fields and hedgerows to provide us with healing. Over time, that knowledge became unfashionable, and people lost the ability to help keep their families healthy by using the pharmaceutical agents of their local vegetation.

This skill is only being re-examined in current times. While the remedies used in this book are based on fact, if you are considering trying some of them yourselves, I strongly recommend seeing a herbalist, or using a herbal textbook. Fiona came from a line of healers and even she had to learn the difference between the benign and the poisonous.

Regarding the dogs in this book, Farley is modelled on the popular breed of Border Terriers. These terriers are affectionate and loving companions and are often too smart for their own good. They do not live to please, as some breeds do, but live to please themselves. All the same, they are the best dogs in the world. Bassett Griffons are also wonderful canines and are indeed, usually, gentle, soft-mouthed, and easy going. They do have beautiful baritone voices, in fact, one sang a lovely solo at my wedding.

The poems and songs used in this novel had been published by the late 19th century and are presented as they appeared in established texts. The place names reflect actual towns and villages in Donegal and Northern Ireland. Any names of people are completely arbitrary and do not resemble any persons, living or dead.

Part One: Fire

Warming hearth and lightning strike,
Wake my heart and fill my life.

Maghera, County Donegal
Ireland
Late 19th Century

A MOTHER AND A SWAN

When one is young, you look at your parents and wonder at their foolish decisions. Why did she marry that oaf? Why have they chosen to stay in this conservative village? Why is he doing a job that he hates? The young look at the old, shaking their heads in disbelief. Surely, this new generation will never make such silly mistakes. How wonderful to be beginning your life and think that you will actually have control over where destiny will take you.

Eala woke Fiona with a tickle and Fiona pulled the quilt higher over her head muttering at her mother to go away. It was too cold to get up this morning. The air was frigid and when she finally poked her head out her breath made a cloud of fog. However, she could smell porridge and Eala whispered that there might be some honey left. Fiona's stomach growled in anticipation, motivating her to crawl out of her nest and hop over to the chair nearest the fire. Fiona's grandmother, Nan, must have risen much earlier to stir the embers and put some oats on as she was already out with her goats, doing the milking. Eala placed a bowl of porridge on the table and doled out some of the precious honey. She also offered Fiona a cup of goat's milk from the pitcher on the shelf. Hunger drove the child to eat quickly while Eala ran a comb through Fiona's chestnut hair, plaiting it out of the child's way.

"How come my hair isn't like yours or Nan's?" Fiona asked, taking hold of the dark plait that hung over her shoulder.

Her mother smiled, "You know that love. You haven't bonded with your creature yet. Your nan and I both have white acolytes, so we have white-blond hair. You will too if you bond with a white animal."

"I want to be like you!" the child insisted, tugging at her plait in dislike.

"Soon, Fiona. Your nan and I have been talking. She thinks it might be easier for you to bond strongly with something we can keep a little bit closer to home than my Ban."

"Don't you have a strong bond with your swan?" Fiona asked frowning. It would be horrible to have an acolyte and not be able to be with it every day.

Her mother looked out the small window towards the loch. "Our bond is very strong," she sighed. "That's why it's so hard, so very hard to be apart so much."

"I guess that's why we have to go to the loch all the time," Fiona said glumly.

It was a grey day, no rain yet but the wind was biting and coming from the north, definitely not the weather for a visit to the water. Yet, Eala had to go, and Fiona had to go with her, so Fiona walked obediently behind her mother, though as slowly as she dared, to let her mother know her reluctance. Eala visited the loch daily once the swans had made their migration from farther north. Sometimes Eala's friend Ban stayed through migration, if there was food enough to share but often, he had to make the flight.

Eala had her way of talking with Ban and sometimes he came ashore and sat with them, Eala would stroke the feathers along his back and he, in turn would lean his long neck across her shoulders. On warmer days, Eala stepped through the reeds and her swan would glide up to her. She would rest her hand on his wing and listen. Fiona

2

had seen the swan dip his head to the side and lean into Eala as if he was whispering into her ear, and she would smile and stroke his long neck. When Eala finally left the loch, she would turn slowly towards the shore, as if unwilling; always stopping to look back, seeking contact once more with her swan.

Fiona's nan had a billy goat that followed her about. Fiona thought Billy was a much better friend because you didn't have to get wet and cold to play with him. She liked Billy and occasionally he would play a bit of a chase game with her. Once Eala had bought her a toy ball and she had tossed it to Billy, who kicked it back repeatedly, until the ball popped and was no more a plaything. Eala's friend, Ban, didn't like playing though. Mostly, he ignored Fiona and once or twice had even hissed at her, as if she were a nuisance.

No, Fiona definitely did not care for Ban and was not over enthusiastic about these frequent visits to the loch. She didn't even like water that much; she felt she had enough of being wet with all the rain. Eala had tried to make the visits pleasurable. She had taught Fiona to swim, a rare skill in a young Irish lass but essential, especially for a child who spent so much of her free time at the water's edge. Unfortunately, Ban always seemed to visit at the coldest time of the year when it would have been far more enjoyable to be sitting by the fire in the cabin, or at least running through the fields with the goats. Running kept you warm. Swimming was well enough in the summer but wading about on a muddy shore in the winter just seemed like some sort of punishment.

When they arrived at the loch, Eala let out a flat 'hoo' sound to call Ban to her. He streamed towards them, around a bed of reeds, and Eala waded out to him, reaching for him, as he craned his long neck towards her. There was an embrace between the swan and the woman, almost embarrassing to witness in its intimacy, and then Eala turned to Fiona.

"Come *a leanbh,* say hello to Ban!" Fiona stood on the shore, staring. She wrapped her shawl tightly around herself and with her toes, prodded at a stone in the mud. Her feet were already freezing, and she didn't want to say hello to Ban. If it weren't for him, they could be home now in the warm, sorting the herbs or helping Nan with the goats. Why did Ban mostly visit in the winter, and why could he never come up to the cabin? Why did they always have to trudge down to the freezing loch and visit him? He always got his way. It wasn't fair Fiona decided. Her mam should pay more attention to her, not some big bird. Fiona pushed out her bottom lip and shook her head defiantly. No to Ban. If Eala wanted her, she could come back and get her.

Eala sighed and lifting her skirts, stepped along the banks of the loch to Fiona.

"Please little one, I want you to be friends with him. It's important Fiona," but Fiona sat down solidly on the ground. Eala shrugged and then scooped up her daughter. Resting her on one hip, she strode out to the swan on the loch. The child and the swan eyed each other. They both wanted the same thing and one of them was going to lose.

Struggling to be let down, Fiona was taken to the shore where her mother placed her gently on the ground. For the rest of her life, Fiona would remember standing on the edge of the loch watching her mother drift away.

She would remember her throat, torn sore from calling and calling but Eala never turned back, and then the screaming sobs, subsiding into hopelessness as she realised that Ban had won.

It was drawing on towards evening and Eala had not returned with the child. Nanny sighed and wiped her hands on her apron. She had just finished corralling the goats for the night and was thinking about what she could prepare for supper but first, she would have to go look for the pair. Eala spent far too much time down at the loch. Nan understood that it was difficult with Eala's acolyte being a water bird but a bit of extra help with the goats and the cheese would not be unappreciated. Besides, it was clear that the child would not be linked with a bird. Fiona was comfortable with the goats but had shown an obvious dislike to the swan. It was probably going to be some domestic animal. Nan thought it would be wise to choose something that would be easy for the child to bond with and stay nearer home. It was regrettable that Eala had bonded with a swan, if not downright inconvenient. Something that could live indoors would be much less complicated. Maybe Fiona would bond with a dog or a cat, even a songbird could spend some time indoors. No, not a bird. The child would forever be up trees and again be of no use around the small holding, and ideally not a cat, as she'd be slipping out every night and getting up to all sorts of trouble. Let it be a dog. Yes, a dog would fit nicely. Nan would start watching the local bitches an look for a pup for Fiona to bond with.

After putting away the milk, Nan threw a shawl over her shoulders and trudged down to the lake. It was nearly dark, and the child would be starving. By the time she got to the loch, the moon

5

was beginning to rise, illuminating the lake with a rare beam of moonlight – there were so few clear nights at this time of year. Close to the shore, Nan could make out a swan gliding past, no, not one, but a pair. Nan's heart stopped cold. A pair. She began to run, shouting out, "Eala!!" One of the swans paused, turning its expressive neck to look at her. Then both swans took wing and flew away.

Nan found Fiona curled up at the edge of the loch, shaking from the cold and weeping weakly. The child was limp from hysterical crying and had screamed herself hoarse. Nan sunk to her knees beside Fiona and stroked her back.

"I'm ever so sorry *girseach*, I'm ever so sorry," and taking the little girl into her lap, she rocked her, and they wept together.

Fiona has been quiet since her mother's departure, rarely prattling as she had done previously and often gazing off towards the loch. Nan worried that she may be rushing things, but it seemed best for Fiona if she was found an acolyte sooner rather than later. There was a litter of pups down at the Nugent cottage. Nan wrapped some cheese in a piece of muslin and took Fiona by the hand, explaining that they were going to look at some pups. Nan tugged gently on the child's hand, and they walked out of the cottage, settling the door on the latch. Passing the goat pen, Nan went up to one of the nanny's and laid her hand on the goat's neck, letting her know that they were going out but would be back soon. Raising her other hand towards the rocks above the holding she signalled for Billy to look out for the nannies. He dipped his head in assent and began leap frogging down the rocks towards the pens.

Nan looked sideways at the mute child walking beside her. "Do you think you like dogs?"

Fiona looked up and shrugged, then bitterly,

"Better than swans." Nan snorted at the reply.

"I'd have to agree with you there. Swans are too much in the wet and cold. Now, a nice pup will curl up by the fire and keep your feet warm. Dogs are a good sort of creature. They can follow you anywhere. You know I love Billy dearly, but I could never have him in the house, all those hooves and horns destroying the place. No, there's nothing quite so good company as a dog. Better even than a cat, though that's quite a useful creature as well." Fiona stared at her grandmother. She rarely extended herself to such a monologue. Why was Nan trying to convince her? Sure, a dog would be fine, or not. Nothing really seemed to matter that much right now. She stamped her foot into a puddle in the road and relished the mud slapping up around her leg. She should have regretted her naughty behaviour, muddying her dress, the only one she had, but she decided she didn't regret it, she just didn't care. Nan pursed her lips but said nothing.

Fiona wondered what it would feel like to wear shoes. When they'd gone to market in Ardara, she'd seen some well-off people wearing shoes. It looked terribly uncomfortable to have one's foot all squished up in a bag of leather. Perhaps they made your feet warmer though. Maybe that is why people put up with them. Well, she'd never know. Nan and her, had calloused feet, that were hard from walking barefoot in all weathers. It would just be a waste to spend money on shoes when it could be spent on food.

The Nugent holding was down the hill, closer to the village and the sea. Fiona thought she could hear the waves. She'd been to the sea to collect seaweed when they'd run out of cabbage. She liked playing in the sand and listening to the crash of the waves. Her mother had found her a beautiful seashell which Fiona had safe on the shelf above the stove. She wished they lived closer to the sea, but the goats were happier up in the hills and the goats were their livelihood, that, and Nan's healings.

As they approached the Nugent place, a dog came racing out barking furiously. They stopped until Mr. Nugent came out, shouting,

"Bloody cur, get yourself inside, you feckin," he stopped himself when he spotted Nan and Fiona. "Pardon ladies," he aimed a kick at the dog, which jumped away avoiding the foot.

"I heard you had some pups Mr. Nugent," Nan began the negotiations.

Mr Nugent eyed them speculatively,

"I heard the child's mam's gone missing. I'm sorry for that."

Fiona looked up sharply. How did he know? It was her private business! It was awful to think of the village all knowing her mother had left her. The shame – as if she wasn't worth staying for. She turned angrily to Nan; had she been gossiping?

Nan sighed.

"Word gets around."

"So, you're looking for a wee pup to cheer the lassie up then? Sure, why not. Children love dogs, don't they." He smiled greedily at Nan.

8

Damn, he was going to strike a hard bargain now. Sometimes a farmer meant to drown the litter and were happy to give away a pup, but she had brought the cheese just in case. She should have remembered the mean nature of the Nugents. The number of times they'd given her an egg, or nothing, for a remedy she'd passed on to them. Well, she could play the game just as well.

"I hear your lad has had a cough this long time. I could drop by some tea and perhaps some leaves for a poultice. I am sure your wife would be glad to see the young one recover. He's your only boy, isn't he?" She didn't add, 'living,' but she knew the Nugents had buried three little ones in as many years. She saw she had hit the mark when Nugent nodded grimly.

"That would be grand and much appreciated." He indicated towards a topple-down shed near the cottage. "The pups are this way."

The stench of urine and faeces was strong in the shed and Fiona wrinkled her nose. They never left their goats to sleep in their own mess. Mr. Nugent obviously wasn't over fond of his dogs. In the dim light she could just make out a small terrier bitch in the corner, sitting up now and growling at them. Three pups reached up to her teats, pulling at her and yipping excitedly.

"There's the bitch, so. You saw the dog when you came in. He's probably gone off ratting. Great ratters they both are. You couldn't find better, but she does have a temper on her. Not too close or she'll have the hand off you, especially with her whelps by her. I'd have drowned them if I could have got them off her," he remarked, forgetting that he was trying to get a good price for one of the pups. "Not sure, how you're going to take a look and pick one. Perhaps, I could throw a sack over her head and grab out one of the pups."

"That won't be necessary," Nan answered, squatting down into the filthy straw. Fiona watched as Nan gazed at the dam and her litter. She'd seen Nan do this before. She looked like she was just resting but she was thinking very hard. Fiona remembered a farmer passing them on the road with his wagon. Suddenly, his horse had shied at some washing that had flown off a hedge. The farmer had gotten down from the wagon to settle the horse, but it continued to snort and roll its eyes. Nan had stood totally still, breathing deeply, and staring just past the horse's ears. In a few moments, the horse quieted, and Nan gave a small smile and turning to Fiona, whispered, "That's how it's done child."

The bitch had stopped growling, so Fiona took one step forward, just past Nan. One of the pups tumbled free, falling off the teat and rolled towards Fiona. She stood perfectly still, trying to breathe quietly as Nan was doing. The pup noticed Fiona then and pranced up to her, attacking her feet. Fiona stood her ground. Then the pup began to lick her toes and Fiona started to vibrate with giggles.

"Go ahead *a leanbh*," Nan murmured. Slowly, Fiona crouched down and let her hands dangle towards the small creature. It took one of her fingers and nipped it sharply. She gasped but did not move. Then, as if making a decision, the pup sat down conclusively on her foot. Fiona bent over and scooped the bundle of fur into her arms, avoiding the enthusiastic tongue, as it searched her face for food.

Mr. Nugent raised his eyebrows but made no remark. Everyone knew the old woman had some sort of strange powers, especially with animals. He couldn't care less so long as he was rid of one of the pups and got something in return. Oh, his wife would make remarks, but she would use the remedy all the same. It wasn't as if they could afford to call in a doctor; even a witch's potions were better than nothing.

"That's decided then," Nugent turned, noting that the bitch had curled back around the remaining pups without so much as a growl in the direction of the young lass. He supposed the bitch would be happy to be free of the burdensome little things. He'd probably have to drown the other two when he could get near enough to them. He needed the bitch back working at killing vermin and keeping strangers off the bit of land he worked. Times were hard and he couldn't keep an eye out everywhere.

Nan handed Nugent the large portion of cheese she had carried under her shawl.

"I'll be back tomorrow with some remedies for the lad." She cocked her head and looked sharply at Nugent. "You know where I am if you ever need recipes."

"Ah yes," he muttered. The damn woman had read his mind of course, hearing his thoughts about her being a witch. Well, what of it? She didn't deny it, and although she always called herself a healer and some called her 'wise woman,' or 'cunning woman' she was a witch and the priest had warned them off. Yet, the priest hadn't given them the coppers needed to see a doctor so Nan was the best they could do and, she did well enough. Tainted or no, her cures often worked. He rubbed his raspy chin awkwardly.

"Well then, we'll be seeing you. Hope the *cailín* is happy with the pup," but that didn't need

11

saying. Already, Fiona had looked into the deep, chocolate eyes and been lost forever. Nan smiled. A dog had been a good choice. With the pup by her side constantly, Fiona would build an excellent, strong bond, learning the listening craft in no time. And the child would have no time to fret about a lost mother who'd chosen a swan over her own daughter.

That night, Farley, as she named him, crawled up next to Fiona, in the bed she shared with her nan. He snuggled under the blankets and laid his head alongside Fiona's, blowing warm, milky breath into her face. She giggled and put her arms around the dog, pulling him close. His warmth was welcome. She had watched Nan touch a goat and close her eyes, listening. Fiona would learn to do this too with Farley, but not tonight. Tonight, he was just a puppy.

MARKET DAYS

It was not a long walk to the town, Ardara, it being only five miles or so but with the heavy cheeses to sell and a small workbench to carry, it felt like an arduous journey. Nan didn't like leaving the goats but found she had to go into town once a month or so to make some coin – some things just couldn't be bartered for. She would put panniers on her two biggest nanny goats and have them carry the cheese wheels. It took some training to get the goats to do this chore for her, as they were more inclined to eat the produce on their neighbour's back then to trek along the road towards town. Nan strapped the bench for her wares to her own back and slung a bag of herbs and ointments over her shoulder. She would lay the cheeses out on the bench when she got to the market on Wednesday mornings but keep the herbs and other remedies hidden away. Those would be produced when requested, and not advertised. There were people about who did not appreciate the cunning woman's craft.

The goat's cheese was not to everyone's taste, but Nan sold it cheaper than the girl with the cow cheese, so she was usually able to distribute most of her stock by the end of the market. The men would wind up at one o'clock and go into the pub for a jar while the women gathered outside to chat or went to the church for a quick novena. Nan did neither, anxious to get back to her small holding and be back with her goats.

When Eala left, Nan was perplexed as to how she would deal with the child on market day. The walk would be long for little legs and sitting by the

13

cheese table all morning would be tiresome for a young thing. It was likely that Fiona would get restless and possibly irritable. Nan couldn't have that while trying to sell her produce. She needed to concentrate on extolling the virtue of her goats' cheese and the health benefits, as well as the economy. It wasn't an easy thing for her to do, not being over-used to communicating with people and much preferring the company of animals. Leaving the goats all day with no one checking in on them also disturbed her. While Eala had often wandered off to the loch and was absent minded about her responsibilities, at least she was a sometimes presence on the small holding. Nan lived in fear of one of her small herd being stolen. She knew each goat intimately and they were all very dear to her. No one else would care for them as she did, and she had rarely sold or bartered a goat. Her goats could only go to the best of homes, where the people would treat the caprine with affection and concern. There were people like this – good farmers who knew well treated stock produced better, but one had to be discerning. There were also lazy farmers who did as little as possible to get by. Luckily, Nan was able to ask the animals the opinions of various farmers, who knew a good home; when the stock there was reported as being well fed, clean and warm in the winter.

After a discussion with Billy, Nan decided that he could watch the flock for the day. She would shut up the nannies in the byre and leave Billy on guard. With his majestic, curling horns and his significant stature, Billy could act as a deterrent to most thieves. Now she just had to decide what to do with the child. Would it be possible to leave her with a neighbour? She had never needed to do such a thing; when Eala was quite young her father had often been around. Nan was aware that mothers often looked after each other's children, though she had never taken in any neighbour children. There was just that tiny bit of suspicion that her home wasn't quite as homely as others, and it certainly wasn't Catholic enough.

The Boyles had been somewhat more friendly than most families in the area. They nodded at Nan when she walked by and had been to see her for various remedies, both for themselves and their livestock. She wouldn't say she was friends with Mrs. Boyle, but the woman had never been rude to her. Their cabin was on the way to Ardara. Maybe she could leave Fiona there for the day?

On market day, Nan loaded up Jenny and Roisin with cheese stuffed panniers. She made sure there was plenty of feed in the byre and had a last-minute conference with Billy. She filled her bag with the usual remedies – nettle rub for joint pain, blackberry tonic, meadowsweet for the runs, self-heal for fevers, willow bark for headaches, yarrow for nosebleeds, and so on. Most women had their own simples, but few had the range, or the efficacy that Nan had. She knew on which cycle of the moon to pick her plants and she said blessings over her herbs as they dried. Not that people knew she prayed over her remedies, but they knew her herbs were better than most.

Nan instructed Fiona to wrap up warmly and gave her two pieces of buttered bread, an apple, and some cheese for her lunch, enough to share with Farley, of course. Strapping the short bench on her back, Nan led her entourage of two goats, one dog and one child down the hill towards the town. On the route, she knocked on the

15

Boyle's door. Mrs Boyle came to the door, drying her hands on her apron, accompanied by a toddler with a sticky face clinging to her skirts. She was surprised to see Nan, as the woman was not known to make calls unless requested for her healing work.

Nan pushed Fiona forward.

"Would you mind terribly Mrs Boyle? I've got to go to the market today and I think it would be a long, cold day for my granddaughter." Mrs Boyle looked confused for a moment and then remembered.

"Ah, of course. I'd forgotten that her mother had gone missing. To be sure, just leave the child with me and you can collect her on the way home." Fiona looked up at her grandmother with consternation. They had not discussed this turn of events at all, and she was not entirely pleased. Mrs Boyle smiled and reached for her, but Fiona hung back. She had never been in someone's house before without her grandmother. What if Nan wandered off like Eala did? What if Fiona had to live with these people forever? Fiona doubted that any of these people could talk to animals or make remedies and she would have nothing in common with them. Fiona shook her head and hid her face in Nan's skirts.

Nan was embarrassed and a bit irked. It was bad enough to have to ask for a favour without the child misbehaving. She peeled Fiona off her and pushed her towards the door.

"You have your pup with you *a leanbh.* You will be fine," but Fiona started to wail.

Mrs Boyle knelt in front of Fiona and took her by her shoulders. She was a mother of seven, five of them living. She knew children pretty well.

"Your nan is coming back lass. She's only going to town for the day and then she'll be back for you by tea-time. I promise." Fiona paused in her protest, trying to hear if Mrs Boyle was telling the truth. "I'm making bread today and we have some jam left. Do you like bread and jam? I bet you do. All children like a bit of jam." Seeing that Fiona was still suspicious, she continued. "How about your wee pup? Does he like bread and jam? Would you like to give him a wee bite?" At that Fiona nodded slowly and allowed Mrs Boyle to take her hand. Farley, aware that food was involved, quickly followed his mistress indoors. Nan adjusted her burdens and continued to walk down the hill towards the town, a bit concerned, and a bit relieved.

Mrs Boyle sat Fiona down at the scrubbed wooden table and put a cup of milky tea in front of her. Eying the woman over the rim of the cup, Fiona drank thirstily. She wasn't used to cow's milk and found the taste sweeter and quite pleasant. When she was halfway through, she placed the cup on the floor for Farley to have his share. Mrs Boyle compressed her lips but said nothing. Her children were less restrained. A boy of eight pointed at Farley and hooted with laughter and a girl, around Fiona's own age complained that dogs were dirty, and she would never drink out of that cup again. Mrs Boyle hushed them both and told them to be polite to their guest.

She was a busy woman and Mrs Boyle had to get on with her baking. She was sure the children would be fine on their own, so she encouraged them out into the yard behind the house to play and get out from under her feet. She kept the toddler by her and occasionally rocked a grizzling baby in the cradle near the fire. The eldest child was out helping his father in the fields. The boy, and girl whom Fiona had already met took her hands and tugged her outside.

"What shall we play?" asked the little girl, a dainty thing with light brown hair braided into even plaits down her back. Her dress was remarkably clean for a country child but like Fiona, she was barefoot. The boy was a bit scruffier, but his clothes were well mended and fitted relatively well, having recently been inherited from the older brother.

"You're poor," the boy remarked, taking in Fiona's dress, cut down from one of Eala's and so worn by washing that it had no real colour at all. Fiona's hair was plaited too, but hurriedly and was already coming loose and gathering around her face in red and brown straggles. Her feet were exceedingly dirty from having walked in the goat byre that morning.

"Then we can play Lord and Lady and Fiona will be our servant," the little girl announced. She turned to Fiona with a severe look, "That means you have to do everything we say." Fiona narrowed her eyes but did not reply. She had no experience of playing with other children. Goats she had played with aplenty. They chased, they feinted, they charged, they even played ball. Goats were great playmates. She wasn't so sure about these two children though.

"What about the dog?" the boy asked, moving towards Farley with intent. Farley lifted a lip and displayed an impressive new canine tooth that had just grown in.

Fiona intercepted the boy, "Leave me dog be."

"Why?" the boy asked, now completely determined to investigate the terrier.

18

"He doesn't want to play," Fiona said.

"How do you know; did you ask him?" teased the boy.

Fiona was surprised. She didn't realise the boy knew about Listeners. Nan had told her most people didn't understand what Listeners did and it was best not to talk about it.

"He told me," she announced.

"Your dog talks to you?" the girl exclaimed.

"Yes," Fiona remarked. "And I listen."

"You're a liar," the boy reprimanded.

"I'm going to tell my mam, you're a liar!" The little girl went running towards the house.

Fiona decided she didn't enjoy these children at all. She thought wistfully of the fresh baked bread with jam but wasn't sure it was worth waiting for. When the boy ran up to Farley and yanked his tail, causing Farley to spin in an instant with a sharp nip, the decision was made. Calling Farley to her, she began running back up the hill towards home.

It was lonesome in the cabin without Nan or her mother, so Fiona went out to the goat byre. Billy inspected her carefully and listened to Farley's report of the morning. Stepping aside, Billy granted them entrance to his abode and Fiona and Farley settled in among the goats. The press of the herd kept them warm, and they enjoyed watching the antics of the younger goats. It was much more pleasant than spending the day with strangers.

At one point, Mr. Boyle came up, calling for Fiona but Billy wouldn't let him near the enclosure. Fiona squatted down behind the goats and made herself invisible until Mr. Boyle gave up and returned home. She heard him muttering under his breath, and he didn't sound too pleased.

She wondered why he was angry, hoping it had nothing to do with her. After all, she hadn't eaten any of their bread and jam, so she was not beholden to the family.

Nan was tired after the day at the market and found carrying the table home exhausting. She wasn't getting any younger. The cheese had sold well, and a number of remedies had sold too, but the few coins in her purse hardly seemed worth the day's efforts. She was worried about her goats and hoped the child had gotten on well at the Boyle cabin. She approached the cabin slowly and leaned on the door to rest for a moment before knocking. Mrs. Boyle answered but her face was not nearly as welcoming as in the morning.

"She's not here. Ran off almost right away. The husband had to leave his work and go looking for her, but he didn't find her at all. It was a right nuisance. We have too much work to do to be running around the countryside looking for a spoiled wee brat."

Nan didn't know what to say. She was terrified that Fiona was down at the loch looking for her mother. And she was mortified that her granddaughter had been called spoiled. The child had been working since she could walk. What on earth had happened?

"I'm terribly sorry Mrs. Boyle, I don't know what got into her. I suspect she's just not used to other people; she's been so much with meself and me daughter."

"Well, that's your own fault, isn't it? Keeping yourself to yourself and not being neighbourly. The children said she wouldn't play with them at all, and then she let that vicious dog bite me poor lad. If you came to church more often, maybe the child

20

would know how to behave." And then the door was shut in Nan's face.

She tried to increase her pace to get home as soon as possible. Please St. Francis, she prayed, let the *wean* and her pup be at home safe. The pup wasn't vicious at all. That boy must have teased it. And of course, Fiona didn't know how to play with children, she played with the goats and her dog quite nicely, but animals aren't cruel like children are.

Reaching the top of the hill, Nan saw Billy, his long coat drifting white in the early evening breeze. He bleated a greeting to her, and she felt calmer. Billy wasn't upset, so things were surely well. The goats shifted as Nan entered the byre, unloading the panniers from Jenny and Rosin and scratching them behind the ears in thanks. As the herd moved towards her, hungry for tea, she spied Fiona curled up against the back wall of the byre, asleep with the dog in her arms. Farley opened one gimlet eye at her, and she heard him asking about a meal. Then Fiona awoke, and leapt up, running to Nan, and throwing her arms around her.

"Don't leave me again, Nan, please don't leave me." Nan smoothed the child's hair, now completely undone and tangled over the small head. How foolish it had been to leave the child behind, so soon after her mother had disappeared. No wonder she had run home to the safety of her four-legged friends.

"I'm sorry Fiona. I thought it would be best for you, but I was wrong. Now let us get inside and feed this poor starving creature of yours."

Nan put off going to market again for as long as possible. It wasn't only the long day and the tiring walk; she was worried about Fiona. The child had lived almost entirely within the close

21

environment of the cabin, and the surrounding fields. She might find the town overwhelming. Nan herself found the town noisy and crowded. There were far too many people, and she was always relieved to turn towards home at the end of the day; to not have to talk, to nod pleasantly and smile at people. None of this effort was required with her goats. They felt her thoughts and she felt theirs. It was simple and peaceful.

However, they needed some flour and oats which she hadn't managed to barter for in her recent healings. She told Fiona they were heading off early the next morning and packed up the cheese and remedies she would sell. Fiona was excited to be going into the town, asking questions about what they would see, what they would buy, how many people would be there, if there would be other children. Nan briefly felt guilty for keeping the child so secluded, but this was the life they lived. Maybe, after a time in the crowds of a market day Fiona would be less interested in town life.

They left at dawn, Nan walking slowly with her load and Fiona and Farley darting off the road into the fields, and then rushing back after flushing a rabbit or inspecting a cow they had not met before. Nan warned them to take it easy or they would be shattered later on, but her admonitions were ignored. By the time they had got to Ardara, Farley was panting for a drink and Fiona was dragging her feet. Nan knew this would happen. The two would just have to sit by the bench and rest before the long walk home.

Nan briskly set up the workbench and lay out her wares. It wasn't much time before a young woman came by and whispered her need for some chamomile, as she was having terrible pain with her monthlies. Another woman then came by and asked for some lemon balm as her husband had dreadful wind. An elderly woman asked for Nan's remedy for piles – a mixture of yarrow tea and lavender oil. The little jars for oils and creams had cost Nan dearly but were necessary for so many of the remedies. Small coins were offered in payment, not enough yet for their supplies but it was still early in the day.

The less affluent housewives were happy to buy the humble goat's cheese at a reduced price. Generally, the people that came to Nan's stall were business like; the women had a lot of shopping to get done before rushing home to make dinner. A few were amicable as they had done business with Nan for years, but none were what she would call friends. There was the odd comment about Fiona, now curled up on Nan's shawl and napping by the stall with the dog dozing next to her. Nan explained that it was her grandchild and there were the usual comments about her being a bonny child, though she was not particularly, but mothers try to be polite, lest the appearance of their own children is described truthfully.

It was only when she had sold the last of the cheese that Nan tidied her bench and counted out the number of coins she had garnered. Fiona was sitting up now and watching the people passing by intently. A few men who were herding livestock they had purchased passed Nan's pitch. The cows or sheep lumbered by; an occasional switch with a light stick prodding them forward. Fiona tried reaching out to them to ask if they minded moving onto a new home but only got a jumble of feelings in return – regret, hope, fear, relief. She was unable to decipher any one single message. She asked Nan what the farm animals were saying but

Nan hushed her, reminding Fiona that they did not talk about listening in public.

It was time to start shopping. Nan did not enjoy this part of market day at all, and because she was not a part of the community, she was not favoured with special deals. Often the merchants were downright rude to her. She held Fiona's hand tightly and instructed the child to stay close and keep quiet. Fiona passed on this instruction to Farley who huffed in annoyance. He was keen to explore the town and sniff the other dogs, and maybe find some scraps of food or pinch a sausage from the butcher. He did, more or less, comply with Fiona's request, although he did make a detour towards a young man, carelessly waving a pie in his right hand. Farley leapt up and relieved the bloke of his dinner, only to be followed by shouts, and the threatening fist of the previous pie owner. Farley was agile though and escaped the aggrieved gentleman. Nan tutted in annoyance; they did not need to be creating any ill will in the town.

The miller's wife was selling flour and oats. She was a stout woman with a red face. She stood behind her wares, hands on her hips, and occasionally slipping a hand into a pocket to jingle the satisfactory load of coins she had collected that day. She lifted her lip slightly when Nan approached. She did not care for the cunning woman. In her white apron, the miller's wife looked down on Nan in her dirty shawl, that had, till recently been a blanket on the ground for Fiona.

"I'd like a pound of flour and half that much of oats," Nan requested. She didn't look the miller's wife in the face, keeping her eyes cast down respectfully. Fiona did look at the wife

24

though, staring at her plumpness and ruddiness. She had never seen anyone so well fed.

"The child is very rude," the miller's wife remarked.

Nan poked Fiona and told her to stop staring.

"But Nan," Fiona explained, "Look at the size of her!"

Both Nan and the miller's wife gasped, and Nan began to apologise profusely. She gave Fiona a little shake and demanded she apologise. Fiona couldn't see why she had to apologise for speaking the truth, but she did so anyway as Nan was so insistent.

"I should refuse to serve you," the wife answered. "In fact, I don't know why I have ever served the likes of you. Everyone knows what type of people you are. And now you are training up the young one, I suppose we'll have another witch around here."

"But we're not" - Fiona began, intending to explain the difference between witches and Listeners but Nan clamped an iron hand on her shoulder and squeezed it, causing Fiona to whimper rather than continue her explanation.

The miller's wife was not really listening though.

"However, I'm a good Christian, and I won't deprive you and starve the child. I will be rewarded in the next life for feeding the hungry in this one. How much money do you have? You know I don't do credit." Nan counted out the coins that were the necessary amount the last time she bought flour, and oats but the wife sniffed. "The price has gone up." Nan offered another coin, but the woman shook her head. After Nan had offered three more coins, the self- avowed 'good Christian'

25

swept the money into her hand and pushed the goods towards Nan. Nan took them without a word and packed them into the goats' panniers. "And take those smelly beasts away from my stall!" the wife shouted after them.

Fiona was confused. Why had the woman been so dreadful? Why did Nan not tell the woman to be more respectful. Why was Fiona in trouble? She tugged on Nan's shawl and the tired, old woman turned to her.

"What is it child?"

"What did I do wrong Nan?"

"Nothing child, don't worry. You did nothing wrong."

"But that lady was very nasty to us. Why was she so horrible?"

"Some people are just born that way lass. And some people don't understand what we do. If you don't understand something, it can scare you. People aren't very kind when they're frightened."

Fiona thought about that for a while.

Then why don't we explain what Listeners do?"

Nan sighed.

"Most people don't want to hear Fiona. And some people have so much nonsense running around in their heads that they can't listen."

Fiona nodded. Sometimes she couldn't listen either. Sometimes she was thinking so many things at once that it was just words and pictures whirling around in her head going nowhere. Nan had told her that as Fiona learned to concentrate, she would get better at listening. Maybe some people never learned to concentrate. It was very hard, and it did make your head hurt.

FIONA'S FIRST HEALING

Fiona watched her Nan moving through the herd of goats, placing a hand here and there, breathing with the goat and then moving on. Fiona was learning to listen like this with her Farley but never thought she would have her nan's ability to work so easily. Fiona still had to focus so hard that it gave her terrible headaches. Yet, she had got to the point where she could place her hand on Farley and pick up on him musing over his next meal, the smell of a rabbit in the wind or the fact that he would like to go for a wander.

Touching him, she could hear what he was saying and sometimes, he heard her thoughts. Last night, Farley shared an image that she had recalled earlier - her mother walking into the lake and becoming a swan, sailing off with her acolyte. Fiona was not pleased to be reminded of this picture and rolled away from Farley, towards her nan. The dog left the matter to rest, preferring sleep to an argument, but someday he would need to understand this memory.

Nan was continuing to work with the goats to assure them that Farley was no threat. This was an ongoing project as Farley was still a bit of a villain. He enjoyed chasing the kids and was known to nip at the odd hock, getting a good hoof in the muzzle for his bad manners. At least Farley realised that Billy, the herd's buck, was not a goat who would be tolerating any misbehaviour. Billy often turned his red eyes on Farley in admonishment, expecting more of an acolyte, though Farley was still only a pup in training. It had been a long time since Billy and Nan were young and mischievous and Billy easily lost his patience with the young dog.

Nan had settled the goats enough to begin milking.

"We'll make some of this into cheese I think," she remarked. Fiona sighed. She hated making cheese. It was a tedious process and it occurred indoors. However, she imagined that Farley would be rather fond of the process as he seemed to be forever hungry, and it was impossible to make cheese without the odd bit falling onto the floor.

"Will we be doing that today?" asked Fiona. Nan smiled up at her and shook her head.

"It's not raining. We should take advantage of the weather and go on a walk. Will you fetch my basket and bring along your wee knife and we'll see what we can find?" Fiona jumped up in excitement, startling the goat and nearly losing the milk. She loved foraging. She wasn't terribly good at it yet, but she and Farley could run through the fields, chasing rabbits, and gathering wildflowers. She'd find some useful plants as well, which meant that she and her dog could avoid the more tedious chores till later in the day.

Grabbing the basket from the table and her knife from under her pillow, Fiona ran back out the door and shouted, "Ready!" Nan laughed and shook her head.

"Well, I'm not. I've to put this milk indoors and cover it and maybe have a quick cup of tea." Fiona deflated. What was with adults and their endless cups of tea? Nan noted the child's dejection and waved her on. "You go along, and I'll catch you up, just don't go too far; my bones aren't as young as yours."

"How will you find where I am?"

28

"Send Farley along to fetch me. I'm sure he can find his way home."

"But will he?" Fiona wondered.

"Of course, he will. Just tell him to come collect me and he'll scent me. His nose is better than yours."

Fiona realized this was a task she had been set. Could she communicate clearly enough with Farley for him to understand what needed to be done? What if Farley decided to run off and chase rabbits instead?

"Are you sure?"

"You've got to learn to trust him sometime *girseach*. Today is as good as any." Fiona nodded tentatively. Turning, she called Farley to her, and they set off down the hill, looking for some burdock. That seemed to be a useful thing to find. After all, people were always after having sore throats. There would be a good bit of nettle down there as well, but Fiona hated gathering nettle. Nan had the knack for it, but Fiona just managed to get covered in a rash. Nettles were good to eat and could be useful for remedies as well, so it would be best to learn how to gather them, but not today. It was probably too late to harvest them anyway. The sun was out, and she and Farley were content to potter about sticking with the plants they knew best. Maybe they could go under a hedge and look for rabbit holes. Farley took such pleasure in digging. It always made her, and Nan laugh to watch his frantic scratching at the earth, as if he were trying to dig to the other side of the world.

Eventually, Fiona remembered she was supposed to be doing something other than wandering through the fields throwing sticks for her dog. She found a patch of burdock and began harvesting the burrs. This was prickly work, so she wrapped her hand in her apron to pry off each burr. She did not attempt to open any burrs. Nan could do that. The seeds were good for cough tinctures but opening the burr was a dangerous business. Seeds could fly anywhere and the down inside the burr could itself, cause a cough. Now that she was being productive, Fiona thought it would be safe to send for Nan. She knelt down beside Farley who was busy snuffling in a bush and laid her hand alongside his shoulder. She closed her eyes and counted her breaths down from ten, trying to make her mind blank. At first, he ignored her as the smells under the bush were heady, but she persisted, and he finally pulled his head out from under the branches and sat looking at her. Fiona sent him the message to return to the cottage and collect Nan and return to the verges they were currently investigating. For a moment Farley just stared at her blankly and then Fiona got a pushing feeling. She wasn't sure what it was, so she visualized her message again, sending it to Farley a second time. Again, the pushing feeling, and then Farley turned around to his business and continued to sniff out the rabbit burrow he knew was nearby. It dawned on Fiona that Farley had understood alright, but that he had no intention of complying. With a sigh, she got up and started trudging homewards, with only a few burdock burrs in her basket. She would probably meet Nan part way and then they could forage on their own. Maybe Nan would know what to do with stubborn acolytes, but Fiona didn't have a clue.

Nan did meet Fiona coming back up the hill and chuckled to see her frowning crossly.

"And where is your little fellow?"

"I don't know, and I don't care," declared Fiona. Nan laughed. "Ah, you do *a leanbh*. He's not your servant. I take it you had a bit of a chat though. That's always good. Even if you don't get what you want, you are still practising the skill. Even now I often chat with my Billy, and he doesn't give me the reply I want. Thinking on it, he usually doesn't give me the reply that I want. We've both chosen hard fellows to get along with. Just keep practising lass."

"It's too hard!" Fiona complained.

"Only at first. The more you do it the easier it gets. There will come a day when speaking and listening this way will come as naturally as speaking to me. More so maybe. Just give it time. Now come along and show me where you found that burdock. We should dig up some of the root as well. When winter comes everyone hereabouts will be coughing and spluttering with cold. We'll sell some remedies to them then."

"Nan," Fiona asked, "How did your mam know to choose Billy as your acolyte?"

With creaking knees, Nan sat down on the side of the path. She patted the ground beside her indicating that Fiona should sit as well.

"Me mam had settled. She was the first of our kind to do so. You know my grandmother was with the travelling people. She was bonded with a horse and was well respected among the travellers; they do love their horses." Nan paused and gingerly adjusted herself on the damp earth, knowing she would feel it later in her joints. "But me mam, she fell in love with a farmer, the man that worked this holding here on the hill where we live now."

"Who was your mam's acolyte?" Fiona queried.

"Why, it was Dermot, the blackbird. Such a voice! The tunes he sang for us. And he was a splendid fellow, all gleaming black feathers, and a bright orange beak. His eyes were bright, like shiny buttons that saw just about everything. He was a clever, wee thing. But mam wanted me to keep the tenancy, so she bonded me to a goat. That way I would stay put and mind the byre for the herd. I should have done something sensible like that for your mam, but I let her go her way. I was too soft on her. I'm sorry for that *a leanbh*, for you are the one who has suffered for my mistakes."

Fiona frowned down at the ground and stabbed the dirt with their spade.

"But who was my father?"

Nan reached over and stroked the girl's hair. Already it was changing colour to align with her acolyte. She had been a chestnut - haired lass but now there were highlights of red, blonde, and black - like the terrier the child had bonded with. Soon she would develop more acute hearing and a sense of smell far beyond the capabilities of the normal human. These were good skills for survival. This time, Nan had chosen wisely and felt secure that this Listener would cope better than the ill-fated Eala.

"It doesn't matter little one. He had no love to give so there is no reason to know him."

"Did my mother love him?" Fiona persisted.

Nan slapped the ground with her right palm and spat to her left.

"She did not! Now child, we have work to do. Stop with the questions and show me these burdock roots.

As they were digging, Farley reappeared and joined in enthusiastically. Nan was able to remind

32

him that they needed the root left intact and he proved himself useful, eventually. "Now he's done us a favour," she pointed out to Fiona, "How can we tell him we are thankful for his work?"

"I don't know," Fiona said sullenly. This having an acolyte was hard work. She seemed to always be training or concentrating. It wasn't like magic at all. She had hoped the gift would just come to her and she would be able to talk with the creatures but instead she was constantly being tutored by Nan and corrected when she didn't try hard enough.

"Think child!" Nan insisted. "Why should he help you or even listen to you if there is no advantage to him? You have to make him want to be your acolyte. He has to learn the job as much as you do."

"He likes food," Fiona offered.

"That's very true. He's a bit of a greedy pig. Have you anything in your apron?"

Fiona dug around in her apron pocket and came up with a crust of bread. She crouched down and offered it to Farley, who snatched it and swallowed it in an instant.

"There now," he's rewarded for his good work. Always try to carry a tidbit with you or find a place you can give him a good scratch. Billy likes a tickle behind the ears. Maybe your Farley would like that too."

"Oh, he does," Fiona brightened and demonstrated scratching a special spot along Farley's neck that caused him to writhe in pleasure and fall to the ground. "That's his favourite spot," Fiona stated proudly.

"Good, then. Now, help me up off this ground and we'll take these roots back to the cabin." Nan reached out her hand and Fiona helped Nan unfold herself from the ground. Farley retrieved his head from one of the holes that he had dug, shook the dirt from his ears and trotted along beside them. On the path back up to the cabin, Nan pointed out some more beneficial plants and asked Fiona to stay behind and gather them. A bit worried that Nan would struggle getting up the hill, Fiona began to protest but then Billy appeared. Nan threw her arm over the old goat's neck and leaned on him as she made her progress home, only limping slightly.

Fiona returned with the nettle leaves she had gathered for Nan, unscathed this time. As Nan had predicted, she didn't get stung because it was early in the year, before the plant had flowered. The leaves were wide and juicy, and Nan would grind them down to extract the liquid, making it into a tincture to treat aching joints. She often gave this to the older goats but had been known to trade a bit of the remedy to farmers in exchange for oats or eggs, even potatoes when her own patch hadn't done so well. Most of the men, were too embarrassed to ask for a dose but their wives, who had to listen to their groans and complaints had no compunction when requesting a 'wee bottle for the pain in himself's bones.' It was hard work making the tincture, but Nan had been doing it for years.

"Did you only take the top leaves like I asked? And nothing that was starting to flower? The leaves are useless then." Fiona nodded moodily.

"I did exactly as you said," Fiona sighed, her grandmother still didn't think much of her foraging abilities.

"And what is this you have?" Nan lifted up a bunch of plants, topped with white flower.

"Elder," Fiona retorted.

"Elder! Did you not look at the leaves lass? This is Sweet Cicely, and this," Nan spread the plants across the table, "This, you great eejit, is hemlock! Are you trying to poison us then?"

Fiona shrugged moodily. There were so many plants in the Spring, and they all looked so similar. How could she ever learn them all?

Nan handed her the hemlock, "Take this out and put it down the privy. I don't want the goats getting to it and remember where you got it, so you don't go back there again! When you return, I'll show you how to make nettle juice."

Fiona thought maybe she should have stayed at school. Surely it would be easier than this constant messing about with the plants. Then she remembered how the teacher had locked Farley outside the schoolhouse and how Farley's whining had driven a hole through Fiona's brain, making it impossible to think or feel anything but the dog's anxiety. Never mind, at least this way she had Farley by her side always, even if they would both rather be out hunting than grinding up green things.

Fiona dragged the stool over to the shelf where the mortar and pestle were kept. After reaching it down, she shuffled towards the table where Nan had emptied the bag of nettle leaves on the table.

"Right then, start grinding," Nan chirped. She was doing her best to ignore Fiona's reluctance. "You'll need to learn my recipes *girseach* as I won't be here forever." Fiona looked up sharply at that. "Don't worry lass, I don't intend to pop off any time soon but there's a lot to learn and as your mother isn't here, you have to carry on the knowledge." Fiona wasn't so sure she wanted to carry on the knowledge. Being the local cunning woman had not won Nan any friends. She was useful to the community, but not liked. If they went to mass, there was always space left around them and few people chatted with them on market day. The whiff of witchcraft and faery hung around them.

As if reading her thoughts, something Nan was terribly good at, she lectured Fiona.

"Our knowledge is important. We've saved lives, or at least made people and animals more comfortable. What would they do without us? Most of our people can't afford doctors. And even if they could, sure, don't we know enough to help them, without having gone to fancy schools and earned degrees?"

"But I could just read your book of recipes. My reading is quite good now," Fiona insisted.

"Aye, your reading is coming along, but there's a lot more to healing than what you can find in a book. Now go on with that grinding. When we have a bit of juice, we'll pour it out through the muslin and let it sit in the window a bit. There's a full moon coming, and the moonshine will give the juice some power."

"What if it's too cloudy?" Fiona was choosing to be as obstructive as possible.

"Then it can wait till we have a moon, or some sun. Either will boost the remedy. Patience, little one. That's an important skill too."

Grumpily, Fiona applied the pestle with extra vigour. 'Patience, my foot,' she thought.

"Tomorrow, I want you to gather some comfrey – you know the one with the purple flowers," Nan mused.

"But I'll have to go down near to the loch." Fiona hated the loch. It reminded her of her mother and the day she left Fiona. There were days when she did go to the loch, to look for Eala, but mostly she avoided it. She had seen a pair of swans from time to time, swim towards her with intent, but on seeing them, Fiona had always run off. She had not yet forgiven her mother and, was definitely not ready to meet her in her swan form.

Nan didn't seem to hear Fiona's protest.

"Comfrey is such a good poultice for wounds. The goats always seem to be getting scratched up when they go through the blackthorn. Even your Farley got himself a bit of a gash a while back. Remember how I put the poultice on his leg for a few days and he was as right as rain in no time."

Fiona frowned.

"Whenever is rain, right?" she grumbled. Nan swiped Fiona's bottom with the cloth she was holding.

"Enough with that. You'll spoil my healing with all your dark thoughts."

And so, Fiona's lessons continued, plant craft, remedy preparation, and listening. Her days were as full as if she had been a regular schoolgirl. It was just as well that she didn't care for the village school. At first it had only been Farley's whinging that had made her uneasy. Then she couldn't think straight with worrying about him being outside in the cold. What if he was unhappy? What if he ran off? What if someone stole him? As her thoughts were focussed on her dog, she heard very little of what the master said, and was reprimanded repeatedly. When the master caught her trying to peer out the window and check on her small dog, she was taken up to the front of the room and had her palms slapped with a ruler. Although she did not cry out, Farley heard

37

the noise and smelled her distress, and threw himself against the schoolhouse door, barking vociferously. The master told her to quieten the dog, or it would get a good kicking. Fiona ran out the door, Farley ran in, nipped the master in the ankle, and they were both expelled from school. It was no bother. They had no intention of going back after that day. There was much to learn at home.

One morning, a small boy with a snotty nose turned up on their doorstep. He knocked once and then sprang back from the door, as if it were somehow enchanted and might pull him in. Fiona opened the door, just as the boy had finished knocking, having been informed by Farley that someone was visiting. The boy regarded Fiona suspiciously and then greeted her with the comment,

"You's not the cunning woman." Fiona made a face at the boy and then called over her shoulder for Nan, letting her know that there was a customer at the door.

Nan made her way over to the door and nudged Farley out of the way so that she could peer at the boy who was busily wiping his nose with his sleeve.

"And how can I help you, young man?" she enquired, when the boy was done clearing his nostrils. The boy sniffed mightily and then answered that they had a poorly cow back home. "And where is your home boy? The boy looked startled that not everyone knew where he lived. He pointed vaguely down the hill.

"Over to there," was his less than informative reply.

"Who's your daddy child?" Again, the boy looked surprised.

"He's me Da."

"What do people call him? His second name, I mean." This was a difficult one and took a few moments of contemplation.

"Doherty," he finally managed.

"Of course," Nan nodded. "I'll be along directly. Go along home and tell your daddy we will be coming after you." Before she could even finish her directions, the boy had turned and was running down the hill. Fiona giggled.

"He was after being scared!" she exclaimed. Nan grunted in reply. She was well aware of the tales told about her. She could do without repeating them to Fiona just yet.

"Hurry yourself, Fiona, you'll be coming with me" Nan urged as they picked their way down the rocky slope towards the farm, lower on the hill. Fiona usually stayed at home when Nan went about her work at other folks' holdings, but Nan motioned for her to come along. They shut up the goats and gathered some herbs and set off on their way. Fiona was excited and gratified to see Nan use all the herbs and plants they were forever gathering and drying. Farley trotted along beside Fiona. He wouldn't mind checking out the dogs on another farm and letting them know who he was.

When they got to the cottage, Nan knocked on the faded front door. It may have once been red, but time and weather had worn most of the paint away. A young woman came to the door, with a babe at her hip and another winding in her skirts. She didn't let Nan in. This sometimes happened. Oh, they wanted her skill alright, but she was a cunning woman, and that sort of strangeness wasn't always welcome indoors.

The woman nodded her head towards a ramshackle stable and murmured that her

39

husband was below with the cow. Then she noted Fiona, standing behind her Nan.

"The child can come in and sit by the fire if she likes." Fiona shook her head and took Nan's hand. The thought of sitting in the stuffy cottage with the smell of baby shit, and the smoke of the fire turned her stomach. Nan gave Fiona a sharp look.

"No thank you," she managed and then anxiously glanced back at Nan. Surely, Nan wouldn't abandon her here when she knew Fiona was keen to watch the work. But Nan just smiled and nodded in politeness at the woman, leading Fiona off towards the stable.

There was the slightly too sweet smell of rotting hay and then manure underfoot. Farley immediately began snuffling about, absorbing essence of rat. Fiona tried not to be distracted by his hunting and focus on her grandmother. There was a brief nod and a non-verbal grunt of a greeting from the farmer. They all stood contemplating the one cow, the only livestock in the stable. The cow was obviously one of the family's main sources of nourishment. Should the cow die, at least one of the children would follow.

"I'll be alright so," Nan told the farmer, taking up the milking stool and sitting next to the cow. She waited a moment and then the man turned and left them alone with the cow. Nan preferred to work on her own and the farmers had to trust her or not seek her services. She placed her hands on the cow and leaned her head against the warm hide. The bovine was obviously in discomfort, switching her tail and stamping a hind foot. Even Fiona could see that the cow had lost condition and was wasting away.

After a bit, Nan pushed herself up from the milking stool, and indicated for Fiona to sit. The girl hesitated, unsure what was being asked of her.

"Now you listen to her child and tell me what she says to you." Fiona was astonished. She could listen to Farley and the goats with no problem, but this was not a beast she knew. She wasn't sure if there could be any communication, and this was important. This cow had to survive if the family in the cottage behind her had any hope of survival. Gingerly, she approached the cow and lay both her hands along the animal's abdomen. Farley came alongside and sat on her foot, encouraging her. Closing her eyes, Fiona listened.

There was only the cow's breathing for a while, and the wind outside the stable rattling at the door. And then, a sort of feeling in her stomach and a wash of red colour. Fiona waited, but nothing more came to her. She turned to her nan, uncertainly,

"She's a pain in her belly?"

"Aye, she does. Likely she's ate something that's not passing."

"Can it be fixed?"

"Maybe. I'll tell the farmer to put something under her forelegs so they're a bit higher, to help the food to pass along. Perhaps he can find some paraffin. That can help."

"None of your plants will help?"

"Not yet. Perhaps later." Nan gave Fiona's shoulder a squeeze. "Well done lass."

The cottager was able to prop the cow up on a small bale of hay and had her chained to stand so. He was less pleased about the request for paraffin.

"I'd have to buy some down the town. That'll cost me."

Nan pulled her shawl around her and sighed.

"Losing the cow will cost you more." He nodded in reluctant agreement.

"The wife's sent you this," he offered, handing Nan a small basket with 3 eggs.

"Well, that's very kind of her, if she can spare them."

He rubbed the side of his face. Of course, she couldn't spare them, but a man had his pride.

"Tell her, I thank her well. We'll have a lovely tea then this evening. You send your boy along if the cow isn't right in a few days." The cottager nodded again as Nan turned to go.

"The wee one," the man called after her, "Is she to be a cunning woman as well?"

Nan smiled down at Fiona,

"That's up to her now, isn't it?"

Nan rarely provided remedies for the Brennans. They were better off than most families in the area and usually consulted a doctor for their own ailments and were not so worried about losing livestock that they would go the extraordinary measure of using a cunning woman to save them. However, Mr. Brennan had terrible wind and only Nan's mallow and meadowsweet tea seemed to alleviate the problem. Every couple of months, Mrs Brennan would send to Nan for a pouch of the mixture. She didn't condescend to barter and always paid with a coin, which she dropped into Nan's hand as if she were humouring a beggar. Nan was feeling pain in her back today, and decided she wasn't interested in dealing with Mrs Brennan. She thought she might make herself a cup of mullein tea and rest by the warm fire. Fiona would have to deal with the formidable Mrs Brennan today. She gave the girl a large bag of the tea and told her that Mrs Brennan should pay a shilling for the supply.

Fiona was not best pleased to be going to the Brennan's. She had to walk down to the church and go up the hill to the shop – the Brennan's lived above the shop. Fiona and Nan rarely used the shop, gaining most of their needs, from bartering or foraging and Fiona always felt stared at when she entered the place. Indeed, Mrs Brennan watched Fiona vigilantly, assuming the poverty of the child and her lack of schooling made Fiona a potential thief. In truth, it was only Farley who had ever lifted anything from the shop, once helping himself to a cake that had carelessly been left on a shelf he could reach. Fiona had to apologise and pay for the cake, still coming up a farthing short. This involved a long walk home, returning with the coin later in the day, and Mrs. Brennan didn't even thank Fiona for the prompt settling of her dog's debts. Farley was banned from the shop and so waited outside, making a habit of pinching the odd loaf from people who stood outside too long to natter.

It was a bitterly cold day, causing Fiona and Farley to keep a rare pace until they got to the shop. Reluctantly leaving Farley outside, Fiona rushed into the shop and waited impatiently while Mrs Brennan served a customer. Spying Fiona, Mrs Brennan looked down her nose and enquired what messages Fiona had come for.

"Nothing, Ma'am. I'm to deliver your tea," Fiona produced the package and placed it on the counter. Then a voice came from the back room of the shop.

"Who's that now?"

43

"Why, it's the girl from the goat byre up the hill," Mrs Brennan replied, gyrating her head to include the speaker. She turned back to Fiona, "That's my brother Aiden visiting me. He used to be in the army before he lost his sight. He was a lieutenant."

Fiona was disinterested and made no reaction. She wanted this transaction over with as soon as possible as Farley was waiting in the cold.

"Me nan says that will be one shilling."

"A whole shilling!" Mrs Brennan exclaimed, "That's very dear."

Fiona shrugged.

"Mallow's not so easy to find sometimes."

"Is that the cunning woman's daughter?" Aiden queried anxiously.

"No, I told you the daughter is long gone. This is the granddaughter."

"The granddaughter? Is she Eala's then?"

Fiona tried to look around Mrs Brennan into the back room. Who was this man asking about her mother? She'd never heard of any Lieutenant Aiden.

"I guess she is," Mrs Brennan answered her brother.

"Tell her to come 'round to me then," he ordered.

Fiona drew back. She thought maybe she should go and come back later for the money, but then Nan would be cross.

"Ma'am," she interrupted, but Mrs Brennan came around the counter and grabbed Fiona by the arm in a rather painful, pincer like grip.

"You heard the man; he wants to meet you." She dragged Fiona over to the former soldier, who was sitting by a warm stove, staring into the space where he could hear the approach of his sister.

Mrs Brennan gave Fiona a shove, nearly pushing her into the man's lap. "He's blind, you have to get up close to him, so he can feel you're there."

Aiden reached out and managed to take Fiona's hand, pulling her even closer to him. He reached up his large hands, hair sprouting on the knuckles, and stroked her face. Fiona pulled back abruptly and scrubbed at her cheek, trying to rub away the strange touch.

"He can't see you, so he likes to feel a face to see what it's like," Mrs Brennan explained. "He was blinded by a swan you know. You must have heard the story, though it happened before you were born, I think."

"A swan," Fiona swallowed.

"Yes, that's what I said. Aiden was a great one for fishing, weren't you brother? Then one day, a swan just attacked him for no reason, and he went blind right after. Had to leave the army and go back home and live with our mam, didn't you Aiden?"

"What colour is your hair girl?" the man broke in.

"It's a terrible mix of brown and black and red," Mrs Brennan offered. "Never seen anything like it. It's not any proper colour at all."

"Your mother had hair so fair it was nearly white," Aiden said dreamily.

"Hair the same colour as a swan," Fiona answered. Farley began to bark outside. "I have to go now Mrs Brennan: me nan is waiting." She looked meaningfully at the box behind the counter where the cash was kept.

"Very well," Mrs Brennan said, annoyed at the child's abruptness, but what could be expected from a beggar child from the hills. She extracted the coin and handed it to Fiona. "You won't lose

45

that will you?" Fiona shook her head and then fled the shop. The whole encounter had made her most uneasy.

When she got back to the cabin, Nan was out in the byre beginning a milking. She was perched on her stool, next to the light brown nanny with the one white ear and one white flash on her left hind leg. The nanny was standing patiently while being milked but shifted a bit as Farley announced his arrival with a few yips. Farley was fond of milking.

"I got the shilling, though she said it was dear."

"It was," Nan agreed, "I always overcharge her."

"Why?"

"She's got a tongue like a razor, and it's always flapping about someone else's business."

Farley gave a yip and Nan squirted a stream of milk in his direction. She missed and Farley got it between the eyes. He contorted himself trying to lick the drips as they came down his muzzle and Nan laughed to watch him. Fiona wasn't laughing though. She stood with her arms crossed, almost glowering. Nan waited a few moments and then spoke, "And what is troubling you *girseach*?"

Fiona kicked at a stone on the ground. Farley pounced on it and brought it to her to toss but she ignored him.

"Fiona," her grandmother insisted.

Fiona sighed and looked down the hill towards the loch.

"There was a man there, in the room behind the shop."

"Was there now," Nan had finished with this nanny and gave it a pat on the flank. The goat trotted off, but Nan stayed seated. Fiona went to take the bucket, but Nan stopped her.

"What sort of a man?"

"He was her brother. He said something about me mam."

Nan spat liberally, to her left side and whispered something under her breath.

"Would it be Lieutenant Aiden?"

"That's the one. Mrs Brennan said a swan blinded him."

Nan snorted.

"He was going blind from the day he was born. A weak sighted man always."

"She said everyone knew the story of how a swan attacked him," Fiona added.

Nan swatted Farley away from the bucket, where he was having a good drink.

"A swan did attack him, and he deserved it, and more besides."

"Why?" Nan shook her head and put her hands on her thighs, pressing herself up into a standing position.

"He was an evil man and that's all I'll say of it. Now take that milk inside and let's have ourselves some tea *a leanbh.*"

Glenties, County Donegal
Ireland
Late 19th Century

"Donal, you eejit, what are you like?" Kathleen exclaimed. She and John had finished the milking and were carrying the buckets back to the house, when they heard a loud, 'Moooo,' of distress. Donal, had lifted Kathleen's small brother on to one of the cow's backs and was encouraging him to, 'Race 'em jockey.' The small boy on the cow was laughing and kicking the cow's sides, shrieking, 'Giddup, giddup!' The cow was having none of it though and actually bucked. Kathleen hadn't known that cows could buck, but there it was and Ciarán lay in the muck in the byre. She put down her pail and rushed to him to make sure he was all in one piece. He must have been well enough because he stood up, red-faced and stamping his foot. He ran up to the cow and punched it with his puny fist, shouting 'Bad cow, bad cow.' Donal was doubled over in laughter and Kathleen had to struggle to keep a straight face as Ciarán was covered from head to toe in cow shit. It had smeared all down his back, his trousers, and even plastered his hair. He was painted with the muck. Finally, Kathleen gave in and doubled over in a fit of giggles.

As always, it was John who put a stop to frivolities.

"Look at the state of him! It will take ages to get his clothes clean. What will Mam say? And he'll definitely have to have a bath. He won't be sharing with me, smelling like the privy." Kathleen sobered and Ciarán's face screwed up ready to cry.

"Ah sure, John, we was just having a bit of a laugh. No harm done. The wee lad won't suffer from a bit of soap," Donal consoled, but John was having none of it.

"Maybe your mam doesn't mind extra washing, but I can tell you mine does. This is just one more chore for her and for Kathleen," John pointed his finger at the other boy. "Do you not think before you do things Donal? Actions have consequences you know." After sharing his bit of superior knowledge, John picked up both buckets of milk and began trudging up to the house. He shouted over his shoulder that it was Kathleen's responsibility to get their little brother cleaned up before tea. Donal and Kathleen looked at each other for a moment and then burst out into another fit of giggles, causing Ciarán to stamp his feet again and erupt into another round of tears.

"Ah laddie we're not laughing at you, sure," Kathleen reassured him, though this was partly a lie. "It's John and the way he acts the old man, he's right full of himself."

Donal took the younger boy's hand,

"Come on mate, I'll take you to the well and rinse you off. Maybe your sister will go along and collect you some clean clothes."

"Will you not be late for your tea Donal?" Kathleen asked, but the boy shrugged. He had been loitering with the Gallagher children, hoping he would be asked into sup with them but obviously that was out of the question now. He was in no hurry to rush home, a damp and dark cabin where his mother may or may not have some bread and a thin spread of dripping for him. Kathleen, added awkwardly, "I would ask Mam if you could join us for tea but I'm sure John has already been in telling her tales."

Donal smiled at Kathleen,

"No worries *cailín*," it wouldn't be the first time John had disparaged Donal's reputation and it probably wouldn't be the last. Without a father, Donal had been allowed to run wild, as the Gallaghers were told, and he wasn't the ideal company for a family that were trying so hard to get up in the world. Donal's father had been arrested for his vociferous support of the failed Home Rule bill of 1893. He had been imprisoned in Donegal Town and caught a fever in jail, passing away shortly thereafter - this political taint was not in Donal's favour. Kathleen didn't care though. She found the red-haired, blue eyed boy much better company than her serious older brother. She had already decided she would marry Donal when she was old enough and she was fairly certain he would agree, when she told him. Determined to pinch a slice of bread or an apple for Donal when she went indoors to find clothes for Ciarán, she waved at her husband to be, gathered up her skirts and ran up to the cottage.

The Gallaghers lived on a modest farm, but their cottage had three bedrooms, which was a good deal more than some of the mud cabins nearby. They had 2 cows, a dozen chickens and a small herd of sheep. There were fields for barley and potatoes. It was a small holding compared to their uncle McGovern's farm. However, the land was their own; an achievement that had only been accomplished by the previous generation, when the Land Act had made ownership of a farm possible for the smaller farmer.

There were three living Gallagher children. John was the oldest and filled with the sense of the duty of being the heir to the farm. Next came Kathleen, quiet and clever with her hands. She could knit, sew, make lace; people were already asking her to crochet collars and trims for them, and her mother let her keep the money she earned to put by for her bottom drawer.

Ciarán the youngest, was horse mad, continuously begging to be given a riding horse, or at least a pony. He had to be content with the old plough horse that worked the farm, but his father had promised him a mount when he was older, *if* he worked hard in school and passed all his exams.

The national school was a one room building next to the church. It was a two-mile walk for the children, which was all too often unpleasant in the predictable Irish weather - rain was a constant. The Gallaghers, being from a wealthier cut of society, had shoes but Donal walked barefoot in all weathers. The children of the school were all instructed to bring peat for the stove, but many had no peat bricks to spare so often the schoolhouse was unheated, but at least it gave the children a break from the routine of farm labour.

Kathleen tried hard at school. She didn't want to be shouted at, or worse still, smacked with a ruler. However, she found the maths confusing, and would get terribly anxious when called upon. John was quite good with maths but disliked literature as he saw little point in it. Donal, on the other hand gave brilliant declamations of poetry, and was known to have a lovely singing voice. In another place and time, he may have found his way on to the stage, but in a rural Donegal school, he mostly found his place under the cane. Ciarán was fond of reading stories and was interested in geography – the world was full of so many interesting places to visit. Hopefully, one day he would leave his small island and explore France and Egypt or maybe even India. In the meantime, he too found himself often under the cane, as he, was, already in awe of Donal's audacity and had become a disciple of the mischievous older boy.

At the end of the year, all the children were required to participate in a talent show. It was generally a tedious affair with children stumbling through poorly remembered poetry, songs warbled out of tune, and Irish dancing with many a misstep. The very unlucky, had to endure a child attempting to strangle a ballad out of an ancient, untuned fiddle. However, it was a chance for people to gather, and most parents did attend, proud, or pretending to be so, of their children's rough talents.

The school room would be packed on 'Presentation Day,' steam rising from damp clothing, with awkward farmers cleaning their boots before entering. The teacher gave out awards for the best scholars in each subject before the students shared their more artistic gifts. Parents clapped with enthusiasm, with some of the more exuberant stamping their feet and cheering. It was agony for a girl like Kathleen, who preferred to stay well clear of the limelight. She did manage to get to the front of the room and hold up a large lace doily that she had crocheted for her mother's dresser. She whispered the stitches she had used and how long it had taken her to make it. Many of the women leaned forward for a better look and several asked to finger the work afterwards. They were actually impressed, and Kathleen flushed in embarrassed delight, crossing her fingers in hopes that she would get a few more orders from her classmates' mothers and aunts.

Ciarán had recited a poem, 'The Stolen Child,' by that new poet Yeats. It was ever so long with several stanzas, but he had practiced with his mother and was able to make it through without too many omissions. It helped when the assembled encouraged him by joining in on the refrain:

Come away, O human child!
To the waters and the wild
With a faery, hand in hand,
For the world's more full
of weeping than you can understand.

A few of the mothers, wiped away a tear, thinking of the small graves in the churchyard nearby where their own children had gone away. Ciarán looked for his own mother, remembering the lost siblings she had mourned, and she smiled bravely at him. It was a moment he remembered forever, her smiling up at him, her dark hair, laced with silver, framing her heart-shaped face. It was the last time she ever came to a presentation.

John had escaped a performance, having finished school the year earlier but Donal was in his last year. Everyone knew he would sing, as he had a fine voice. In the school yard he was better known for his parodies of popular ballads, often making fun of the school master but it was hoped his final school performance would be universally acceptable. As usual, his mother had not come - she rarely left home except to go to mass, still overwhelmed with the shame of her husband's arrest. How his mother could ever be ashamed of his father, a hero, was something Donal would never understand. And so, completely at ease with his audience, Donal climbed up onto the podium, in front of the community and sang the popular ballad, *The Banks of the Daisies.*

*"Kathleen fair beyond compare, asleep upon
a bank I spied,"*

he sang, looking down at Kathleen Gallagher, who
blushed furiously and hid her face in her crochet
doily. Of course, everyone looked to where Donal
was directing his intent, and there were many
nudges and whispers. He continued,

*"All upon tiptoe I sought her side and kissed
her down in the daises."*

At this, there were downright sniggers and
the priest considered interrupting, but the lad had
such tone. Besides, the misty eyes of the mothers,
remembering their own days of youth and
romance, was a hard thing to destroy. He let the
lad finish to rapturous applause and calls of,
'Encore, Encore!' Donal bowed and looked to the
school master, who decided, as it was the last day
of school, what more could the boy do, and
shrugged his assent. Donal then broke into a
resonant rendition of 'A Nation Once Again.' At
this, the priest looked positively terrified but there
was no stopping this piece. One by one, the men in
the room began to join in, and when given the nod,
the women began to stand up from their seats,
their voices joining in with Donal's rich tenor.

*So, as I grew from boy to man
I bent me to that bidding
My spirit of each selfish plan
and cruel passion ridding
for thus, I hoped one day to aid
oh, can such hope be vain?
When my dear country shall be made
A Nation Once Again.*

A Nation Once Again,
A Nation Once Again
and Ireland long a province
be a nation once again.

With this proclaimed, many fists punched the air, and the schoolmaster dropped his head into his hands, making no effort to dissuade the patriotic fervour, but the priest sidled up to the master and shook his arm, "Enough now! They certainly don't sing their hymns like this." The school master rose resignedly and tapped Donal on the shoulder. All smiles at his triumph, Donal clasped the school master's hand and declared it all good craic.

And so, the children grew towards adulthood, the three Gallaghers and their ungovernable friend Donal. The potato famine was decades behind them. Home Rule had been proposed twice and the Land Reform Act had improved tenancy agreements for the small farmer. Ireland was taking off her shroud and moving towards the twentieth century. They believed their futures had promise. It was a shock then, when Mrs. Gallagher came down with typhus, probably contracted from visiting the poor, for she had never let a louse live long in her own house.

Mr. Gallagher struggled on for a few years after his wife died, but he had married as a mature man and the death of his helpmate had taken a huge toll on him. He too, passed, a few years after his wife, leaving young John, only twenty-two at the time, in charge of the farm. John promptly married, realising he needed an assistant and wisely chose the formidable Maire, a widow who was a few years his senior and an adept housekeeper. John was a grand manager for the work, but his siblings did not enjoy being ordered about like lowly privates in John's personal army. Kathleen took the opportunity to marry Donal and remove herself from the family home. In doing so, she moved from a comfortable cottage to a barely weather tight cabin and a husband that was not quite scraping by. However, Kathleen, shy and retiring on the surface was incredibly stubborn, and had made up her mind that Donal would find his way in the world.

Ciarán was able to survive the loss of both parents by focussing on the belligerent stallion his father had bought him when Ciarán finished school. However, John strongly believed that his younger brother would not benefit from the influence of his reckless brother-in-law and requested that Ciarán be sent to his uncle's farm. Ciarán could learn about managing a larger holding and help William McGovern build up his stables. Uncle William was happy to take on the lad, as he obviously had a gift with horses. Ciarán was also good company for Liam, William's son, an only child who was growing perhaps a trifle too full of himself, with no sibling competition. As there were only twenty or so miles between the two farms, visits were not impossible, especially on Ciarán's rambunctious horse. Liam often accompanied Ciarán on visits as they liked to race their horses down the roads and were always happy to get away from the overseeing eye of William McGovern.

Donal and Kathleen lived with Donal's mother in the Hegarty cabin, a few miles from the market town of Glenties, and far enough down the road from John's house that Kathleen felt she had moved away to her own life. There only being the one room in the cabin, marital relations were somewhat stifled by the presence of Mrs Hegarty senior but luckily, she was going deaf. Donal's mother kept threatening to move in with her sister, but wanted to help out the young Kathleen, just until she could keep house on her own properly. Kathleen couldn't wait for that day to happen.

While the cousins, Liam and Ciarán always stayed with Ciarán's brother, it was at Donal's and Kathleen's house they spent their time, it being a far more relaxed meeting place. Gathered around the fire, with the table pulled as close to the warmth as possible, they would drink their cider and discuss their plans to free Ireland from England's yoke. Kathleen smiled at their talk, assuming it the bluster of young men. Liam had always had a comfortable life on his father's farm and was well aware that part of his father's success was based on his obsequiousness with Protestant neighbours and deference to British rule. Liam enjoyed the concept of a free Ireland, particularly if that included land reform, so that he could own his own farm rather than pay rent to a landlord. However, Liam was not so sure that he was willing to make any sort of sacrifice to be rid of the current system. Things were well enough for him in his life. His father had actually been able to buy some of the family farm. Ciarán was more romantic and would stand up and sing the rebel songs with all the emotion required. He knew he didn't have a chance of ever owning land and he was not so good at the bowing and scraping as Liam was. It was Donal who had anger behind him. He had already lost a father to the cause. He was used to sacrifice. Donal read the papers closely and studied the rise and fall of the hopes of Home Rule. Donal's mother had often had trouble meeting the rent after her husband's death, and

Donal knew that she had needed to borrow from the Gallaghers on more than one occasion. He had experienced the bailiffs in his home, taking away a cow to cover arrears, and threatening his mother, that they would be put out on the road. Donal was ready for revenge.

Kathleen was in the latter days of pregnancy and tired easily, so she made her excuses and took to bed early, leaving the men muttering at the table. Donal leaned forward and lowered his voice, drawing Ciarán and Liam closer.

"I've a plan to make a wee protest. You've seen the estate house. It's painted white, with great windows looking over a lawn. Now, how do you think it would look with a blood splashed across it? Then written on the door: 'Enjoy your blood money.' I could time it with the rent collection. That would put the fear of God up them."

"You're mad," Liam commented, amused.

"To be sure, you'd be caught. And how would you even get that close to the manor? And where would you get the blood?"

Donal slapped Ciarán on the back,

"You're full of doubts brother. Sure, don't I know the gamekeeper that works on the estate? And as for the blood, your brother has a pig that he's butchering next week."

"Aye, and his wife is using the blood for pudding," Ciarán countered.

"But my Kathleen will be helping her and will steal away a fair portion of it for meself."

"She'd have to be quick to get past Maire," Liam put in drily.

"Well, yes, I will need to figure that one out," Donal considered, "but it can be done. Sure, and desecrating a landlord's house! It would make all the papers."

"It would," Liam answered, "but what would it achieve?"

"It would make them feel very unwelcome, I hope. It's time the British landowners left Ireland for the Irish."

"They'll hardly do that Donal, they make too much money here," Ciarán added sourly.

"If they get scared enough, it won't be worth it to them. You've heard of the houses being burned and such. You can bet those landlords aren't present anymore."

"But their agents are," Liam argued.

"The agents are easier to eliminate. They aren't guarded in big houses. We can get rid of them next."

"We?" Liam asked.

Donal tapped the side of his nose. "There are a few of us that feel the way I do. Are you game to join us boys?"

Ciarán looked at Liam, but Liam shook his head with determination.

"My father would find out and have my face off. It's his life's work to kiss the arse of the landed gentry. There's no way either of us can be found mixed up in any Fenian business." Ciarán felt disappointed but knew Liam was right. William McGovern was providing him with a living, and he couldn't jeopardize that.

Donal crossed his arms and leaned back in his chair,

"The two of you don't have a pair of balls between you."

Ciarán tried to defend himself,

"It's not just Uncle, John would have my head off as well. I can't risk it." He sighed, deflated. He didn't want to be cautious like John, he wanted to be impetuous and reckless like Donal. Donal even had a wife and a child coming – yet he could leap at a cause and try for change. "I'll do this for you, if I'm here when the pig is slaughtered, I'll steal the blood out of the kitchen before it's cooked."

Donal roared with laughter,

"Taking on the formidable Maire, you are a brave one there!"

The gamekeeper had led Donal to the manor house, through the estate and the pheasant pens, and up to the back of the house. On his own, Donal had crept around to the front of the house, but a dog had started barking. So, Donal had hurriedly splashed his bucket across the door, scrawled his epistle of accusation with the sticky blood, and was running off when someone let out the two mastiffs, who had eventually overtaken him and pulled him to the ground. Unable to escape their massive weight and drooling jaws, (he smelled ever so delicious being tainted with pig's blood) Donal was apprehended by two footmen and three stable boys. He was collected by the constable the next day, after spending the night in a stable, well-guarded by the mastiffs.

The local assizes would not be held for many weeks, so it was decided that the prisoner should be transported to Donegal Town where he could face trial and be convicted promptly. A heavily pregnant Kathleen appeared on her brother's doorstep, begging for his intervention.

John had no intention of putting himself in jeopardy by taking sides with republicans. Donal's family had already been tarred with the brush of rebellion, via his father's actions, and now this. Of course, it was terrible luck for Kathleen, but she had been warned that it was a foolish match. He had told her, 'Use your head, not your heart, lass,' but she hadn't listened and would now have to pay the price. John looked to his wife to sort out the hysterical young woman. Maire took Kathleen by the arm and persuaded her to come and lay down, for the baby's sake, and she'd bring her a nice cup of tea with a wee drop to calm her nerves. As she was towed away, Kathleen looked back beseechingly at her brother,

"You will help us, won't you?" But John only made a noncommittal sound.

As Donal had predicted, the news of his attack on the manor house did make the papers, and Liam and Ciarán read of the arrest with much consternation. Obviously, they hadn't tried hard enough to talk Donal out of his mad plan. They had genuinely believed it had been the drink talking. What an arse Donal had been, risking his life over something that was little more than a statement. He hadn't even achieved anything! Mind you, the news story did play up the image of the suffering wife left behind, soon to be a single mother. He had got his publicity and maybe, just maybe, there would be some support for Donal's call for independence. Blood money indeed. In more ways than one.

It was not difficult to explain to William McGovern that Ciarán had to return home to check on Kathleen, as tragedy had struck her. McGovern was soft hearted towards his sister's children. She had been a loving older sibling, almost like a second mother to him and he felt her loss keenly. He could only imagine how bereft her children had been when she died. However, he was less indulgent when Liam announced that he would be accompanying Ciarán. He only allowed it grudgingly, knowing that Liam was a great support to his cousin and Ciarán did seem quite devastated by this blow to his family.

The lads set out from Balleybofey as soon as they could, packing only a change of clothes and enough food for a day. They would be at the Gallaghers by nightfall, hopefully before Donal's transport had been arranged. Guilty of not supporting Donal in his crime, the least they could do would be to see if they could help him avoid the trial, or at least the sentence.

John was not surprised to see his brother and Liam, but not altogether pleased. He had put Kathleen in the spare room and would have to shift his children into his own bedroom to accommodate two more in the cottage. Maire was not as worried about the logistics but was suspicious of the precipitous arrival of the two lads. Ever blunt, she eyed them both and said,

"I hope you're not planning anything foolish. We've had enough of men who can't be bothered to think before they act." Ciarán had the good sense to look down at the floor, but Liam just smiled as Maire charmingly.

"And how is my dear cousin Kathleen?" he asked.

Maire got an even more severe face on her.

"How do you expect? She's sick with dread. If she doesn't lose that baby, I'll be surprised, I will. Whatever was that man thinking? Nothing, I'll tell you that for free, nothing at all. The poor lass loves him to distraction but that's love thrown away as far as I'm concerned," and she stomped out of the room, leaving the cousins alone with John.

He glowered at them,

"What are you doing here?"

"We've come to help," Ciarán said, standing up straighter and trying to look John in the eye.

"What? You'll help with the nursing of your sister? The two of you?" he raised his eyebrows at them in obvious disbelief.

"Surely we can ask around and see if there is anything we can do. We could go to Donegal Town and make a statement at the trial," Ciarán replied, deciding to ignore his brother's obvious sarcasm.

"A statement would be useless, he was caught red-handed, literally red-handed," John snorted in disgust, "Bloody eejit. so, no, you won't be going to any trial and making a spectacle of yourself. You can pass your condolences to your sister and then be off back home, both of you," and he too, turned and left the room.

Ciarán and Liam sat at the table, finishing the late supper Maire had set before them. Both were quiet, Liam resigned, but Ciarán's mind was still racing.

"I know a fellow that might help us. He used to look in on Donal and his mam. He lives up towards the hills. I'll have a word with him tomorrow morning. I think he'd be glad enough to help us."

"Help us?" Liam asked tentatively.

"Free Donal of course! I'm not going to leave my sister a widow. Sure, there won't be that many on a single prisoner detail. A few men could scatter the soldiers and slip in there and rescue a man. Conall can carry two of us as easy as one."

Liam looked doubtful. "Come on now Liam, we have to do something worthwhile with our lives. It can't be always what your Da or John wants. We need to be our own men."

Seamus had been in prison for a number of minor offenses, most often drunkenness, but he was a game fellow. He was a good bit older than the lads and had been involved in minor skirmishes for the Fenian cause over the years. Moreover, he had been close friends with Donal's Da and had taken on a protective interest in young Donal. He was aware of the incident and all too ready to help arrange a plan. And so, it was arranged, there would be four of them, a fellow Seamus knew being recruited, and that they would have the power of surprise, and the knowledge of the area. There would be no problem with them taking on a few soldiers. Donal would be freed, and Seamus would hide him in a derelict cabin in the hills. They had only to watch the gaol and be prepared for the transfer, though word had leaked out that it would be soon. Liam had coin enough to bribe one of the goalers to keep them informed and they were soon told that the prisoner would be moved at night, to prevent any interference from the locals. With another coin as prompt, they were told it might even be that same night.

And so that evening, the young men prepared to set out on their rescue mission. Ciarán, saddling his horse, had to make a second attempt to cinch the girth. His hands were shaking, and it wasn't the cold. Liam was already in the saddle and smiled down on Ciarán.

"Second thoughts Cuz?" Ciarán shook his head, not looking up at Liam. How could his cousin be so cavalier about it? They could succeed, save Donal, or they could both be shot.

They could all end up dead. But Liam never worried. Not like Ciarán, who had been born worried. He had always wanted to be carefree like Donal, or confident like Liam, but instead he saw how all that could go wrong. Like his country, he was anxious. It was as if he had absorbed the terrible history from the soil - years of starving, the evictions, watching family farms turned over to be a landlord's sheep pasture. There was only the church to turn to, to keep the fear at bay, the church, and the Republican movement. If Ciarán could be a part of the Republican movement, maybe he could hope for something better, a change at least. As a second son, on a farm that barely broke even, he knew he had no real place in the world. His uncle had arranged a match for him that promised a bit of land but that was his uncle's dream, as the land lay adjacent to the McGovern farm. For himself, Ciarán had only vague hopes.

Ciarán tried to get command of himself. He had no wife or family, so what did he have to lose? Well, his life, but look at Donal, his brother-in-law, he had done his bit even as Ciarán's sister was about to bear their baby. What if Donal never got to see his own child? What if Ciarán had to return to his sister and tell her he had done nothing for her husband, had just let him go to his death? That could not happen. Gritting his teeth, Ciarán mounted his enormous grey stallion, settled into the saddle, and gently prodded his horse forward.

"Let's go then," he announced, trotting down the road into the fading light. Ciarán and Liam knew the road well and could take it at speed. The soldiers hadn't that advantage, plus they were transporting a prisoner in a heavy wagon. The plan was to distract the soldiers with an altercation and then pull Donal from the wagon, throwing him onto Conall, and galloping away. It was a simple enough plan that shouldn't have too many loopholes. Liam and Ciarán would be joined farther down the road by Seamus and his friend. The guard detail for the prisoner was supposed to be six soldiers. Surely, the four of them, attacking in surprise, would be able to handle six soldiers that were totally unfamiliar with the territory. It was lonesome country between Glenties and Donegal Town.

Though Liam had not grown up in this part of the county, he had visited his cousin enough, so that he was secure in his knowledge of the track. With the confidence of a young man who had never wanted for anything, he almost considered the operation as an opportunity for good craic. They'd give the soldiers a bit of a rout, screaming like banshees and shooting into the air. They had no intention of killing anyone. However, if any of the party were caught, the penalty would be death. They just wanted to scatter the guards and rescue Donal. Sure, there was no harm in that, and the only concern Liam had was his father finding out. His father would be incandescent if he discovered that Liam had done anything to jeopardise the family's hard-earned position. William McGovern enjoyed prosperity and felt fealty to family was far more important than to country. Liam wasn't sure what he, himself, believed, but his bond to his closest cousin bound him to support the enterprise. And what fun it was, to pull one over on his father.

The only sound was the clopping of hooves on the hard-packed dirt road. They had been lucky with the weather. Muddy going would have slowed them down and having some light, as the moon peered occasionally from the clouds, was an advantage, although also a gift to the soldiers. Despite their ears being keenly pitched; they were still surprised when a man stepped out from the hedge alongside the road. Settling their startled mounts, they tardily recognized their erstwhile comrade.

"No horse Seamus?" Liam asked, suddenly feeling slightly uneasy.

"Ach, nothing but donkeys, and sure that would only slow me down."

"And where is Christy?"

"Home with a sick wife he says. I'm thinking more that he's got the willies."

"Can we do this with just the three of us?" Ciarán worried.

Seamus shrugged philosophically,

"Maybe. I've got a gun anyways, and if you'll get me on the back of your mad beast, I can ride along with you."

"Yes, but where do we put Donal if we're both up on Conall?" Seamus was non-plussed.

"Ah, well, I'll just sort of melt off into the fields you know. They won't be able to follow me in the dark. Sure, it will be fine. Let's get on with it. Your man Donal is waiting on us."

Ciarán gave Seamus an arm but there was no getting him on Conall, who was not over fond of the idea in the first place. Without a mounting block, the size of the horse was an obstacle too far. Finally, Liam had to dismount and give Seamus a leg up while Ciarán yanked the man's free arm and then Seamus fell heavily onto Conall, who grunted in disapproval.

"Sorry mate," Ciarán apologized, patting the horse's broad neck.

"And what about me?" Seamus complained. "I've had my bollocks nearly torn off trying to clamber on this elephant."

"Will the two of you shut it?" Liam retorted. He had stopped enjoying the night out now that the odds against them had been substantially raised. He pressed his horse into a trot and Conall, with the two men, followed with an irritable toss of his head. Turning, Liam warned Ciarán, "And if your bloody horse bites my mare in the buttocks, I'll have your head on a plate."

Ignoring his cousin's threat, Ciarán wondered aloud,

"What's our plan now, with only the three of us?"

"The same boyo," Seamus answered. "When we hear them, we'll break off into the fields along the road and come at them from the front, yelling like banshees and firing our guns, then you dash in, and grab hold of Donal while the rest of the Peelers come looking for us. Only, they won't find us, will they? Bloody eejits will be up to their neck in ditch water or caught in the blackthorn. No worries, lad. Just get your wee brother onto the horse and be off with you." Ciarán swallowed hard. He did worry and somehow, the plan didn't sound nearly as good as it had when they discussed it at Seamus' cabin.

They heard the soldiers after about another thirty minutes riding, and without a word, Liam jumped the stone fence on the side of the road to travel through the fields alongside. Seamus dismounted with a great deal of whispered cursing and clambered over the wall on the opposite side of the road. Ciarán waited until he hoped the other two were ahead of the prisoner's party and hoped they had not made too much noise crashing about

71

in the dark. Then, cautiously, Ciarán trotted towards the soldiers. It started then, the shouts and the gunshots, and Ciarán urged Conall forward as fast as he could go, reaching the wagon where Donal was laying on his side, hands secured behind his back. Ciarán leapt from his mount and jumped into the back of the wagon, using the butt of his rifle to knock out the driver. He reached for Donal and tried to raise him to his feet, to leap off the wagon and run for it, but Donal had been beaten and had no strength left to stand.

"Ciarán," he whispered, "Get out of here. You'll be killed!"

"No!" Ciarán protested, "I promised myself I'd bring you back to Kathleen!"

"Who will look after her if we're both dead? Go! Now!" but it was too late, a shot rang out and Ciarán fell, dropping hard onto the floor of the wagon, thumping his head on the way down.

Liam had to break his promise to himself not to kill anyone and shot the soldier approaching the wagon. The driver was still unconscious from Ciarán's blow and the other four were running after Seamus, who to his credit, had goaded on the soldiers with sordid insults and promises of a good fight. Running to the wagon, Liam was going to pull Ciarán out but was stopped by the bulk of Conall, the great horse reaching into the wagon and picking up Ciarán, teeth embedded in his jacket. He pulled his rider's body free, and Liam was able to shift Ciarán's weight into his arms. Just then one of the soldiers returned from his unsuccessful pursuit of Seamus and approached the wagon. Conall reared, screaming, and came down on the soldier, crushing him into the dirt of the road. With three soldiers still unaccounted for, Liam hurriedly lay Ciarán across the horse's saddle, hastily whipping off the horse's reins and using them to tie Ciarán in place. Conall took off without needing any prompting and Liam whistled for his own mount. They departed at what speed they could manage, with a man draped across his horse's back. A shot rang after them before they slid into the darkness of the night.

Donal was left to the remaining soldiers, who returned, furious and vengeful, kicking the bound prisoner repeatedly until there was little point in hanging him.

The morning light was beginning to appear on the horizon when Liam brought his burden up to his cousin John's farmhouse. He knew that John would not welcome them, so he urged the horses towards the stables. He untied Ciarán and let his body slip onto a bale of hay. Conall nuzzled the vaguely conscious man.

"Donal?" Ciarán managed.

"No," Liam replied tersely. "You've been shot. I'm going indoors to speak to your brother."

Ciarán reached out weakly and grabbed Liam's coat,

"Kathleen?"

"I'll say nothing just yet. We need to sort you out first. Now lie steady. Conall will look after you." The stallion rolled one red eye at Liam, causing Liam to step back uneasily. "Right then. I'll be back." He ran towards to the back of the house and rapped insistently on the kitchen door. It was the kitchen maid that answered, in her nightgown, with her shawl pulled tightly around her.

"Whist, what ails you?"

"I need your master, my cousin John, fetch him quickly!"

"For what do you need the master? He'll have me face off for disturbing him."

"His brother's taken a bad wound; he could be dying even now. Get you going!" The woman gasped and leaving the door ajar ran up the stairs. Liam stepped indoors and stretched his hands towards the fire, still faintly warm from last night's smooring. It was only a moment before he heard the heavy step of his cousin John.

John was in his night shirt with his trousers pulled on over his bare legs. His expression, in the dim light, did nothing to alleviate Liam's anxiety.

"What's happened then?"

"Ciarán's been shot." Liam swallowed, realising he had tears in his throat. "It's bad."

"Where is he?" John's voice was steady, almost steely. How could he be so cool?

"In the barn. Will you help me bring him indoors and then I'll go fetch a doctor," Liam pleaded.

"Was he shot doing Fenian business? Because if he was, I won't have him under my roof." John crossed his arms and walked to the door looking out, as if soldiers were even now approaching his home.

"By God man! He's your own brother. Are you going to leave him to bleed to death in your barn?" In his anger, Liam was shouting.

"Will you shut it? You'll have the whole house awake." John hissed back. But it was too late, feet could be heard on the stairs and Maire appeared.

"Whatever is going on down here? I finally got Kathleen settled and there's the children about to wake up." Her hands were on her hips as she glared at the two men.

74

"Your man here wants me to take in a Fenian rebel," John retorted.

"His own brother! Bleeding out in your barn right now. For the love of God, you have to help him." Liam was desperate at this point, the long ride with Ciarán slipping in the saddle, the blood dripping along the road, him not knowing if it was best to see to the wound or get to safety as soon as possible. The only piece of luck had been the rain, washing away the trail of red as it fell. It had meant to be an easy mission, cause a commotion, rescue Donal and everyone happy at the end, but now it was all a disaster. Was no one going to help him? He collapsed in a chair and put his head in his hands to hide the tears.

Maire was not quite as rigid as John, hard woman though she was. She put a hand on Liam's shoulder.

"We'll have him in the house for now and fetch a doctor," she gave her husband a steady look, daring him to interrupt her, one as stubborn as the other. "He can stay the one night and then we'll put him down in Kathleen's cabin, now that the mother has left. Or maybe, he'll be well enough by then to go back to your father's Liam. I'm sure your father will be anxious to have you home, no?"

John grunted disapproval but didn't carry it any further.

"I'll make up a bed and we'll be as quiet about this as possible. I've given Kathleen a sleeping draught and I don't want her to awaken and see her brother blooded, and God only knows where her husband is ..."

Liam lifted his head,

"Dead by now I should think. We were trying to rescue him."

75

Both John and Maire raised their hands for silence.

"Say no more. We don't want to know. I'll get Ciarán's room ready, and you bring him up there. I'll move my boys out for the time being. Go on John, and mind you don't make a mess of the floor in here. The less explaining we have to do the better."

GOODBYE MY HOME

Fiona lay across from Farley looking deep into his eyes. They were dark brown like her own, the full mahogany depth of them filling the globe. She held his gaze, sharing their thoughts. It was cold and they were both hungry. It felt like the travelling had been going on for days and they had no idea of where they were going, other than 'away.' Farley had caught them a rabbit yesterday, and they had eaten every bit of it but the eyes. Farley would never eat the eyes and Fiona couldn't bring herself to do so either. Farley had no trouble with the intestines and organs, but Fiona stuck to the meat and marrow, when hunger did not dictate otherwise. Ordinarily, she would have saved the skin, as skins were always useful, but she had to wastefully leave it behind or they would have been swarmed with flies. She buried it so there was no trace of their scant meal, and then they moved on, farther from the goat byre and her grandmother's cabin. There would be no mercy for a quare girl that talked more to animals than people. No one would listen to Fiona's explanation or care for her vengeance. She was not even sure herself why she had done it. Mad rage, perhaps. She had thought she was not human enough to have that feeling, but apparently, she was just as bad as the rest of them.

Fiona tried to piece together what had happened to destroy her home and her place in the world. She had only gone to the well, hadn't she? It was just across two fields. She heard her nan shout, she had Farley to thank for her keen hearing, and they had both stopped in their tracks, Fiona putting down the bucket. Then they had run back towards the cabin. They could hear Billy as well, running from the opposite direction, higher up the hill. When they got to the cabin, there was a soldier leaning over Nan, Nan laying against the wall of the byre, her head at an odd angle. They smelled blood. Billy got there first, ramming his horns into the man, who dropped the bleating kid imprisoned under his arm. Billy drove the man against the side of the pen and then reared up, bringing his hooves down hard against the man's chest. The nannies were gathering around, pressing in on the man, bleating and nipping. He was pulled to the ground, whence Billy reared up again, bringing his forefeet down hard on the man's abdomen. When Fiona got there, the work was nearly done. She took the knife from her apron, grabbed a fistful of the soldier's hair to pull the throat taunt and drew her knife across his vessels. The blood spurted into her face and across the front of her dress. Ripping her apron from her waist, she wiped her face and crossed to Nan, crumpled against the stones. She knelt by her grandmother and took her in her arms, knowing the form was lifeless, and she keened, a searing howl fit for the Morrigan's ears. Billy stepped over, folded his feet under him, and settled next to his Listener. Laying his head in Nan's lap, Billy sighed one, long, wretched sigh and then followed his Listener.

There had been no way to move the goat and the old woman, so Fiona fetched a blanket from the cabin and covered them. She left the uniformed man to the elements. The goats she freed by opening the byre and inviting them to wander the hills. They would make do. If people chose to chase them, the goats would either willingly be caught, or trot away free, depending on each nanny's wishes. Making a knapsack of the other blanket, Fiona packed Nan's book of recipes, some food and as many herbs as she could transport. The herbs and the book were the only thing of value that they had possessed. Then she closed the cabin door and left the place where she had been born, bonded to Farley, and grown into a Listener.

Food, Farley said, and Fiona was relieved to end her reverie. It was time to get up and hunt again. She stood up slowly from the damp ground and made a vague gesture at brushing the weeds off her skirts. She didn't know why she bothered. No one would see her, hopefully, and she would only get grubbier as their journey continued. They began to move cautiously through the fields, looking for mounds and rabbit holes, or even a stream where Fiona could catch fish. Farley grazed on grass intermittently and Fiona tried to do the same but found she liked greenery better cooked. Making a fire was worrisome though. The smoke might be seen, and people could approach, asking awkward questions. A cave would be useful to hide in for a bit, but they were too far from the coast. Fiona wasn't sure if there would be any mountainy bits nearby, she had never ventured so far from their small holding. It would certainly rain later, it always rained in Ireland, and spending another night shivering against a stone wall did not appeal. With all the evictions and fevers over the years, surely there had to be an abandoned cabin or stable. Even a ramshackle structure with half a roof would be some comfort.

Farley, as usual, was successful in his hunt. Combining his canine skills with superior intelligence made hunting less challenging than it was for most dogs. He was small, at seven or eight kilograms (of pure muscle of course) so he couldn't bring down big animals, but rabbits and the odd filched pheasant were easy work. His grizzled, coarse coat helped him to blend into the undergrowth and slip through thorny bushes relatively unharmed, and Fiona could gut the kill and split it between them. When they had been home, there was always a pot over the fire with a stew going. Bits of rabbit, some root vegetables, and anything else edible that Nan had gathered. The goats were good at pointing out prime spots for foraging. Between the two of them and their acolytes, Nan and Fiona had perhaps eaten better than their neighbours, although that was hardly saying much. At least they had not relied entirely on potatoes. Now, Fiona's stomach grumbled in memory of those hot stews. Home had only been a cabin with a dirt floor, but it had some warmth to it and Nan had been there, with an elaborate story for the evening's entertainment or a new recipe to teach her granddaughter. Fiona brushed away a tear. No more.

Farley enjoyed the mouse he had caught and returned later with a small leveret. Fiona quickly prepared it and ate as much as she could raw and left the rest for Farley - as long as he stayed strong, that was what was important. She knew she would have to find some kind of shelter and start preparing proper meals soon, but it was more important to get distance between herself and the cabin, and the man she had despatched. She imagined again, her nan, thrown aside, hitting the stone wall, and then sliding slowly into a heap. There had been a lot of blood. Blood caused by Billy, blood from her knife and a trickle of blood, inexorably flowing out of Nan's ear. So much blood. There was nothing she could do about it;

no way could she adequately explain it to anyone in authority. Revenge, defence, whatever – she had killed a British soldier and she was a powerless Irish girl; the only action open to her had been to flee. More than anything, she had left to escape the horrible sight of her nan, dead upon the ground. Fiona felt no guilt over slicing the man's throat. It had been no different to her than ending the life of a rabbit or fish, only this wasn't for the purpose of food, just revenge. She did feel guilty at not being able to bury her own grandmother, but at least Nan was resting with the great buck Billy beside her; as long as Nan and her acolyte were together forever, they would rest peacefully.

The third day of travelling was a day of filthy weather and Fiona slogged through the mud in the fields, which tired her legs unduly. She was afraid to go by the road in case soldiers were about but felt she was making little progress by the back ways, if she was, indeed going anywhere at all. She had left without much of a plan. She had packed well enough taking the necessaries, and the all-important recipe book but she had no map or any real knowledge of the country. She and Nan had only ever gone down from their cabin on the hill to the local market in Ardara, but no more places than that. They had made no alliances while selling their goat's cheese and some of Nan's remedies. People had looked askance at them, and Fiona had no one to turn to.

Now she was lost in a wet, cold country, recently recovered from plague, and decimated by emigration. Where would she find a place to settle and be safe? If it weren't for Farley, she might not have seen much use in going on. What life could she make for herself with no education, no money, and no family? She could be a servant but knew that would never last, not with her nature and her need to listen to the animals. And what if she were caught and accused of her crime? Would she hang? Most likely and that was not serving her purpose at all. She needed to be the Listener she was trained to be. There weren't many of them about and the need was great.

As night drew in, the rain grew heavier. Fiona slogged along a bit farther, looking for a hollow under some bushes to seek shelter. Hedgerows were not common in Donegal, farmers relying on stone fences due to the lack of lumber. There were a few old places where the hedge schools had been, the fairy ways. These hollows along walls offered some shelter, but even they soon developed muddy streams within them and there was no dry place to rest at all. They had stopped in one of these hollows last night, but Farley was not impressed and periodically shook out his coat and huffed in irritation. He understood why they had left but that didn't mean he was happy about being away from a warm fire and a pool of blankets. Bloody people, he thought, always arguing about something. They made life so complicated.

There was something darker and more solid in the darkness ahead – could it be a cabin? Fiona slowed her pace and turned to Farley for confirmation.

A dwelling, occupied. Horses. Maybe two, and people. Men, not so many. One is quite ill.

Do you think it's safe? Fiona asked.

Hardly. There are men. But the horses are outside. Perhaps there is a stable. You will have to remind the horses to be still. They are nervous creatures and will not like the smell of me. Can you do that? Fiona was unsure. She knew she could communicate effortlessly with any dog and could certainly speak to most farm animals as she had experience with them when farmers came to ask her grandmother for healing. The few horses she had encountered had been heavy draught horses, were these that type? But farmers rarely had more than one horse. If there were two together, maybe they were riding horses. Would they require a different sort of communication? She imagined that riding horses were of a different class and would expect to be treated with a higher level of respect and deference.

I'm drenched and half frozen Farley. It's worth a gamble. If there is any trouble, we'll run. No one will come looking for us in this weather. Waiting till the cabin went dark, she stumbled towards what they presumed was the stable, exhausted, and desperate for a roof of any sort. She hoped that whoever owned the horses was snug and warm inside and would not begrudge her a bed in the straw.

They approached downwind of the horses and slipped into the stables. Farley was right – horses are flighty creatures, and these were stabled away from home, in a location they did not feel comfortable in at all. There was a loud whinny and stomping of hooves as Conall and Bride became alert when they heard the dog. The horses, as a rule, didn't dislike dogs, but they were not in their home barn and this dog smelled somewhat unusual. Farley let out one clear bark of parley and waited. The horses shuffled suspiciously. Fearing they would alert the people in the cabin, Fiona felt forced to approach, though not without trepidation. Conall, was one of the largest stallions she had ever seen and exactly the colour of the moon on a winter night. It was obvious that he was a of very high status among his kind.

Slowly and gently, she placed her hands on the point of the stallion's shoulder. He tossed his head and attempted to bite her, but Fiona anticipated his intention and managed to avoid him neatly. She made sure to stand to the side of Conall so she could be fully seen by him.

Hush, oh great stallion, she greeted him. *We mean you no harm. We come only to shelter from the rain and beg leave to share your presence.* She felt a bit silly using such glorified language but sensed it was necessary in the presence of this stupendous beast. Farley sat down and chewed on a foot, to let the horses know that he was not interested in anything untoward.

Mollified by the girl's proper greeting, Conall, named after the great warrior Conall Cearnach, of the Red Branch of Ulster (he liked to remind anyone that listened of this dignified title) ceased his attempts to remove Fiona's fingers. He snorted deeply, blowing hot air over Fiona's head. It was the first warm thing she'd felt in days, and it gave her the impetus to continue her grandiose speech.

Oh, great one, you honour me, and she bowed her head respectfully.

After a time, Fiona began to hear Conall:

Strange girl and small dog. Wet and cold. No threat. I suppose they just want to share the stable.

What?

She, the girl, she can hear me! She is a Listener! A true Listener. I thought they were all gone from the land. But she is here, with me now and can hear me! Girl, who are you? Why are you here?

Fiona let her thoughts flow into him,

I am a Listener, as you say, from a long line of Listeners but there is only meself and my acolyte remaining. Thank you for allowing us into your abode. May I introduce you to me acolyte, Farley. He is a true dog. I hope that you will both permit us to rest here this one night for the sake of St. Francis, who loves us all. At the mention of the saint, Conall blew and settled his hackles. This one had taken the vow to serve the furred and feathered. They could rest easy.

Bride was getting nervous as the girl stood so long by Conall's side. Was she trying to steal them? She had heard of horse thieves and did not like the idea of leaving her rider or the good life she normally had at her home stables. She snorted for attention and reached her muzzle towards Conall.

He turned to her with excitement – *the girl is a Listener! She can hear us. I can hear her, and she brings an acolyte with her.* Bride whinnied and stamped her foot in astonishment. Fiona stepped around to Bride and laid her hand alongside her shoulder and let Bride know her. Bride shivered all over. Never in her life had she ever expected to meet a Listener. So many things she could ask her to tell her rider. She was speechless with the thrill of the moment. Fiona smiled. She had not spoken with horses of this ilk before and had wondered if it would be difficult. Dogs she could speak to sometimes without even making physical contact and goats she knew well too but horses had not been part of her day-to-day life. Now these two flooded her with their joy at having someone to communicate for them.

Conall shook his head, calling her back to him. She respectfully asked him again if he would share the shelter and he tossed his head impatiently.

Of course, my listening friend, but would you not be more comfortable going indoors with the humans? Fiona tensed.

I do not know your people, she said, *and perhaps they would not welcome a traveller of unknown origin.* Inwardly she groaned. What if they were soldiers? What if she had chosen the wrong place altogether to seek respite. She sent an image of soldiers to Conall with a question, and he promptly tossed his head in anger.

No soldiers here! Hate soldiers. I would stamp on them. They have hurt my rider!

Fiona stepped back quickly to avoid Conall's anger and Farley stood up, wary of the situation. For the first time he approached the great horse, who eventually settled enough to lower his nose and try to touch Farley on the muzzle in a careful greeting. Farley stood between the horse and Fiona, sending his thought pictures to Conall, who clearly saw they had a mutual enemy. From Conall, Farley gathered the story of the night attack, the failed raid, and the wound to Ciarán's leg. His knowledge flowed to Fiona, and she grimly understood the situation.

Your rider lies within, gravely injured.

Conall let his head drop. A rider and a horse, while not as close as a Listener and an acolyte, have their bond. Moved, Fiona went to him and laid both hands across Conall's flank.

I have little skill great horse, but I do have my nan's recipes and her herbs. If there is aught, I can do, then I will offer my services.

Will you save my rider? The great horse beseeched.

86

I will try, promised Fiona. *I would like to do this for you as I know what it is like to lose one you love and I would not wish it on you or any other creature, but I cannot go to him now. A beggar on the doorstep in the night would not be welcomed.*

When Bride's rider comes to check on us, speak to him. Let him know you have come to save my rider. Fiona offered her assent and sat down to wait. It was draughty in the old stable, but the horses had warmth to share, and Farley curled up pressing alongside her. The animals did what they could to keep the frail human warm until it was time for her to deal with the riders.

Liam woke from his uncomfortable bed on the bench and rolled onto his side, stretching his aching limbs. He gathered himself and stood, stepping carefully over to the rickety frame bed in the corner of the cabin. He feared the worst and steeled himself to kneel beside his cousin, feeling his forehead. But it was not cold, in fact it was beaded with sweat. Ciarán lived, but still deep in a fever. The only response he got from his cousin was a low moan. The pain must be wicked to feel it beyond the reaches of the fever. Liam sighed and stood. He would have to send for the doctor again – the useless quack that would again need to be bribed for his silence. 'Blast him,' Liam swore softly, not sure if he was referring to the feckless doctor or his rash cousin, forgetting that he, himself, had been just as willing to participate in the mad escapade. Well, he would stir up the fire and make himself a cup of tea before venturing out into the weather. He would have to do his best to put Conall out to grass, somewhere inconspicuous, and get him hobbled so he didn't run off. Ciarán would never forgive him if his

precious horse disappeared. Damn them both –
one as headstrong as the other.

After struggling over the hearth and reviving
the smoored fire, Liam filled the kettle from the
bucket by the door and set it to boil. He decided he
would go deal with the horses while the kettle
warmed. Pulling a burlap sack over his head to
keep the worst of the rain off, he strode towards
the stable.

Farley had heard the stirrings of the man
and alerted Fiona. She stood up and brushed the
straw from her skirts, picking a few pieces from
her hair. It was a fruitless effort. She would never
be able to make herself look presentable, not after
three days wandering and no proper meals. She
stepped to the stallion and laid her hands on him.

A man approaches. Can I trust him? Fiona
asked the horse.

He'll not harm you, Conall reassured. *Will
you go with him and see to my rider? I fear he is no
better.*

Fiona wondered if there was anything she
could do. She had some healing skills, but all her
patients had been animals. Her grandmother had
taught her the herbs and how to mend wounds,
but Nan had done all the healing for people. Did
she even want to get involved? It was probably
best to keep moving. No one knew she had killed
the soldier, but it wasn't impossible that two and
two would be put together. Besides, people had
never been kind to her. If only the stallion has
asked her to tend to one of his wounds, now that
would have been easy. Conall nuzzled her,
something he rarely did as he preferred biting
people. *Please* he almost begged, even though a
stallion does not beg.

Liam has been standing back watching the small girl, or was it a woman? Hard to tell in the dim light. Why wasn't Conall biting her or stomping on her foot? How had she even got past the stallion and into the stable? That damn horse didn't let anyone but Ciarán near him. Speaking of Ciarán, he needed to sort these horses and get back to his cousin. In the state the lad was in, anything could happen, even in a short time. Death, even. Liam swallowed hard. How dare he think such an ill thought about his cousin? Even if there was truth in it.

"You there," Liam interrogated, taking a step in the girl's direction, "What is it you're doing here?"

Fiona was silent for a moment. She could sense the anxiety of the man but more strongly she felt the great need from the large stallion.

"We're getting out of the rain," she ventured.

The man eyed them suspiciously; he certainly was uneasy,

"How do I know you aren't a horse thief?" Fiona sighed - men and their need to own things!

"I've never ridden a horse so it's unlikely I'd want to steal one," she offered drily. He considered her as well as he could from a distance. It was clear he didn't want to get too close to the stallion and Conall was revelling in the man's fear and kept tossing his head and showing his teeth. Fiona decided that the best course would be to consult with Conall.

Why do you disdain this man?

Conall tossed his head again and neighed triumphantly. *I enjoy teasing him. He's not so bad but he is not like my rider. My rider has some of my language, but this one is mute. His horse tolerates him, but I never would. He has no skill and no words for us, a man entirely with no link to our world.*

But he doesn't beat his horse? Fiona queried.

Conall snorted.

I wouldn't allow that, he replied. *That is Liam. Bride's rider. You will need to convince him you are here to help. He may be a bit suspicious.*

Fiona took a deep breath and stood a bit closer to Conall for reassurance. Surely, this man wouldn't wish her harm if they had the same enemy. Farley sat on her foot, as further reinforcement. She had her allies at any rate.

Liam was stumped by the girl practically clinging to Conall. The stallion hated people. He bit them for amusement; he kicked them or tossed his head wildly, knocking the unwary senseless. But here was a mere slip of a girl, stroking him and murmuring to him. For a moment, Liam was sure he was in the presence of one of the fae, no mere human could have this effect on Conall.

"Who the devil are you?" Liam shouted, choosing to intimidate, rather than give in to superstition.

"No one in particular. Just a *cailín* looking for some shelter. Your horses were kind enough to share their stable last night and I am grateful for that. I mean no harm."

"Well, away with you. We haven't anything to offer you," Liam dismissed her roughly.

Fiona swallowed hard. She hadn't expected such a gruff reception. She turned to the Conall for guidance.

What do I do? He wants me gone!

Conall dipped his great head and blew warm breath on the girl. The sign of affection was beyond Liam's comprehension.

"How in the name of our sweet Lord have you got that horse twisted around your finger? Are you some sort of witch?"

Fiona jumped away from Conall in fear.

"No witch. I'm no sort of witch at all. Me nan was a wise woman is all. I have some herbs and her recipes for helping poorly folk. There's no witchery there, I've just learned some healing for those that can't afford the fancy doctors." Liam stared at her, wondering if this girl would be of use to him and how odd that she appeared just when he was planning to call the doctor. The silence unnerved Fiona further. "I'm better with animals I must confess but me nan would help anyone, and I have her recipes."

"And where is your nan now?" Liam queried, eyeing the girl, and thinking she probably was too young to know much of anything at all.

Fiona didn't think she could speak. She swallowed hard and looked away for a long moment. Finally, she whispered,

"Dead."

Now Liam was silent, abashed at his coarseness.

"And the rest of your family?"

"Gone," Fiona thought of Billy, lying next to nan, of the flock filtering through the open gate, wandering away from what was home. And her mother, wherever she was, on wing, or gliding gracefully by. All gone. Except Farley, there was always Farley. She reached down and offered, "I have me dog. He is all me family now."

Liam nodded, speculating,

"I am sorry for your loss," he muttered. Could he take a risk and bring this girl indoors? Would she know anything that would help Ciarán? And would she keep her mouth shut?

Fiona knew she had to clarify her allegiance. She lifted her head with defiance,

"Well, the soldier that killed her is sorry now too," she spat out. Liam, stared hard at her and tentatively asked, "How sorry?"

"Dead sorry," Fiona declared.

"What? Dead? How's that?"

Fiona shrugged.

"I cut his throat. I had some help from a goat I know named Billy."

"You killed a soldier? Jaysus, lass, you must be out of your mind!" Liam shook his head. "Bloody hell. You best come indoors and tell me the rest of your story. And if you have some recipes for a sick man, I'll need your help and your silence, but I don't suppose you'll be running to the constables with tales anytime soon."

Fiona swept her hand down Conall's mane to let him know that she would be helping his rider. Then she turned to Liam,

"Will I lead out this horse so that it can get some grass?"

Liam smiled and nodded.

"You can do that too, but mind you hobble him, so he doesn't wander off."

"Oh, he won't leave his rider, there is no risk of that. And I'll point him away from the road so he can't be seen. He's such a fine creature, I suppose he would get easily noticed."

"Bless you," Liam said and slipped a harness over Bride's head to bring her out into the field and get her hobbled.

When Fiona entered the cabin, she inhaled the stink of purulence immediately. She went straight to the man lying on the cot and felt his fever. He was young but drawn by illness, and what might have been a ruddy complexion had taken on a greyish hue. His black curls were damp with sweat, and his blue eyes were uncomprehending. With no further ado, Fiona stepped up to the prone body and removed the blanket from the left leg. A large, oozing wound was poorly bandaged, and stained with blood and pus. She shook her head in disgust. What a mess! It would take ages to put this right.

Kneeling down next to the injured man, Fiona started listing in her mind exactly what she would need to proceed. He was feverish too, so the wound had also poisoned his blood. She would need to treat the fever along with the wound. She was grateful that she had collected much of Nan's herb supply when she left home – she knew they would come in handy and now they had. It made her feel like Nan was looking out for her. She said a quiet thank you to her grandmother and then set about the task.

She turned to Liam,

"Could we boil up some water and do you have an extra linen I can use for bandages?" Liam immediately began building up the fire, relieved to finally have something to do that might help Ciarán. Fiona began searching through her satchel for willow bark. She hoped the man would be able to take some tea. 'The man,' she thought, she needed more information than that. She turned to Liam, "Does he have a name?"

Liam rolled his eyes,

"Aye he has a name and so do I. He's Ciarán and I'm Liam. And yourself?"

"Fiona, and this is Farley,"

"Of course," Liam said, "you have to introduce the wee dog as well."

He glanced around the grim little cabin, wondering if there was any spare linen. He had been in this cabin many a time, drinking and talking with Ciarán and their friend Donal. He had never bothered to look for basic necessities though. It was Kathleen's and Donal's home, and neither of them were here to help. "What do you need the water for?" he asked the ragged girl before him.

"To steep a tea and to mix with salt for cleansing the wound. Then I'll need to dip the bandages in the water and place them wet over the wound. I could do with some honey as well."

"Demanding little thing," Liam muttered, then more audibly, "The doctor thinks the bullet passed through and the leg is broken. He was in an awful hurry to stitch up the wound and stop the bleeding. We needed to move Ciarán quickly. I'm not sure the wound was cleaned properly, or even if the leg is set."

"You paid this doctor?" Fiona queried in disbelief.

"More for his silence than his skill."

"Well, that's good then for there wasn't much skill involved." Fiona shook her head. All the good Nan had done with her bits of herbs gathered freely, only asking a loaf here or a few eggs there, for years of wisdom. Yet, people were suspicious of a cunning woman, but trusted the modern doctor. "I'll need to remove the bandages and take a look at the wound, though I can smell right now that it's gone septic."

"I'm afraid you'll see a fair bit of the rest of him as well."

Fiona shrugged; she hadn't seen a man naked before but how ugly could they be? She untied the knot holding the bandage in place and began to expose the wound. The leg was angry and red, oozing pus, some of it green tinged. The edges of the wound were starting to blacken. Fiona gasped. How foolish these people were to let things get so bad. The man was likely to lose the leg, if not his life.

"That bad?" Liam asked sadly.

"And more so," Fiona replied. "But I've promised that great horse out there that I would return his rider to him, and I won't break a vow to such a creature as that. Now, I need the cloth and hot water with a bit of salt in it. Let's get to work."

Liam took one of his shirts and, under Fiona's instruction, began to tear it into strips. The strips were then soaked in the hot water from the now warm kettle and Fiona took a pinch of her precious salt and added it to the bowl of bandages. She used one strip to gently cleanse the wound with the warm salt water, but even her mildest ministrations generated groans from the patient. Once she had removed as much debris as possible, she began to lay the strips across the wound, creating a wet dressing that would soon dry, sucking up the muck of the wound and cleaning it of some of the devitalized tissue. As she dressed the wound, she reminded herself that it was not that much different to a goat's leg and tried her best to ignore the signs of pain from her patient. At one point, she had to ask Liam to hold the leg still, but she was able to finish the dressing, without causing all out howling from Ciarán.

"I'll keep those dressings in place until tomorrow and then we'll pull them off." She looked levelly at Liam, "It will hurt like the divil when we pull off the dressings as it will take away all that is dead and rotting. You may need to tie him down. Then, likely, I'll have to do it all over again the day after to get all the poison from the wound. Will that be alright?"

Liam swallowed hard, not looking forward to the procedure, but he nodded in agreement.

"At least you're doing something, whatever it is. And the fever, is there anything we can do for that?"

Fiona frowned.

"White Willow bark will be good for that, but I need to add something else to help fight the poison spreading from the wound to his brain. I'll need to check Nan's recipes. I could make a tincture, but it won't be easy to get down him, the state he's in. And I'll need to collect some herbs for a poultice when we dress the wound tomorrow. Do you think you could get me some honey?"

Liam nodded.

"I'll go up to the big house. Maire might have some simples you can use as well if you tell me what to ask for. But first, I'll get us both a cup of tea. When did you last eat *cailín?*"

"I had a bit of a rabbit with Farley a day ago," Fiona answered, looking longingly at the stool by the hearth. She was that tired, and it didn't look like nursing this young man was going to be an easy job.

Liam noticed her envious glance and motioned to the stool,

"Sit yourself down and I can get out the loaf and wet the tea. While we are eating you can tell me how you came to kill a British soldier and I had best tell you how my cousin and I are in this predicament."

Liam sliced some bread from the loaf brought over from John's house and cut a piece of cheese for Fiona. She settled on a chair near the stove and broke off pieces of cheese and bread for

Farley before devouring the rest of the sparse meal. Liam noted her attention to the dog but merely raised an eyebrow. You honour what family you have, he mused. The hot tea was heavenly, and Fiona felt her strength returning. She collected the last few crumbs on her fingertips and let Farley lick her fingers appreciatively before he curled up next to the warmth of the fire.

"Is this your cabin?" Fiona queried, though she knew it wasn't. Liam was well dressed, if filthy, and the horses were too fine to belong to simple cottiers. There was a lot she needed to figure out about these two men.

He nodded to his stricken cousin,

"This is his sister's cabin. She shared it with her man before he was arrested."

Fiona nodded and then asked,

"Why isn't Ciarán with his sister then?"

"Ah yes," Liam sighed, "That is a question. Kathleen isn't well at the moment – she's just lost her husband and now it seems she's lost her baby as well. She's up at the older brother's house – John. My cousin John is very eager to avoid any involvement with his brother's troubles. As a matter of fact, John is keen to avoid any involvement with his brother at all."

"You mean his own brother put him out of the house when he was injured?"

"Not exactly. Ciarán was living with my father and myself anyway. We only went to John after the accident with the soldiers. And to give him is due, John did have us for a night and called in the doctor but then he was sure we were endangering his home and decided we'd be safer out this way – in case anyone came looking. In the meantime, his wife, Maire, is sending over food and necessities. They haven't completely abandoned Ciarán, and they do have poor Kathleen now to deal with. You see, it was her husband we were trying to break free from the peelers. Obviously, we failed."

Liam paced across the room and ran his hand viciously through his hair. His voice rose as he explained,

"One of our fellows didn't show and with just the three of us, six guards were too many. Donal is meant to be hanged, if, he survived the beating he got during our failed rescue attempt. Her husband being arrested was too much for Kathleen and she lost the baby. Of course, seeing Ciarán this poorly wouldn't be doing her any good either. It really is best we're out here. And if soldiers come looking, it's only us that will suffer."

"What did you do exactly?"

"We attacked a group of soldiers transporting a prisoner to gaol. Donal was a bit of a republican, or at least that's what he thought of himself. More a bit of a fool. He was caught 'defacing' a landlord's property last week. He was being transported to the gaol at Donegal Town. We thought we could overcome the guards and sneak him out of the country, sending Kathleen after. You see, there was meant to be four of us. And now Ciarán has been shot and we may end up having lost the both of them." Liam looked down into his now empty cup of tea.

"Surely, they'll come after you!" Fiona was alarmed. She seemed to have stepped into danger, not away from it.

"It was well dark, and both Ciarán's brother and my father are known to be quite friendly with the local constables. They'd never suspect Ciarán and myself."

"But they'll be riding all over the country looking for someone with a grey stallion!"

Ciarán nodded, "Well, yes, that is a bit of a problem. But surely, they'd never look in this broken- down cabin. And I'm grazing the horse well out of the way. We should be fine. Ciarán just needs to make an effort and get himself better. The thing is, I think he blames himself for failing and letting his sister down. He is very fond of Kathleen, and it was terrible to hear her shrieking and wailing when she realized she'd never see her husband again. I wonder is Ciarán trying to die out of guilt."

Fiona was not entirely reassured by Liam's reasoning. However, she'd promised Conall she would try to heal his rider, and besides, it felt so good to be warm indoors again with some food in her belly. If any soldiers came looking, surely there would be time for her to run and hide, Farley would warn her well in advance. Perhaps, also, this rescue attempt deflected some of the attention from herself.

As if reading her thoughts, Liam asked,

"And what is your tale then young lady?"

"I'm afraid I'm no glorious revolutionary hero. Me nan and I lived on a small holding with our goats and Farley. We kept ourselves to ourselves. I think the soldier that came wanted one of our goats, but we would never sell them. He must have insisted so nan tried to stop him. He threw her off him and she hit the stone wall. I was too far across the field. It was done before I could even call out. Billy attacked the man so that there was little left to do when I arrived. I just knelt down and slit his throat."

"Holy Mary, mother of God," Liam breathed, "Remind me to never get on your wrong side. And you, only a slip of a girl." He shook his head in disbelief. "Seems you've got more spirit than many of our brave republicans. Did no one see you then?"

"No, it was only the one soldier. He was probably a deserter now that I think of it, being so hungry as to want a goat for meat. But we weren't so friendly with our neighbours. If someone came asking questions, they would likely talk against us."

"Who is Billy, and where is he now?" Liam asked.

Fiona speculated. Conall had said Liam couldn't speak to his horse He wouldn't understand.

"Billy was our buck and he's dead now. I opened the gates and let the rest of the flock go where they wanted. I couldn't hide the soldier and I had to leave any way. I couldn't ever again look at that wall without seeing her lying there, her head twisted at an odd angle, her eyes seeing nothing."

Abashed, Liam stood up and moved restlessly about the cottage.

"I'm sorry for your loss," he muttered, as he had before. Well, there never are the right words. "Is there anything you need?"

Fiona lifted out of her thoughts and looked at him.

"For what?"

Liam sighed uncomfortably.

"For yourself. Is there something I can get you when I go to John's house?"

Fiona was surprised but decided to test his offer.

"I could use a blanket for meself to sleep on, if you're asking me to stay here."

"Well, it would be a blessing, if you can manage it in your busy schedule," he smiled at her and hoped she would take the jest.

"I guess this place is as good as any," Fiona smiled back, albeit weakly. Then she opened her parcel and started looking for white willow for fever, garlic and burdock root for a poultice and some comfrey for the bone. She could hear Nan's voice in her head and see the gnarled fingers moving through the pouches, pulling out the remedies that were needed.

IS A MAN THE SAME AS A GOAT?

Fiona lifted her head off her arms. She must have fallen asleep curled up in the chair. She had only been nursing Ciarán a few days, but it was already taking its toll on her. Stretching till her bones popped, she stood and walked over to her patient. He lived. She watched the breath rise and fall, a bit too quickly, so she lay her hand across his forehead. Still feverish. She slipped out to the kitchen and groped for a candle. By the weak light she was able to locate the willow bark infusion she had in the window and poured out a cup. She considered adding some hot water to dilute it, but doubted she'd get even half of this cup down. He'd have to take it bitter. Maybe when Liam got back from the big house, he would have honey with him to sweeten the brew. It was foul stuff and as he regained his strength, if he regained his strength, he would refuse to swallow it. At least that is what happened with the goats. Fiona figured people weren't that much different.

Carrying the candle and the tea, Fiona returned to the sick bed and surveyed her patient. She would have to prop him up to get the infusion down him and that would not be simple. He was a good deal heavier than she was used to lifting. She placed the candle in the window, being careful to pull the curtain material aside and placed the cup next to it. What she needed to do was insert something under him and boost him that way. There was no possibility that she could lift him while simultaneously feeding him.

Casting her eye about, she noticed a chest at the foot of the bed and went to open it. As she had thought, it was full of linens. This must have been the hard work of the young bride, now a widow and mother to a dead baby. Sending Brigid, a quick prayer for the bereaved, Fiona began pulling out sheets and a tablecloth and rolling them up into a large cylinder. She took her make-shift prop and slid it under the pillow of her patient. He stirred slightly and rolled his head towards her, opening his eyes into the dim light of the room.

Ciarán stared at the girl trying to hoist him into a sitting position. Some part of him told himself he should move and make it easier for her, but he could find no strength. He lay there, limply, wondering where he was and why he was still alive. The girl, realizing he was conscious, began to speak softly.

"I'm just trying to lift you a wee bit now if you don't mind. I need to get you to drink something to get your fever down. It's a dreadful brew but you'll drink it all the same. You'll have to, I'm afraid." Fiona went to the window and retrieved the cup. She could hear Farley patter alongside her; he had heard her voice and had decided to investigate the situation. "And here's Farley come to make your acquaintance. Farley this is Master Ciarán. Oh, and I'm Fiona. Your cousin hired me to nurse you and don't worry, I hate soldiers too." She tried to smile at the young man but was afraid it came out more as a grimace. She wasn't used to talking to strangers, and she certainly wasn't used to nursing them. Why had she agreed to this? Oh yes because the horse had asked her.

"Your horse, Conall, he asked me to look after you. That's why I'm here. I hope you don't mind. He was very insistent."

"Conall ..." Ciarán whispered.

"Aye, that's what you call him isn't it? He has a grander name for himself, but you call him Conall, right?"

"He is ... Well?"

"Oh yes, just pining for you. When it's full light outside, I'll go out and tell him you are on the mend so. He'll be that pleased," and then she lifted his head and offered the cup. It felt terribly awkward. He wasn't a dog, or a goat, but a man. However, he was ill, and she had promised, so she poured a sip into his mouth.

Ciarán screwed up his mouth and would have spat if he could find the energy. Instead, he just let the liquid dribble out of his mouth.

"Now, none of the that! You have to drink the stuff. I told you it was horrible. Just swallow it and get it over with. Otherwise, I'll never get this fever down and you'll likely die. What would Conall think of that?" She nodded emphatically and brought the cup to his lips again. "Swallow it fast. I've asked for honey from the big house but for now, just get it down you."

'Bossy cow,' he thought but endured the ministrations and swallowed the contents of the cup, nearly gagging as the last bit went down. Then he lay back on the pillow, utterly exhausted.

"I've got you propped up like. It's maybe not so comfortable but I'll leave you like that a bit to make sure the tea stays down. Maybe you can take a bit of broth too? Farley caught a rabbit earlier and we made a good meal out of it. We've eaten most of it, but I kept a bit by in the pot in case you woke. It would be good to get some nourishment in you. Your cousin says you have been in and out for the past three days and haven't taken any food at all." She crossed the room, making her way carefully in the dim light, to get a bowl of the rabbit stew. Briefly she turned back to him and narrowed her eyes, "And don't you dare die while I'm not looking."

When she returned with the broth, she tried to spoon it into his mouth, but he waved her away.

"I'll do it myself," and he took the bowl in his trembling hands, and attempted to spoon the liquid into his mouth, missing often and feeling it dribble down his chin. Silently, she took the bowl from him and handed him a cloth to wipe his face. He leaned back, completely shattered. "Are you the witch that ripped my skin off?"

"Aye, that's right. I soaked some bandages in salt water and set it to dry on your leg, then ripped it off, taking away some of the badness with it. I bet it hurt like the very flames of hell."

"It did," he muttered, vaguely remembering screaming oaths and Liam holding back his flailing arms. He was fairly sure he had promised to rip her head off and may even have tried to do so.

"Your cousin is up at your brother's house this night, collecting some food for us. He should be back soon." Ciarán was annoyed that the girl had answered his question before he had asked it.

Fiona decided as Ciarán was awake, that she should fill him in on the plans. "I'll be putting maggots in your leg next. Tickly wee things but they'll get the rest of the rot out. Your man, the doctor left a bit of cloth in when he was digging around. It was a right mess. It's been a terrible lot of work to get it clean. I don't think you'll lose your leg though." She did not intend to be unkind, but all her former patients had been four legged. Goats and cows didn't take kindly to euphemisms. You had to be straight with them and she hoped men weren't too much different. This one seemed a bit astonished at her bluntness but finally murmured

105

'thank you,' before dropping off to sleep again. Fiona went back to the pot and noticed a bit of broth left which she poured into a bowl and put on the floor for Farley. Her lovely boy was partial to a drop of rabbit stew.

Liam returned in the morning with more blankets so that there was something besides her cloak for Fiona to sleep on. He brought what food stuffs Maire could spare and simples that Maire thought might be helpful for healing: honey, salt, comfrey, nettle, and burdock. Fiona was very grateful for the simples, as she had only the small supply, she'd brought with her when she fled. She could always gather more, but the time of the year wasn't right for some of the plants, and she hadn't much time to forage when she was nursing the sick man.

"I'll need to get back to my own home soon," Liam announced. "My father will be wondering what happened to us. Ciarán and I were only supposed to be visiting his family." He paused, worrying at his lower lip. "I guess I'll tell him Ciarán had a fall from Conall. Sure, anyone will believe that; the horse being the wild creature that he is."

"Hardly fair to blame the horse when he saved your man's life." Fiona retorted. Liam had told her of Conall lifting Ciarán in his teeth and pulling him out of reach of the guards.

"My father doesn't support the cause. And we never meant to get involved, not seriously. We just wanted to rescue Donal." He looked down, deflated by their failure. Kathleen was still being given laudanum, sleeping till she could bear to face the fact that her husband was dead and that she had lost the baby. How long would that take?

"So, I'm to stay here? Or will his family take him home once you've left?"

"Ach, no, John won't have him at the house. It's too risky what with Kathleen being so delicate. No, he's best off staying here and sure, you're doing a grand job aren't you? You got some food into him today, did you not?"

The thing was, Fiona wasn't sure she wanted to stay. She found being tied to the cabin confining. She was used to more time out and about. She and Farley had been doing most of Nan's foraging as Nan's hips and knees had started giving her gip when she walked too far. There had been the goats to tend to, journeys to other holdings to help with healings, and the odd visit to market in Ardara to sell their produce. On the other hand, she was growing fond of the stallion, Conall. She had slipped out to the stable as often as possible to listen to the great horse and on his request, let him out of the stable to graze, though she was vaguely aware that Liam preferred the horse shut up as much as possible. She had reminded Conall that he had to keep well away from the road, so no strangers spied him, and the horse reminded her that he wasn't born yesterday.

"We will pay you for your service, you know? It won't just be food and keep. I'll see to it that you get some coin as well," Liam reassured her.

Fiona looked surprised. She had never had a job before and wasn't sure if she should have made some sort of agreement. Then again, she hadn't any choice, had she? She had made a promise to Conall, and she kept her promises to animals. Maybe now she would need to make a promise to a man. That was a frightening thought. Abruptly, she answered Liam,

"Sure, I've nowhere else to go."

Liam left the next morning, still not sure if he was doing the right thing. The longer he was away, and it had been over a fortnight now, the less time he had to manage any rumours that might have reached his father's ears. In Ballybofey, they would have heard of the altercation between the prisoner's guard and some 'rebels.' Would William McGovern Senior notice the coincidence in the timing of their visit to Glenties, and the attack? Their reason for the visit had been to visit Kathleen, hoping to arrive in time to see the new baby. McGovern knew Donal had been a prisoner and yet he had been sympathetic regarding his niece. William Senior saw himself as a sort of patriarch, looking after his dead sister's family, especially since the Gallagher's father had died as well. He had not approved of Kathleen's match, but he didn't begrudge the girl her anxiety. Surely, the tale of the baby's death, alongside Donal's would distract William long enough, so that he did not dwell on the unfortunate incident of Ciarán's injury. Liam's father would be annoyed to have Ciarán away from his duties on the farm for an extended period, but annoyance was far better than suspicion.

And the girl, could Liam trust her? She was a rare healer, that was obvious, far better than the useless doctor that had first tended to Ciarán. She was that bit strange though. She kept herself to herself mostly, though she had a running conversation with that dog of hers. She had been in the stable, far too often for his liking. Could she really be tending that brute of a horse? How? He could barely get near Conall on the best of days and was scared for his life the rest of the time around the horse. Well, he had no choice really. John wouldn't take Ciarán into his house and there were no other skilled women about to nurse Ciarán. Fiona would have to do, odd thing that she was and all.

It was late on the afternoon after Liam left that Farley suddenly stood up, body vibrating with a deep-throated growl. Fiona went to him and laid her hand on his shoulder and gulped at the sense he gave her. Horses, three or four. Men on horses. A group of men on horses could never be a good thing. She rushed to Ciarán's pallet and shook him sharply. His eyes peeled open, and he attempted to press himself up into a sitting position.

"No," she hissed, "Stay down. I'm going to cover you over, almost completely, and you're to stay faced to the wall. Some men are coming. You need to be feverish or unconscious. Just make sure you're insensible. Do you hear me? Don't speak, don't move. Can you do that?" Ciarán figured he didn't have much choice. As he couldn't sit up without help, he could hardly defend himself, or her for that matter.

Fiona threw a block of peat on the fire, and when the smoke billowed up, she stuck her face into it, making her eyes run with tears. She took some ashes and rubbed them into her face, making her wan and sickly looking. The hoof beats were fully audible now. She laid her hand on Farley for reassurance and reminded him to act with restraint. Then the knocking came.

Lieutenant Distaff and two soldiers had been given the detail of searching the countryside for the Fenians who had attacked the prison guard. They had lost two soldiers and though the prisoner had been dispatched, the attackers had escaped scot-free. They were rat terriers, these Fenians, running out, taking a quick nip, and then hiding

109

down some hole. Distaff hated dogs – bloody, sneaky creatures they were. He was not best pleased when he heard barking coming from the cabin they were approaching. Stupid Irish, look at that mud hut before him. Obviously, peasants that didn't have two ha'pennies to rub together, and then they take on a useless dog to feed as well. Idiots.

Fiona opened the door a crack, leaning heavily on it as if she were bereft of all strength. She did not like what she saw. Three uniformed men. She felt her stomach turn and the anger she felt over Nan's death rose in her throat. She'd be happy to dispatch these three fellows as well, if only she could. She'd really have to get control of her anger. She couldn't go around wishing death to every soldier she met, well she shouldn't anyway. She waited, letting them speak first.

One of the men, clearly an officer for he wore more braid and bangles than the other two, stepped forward.

"We are searching for fugitives. We need to enter your home," he sneered at the description of the cabin as a home, then continued. "To ask you about any men passing this way, and to make sure you have no one in hiding."

"You don't want to be coming in here," Fiona wailed. "We've the fever. My brother is near dying and sure, I'll be following him close after." She thanked St. Francis that she had freed Conall from the stable right after Liam left. He would be wandering up in the fields above the cabin as he had a yen for fresh grazing. Liam had told her that if anyone came, they would be looking for a grey stallion, as if she didn't know that already.

The two soldiers stepped back, and one pulled out a cloth and covered his mouth. Distaff looked disgusted at his inferiors. He pointed at the private covering his mouth,

"You, get in there and do a thorough search, and make sure to have a good look at the brother."

"But sir,"

"Now!" Distaff ordered. He pushed the door open, and Fiona fell back, nearly tripping over Farley who had been pressing against her legs. "Control that cur," he shouted at Fiona. Fiona picked up Farley and placed him on Ciarán, right on top of the injured leg. She heard Ciarán moan, just as she hoped he would, to scare the soldiers even more. The private crept towards the bed and reached out to turn Ciarán as Farley's growl reached a more intense decibel. Fiona laid a hand on Farley. Still covering his mouth, the private pulled on Ciarán's shoulder and took a quick look at the face, red and mottled from pressing into the straw pallet, a string of spittle hanging from the lip. With a jerk, the soldier leapt back and wiped his hand on his trouser.

"I think he's dead, Sir."

"He's not dead you dolt! I just heard him moan."

"Maybe that was his dying breath," the other soldier offered.

Distaff sighed deeply.
"Just finish searching the place," not that there was much to search, the table, chair, a bench, the chest, and a cupboard.

"They've got a fair bit of food for peasants," the private remarked.

Distaff turned to Fiona with an upraised eyebrow.

"Sure, people are generous, so they are," she quickly improvised.

Distaff was not satisfied. They had made no progress in their assignment at all. The people around Glenties were either all liars or too thick to string a sentence together. Even at the big house, where the farmer had lived, very little had been said. It was well known that the farmer's sister was the widow of the prisoner, but he hadn't been allowed to see her. She was ill he was told. He was going to force the issue, but report had it that the farmer, John Gallagher, had always been cooperative in the past and that he had never had any doing with the Fenians. John had agreed with Distaff that the attack had been an outrage and an insult to the Queen's justice. Distaff had chosen to look in more remote abodes, that was where the rebels usually hid themselves. He couldn't have gotten more remote than this sordid cabin at the back of beyond. He advanced on the girl, who had sunk onto the bench as if her legs could no longer hold her, which was only the truth, as Fiona was shaking all over.

"Have you seen any unusual characters? We're looking for three men, one riding a large, grey horse. Have you seen any one like that?" He spoke slowly, aware that many of these country people could barely understand English.

While she was keen to get the soldiers out of the cabin, she couldn't resist playing with the Lieutenant for just a moment. "Horse?" she asked, trying her best to look confused.

"Yes, a horse. Big, white," Distaff felt himself gesturing with his hands and felt even more irritated, if that was possible.

"Horse?" Fiona said blankly. Then, after a moment's reflection, "Ah, *capall! Capall bán!*" she said triumphantly.

"A horse," Distaff insisted. "A big, bloody horse!"

Fiona smiled and shook her head.

"No horse. Only donkeys around here."

The private had finished his search and both he and his companion were eager to go and get away from the reach of infection. They hovered by the door and then the one with the handkerchief over his mouth summoned the courage to say a muffled,

"Sir ..."

Distaff withered him with a look but decided there was no point in continuing to interrogate an illiterate, ignorant girl with very little command of the English language. For good measure, Fiona began an intense coughing fit and doubled over, clutching her sides. Both inferiors moved quickly out of the door and into the yard.

"We'll check the stable," they called over their shoulders.

Distaff gave one long look to the body on the bed and then asked the girl,

"What will you do when he dies?"

Fiona, recovering from her self-induced fit, sat up and wiped her eyes.

"Bury him." She was tired of the performance and wanted the man out of the cabin now. Distaff waited one more moment.

"At least you'll still have that flea-bitten varmint," Farley bared his teeth at Distaff and the Lieutenant left the cabin. She waited until the men had finished searching the stable, hoping there were no droppings left – she had cleared it when Conall went out earlier, but was it clear enough to look uninhabited? Apparently so. She heard the men leave, their horses trotting east. She motioned Farley off Ciarán's leg and went to his side.

113

"I'm sorry I hurt you. I didn't want them to smell the wound. Are you alright?"

Ciarán rolled onto his back and lifted himself up onto his elbows.

"You are bloody brilliant girl!" he smiled at her.

As Ciarán regained his strength, he began to make brief forays out of the sick bed. The first goal was managing the chamber pot on his own, as it was incredibly embarrassing to have to ask Fiona for help. She seemed nonplussed though, and her business-like manner did much to ease his chagrin. She had spent so little time around people, she hadn't learned to become ashamed of bodily functions. Dogs, goats, sheep, and cows had defecated in front of her, why not a person? But Ciarán had been raised in a strict Catholic family and attended a school with strong rules about appropriate deportment and so found intimate nursing a bit too personal. It was a small goal, but he was hugely relieved when he achieved it. True, Fiona still had to empty the chamber pot for him, but he would manage that soon he promised himself.

The next milestone was to take the few steps to the bench so he could sit up at a table to eat. The pain in his leg was incredible and Fiona warned him not to use it too soon or the bone wouldn't set right. She had asked for a walking stick from the farmhouse and a blackthorn cane had arrived eventually. Ciarán felt like an old man using it, but it did ease the agony to put some weight on the stick. Fiona encouraged him to lean on her, declared she was quite strong for her size, but to him, she seemed a tiny, wee thing and he didn't want to break her. Over the course of a week, he built up the strength to take the few

114

steps to the bench and was inordinately proud of himself. It was then that he began to get bored.

It is all very well to lay in bed when you are delirious with fever and weak with pain, but when you have begun to heal, the confines of a bedchamber can be imprisoning. Ciarán was desperate to see Conall, so, Fiona brought the stallion to the door every morning and Ciarán could call out to the horse from where he sat. He hoped to be able to stand long enough soon that he could stroke Conall's muzzle and scratch behind his ears. He promised Conall so. The horse nickered to him anxiously and did try to get in under the lintel of the door, but he couldn't manage. Ciarán had to laugh at the big horse trying to force his way into the miniscule cabin, but Fiona scolded him. Conall was frustrated and unhappy to be so close and yet unable to touch his rider; it was cruel to laugh at him. Ciarán apologised profusely, relieved that the girl had his horse's best interests at heart.

When Fiona next went up to John's for food, Ciarán asked her to request some books. The Gallaghers hadn't owned many books, but Ciarán knew there was a Dickens and a book of Greek myths, and didn't Kathleen have a Hardy novel somewhere in the cabin? Maybe re-reading those volumes would ease the tedium of the long hours. Returning with a loaf, some butter, some potatoes and a few eggs, Fiona produced the three books and a bonus extra, Fairy and Folktales of Ireland. The last belonged to John's son, but it had been decided that Ciarán could borrow it. Fiona cleared the table and placed the books down, almost reverently. She stroked the cover of the fairy tale book but didn't dare to open it. Ciarán watched her, amused.

"Did you not have any books in your home?"

"Aye," she replied, "We had Nan's book with her recipes. She taught me to read with that book."

"Had you no story books at all?" Fiona shook her head. There had never been money to waste on a story book. All the stories she knew came from Nan's imagination.

"But you can read?"

Fiona was offended.

"Of course, I can read, and figure too. I went to school for a time, but the teacher wouldn't let Farley indoors, so I couldn't keep it up, but Nan taught me."

"You were let off school because of your dog?" Ciarán had trouble believing this.

Fiona looked away and shrugged.

"I don't think they were too keen on having me there. When I stopped going, no one bothered to ask me back."

Ciarán wasn't sure what Fiona meant by her remark. A lot of ragged children attended school. Maybe, it was because her grandmother was a cunning woman? Perhaps the parish priest had turned the community against Fiona and her nan. It wouldn't have been the first time. He reached over and picked up the Dickens, fondling it with anticipation, "*Nicholas Nickleby.*" He had loved reading the novel when they first got it as a family Christmas present. Kathleen had read it first, then himself and then John had got around to reading the story. Then they had all taken turns reading it aloud to each other in the evening. He looked up speculatively at Fiona.

"We used to read these books to each other of an evening ... would you like to do that?"

Fiona blushed,

"I wouldn't say I'm that grand at reading out loud."

"That's alright," he added quickly, "I can do all the reading. It's only fair. You do all the rest of the work." She laughed at that and readily agreed. "We'll start with the Dickens. He's an English writer but still very good. It's a story about a boy, Nicholas, his father dies, and he is left to take care of his mother and sister. His uncle promises to help but turns out to be a rare evil fellow. Nicholas has all sorts of adventures, but I can't tell you everything or I'd spoil the story for you."

"Your father has passed, hasn't he? And your uncle looks after you? Is that why you like the story?"

"No, my uncle has been awfully good to me. The uncle in this tale is right wicked."

"What about the sister? Does she have adventures as well?"

Ciarán paused, "Well, she does, and she doesn't."

Fiona gave a small snort.

"Me nan told me stories where women were important. She told me about *Airmid,* how she learned all the herbs to save people, even though her cruel father tried to destroy the knowledge. And she told me about the queen over the water that killed all them Roman people – Boudica. That was a good tale."

"I know about Boudica. I learned that in school. She was a warrior queen, like our Queen Maeve."

"Oh yes, Nan told me about Queen Maeve, she could be a bit wicked. But I liked her, she got back at that Cuchulainn for killing her pet stoat, she did."

Ciarán roared with laughter.

"God forbid any man get between you and your pet," he gestured at Farley.

"Indeed," Fiona said primly. "We look after each other, don't we *asthore*?" she enquired of Farley, bending low to kiss the top of his head. Farley licked her nose in agreement.

They began the habit of reading that very night and it was an enjoyment, sitting close to the fire and reading by the candlelight. Ciarán felt comfortable with Fiona and was able to act out the voices of each character, though the playacting reminded him of Donal. His brother-in-law had been a great mimic, having them all in fits of laughter after imitating the schoolmaster or the priest. It was a good memory to hold onto. He hoped Kathleen could save the same memories of when they had all been younger, when their greatest fear had been that of a thrashing from the teacher.

After reading, sometimes the two would chat, Ciarán trying to find out more about his curious helper; her life had been so different from his. She was interested in hearing about his school days, his mates, and his siblings, and especially his mother. His mother had been so gentle and quiet, very like Kathleen. She had lost as many children as she had living but had not given in to mourning, reminding the family how lucky they were to have a roof over their heads, shoes on their feet and food to eat. When she could spare a bit, she would visit cabins where food was lacking, bringing a few eggs and potatoes, sometimes a pail of milk. She had visited Donal's cabin often enough, even though she found Donal's mother a sour woman, blaming all her woes on her deceased husband.

With her own children, she had been firm, expecting them to put in every effort with their schoolwork and not shirk their chores. Yet, there had been praise for every achievement, real joy when they mastered a skill or did well in an exam. She had done her best to tread the fine line between being respectful of the church without bludgeoning her children with the burden of sin. As a result, Ciarán wore his religion lightly and was not shocked to hear that Fiona had been a less than regular mass goer.

Fiona's excuse had again been that Farley wasn't allowed in the chapel and it grew too cold to hear mass in the vestibule during winter months. Also, it was a difficult climb down the hill for her nan, and well, Fiona drifted off and Ciarán waited. Finally, she looked up at him and admitted,

"No one really wanted us around. We weren't proper." Ciarán waited to hear what proper meant. Fiona picked up Farley and went and sat on the floor, farther away from him.

"My nan was friends with a traveller. He was me mam's da. He came by every few months to see me mam until she was, maybe five or six years old. Then he stopped coming. Nan's not sure what happened. Perhaps he got a family, maybe he died. It was no matter. Nan never expected him to stay, and she had her Billy, the ram of our goat flock, so she wasn't lonely. And of course, she had me mam."

"Ah, so she wasn't married to your grandad." Fiona nodded her head. "Well," Ciarán tried to think of what to say, "People do have opinions. I guess we are told by the church that we have to marry. But maybe that's just so there's someone to care for the women and children. You mostly need a man for that." Fiona gave him a furious look.

119

"Obviously, your nan didn't need a man. She just did fine on her own," he back pedalled quickly. "And your mother, did she marry?"

Fiona went very quiet for a while. She stroked Farley's ears, a velvety texture that reassured her.

"I think I met my father once. No one ever told me he was my father, but it was the way he asked after me mam and touched me face," she touched her own face, remembering. "And he had been attacked by a swan. I know anyone who had hurt my mother would definitely end up being thrashed by a swan."

"Your mother's pet was a swan I take it?" Ciarán chose not to ask any more about a liaison that had obviously been rape. No wonder Fiona preferred her stories to be about women. She certainly hadn't met many worthy men.

"Yes."

"A swan is a lovely creature. They look like peace itself, gliding along a loch."

"Me mam was lovely. She had hair so light it was nearly white, all long down her back and she was tall and slender, with a graceful neck. She would look at me just so," Fiona craned her neck to one side in imitation.

"What happened to her?" He knew Fiona had left home because no one was there anymore, and the slight matter of having killed a soldier.

Fiona looked into the fire, watching the flames burn blue against the heat of the peat.

"She went to the loch one day and never came back." Standing up, she gently put Farley onto the pile of blankets and crossed to Ciarán, "You'll be tired now with all that reading, shall I help you to bed?"

They worked their way through *"Nicholas Nickleby"* and Fiona wondered why Kate didn't carry a knife in her pocket. She'd have kept those filthy men out of her way if she'd had a good knife, or better yet a dog. Ciarán almost asked her if she'd really use a knife against a man and then remembered, Fiona had. This was a girl that had grown up without the protection of a man, or even her community. She had been born of violence and had no intention of letting it happen to her. No one in her family had married. None had ever birthed boys. He was surprised she had agreed to nurse him at all. Perhaps that is why some of her 'cures' had been on the painful side.

"Why is it that you stayed here?" he asked one day. Fiona was plucking leaves and flowers off the stem of some cocklebur. Every now and again she muttered threats at the burs and gathered them up and threw them into the fire. He was lying on the bed, having woken after a nap, and had tired of staring at the ceiling. Without looking up from her work, she replied.

"I told you, your horse Conall asked me."

"But I'm better now, just taking my time mending. I'm sure they could find someone else to mind me."

She looked up then and wiped the hair out of her face with the back of her hand so that she could see him clearly.

"Is that what you want?"

"Not at all!" He assured her. "It just seems odd work for a lass like you to be doing."

"And what kind of *cailín* am I at all?"

He couldn't tell if she was annoyed with him or curious of his opinion. He decided to be honest.

"A very strong-minded lass, with no particular affection for people in general, and certainly not for men."

She considered this.

"I suppose that's fair enough. I can't say I'm over fond of your cousin Liam, he thinks I'm a servant and barely trusts me. However, I'm useful to him at the moment." Ciarán nearly gasped at her directness. Was she correct in her assessment? Probably. Liam had grown up spoiled and used to household staff, and Uncle William did have a manner of looking down on the poor as if it were their own fault, or laziness that had deprived them of a viable income. Likely, Liam had absorbed some of this prejudice. Yet, Fiona continued. "As for your brother, turning his own blood away from the door for fear of being tarred a Fenian supporter," she wrinkled her nose in disgust, "That lacks courage and loyalty. A dog would never treat you so."

"Do you compare all people to dogs?"

"Why not? Dogs aren't sly or two-faced. They either love you or hate you, and if they love you, it is steadfast and constant, even if it threatens their own life. How could any man, or woman, better that?"

"You have a point," he admitted. "You still haven't answered me though."

She waved her hand as if brushing away his concern.

"You aren't like them. Your horse wouldn't love you so if you were."

He raised himself up on his elbows.

"I take that as high praise then?"

"Oh, I wouldn't say high praise, but you'll do. I'm happy to mind you till you heal. Besides,

I've nowhere else to go for the time being, and your family is paying me."

He leaned back and smiled. Maybe she was just staying for the money, but he didn't think so. She was too much like a dog herself. She either loved you or hated you, and if she couldn't abide him, she would have strayed by now.

Fiona wanted to know about his schooling and seemed somewhat regretful that her own education had consisted primarily of herbology and the caprine care. She asked him about history and geography. He told her that he had won a geography award once for memorizing all the capitals of Europe. She made him list them out and tell him everything he knew about each capital, which wasn't much as he had never visited them. "Paris is full of French people, which apparently we like, as they supported our uprising in 1798, though, we could have used an army more than just uplifting rhetoric. Rome is where the Pope lives, Athens is where the classical scholars lived." He paused; did she know any Greek myths? She shook her head. He explained about their plethora of Gods and how they were always involved in mischief. She found that quite amusing and looked forward to him reading the book of Greek stories.

He told her of their presentation days at the end of the school year, how Donal sang each year, and that everyone said he had the voice of an angel and should be on the stage. He was very conscious of being in Donal's cabin, a place his family had found pitiful. Yet, Kathleen had chosen to live here and had hoped to have a life with Donal. Ciarán felt again, the sharp knife of having failed. His sister's dreams were shattered now. No husband, no home, no child and wasn't it all his fault?

As if reading his thoughts, Fiona asked after Kathleen. What talent did she have? He smiled, remembering all the times Kathleen had stood between him and the paddle, making excuses for him and always seeing humour in Donal's many pranks.

"She is very clever with a needle. She sews and crochets. She's been selling her lace since she was a girl, but her real gift is as a peace maker. She was always telling Da it wasn't really my fault; it was accidental like. The number of times I spilt the milk bucket, and she swore up and down that the cow had kicked it instead of me just not minding where I was going. And at school, Donal was forever getting in trouble – usually arguing some point in history. Kathleen always took his side, saying that Donal was helping us to see a different viewpoint. Now, she is loyal. You'd like her, I think. Fiona nodded, though she couldn't understand why anyone would want to be good at tatting and sewing.

"And what did you do?" Fiona continued.

"My mother always had me learning poetry. She loved the poems, she did, so. I would learn one off by heart each year and speak it at the presentation. I never declaimed them well, but I usually managed to get all the words out."

Fiona nearly clapped her hands in delight.

"Tell me a poem then. I'd love to hear what a poem sounds like." Had she really never heard a poem? No wonder she was so good with plants and animals – she'd never filled her brain with anything else. He didn't envy Fiona's narrow childhood. She had freedom, but little else.

"It's been an awful long time. I'm not sure I remember any," he began but couldn't bear the disappointment on her face. "I will have a go, but you mustn't laugh when I stumble."

"Sure, how would I know what a mistake was? Just go on."

He racked his memory but knew, the poem that had stayed with him would have to be the last one his mother heard, Yeats' *"The Stolen Child."* He closed his eyes a moment, seeing the stanzas arranged in his mother's book and then cleared his throat. At first, the words came slowly, and then it was as if a drawer in his brain had opened, and the pages were handed to him. He found the flow and was able to sing out the last stanza,

Come away, O human child!
To the waters and the wild
With a faery, hand in hand,
For the world's more full of weeping
than you can Understand.

Away with us he's going,
The solemn-eyed:
He'll hear no more the lowing
Of the calves on the warm hillside
Or the kettle on the hob
Sing peace into his breast,
Or see the brown mice bob
Round and round the oatmeal-chest.
For he comes, the human child,
To the waters and the wild
With a faery, hand in hand,
From a world more full of weeping
than he can Understand.

He saw Fiona, her knees pulled up to her chest, staring into the fire. With her sleeve, she wiped away a tear tracking down her face and sniffed loudly.

"How did he," she asked, "How did the poet know how me mam felt?" Ciarán reached out and squeezed her shoulder.

"Sure, poets are good like that. They have a way of looking inside of us and putting all that whirling and worrying into beautiful words."

Fiona stood up and kissed him lightly on the cheek.

"I thank you," she said and then slipped out of the cabin, her dog following her.

A HORSE RIDE AND A SWIM

His leg was murdering him. He tossed restlessly on his pallet wishing he had a bit more poteen to take the edge off the pain. Rolling onto his right side, he heard the girl sobbing. She was obviously trying to be quiet about it but there was no mistaking the sniffing and hiccupping. He waited a moment to see if she would stop, but then he heard her heave a great sigh and in the dim light from the fire could see her shoulders shaking. She was beside herself. He was surprised. Fiona had seemed such a contained little creature. He hadn't realized she had any of the softer emotions.

"*Cailín*, what's ailing you?" but there was no answer, except a concentrated struggle to swallow a sob. "Fiona? Will you tell me what's wrong?" he whispered. He didn't want to wake Liam who was sleeping on the bench by the table. Ciarán got no answer though. He tried to sit up but was still unable to walk without the noisy stick, so it was pointless. She was silent now, but he could still see her shaking with each sob, choking them down.

Unable to go to her, he did the only thing he could - reaching out, he grabbed the cloak she slept in and pulled it towards him. Fiona sat up with a gasp and shot him a look of reproach, then she turned away from him and rolled herself tight into a ball around Farley, shutting Ciarán out.

"I'm sorry. I couldn't sleep and I heard you. I don't mean to intrude, but if you want to tell me ..." He gingerly laid his hand on her shoulder and immediately felt all the muscles stiffen under his touch. It reminded him of a colt, skin twitching under an unfamiliar hand. With a colt, he would

127

persist, gently, quietly, stroking and calming it. He let his hand slide down her arm and then back up to her shoulder, softly moving down the thin arm, waiting patiently.

"I miss me nan," she finally muttered in a strangled voice.

"Of course, you do," he answered, continuing to stroke down her arm. He began to feel the muscles loosen slightly and moved to her back. His mother used to stroke his back when he was ill. He remembered that. It had always made him feel sleepy. Bit by bit Fiona's breathing began to even and the catching sobs lessened. The tight ball began to unravel and finally she was only sniffling. She reached up and scrubbed her face with her hand.

"I'm fine."

"I know you are. It's been very tiring taking care of me, I'm sure. You need to sleep now," and he continued to stroke her back. Farley leaned his muzzle over her side and eyed Ciarán intensely. He wouldn't put it past the dog to have his hand off. He met Farley's gaze and they stared at each other over the recumbent girl. Then Farley stood up, circled three times and with a thump settled himself back to sleep. Fiona quieted soon after and Ciarán felt her drifting off. It would be good if she could escape her pain in sleep.

Later in the night, Fiona whimpered in a dream and unthinking, Ciarán pulled her closer to himself and draped his arm over her body protectively. Farley gave his hand a questioning lick but accepted its presence. The three of them fell asleep, huddled against the chill of the past.

Liam, who had managed to get away from his father's farm for a few days, had come for a flying visit to check on Ciarán. He had slept on the bench uncomfortably and woke up early to peer about the room in the morning light, noting that the girl and her dog were curled next to Ciarán's pallet and encircled by one of Ciarán's arms. Oh, dear. Now that was going to be a problem. He got up as quietly as possible, but the girl's eyes flew open. She stared wide-eyed at Liam and then, realizing where she was, slipped out rapidly from under Ciarán's arm and darted out the door, followed by her dog. At their exit, Liam found no more reason to be quiet and clattered about pulling the bench he had slept on back under the table, hoping to wake Ciarán before Fiona returned, if she returned.

Ciarán woke up to see Liam glaring down at him.

"You do remember you are promised, don't you?"

"What?" Ciarán asked and tried to sit up without causing too much agony in his leg, while simultaneously trying to figure out what his cousin was on about.

"Promised," Liam enunciated, "To the lovely Gráinne, and her fields and dowry."

"Ah Yes," Ciarán sighed. He was fond of Gráinne. Well, he found her very attractive anyway. He knew his uncle and brother had managed the match to help him gain some place in the world, but he also knew that his uncle was desperate to get his hands on the wee bit of land that came with Gráinne. It seemed a bit unfair on the lovely lady but that was the way of things.

"You can't risk losing that, you damn fool!" Liam hissed. He rolled up Fiona's blankets and threw them in the corner of the cottage with a trifle more enthusiasm than necessary.

"Ach, I was just comforting the girl. She was crying in the night. The poor wee thing has no family and no home," Ciarán shrugged and looked away. Liam was so good at making him uncomfortable at times. He had nothing to feel guilty about. He *was* just comforting Fiona, as if she were a little sister, maybe.

Liam stood over Ciarán, who had finally managed to get himself sitting upright. He needed to have some sort of presence to deal with Liam's arguments. Liam crossed his arms and stood glowering down at Ciarán.

"You'll also remember the poor wee lassie is a murderess."

"Ah sure, it wasn't murder, it was revenge," Ciarán shrugged off the incident as if it were hardly worth mentioning. Liam's face continued to beam disapproval.

"Either way, she's not needing our pity. She's more a wild beastie than a girl. I've never seen anything so quare as her and that hedgehog of a dog she has. The two of them give me the willies. I'd say she'd as soon scratch your eyes out as curl up in your lap."

"Well, you're right," Ciarán agreed, "she is a bit of a wild creature."

"And that bloody dog is too clever altogether. I'm not convinced it isn't some sort of fairy or demon taken the form of a dog," Liam continued. "And now you want to tame its mistress, God help you."

"Tame her?" Ciarán laughed. "What would be the fun in that? She's far more interesting as a wee beastie. Leave me be Liam. I know what I'm doing and I'm not going to chase after some feral little girl and lose my match to Gráinne. Besides, I'm in no condition to chase after anybody right now. Now, will you help me stand up so I can go outside before I piss myself."

After assisting Ciarán, Liam saw to the horses, avoiding Conall's nips and kicks as best he could. He could see that Fiona had been looking after Conall as the stallion seemed fairly well groomed and certainly in good condition. He was pleased with that, though not sure how the girl knew what to do, as she had explained she'd never had any prior experience with horses.

When he returned to the cabin, Ciarán was sitting up with a book that he had from his brother's house, he greeted Liam cordially and begged for a cup of tea. Liam was only too happy to oblige, feeling a bit thirsty himself. He noticed small bags of herbs in the corner of the cupboard and sniffed each one, till he found one that seemed to be ordinary tea. He remarked to Ciarán that there were an awful lot of simples and Ciarán groaned in reply, stating that they were all horrible and designed to make him sick at his stomach. Hoping he had indeed made tea, Liam poured them both a steaming cup and dribbled some milk in. The jug was getting low. He'd have to go over to John's tomorrow and collect some more supplies.

Fiona came in much later in the day with a bag full of plants she'd collected and a freshly skinned rabbit. Without speaking to either of them, she threw the rabbit on the table and began chopping it into smaller bits. She was a dab hand with a knife and Liam decided to never get between her and a chopping block. When Fiona was satisfied with her butchery, she threw the pieces into a pot of water that hung over the fire. She added some of the greens she had foraged and then explored the cupboard for a few potatoes. These were peeled and added to the stew.

"There's a lot of shrubbery you have there," Liam observed as Fiona began separating her foraging into separate bundles. She looked up, surprised to be addressed.

"It's late Spring. Best time to gather leaves. There's dandelion and nettle in the stew. I've got some comfrey here for his wound and elder flower in case he throws another fever. Honeysuckle, also good for the wound, and it smells nice in the cabin."

It was the most he had ever heard her say altogether. Liam picked up a honeysuckle flower.

"We used to suck on these like sweets when we were boys, do you remember cousin?" Ciarán remembered.

"How is it you know all this healing flora when you're not much more than a child?" If Fiona took affront at Liam's reference to her immaturity, she didn't show it. She continued to sort the vegetation and then eyed the ceiling, trying to see if she could attach something to the thatch from which she could hang her herbs to dry.

"Me nan taught me. She was a wise woman. People often came to her for remedies, sometimes for their creatures, sometimes for themselves." Ciarán looked at Fiona then, remembering her tears from the night before. Fiona caught his eye and then looked away hurriedly. She was embarrassed to have been heard crying. She didn't want to seem weak and childish, even if she often felt that way. She was on her own now, well, on her own with Farley and they would do alright. Sympathy wasn't necessary.

The stew was remarkably tasty, though Liam had been a bit leery of the nettle and dandelion leaves. He was used to cabbage and carrots as vegetables and had never had to eat what could be found along riverbanks or in the fields. When they were finished, Ciarán read for a bit by candlelight, generously sharing the story. After which, Liam and Ciarán chatted idly about how John's farm was doing and whether he'd give up the fields entirely to sheep or keep some acreage for sowing. Fiona had scrubbed their few utensils and left them in the cupboard, away from any vermin that might wriggle in via the thatch. She sat by the hearth checking Farley for ticks and throwing the odd flea into the fire, listening to the spit as the blood engorged creatures exploded. They retired early, Fiona in her blankets by the hearth, carefully situated far enough away from Ciarán to be seemly but close enough to hear him if he needed any pain relief in the night. She had made him a hops bag to slip under his pillow to help him sleep so she was hoping for a peaceful night. Liam wrapped himself in his cloak and stretched out on the bench. Farley patrolled the cabin for any foolhardy rats or mice and then settled himself next to Fiona.

The next morning, Liam was seated on the bench, eating some old cheese and hard bread. He was still bleary with tiredness but was watching Ciarán's sleeping form.

"I could hear you chewing if you were in the next county," the prone form of Ciarán muttered. Liam huffed and continued to gnaw on his breakfast.

"Hungry?" Liam proffered. Ciarán struggled to an upright position and began the arduous process of trying to stand up. He still felt weak from the fever and his leg resisted any orders he gave it to move. The dampness and chill in the cottage didn't help much either. He would have liked to curl back up on the bed, but he knew he would never get better unless he pushed himself. Haltingly he approached Liam and reached for the bread.

"I'd rather have food, but I'll eat whatever you're offering," Ciarán grunted. Liam handed him the remainder of the loaf and perused his friend.

"Well, at least you're standing," Liam wiped the crumbs from himself and stood, looking about the cottage. "Where's the girl?"

"Fiona?"

"Of course, Fiona, you eejit. Unless you have some other girl hidden in one of the corners. I didn't hear her go out. I suppose she and her dog are off somewhere hunting. I hope they bring us back something to eat."

"You could go out hunting yourself you know," Ciarán remarked, but Liam ignored him.

"Well, I can't ask the girl to see to the devil horse, so I suppose I'll have to do it myself," Liam complained. "Do you know if John brought over any hay?" Ciarán just shook his head. "Do you want to try walking out to the stable to see your great lummox?"

Ciarán would very much like to see Conall, other than in the door frame. Up to this point, he had relied on reports from Fiona, as she was not strong enough to help him out to the stable. He told Liam as much and then looked about for his trousers, sitting himself back down and painstakingly pulling them over the bandages on his leg. Liam reached down and levered Ciarán back onto his feet, helping his cousin limp towards the door. They stopped to lean against the cabin wall for a bit of a rest. Ciarán was already sweating from the pain, but he was determined to make it as far as the stable.

Liam stepped around the corner of the cabin towards the stable, walking as slowly as he could without seeming to patronize Ciarán. He needed Ciarán to get on the mend quickly and was appalled at his cousin's still apparent weakness. There was only so long Liam could keep up the pretence that Ciarán was at home with his brother, convalescing from a bad fall off Conall. Ciarán would need to be able to ride again as soon as possible and get back to Ballybofey with Liam.

"Shite!" Liam exclaimed when he reached the shed. Only one horse stood within. Conall was gone. "She's stolen your horse," Liam turned to Ciarán, afraid of how this new blow would further weaken his cousin.

"That's impossible! She couldn't control him." Ciarán felt confused. He had come to like the girl's company. She didn't seem like the type to thieve from him, especially since she knew that he had a strong bond with the horse. Conall was more than his companion – Conall was the one being he felt perfectly at home with. He knew that Fiona could understand that as she had the same relationship with that wiry terrier of hers. He wanted to sink into the mud where he stood. "How could she?" he gripped the stable wall, feeling as if the world were starting to spin away from him.

"She's a wee witch, I say. I've thought it all along and now we have proof. No normal lass could lead off that beast and betray our trust after we've fed and sheltered her these past days." Liam was kicking himself for having left his cousin in the care of the girl. Why hadn't he stayed with Ciarán? Why had he been so worried about what his father would think?

"To be fair," Ciarán interjected, "She did work rather hard for her food and shelter,"

135

thinking of the bandage changes, the cleansing of the wound and probably all the time she had spent dealing with him in a delirious state. Liam only grimaced at him. Still, his horse, his Conall, how could she?

Liam cursed vociferously and led his gelding out to graze. He led the horse to a pasture behind the cabin and hobbled her so she could not wander far. "Well, will I wait here with you or go look for her? Would you be alright on your own for a bit?" It was embarrassing to have to ask, but Ciarán looked none too good at the moment.

Ciarán waved a hand at him vaguely,

"I'll be fine. Find my bloody horse will you." He started to limp back in the direction of the cabin but had to reach out and grab Liam's arm for support. Liam got him to the side of the cabin and let Ciarán use the mud and wattle wall for support. It was then that they heard hooves coming across the field. Both men looked up to see Conall trotting towards them with Fiona on his back. She and the horse slowed as she saw the men staring at her. The horse came to a stop by the shed, bowed extravagantly low and Fiona slid off his back. Farley loped up behind them. She made no effort to restrain the horse and Conall walked up to Ciarán and nosed him solicitously.

Liam grabbed Fiona's arm almost as soon as she hit the ground,

"What the bloody hell do you think you are up to?" he shouted into her face. Fiona shrank back and tried to pull away from him.

"I just wanted to see what it was like to ride a horse."

"You don't go taking other people's horses. Horse thieves are hanged you know!" Liam bellowed. Conall was not enjoying the noise and began to toss his head and blow, his disgruntled sounds interspersed by the steady growling coming from the small, but rather vicious looking terrier at Fiona's feet. Ciarán managed to step forward and hung off Conall's mane.

"Will you stop shouting next to the beast. Shall we hobble him with your one and take the *cailín* in for interrogation," he said it half-joking, reassured that his horse was well, and that the girl had not deceived him. Fiona didn't hear the humour in his voice and rounded on him, defensive and insulted.

"I didn't steal him. I asked Conall and himself said he would teach me to ride. He gave me permission!" she insisted.

"You asked the horse?" Liam sneered. Fiona swallowed hard and looked at the ground.

"Will you let go of my arm please?" Liam reluctantly released her and pushed Fiona over to Ciarán,

"Help him indoors. I'll sort out Conall and then we'll discuss your story."

"He doesn't like being hobbled!" Fiona's voice rose and Farley decided it was time to start barking.

"Quiet," Ciarán begged. "How are we going to keep the horse by if we don't hobble him?"

"He won't leave you," Fiona was astonished at Ciarán's question. "Why would he leave you? Just trust him." She made a slight motion at Farley, and he quieted. Liam observed the interaction, which just confirmed his suspicious further. Throwing up his hands and muttering, he stomped off to hobble Conall, hoping the horse wouldn't try to kill him in the process. Too bad he couldn't make the girl do it.

Ciarán, leaned on Fiona's shoulder in order to propel himself into the cabin. When she had got him seated indoors and he had caught his breath, he spoke,

"*Cailín*, do you not realize how dangerous that horse is? He could have easily killed you. And how did you even get on him and ride him without saddle or bridle? And the wee bow, so you could get off. When did he learn that trick?"

Fiona chewed her lip. There were still some that feared witches and they would likely think her one if she told the truth, but she couldn't think what else to say.

"I asked him, and he lowered his neck and let me climb up." She forgot for a moment the trouble she was in and remembered the feeling of sitting astride the powerful beast, his muscle moving underneath her. "Ah, it was a beautiful feeling, to be up so high and on so noble a creature. At first, he walked slowly, so I could get used to his way of moving and then he told me to hold his mane and he started to trot. That was a bit unsteady." She frowned, her bottom still sore from the experience. "When I felt safe enough, he stretched out his legs and just flew. We were flying, like the great winged horses in the stories, what are they called?"

"Pegasus," Ciarán answered.

"It was the most wonderful thing. Do you feel that every time you ride? Is it always like that?" Ciarán smiled at her, relieved and more than that. No one but himself had ever cared for Conall, wicked horse that he was. Then, here, this slip of girl had ridden him and extolled his virtues. She couldn't be a thief, not this girl that loved his horse.

"Aye *cailín*, it is sometimes like that, though you feel a bit less magic after eight hours in the saddle on a rainy day. The thing is, Fiona, I'm not sure how you 'talked' to him." He watched her shining face fade back into one of fear and was sorry for that. Liam reappeared at that point, glowering at Fiona, and looking none too pleased with Ciarán either. It was clear to Liam that he would have to take matters into his own hands as Ciarán would be too soft on the girl. Ciarán felt some sort of debt to her for saving his life and the two had been some time together with no other company. All bloody John's fault for not letting Ciarán stay at the big house. They would have to get rid of Fiona as she obviously wasn't trustworthy, but the problem now was how to keep her silent? It would do them no good if she started telling the tale of how she cured a young fellow of a gunshot wound to the leg, a young fellow with a grey stallion. She'd be sure to give them away as the men who had tried to free a prisoner on the road to Donegal Town.

Liam closed the door behind him and stood in front of it, making it obvious that he meant to block Fiona's escape, should she try. Fiona and Farley stood between the two men, switching their gaze from one to the other.

"So, are you going to explain yourself then?" Liam pressed. Fiona shifted slightly and looked at the door.

"I guess I have no choice."

"You don't," Liam crossed his arms and glared at her. Ciarán made to interrupt but Liam silenced him with a glare.

"What will you do to me when I'm done telling you? I've done naught to you but help your man. So, I borrowed the horse for an hour - he

139

was glad of the exercise. Is that what I'm standing trial for?"

"You know full well that's not what we mean. What is this nonsense about asking the horse? What sort of fool do you take me for? Tell me now, does Conall prefer English or the Irish?"

"Irish, obviously," Ciarán interjected. "He is named after Conall, the Red King of Ulster." He tried to smile encouragingly at Fiona. There had to be some logical explanation. He often chatted to the horse. He sometimes thought Conall could almost understand him, and young girls were prone to fancies, that was all it was. At the same time, she had managed to get near a thoroughly fractious horse and ride him, all without any sign of injury. This was more than could be said for Liam, who sported a large bite mark on his arm from his efforts to hobble Conall.

Fiona decided the best tact was to address Ciarán and try to ignore Liam, who quite frankly, was beginning to irritate her. Ciarán had told her how fond he was of his horse and even Liam had told her that Ciarán was 'magic' with horses. Surely Ciarán would understand.

"You've heard of St. Francis?" she ventured.

"Of course, we've bloody heard of St. Francis," Liam spluttered. Turning away from him, Fiona continued.

"There are people who follow his ways, who believe that all the Lord's creatures are precious. These people take a vow to protect our friends with no voices. They train from a young age to hear the needs of the beasts and try to fill those needs. We call ourselves, 'The Listeners'," she finished, looking at Ciarán. Did he believe her?

"You said you asked Conall," Ciarán watched her face. She wasn't lying. "So, you can speak to beasts as well as listen to them?"

Fiona nodded,

"Some, yes. Conall is used to you chatting with him. When you ride, you give him signals with your legs and hands and you use words with him as well. He is comfortable with humans. Frightened animals can't hear me right away, but Conall was never afraid. He could hear me from the first. The other horse, Bride, she can understand feelings but doesn't send me back clear pictures yet."

"Is that how it is? They send you pictures that you see in your mind?"

"Yes, it's like that with Conall, but I only get feelings from Bride. With Farley, it is different again."

"The dog is your familiar, isn't he?" Liam suggested. Fiona looked down at the floor and sighed. She thought she had maybe gotten through to Ciarán, but Liam was determined to brand her as a witch, with all the complications of that title.

"We follow the ways of St. Francis. How could I be a witch and follow a holy man?" Nan had told her no one would understand. But perhaps Ciarán did? Conall had suggested that the man was more gifted than most.

"How come we've never heard of you Listeners before?" Liam drew near to Fiona, but Farley began to growl, rumbling reassuringly beside her.

"Leave her Liam. She's telling the truth. And I have heard of Listeners. My mother used to tell us stories. She even said I was like one with the horses." Liam, surprised, glanced at Ciarán, who continued. "And I know my horse. You've seen him when he takes a dislike to something, no one can get near him. But he trusts Fiona. Animals can know things that we're sometimes too thick to see. He'd have thrown her and broke her into bits and pieces. But he didn't. Jaysus, Liam, she was riding him without a halter or saddle. I can't even do that. She could only have done that with Conall's consent."

"You don't think she put an enchantment on him? She could be faery folk - she could have enchanted you for all we know. We don't know what was in all those teas and potions she's been feeding you."

"If that were the way of it, why would she have bided her time this long? All these weeks tending my wound and waking in the night to break my fever? What would be the point in that? The wee lass has mistaken me for one of her beasties and tried to help me, that is the only thing she's done wrong here." Ciarán was getting disgusted with Liam's distrust. Why, it was Liam who had hired her in the first place. Why was he so accusing? Maybe he was jealous Ciarán realised. Liam and Ciarán had always been the closest of cousins and now Liam could see that Ciarán was rather fond of the odd young healer.

Liam spat on the floor and shook his head. Striding up to Fiona, her grabbed both her arms and leaned in close to her face.

"Whatever you are, I don't trust you and I'll have my eye on you," Farley nipped him on the leg just then and he went to kick him, but Fiona pushed between them.

"You don't ever hurt my dog, ever. If you so much as touch a hair on his head, I'll have your bollocks off. You can trust that." Ciarán nearly fell

142

off his chair laughing. Enraged, Liam stomped out of the cabin and took his horse up to John's house. He would try again to persuade his stubborn cousin to take his brother back home.

When he had left, there was an awkward silence. Fiona went to stir up the fire and brought Ciarán a cup of tea with some willow bark and nettle for the pain. She remembered to add honey to hide the bitterness of the bark. He lifted his eyebrows when she handed him the cup.

"Can I trust that you're not bewitching me with some of your magic herbs?" but this time, she could hear the smile in his voice.

"You can trust me as far as you can throw me," she snapped back.

"Which is not at all at the moment," he grunted as he shifted his sore leg. "You know, I do appreciate all the healing you have done for me *cailín*." Fiona shrugged, but he reached out and caught her with his free hand. "Tell me, Fiona, is Liam or my brother paying you for all the work you've done?"

She yanked herself free.

"They are, so, but that's not why I'm doing it. Sure, I could get easier work elsewhere and not have to put up with your buck eejit cousin. I promised your Conall. He asked for my help the night I went to his stable to get out of the rain. I don't break promises made to animals."

"Fair enough *cailín*, I didn't mean to insult you. I just want you to know I appreciate the kindness you have done me, even if it's only for my horse. I think I might have died without your help."

"Oh, you surely would have. That doctor was worse than useless. I think Liam could have done a better job." They both shared a laugh then. "Did

143

your mother really tell you about Listeners?" Ciarán thought of his mother, how they would sit around the fire while she told them stories during the long winter evenings. Kathleen and he had adored those times, John less so, but he was older and impatient, wanting to be seen as too mature for childish things.

"She did, it is a common enough tale, though I wasn't sure if it was true until today."

"You believe me then?"

"Like I said, Conall is not over fond of people. If he let you ride him, you must have some sort of gift. But tell me lass, why is your wee dog so important? Is it just that he's your family, or is it like Liam said, he is some kind of familiar?"

She eyed Ciarán carefully and then sat on the floor by his feet, taking Farley into her lap and fondling his ears.

"Farley is my acolyte," she said, "My helper. He teaches me to listen, and he listens to me."

"How long has he been with you?"

She looked down at the rough terrier and considered. "Maybe thirteen, or fourteen years."

"That's well old for a dog. What happens if ..." But Ciarán felt it would be rude to finish the thought.

"He won't die," Fiona said sharply, looking up into Ciarán's face. "We are bound. He will live as long as I do, and I will live as long as he does."

Ciarán looked worried, "Do you mean if the little cur gets run down by a cart or some drunk takes to kicking him, you would pass along with him?" Fiona nodded.

"Holy Mary, mother of God, that's a worry."

"Why?"

He ran his hand through his hair, struggling to put it into words,

"Animals lives aren't valued in the same way. You slaughter a pig or a sheep without thinking about their soul. It's not murder to kill a dog. Their lives are cheap."

"No, they aren't. They have as much value as we do."

"That's not what the church tells us and it's not what people believe."

"Well, it's what I believe," Fiona flounced to her feet and took his cup. "I need to go gather some more plants. I'll be back later."

"Wait!" Ciarán called, "I surely know that Conall is worth more than many a man I know." He was gratified by the smile Fiona gave him before collecting her basket and going out the door.

Liam had a terse discussion with John who absolutely refused to have Ciarán in his house. There could be a constable or two still looking for a young man with an injury who happened to have a grey stallion. John could not have trouble in his home, brother, or no brother. Ciarán was a risk to his family, and it was best he stayed in the cabin, cared for by the cunning woman Liam had found. As there had been a visit to the cabin by soldiers, Liam could not deny the concern. Kathleen was still in a delicate state after her double loss and if her brother were arrested as well, it was unlikely that she would ever be able to regain her strength. Liam collected some provisions for the cabin and returned in a grump. He dumped two loaves of wheaten bread, a few eggs, butter, and more honey on the table.

"Why do you need so much honey?" he complained. "Maire says you are using up all she has harvested."

"She puts it in the foul brew she makes for my pain," Ciarán explained, "and on my wound."

"On the wound?"

"Aye, it helps with the healing." Liam grunted but had to admit that Ciarán's wound was no longer seeping foul smelling pus and that his fever had abated. Fiona was a half decent healer, and she wasn't a horse thief after all. Why did she make him so uneasy? He pondered the question throughout the evening. Fiona did not directly speak to him, instead playing a game of tug with an old rabbit skin of her dog's.

"Could you not have used that skin to make gloves or something?" Liam finally asked her.

"I could have," Fiona replied, continuing to shake the skin and then pull it away at the last moment, as the terrier leapt at it, latching on, and hanging, "But Farley caught the rabbit. We all ate it in a stew. The skin is his." Liam rolled his eyes, but Ciarán laughed.

"Bring it here, let me see if I can get it off him," Ciarán asked. Fiona dragged the skin, attached to dog, and handed it to Ciarán. Farley play growled and shook his head wildly as Ciarán yanked. "I can't believe how much strength I've lost," Ciarán worried, "This wee dog is defeating me."

Suddenly, Liam stood up and wrenched the skin from both Ciarán and Farley, he tossed it into a dark corner of the cabin, where Farley chased after it and pounced on it in with a delighted yip. "Ah now, you've ruined my game cousin. I was enjoying myself." Liam ignored Ciarán's complaint and walked past him to add another brick of peat to the fire.

"I spoke to Gráinne in the week," Liam began, watching his cousin for a reaction. "She had come with her mother to have tea with my mother. She asked after you. She wanted to know when you'd be well enough to come home. I told her it would be soon. She seemed right glad of that. I think she misses you."

"Well," Ciarán hesitated, "Sure, that's nice to hear."

"So, will you be setting a date with her when you get back?" Liam asked. Ciarán scratched his sore leg and watched the flames in the fire.

"I thought your father and hers were still wrangling over the land parcel. I'm in no hurry to become a married man. I'd need to be fully recovered anyway to support a wife. That won't happen tomorrow."

"She's a very pretty girl," Liam offered.

"That she is," Ciarán agreed matter-of-factly.

"You're not worried some other fellow might snap her up?"

Ciarán laughed,

"Are you keen on her yourself Liam? Ach, no, your father has set his sights higher for you. Sure, none of us gets to decide anything without his permission."

"You've done quite well by my father," Liam replied acidly.

"I have indeed and am not complaining. Just stating the facts. Now, as I've no more entertainment, I'll be off to me bed," he began to push up from the chair and Fiona went to assist him, but Liam intervened.

"It's alright, I've got him," he told her, trying to see her face but it was unreadable in the dim light. Had she known that Ciarán was promised elsewhere? Did the girl have designs on, what to her, must seem to be a wealthy young man? He wasn't satisfied with Ciarán's remarks regarding

Gráinne. He knew it was an arranged match, but Ciarán had seemed more enthusiastic previously. Perhaps, he just needed to see the golden-haired girl again. Granted, Gráinne wasn't the sharpest knife in the drawer, but she was easy on the eye, and with her bit of land, Ciarán would have coin enough to hire a housekeeper to run his home.

Liam slept on the bench by the table, wrapped in his coat. Fiona, as usual, curled up in her nest of blankets on the floor by the fire. Farley, circled a few times, ignoring the limbs he trampled and then collapsed himself on Fiona's legs, still holding his rabbit skin in his mouth. Liam felt as if the dog were watching him and rolled over to face the table. There was something not right about that dog.

In the morning, Liam reported that he would be returning to Ballybofey and his father's holding. He was pleased with Ciarán's progress, in terms of health, but was disturbed by the relationship that had established between his cousin and the girl that had been hired as a healer. Well, it would come to naught. Now that Ciarán was on the mend, he would be eager to get back to his old life, working with the Ballybofey stables, helping manage the holding and hopefully, soon, marrying a girl that would bring him an income of his own. They would pay Fiona for her work and send her on her way, maybe with a reference so that she could get a position with a decent family. All would be well. Liam was worrying for nothing. As he gathered his things, he noticed again, the terrier sitting, watching him. He made a rude gesture at the dog, who actually snorted, then got up and trotted out of the cabin. Jaysus! He was getting carried away now. It was only a dog for the love of God.

He clasped Ciarán's hand and promised to come back again when he could get away. Ciarán reassured him that they were grand, Fiona was able to collect supplies from Maire, and Liam shouldn't trouble himself. He could stand now, Ciarán boasted, and would be running races in no time. Then he'd be able to ride again and would be back at the McGovern farm, holding Liam's hand. Liam gave him a gentle shove at that, but only gentle. His cousin was a long road from healed just yet.

Fiona had been standing on the table, hanging some herbs from a bit of rope she had strung from the thatched roof. They would soon dry in the smoke from the fire. Liam nodded at her, feeling slightly guilty. The girl was tireless. If she wasn't collecting greens, she was making tinctures or poultices. Surely, Ciarán would not have done so well without her. He cleared his throat.

"I'm sorry we had words yesterday," he blurted out. She continued with her task but answered.

"They was only words." He supposed that was the best he would get. With a quick nod, he left, hoping that the next time he saw Ciarán, it would be at Ballybofey, without Fiona and her bloody dog.

When Liam had left, Farley came up to Ciarán and pawed at his hand. Ciarán understood that this meant he was supposed to scratch behind the left ear. He dutifully complied until Farley, sated with scratching, lay down, let loose an airy fart and fell asleep. Fiona had finished her herbal arrangement and stepped down from the table.

"Will you have a cuppa tea?" she asked Ciarán.
"Will you sit with me and tell me more about your little friend here?" Ciarán gestured toward the sleeping, though still fragrant Farley. She nodded, threw some tea leaves into a pot, and poured hot water from the kettle hanging over the fire. She filled the cups and then took the milk from the press, sniffing it for freshness – it didn't have much time left but she poured it into the pitcher as it was.

She'd have to collect another bucket from Maire tomorrow. It was a shame Liam hadn't brought back fresh milk; it was clumsy to carry the bucket from the big house.

"Now Farley, here," Ciarán reached out with his bare foot and rubbed the dog's backside with his toes. Farley mumbled in his sleep but remained steadfastly somnolent. "He's quite a clever dog. More than most I've seen. But what did you mean yesterday about him being an 'acolyte?' Can you explain it to me?"

"You don't think I'm mad? Or fey?" She asked cautiously.

"Well, you could be," was his laconic reply, "But I'm sure I'm not bothered. Go on and tell me some more about this fellow here," again he indicated to Farley with his foot. This time Farley did grumble. There was only so much interference a dog could take.

Fiona pulled the bench over closer, so she was nearer the fire. She set down her teacup beside her and began,

"A Listener must have an acolyte, to help her join in the animal world. Me mam had a swan," she paused, not wanting to go into that story today, "Me nan had a goat, a billy goat, and I have Farley."

"How is it decided, which animal a child will get?"

"It's usually the mother that decides, my mam had gone, so Nan decided for me. And it's only a girl child. At least in our family. No one has ever had naught but girls, and only the one."

"I'm sorry," Ciarán interrupted. "Were you very young when you lost your mother?" Fiona nodded but did not dissuade him of his misconception. Many mothers died when their children were still young. None but hers had turned into a swan.

"Nan chose a creature that could be by me always, as I was missing me mam so. Billy, Nan's acolyte didn't care to come indoors and of course me mam's swan ..." She had to leave the sentence unfinished. "So, Farley is with me most times of the day. That has made our bond even stronger than most. I don't have to touch him to hear him. I can feel his thoughts," should she say the rest? "And he mine," she admitted. "And I can feel when someone hurts him, like to kick him or something."

"And he can feel when someone hurts you?" Ciarán encouraged her. She nodded. "Now, that is powerful. Though, I can imagine it could get a bit awkward at times?" Fiona blushed, there had been that time when Farley went after a bitch in Ardara. Seeming to read her thoughts, Ciarán asked, "What will you do when you marry? Surely a husband would not be so keen on Farley sharing the private moments with his wife."

"Oh, I won't marry," Fiona said hurriedly. "It wouldn't suit me at all. I can't have some man

151

telling me what to do and where to go. I've got me own mind."

"And Farley's," Ciarán added.

"Yes, and Farley's and he's a rare stubborn creature." She got up then, took the cups and rinsed them in the bucket she kept for cleaning things. "Are you well enough now on your own?" She asked over her shoulder. "If so, Farley and meself will go out and see if we can't find another rabbit."

Ciarán was eager to be up and about, but he was still quite weak. Fiona didn't fancy trying to support him as he practiced walking. He was a good deal taller and heavier than she was and she was sure any extended period of exercise would lead to her collapsing, with Ciarán following suit. She could manage to get him up to use the chamber pot, him balancing himself by leaning on the bedstead while she discreetly stepped away. She had got the stick from Ciarán's family, but he was so reluctant to use it. She would have to push him harder. There was a small loch that wasn't much of a distance. Maybe if she could get him that far. She remembered putting a lame goat in the water and getting it to walk where it might weigh less. Had Nan told her to do that? Or had the goat? She couldn't remember, but the goat did heal quick enough with regular exercise in the loch.

Clothing might be a problem. As soon as Ciarán realized he was being bathed and nursed by a woman, he had become terribly self-conscious. He'd have to take off his clothes to walk in the loch and she didn't want to leave him on his own in case he fell. She would have to think of something.

Fiona put the eggs in the pot to boil for their dinner and sliced some pieces of bread. There was a bit of cheese left so she brought Ciarán a slice of bread with cheese and butter. She and Farley shared some bread with butter and honey – she had some honey left from dressing the wound. She gave Ciarán time to finish his meal and a cup of tea and then presented him with his stick.

"We're going to walk down the loch today," she announced.

"You know I can barely make it to the stables," Ciarán frowned.

"That's because you're embarrassed to use the stick."

"Sure, I'm not going to limp around with a stick like some old man!"

"And who's going to see you? Fiona placed her hands on her hips and glared at him. "I'm certainly not going to carry you."

"Well, I've no need to go at all."

"You do."

"And why is that?"

"You're going to walk in the water. Not on it mind you, don't get any grand ideas. Just in it. It will be great healing for your leg."

"Hmph! Another clever idea of your grandmother's I suppose" Ciarán remarked acidly.

"You'd be long dead if it weren't for me nan's clever ideas. Now get up with this stick, and we'll get out the door already."

There ensued a staring match between the two of them, Farley watching with much amusement until Ciarán realised he was beaten and took the stick, banging it to the floor. Farley jumped and gave a warning growl – he was not fond of loud noises.

"Sorry young man," Ciarán offered politely to Farley. It wasn't the dog's fault his mistress was so stubborn. "Right then, off we go."

It was a terrible, plodding pace. What should have been a few minutes' walk took nearly twenty, with frequent stops to rest. Ciarán was dripping with sweat and pale with fatigue when they finally reached the shoreline. Without a word, Fiona helped him settle on the ground. Breathing hard he sat, and then stretched out to lay upon the grass.

"Well, that was bloody awful. Excuse my language." Fiona shrugged at his expletive.

"Swear all you like. It's no matter to me." She too lay back on the grass, and they gazed up at the clouds, quickly scudding by. It wasn't going to rain just yet, but it would.

After a long pause, Ciarán asked,

"What would you be doing if you weren't looking after me?"

"I don't know," Fiona admitted. "I can't go back home, and I wouldn't if I could. Not without Nan there and I've let all the goats go so, no way to make a living. I suppose I'd be on the road, looking for work. Maybe, I'd have a place at a farm by now. Maybe Farley and I would be sleeping rough. Maybe we'd have joined up with a group of travellers. Or I could have gone to America, or England."

"Would you like to go abroad?"

"No, not really. I'm content enough on this island. How about you?"

"Am I content? Or would I like to go abroad?"

"Either one. Or both."

"Oh, I'd like to see the world someday, but I'd like to make this one a bit better first. I do believe in the cause you know. It wasn't just because he was my brother-in-law. When I'm better, I will go back and help in any way I can. If I can be of any help with this useless leg."

"The leg is getting better. I imagine you'll be able to ride again, though your walking will be a bit off. Now, what would you be doing if you weren't mending right now?"

"I suppose I'd be at my uncle's farm with Liam. My uncle was teaching me how to manage a farm properly. He's done quite well for himself. I was learning a lot from him. And I suppose I would be visiting Gr-" he stopped himself. Gráinne! He hadn't really thought of her much since he'd been recovering at the cabin. What had Liam told her? Was she worried? Did she care? She was probably well upset that she was engaged to be married to a cripple.

"Visiting who?" Fiona broke in.

He felt a rather uncomfortable discussing Grainne with Fiona. Two more different women, he couldn't imagine. Gráinne with her silk gown, piano playing, and sketching. Her complete lack of equestrian skills, or skills in anything that involved being outdoors ... She was elegant, not utilitarian; a comely woman, trained to be an adornment, not a helpmate.

And then there was Fiona, unkept and often dirty, uneducated in the ways of the world but seeming to know the animals and things of the earth as if she never had to learn them. There was an intelligence born of instinct but an incongruity with general society. It was like comparing the sun to the moon.

He realised Fiona was waiting for an answer.

"Ah well, my uncle is very much in the world you know. We even get into Derry for a ball or a concert."

Fiona cocked her head and stared at him.

"Did you not have many friends when you lived with your nan?" he asked.

Fiona looked as if she were unfamiliar with the term.

"Friends? Me nan was a wise woman. They wanted her help alright, but not her company. And I was ... Well, I don't know how they saw me, but not like any other girl in the region. I once heard a woman call me feral. Do you know what that means?"

"Aye. It means, wild, untamed. I would take it as a compliment."

"Would you?"

"Yes. Certainly. Most young girls are bred to be quiet and gentle, worried about babies and clothes, and things like that. I think it could get quite boring."

"Does your sister bore you?"

"Kathleen, not at all! First of all, she's my sister so, I can't really complain about her, but she was also interested in politics. She'd argue with Donal and me half the night ... Donal, he was her husband, the lad we were trying to save ..." Ciarán broke off and swallowed hard. He would not cry in front of this wee girl; she'd probably laugh at him. Look at how she'd lost everything, and he'd only caught her weeping the one time. She was as hard as nails, not like him. What an eejit he was.

Fiona hugged her knees and looked out over the loch.

"It's time we get you in there now," she said after a decent interval.

"I'd really rather not."

156

"Fine," Fiona agreed, leaping up. "I'll go in first. I need a good wash. Then you have to follow. If a weak, wee girl can manage a swim in the loch, so can yourself." With that, she dropped her shawl and pulled her apron over her ahead. Completely unabashed she removed her skirt and bodice and ran towards the lake in her underclothes. Ciarán sat there, astonished. Why, she'd just undressed in front of him! Certainly, he'd seen her just wrapped in a shawl over her under things while she had nursed him at the worst, but to strip off her clothes without a thought. She was a feral child!

He watched her dive into the lake, completely submerging and then taking several strokes out into the centre. She was like an otter, totally at ease and unafraid. When Farley joined her, they splashed about, him barking hysterically, and she splashing him. It was like two boys, like how he and John used to play in the loch, but she was a better swimmer by far.

Dripping, Fiona returned. She reached out her hand and helped him to his feet.

"Your turn now!"

"How did you learn to swim like that? I've never seen a girl swim at all, much less out into the middle of the lake! And you are indecent! You do realise that?"

"It's freezing standing here! Will you get in the water already? And me mother taught me to swim when I was a baby, and I'm not indecent. I'm dragging down with clothes. We used to swim naked. Now take off your jacket and trousers. You can swim in your long shirt and be decent enough."

"I cannot!"

"Don't be ridiculous. Don't you think I saw every part of you when you were unconscious? There'll be no surprises for me. Now get on with you!" Not wanting to hear anymore from her, he moved towards the water, laboriously shedding his garments.

Surprisingly, Ciarán did find it easier to walk in the water. Although the ground under foot was marshy and unsure, the buoyancy took some of the weight away and he soon found that he could take several strides unaided.

"Go ahead and try swimming," Fiona suggested. "It will be good exercise for your leg."

"Did you do this to your granny's goats?"

"Indeed, we did, and it worked miracles. You can't have lame goats you know."

Submitting, Ciarán submerged and began to take tentative strokes. His leg ached with each kick, but it felt good to use the muscles, to use the leg at all. He wouldn't lose his leg. He would get better. As if in encouragement, Farley came alongside him and paddled industriously, occasionally barking in praise for Ciarán's efforts. Ciarán tired swiftly though and Fiona noticed the grey cast to his visage.

"That's enough for today," she helped steer him back to shore and doggedly climb back to the spot where they had been chatting before. He collapsed onto the ground and Fiona covered him with the blanket she had brought from the cottage.

"Aren't you cold?"

"I've got me shawl."

"Come under the blanket already. You'll catch pneumonia and then it will be Farley nursing the both of us."

Gingerly, she sat down next to him, and he wrapped the blanket around the both of them.

They were quiet for a moment, then she interjected,

"Tell me as soon as you are ready to walk back up to the cottage."

"Not yet," Ciarán breathed. "Still resting from my cross-channel manoeuvres." Fiona lifted her eyebrows in query. "Like swimming from Ireland to France."

"Hardly," she snorted.

"I went to France once, when Liam and I were about twelve years. His father took us. He had business there, buying some dogs, I think. We were too young. It was almost overwhelming – everything so different, yet the same. Farms weren't that much unlike ours, but the people ate strange foods. Of course, the language was different and the women, so beautiful. We were just starting to look at the girls then, and we did a lot of looking. And some looked back and giggled. They must have thought us such country bumpkins." He felt Fiona stiffen. "I imagine you've met a few country bumkins yourself then?"

"Me? And where would I do that?"

"Surely you met fellows after church, or at the market, or even at dances? You've been to dances, haven't you?" He smiled at her teasingly, but her expression was blank.

"Dances? At the market we were working and as for church, she looked away a moment. I told you, we didn't go every Sunday. The priest wasn't so fond of Nan, or meself either. And he wouldn't let Farley in the church. No, I've not been to any dances. We only visited people when someone needed healing or had a sick animal. We weren't always welcome either," she replied heatedly.

"I'm sorry," Ciarán offered. "I ... Your life has been so different to mine. How old are you anyway?"

"Seventeen years," jutting up her chin, Fiona fixed him in the eyes, as if he would contradict her.

"Really?" he was incredulous. "You're awful wee for your age." She scowled at him. "Not that that's a bad thing. Good things in small packages and all of that ..."

"I imagine you think me very ugly."

"What? I never said –"

"I'm small and scrawny and wear worn out clothes that don't even fit properly - me mam's clothes and she was tall and beautiful, with white, blond hair, floating all around her. She was a proper woman. I'm like Farley. Strong and nimble but no beauty."

"Uh, your hair,"

"What about it?" she spit out at him.

"It's amazing. It's every colour of brown and red and even blonde. I've never seen anything like it." Fiona picked up her plait and looked at it.

"It's the same colours as Farley's," she said flatly.

"I noticed that. It's such a coincidence. But it's really, lovely. I mean it," Ciarán floundered. He didn't like the look of Fiona angry. It was rather intimidating.

"It's not a coincidence," Fiona retorted. "Come on now, you've had enough rest. Let's get you back to the cottage and we'll have a hot cup of tea."

"Wait," Ciarán insisted, grabbing her arm. He took hold of her plait and examined it closely. Then he looked at Farley. "Well, he's handsome and you're, well, not pretty, that's not the word. He looked at her face and took her chin in his hands. Staring into her eyes, he noticed how large the iris was, almost filling the eye with a deep brown colour. "You're fascinating," he finally said. Fiona held his gaze one long moment, then leapt up and ran to the cottage.

"I'll get the kettle boiling and come back and collect you," she threw over her shoulder.

Part Two: Air

Teach me to breathe; teach me to fly,
Dreams can soar like birds in the sky.

Ballybofey, County Donegal

Ireland

Late 19th Century

CIARÁN RETURNS TO HIS UNCLE

"You'll be able to go back to your uncle soon now," Fiona observed as Ciarán limped over to the fire to lift the kettle and wet the tea. He was still leaning on the stick heavily, but he could sit on a horse. The journey was only a few hours to the McGovern place near Ballybofey. She watched Ciarán sit down heavily on the one chair, still in pain she noted. She'd send him with some willow bark tea and an ointment made from lavender and nettle. She'd gathered enough nettle before they'd flowered, and she was sure that Maire up at the big house would have some lavender and lanolin for the rest of the recipe. She could maybe go up there later in the day. Ciarán might want to leave as early as tomorrow so she'd have to make quick work of it. She pulled a tick from Farley's ear and flipped it into the fire. Standing, she brushed down her apron and told Ciarán she was off to his brother's for a few supplies. "Shall I tell them up there anything?"

"Aye, you can tell them I'll be off soon. John will be delighted, I'm sure. It's been a terrible trial to him to have me near abouts."

"I still don't understand how your own brother could put you out of his home," Fiona pursed her lips in disgust. "That's not real family, is it? Not that I would know, but it just seems wrong somehow."

Ciarán took a sip of tea.

"Well, you have to understand he's in a very precarious position. He's got the wife of a known rebel living in his house. He has his own wife and children to think about, and his bit of land to care for. It's not easy being a farmer at the best of times, and now, with the landlords selling up most of the land for grazing, he could find himself the lone ploughman in a sea of sheep. He has to be seen as friendly towards the big landlords or he could find his property sold out from under him. He wants nothing to do with revolution. He has no care for politics. He wants a simple, safe life and my being there jeopardises all that. I can only be grateful that he let me stay this long. It's still nearby enough for us to get messages, though far enough from the house that he can pretend he doesn't know I'm here." Ciarán sighed, reflecting. "We've never been close. Kathleen and I are of a similar age, and it was always the two of us that ran about together, causing mischief. John was so much more mature. Really, he was an old man from the day he was born."

"Our people only ever seem to have the one child. Not sure why. I guess that is why we always have our animals. Farley is my brother. No insult meant, but I think I'd prefer Farley to your John."

Ciarán guffawed,

"They're as stubborn as each other but Farley is good craic, you'd never say that about John."

"Hopefully, I'll just see Maire, or maybe Kathleen. She was in the kitchen the last time I went."

"You said so. She looked well enough?"

"A bit pale and ever so thin but she was joining in. I'm sure she'll get better with time. I did leave a tonic for her that one time, but I don't know that she ever used it. Elderberries are very good for you. The goats ate them all summer."

"I hope you didn't tell her that. I don't know how she feels about goats."

"I told her nothing. I've not had a word with her. I left it with Maire, who sort of sniffs when I say anything. I can't tell if that means she doesn't believe me or she's just getting my scent."

"Maire is like John. She's not a great one for trusting people If you gave the tonic to her, it probably went to the pigs."

"That's alright then. Pigs are grand creatures. I've always wanted to have one, but I don't think I could slaughter it, no matter how hungry I got. It would be like eating a dog. Clever souls, pigs are." Ciarán raised his eyebrows and began to laugh.

"You're a caution *cailín*, now go if you're going."

That evening, Fiona stirred the lanolin over the fire, worrying how she'd get all the grease out of the pot to cook in it later. Nan had had the two pots, one for food and the other for her remedies. In the cabin, there were no such luxuries. Perhaps, it wouldn't matter. If Ciarán was leaving soon, there wouldn't be much more cooking to do. She couldn't take the pot with her; it was too cumbersome, and it wasn't hers anyway. John would probably think her a thief. She'd have to be careful to leave with nothing but her scant supply of leaves she'd dried and maybe a bit of food. They couldn't begrudge her that. Liam had given her some coins so she would be able to buy victuals as she looked for work. Surely, she'd be able to find employment in a few days' time, and it wasn't yet so cold that sleeping in the fields would sicken her or Farley. There might be a barn or stable she could pass the night in as well. It was getting too late to help with the harvest but maybe she could work in a dairy or even a stable. She knew it was mostly boys that worked in stables, but she was as strong as a boy. If she cut her hair and got some trousers.

"Are you making more potions little witch?" Ciarán joked.

Fiona narrowed her eyes at him, "You know full well I'm no witch."

"A faery then? You certainly are one of the little people," he grinned mischievously. Fiona raised the spoon she was stirring with and threatened to hit him. He held her off, "Never mind wee *girseach*, it's quality, not quantity that counts." He smiled down into her face and Fiona looked up at him, a moment too long. She felt a thickness in her throat and pulled away abruptly.

"I think I'll leave tomorrow," Ciarán said suddenly. Fiona nodded without answering. She couldn't trust her voice yet. "Will that suit you?"

"It's nothing to do with me," Fiona found her voice come out much sharper than she had intended. "I've no fiancé waiting for me." Damn, she hadn't meant to say that.

"Are we jealous then?" Ciarán reached for her arm and Fiona yanked it out of his grasp.

"What am I to be jealous of?" but she wouldn't turn to look at him.

"Nothing, I'm sure." He was quiet for a moment. "Shall I read to you while you work?"

"Go on then," she acceded. She would miss listening to the stories at night. John had been good to send along the books for Ciarán to read during his convalescence. While Fiona could read, slowly, she'd only ever had her Nan's recipe book to read. Of course, she'd had Nan's stories, wild, fantastic tales of the Tuatha and the Firbolgs, and even the odd mention of a Listener but she'd never read, or even seen a novel. They were currently reading *Tess of the d'Urbervilles*, a book of

Kathleen's. Fiona would never get to find out what finally happened to Tess. They had only got to the part where Angel goes to Brazil, leaving Tess to seek work in a much less pleasant places than her former dairy. That would be her soon, Fiona realised. At least she wasn't married to an eejit like Angel. She let Ciarán's voice, deep and melodious drift over her. Yes, she would miss all this.

It was very misty when Fiona packed her small bag. She took only the recipe book and some bread, cheese and the last of the honey. Farley might get a scratch that needed tending, or a spoonful would settle an upset stomach if he ate something a bit too ripe. Farley joined her as they slipped out the door as quietly as possible, he turned back once to glance at the figure asleep on the straw bed. He'd have liked to lick Ciarán's hand before he left, but he understood their departure was stealthy.

They crept around to the stable and Fiona was relieved to find that Conall was at home. She laid her hand against his great neck and then leaned into him, resting her forehead against his warmth. 'I'll miss you, noble beast. Look after Ciarán, as I know you will.' She dashed a tear from her cheek and Conall blew warm air into her hair. 'May I take a piece of your mane to remember you by?' The stallion lowered his head and with her knife, Fiona cut a swathe of hair, tucking it into her pocket. 'Go with the Goddess, great one,' she managed and then stepped away, slipping out of the stable and starting off down the muddy road, Farley at her heels. She hoped to be long gone before Ciarán awoke. He should be able to sort out his own breakfast.

Ciarán stretched and rolled off the straw mattress. He'd be thrilled to be in a decent bed

171

again. He had an actual feather mattress in the room he shared with Liam at his uncle's house. It would be grand to be with Liam as well. He hoped his uncle had accepted the story that Ciarán had had a bad fall from Conall. Of course, he would though. Everyone knew how cantankerous Conall could get. McGovern had even recommended shooting the stallion a few times, but only in jest. William McGovern had a good appreciation of decent horseflesh.

There was a bucket of water by the fire which Fiona had brought up from the stream the day before. Ciarán poured some into the kettle and stirred up the fire, adding a block of peat. While he waited for the kettle to boil, he used the remainder of the water to wash himself. There was no point in returning to his uncle looking like a tinker. He was sure his uncle had assumed that Ciarán was staying with his brother John, not in a rough cabin at the edge of John's land.

Fiona was often out in the morning, though she seemed to appear when the tea was ready. He imagined Farley would be looking forward to a piece of toast. Ciarán reached for the loaf in the cupboard where they kept it free from mice and noted it was much diminished. So, they had breakfasted without him. Very well then, he would finish off the cheese and honey then. He was annoyed to find that the honey jar was gone and that there was very little cheese left. Perhaps they'd gone up to John's house to beg more provisions. Mildly disgruntled, he ate the cheese standing and toasted the bread over the fire next to the kettle. He spread the toast liberally with butter - they hadn't polished that off at least and then swallowed his tea. He wanted to gather up his things and get on the road. It was bloody irritating that Fiona had decided to swan off without so much as telling him where she was going.

Ciarán placed the books on the table for someone from John's house to collect later. He didn't imagine Kathleen would be returning to the cabin anytime soon, if ever, but he wanted to leave the place tidy for her. He folded the blankets and placed them next to the books. He noted that Fiona's blankets were tucked away in the corner where she stored them during the day. He added them to the pile on the table, put out the fire and looked about him. He hadn't much of anything to pack. Perhaps he should take back the books and blankets himself. That way he could meet Fiona along the road returning from John's. He could tell her to gather up her belongings and be ready to leave upon his return from the big house.

In the stable, Conall seemed more restive than usual. Ciarán unearthed the saddle from under the straw where it had been hidden. He had been angry with Fiona's insistence on letting Conall roam free, but the horse had proved faithful, returning from grazing every evening to settle in the meagre stable. Thank God, Conall hadn't been there when the soldiers had come searching. The game would have been up then. She was a clever *cailín* was his Fiona.

Having brought a stool from the cottage, Ciarán used it as a rather unstable mounting block. However, with his bad leg, there was no way into the saddle without some assistance. For once, Conall held still and almost seemed to lower himself a bit so that Ciarán could get into the saddle. Nonsense really. Conall never made anything easy. He was probably just planning some trick. Once in the saddle, Ciarán felt more

173

comfortable than he had in ages. There was very little pressure on the weak leg, and he was so much more mobile. The limping walk, leaning on a stick, was so tedious. On horseback, he could know speed and flight again.

It was not without difficulty that he dismounted at John's house. He threw Conall's reins to a stable lad, who backed away in terror.

"Never mind," he told the lad and led Conall into an empty stall, which the horse promptly began to kick. "Mind you don't knock the place down before I'm back," he requested, while unloading the bundle from the horse's back. Going round to the kitchen door, Ciarán, rapped once and then entered. Maire and Kathleen were baking, it looked like scones. The women were warm from the oven, sweat causing their hair to stick damply to their foreheads. They both looked up in surprise as he dropped his bundle on the table.

"Walking, and only hardly using the stick!" Maire exclaimed.

"After a fashion," he admitted. Kathleen came to him and enveloped him in an embrace.

"Thank you," she whispered.

"For what? I failed you." He withdrew from her, humiliated.

She placed her hand, dusted with flour, on his cheek.

"You tried. And you lived. For that I am grateful." Then she turned, flying up the stairs, her quiet sobs following her.

Hands on her hips, Maire flared at him,

"Could you not send word that you were coming? Now she's in a state again and God only knows when she'll calm down."

"Surely Fiona told you I was planning on leaving today. Wasn't she just up here looking for honey?"

"That changeling bit? Not at all. She was here yesterday asking for stuffs to make an ointment for you. I hope you packed it with your belongings. She took a fair bit of my lanolin. Not sure what I'll do if I need to make a remedy for my own family." She paused in her tirade, "But as it's for you, it's alright. I suppose you are *family*, after a fashion."

"That depends on John's mood," was Ciarán's sour reply. "Is he about?"

"He's not. He's out with the sheep, checking for foot rot. And you shouldn't be so hard on him. You know he had to do what he did. He didn't turn you out altogether. He just asked you to bide your time a bit away from the house. You know he couldn't risk harbouring a fugitive."

Ciarán grunted in assent.

"I've returned the books and the blankets. Not sure if there is anything else in the cottage you need but I'm sure you can send a lad down to collect it. I'm back off to Uncle's today. I need to get on with things."

"Legal things I hope."

"Aye, all within the law now. I can't be any sort of rebel with a dodgy leg. I'll have to settle down and become a country squire."

She snorted.

"At least you'll get a bit of land with that young lady you're promised to."

"Gráinne. Yes, I suppose so." Somehow, thinking of Gráinne filled him with a kind of dread. He didn't know if he could go back to the game of flirting and courting that was expected with that sort of girl. He'd got rather used to the comfortable conversation he had with Fiona. Gráinne would be a lot more like hard work. Well, he supposed he had to earn her land, it wasn't going to be freely given.

Maire was eyeing him closely,

"You haven't gotten yourself involved with that wee slip of a girl that was caring for you? She's no better than a kitchen maid you know? Worse really. I bet she's never worn a pair of shoes in her life."

"Fiona?" laughing, Ciarán shook his head. "I couldn't imagine her in a kitchen, much less wearing shoes. She's a right savage, that one. She'd as soon bite a man as cuddle him. You've no worries there."

"That's good. I never felt right about having her stay with you on your own. It didn't seem proper. But what were we to do? I didn't have anyone from here to spare and Liam did say she knew a bit about healing."

"Well, I'm not dead anyway."

"No, thank God. Now let me pack up some food for you on your journey." She took some scones from the oven and cutting them open, slathered them with butter and jam. Wrapping then in a cloth, she handed them to her brother-in-law. "God Speed Ciarán. I'll give your love to your brother."

Riding back to the cottage, Ciarán looked out over the fields for a small woman and her dog but saw nothing of the pair. He was starting to get worried. Where could she be? Should he go on and leave her a note? But surely, she'd be at the cottage when he got back. She knew his plans.

She wasn't there. It was cold and now damp, with the fire out. He realised he didn't have any paper, so he scrawled with cinder on the table,

"Started down road. Please follow," and returned to the stable to load his bag onto Conall and then himself.

They did not trot, as his leg still couldn't take the pressure but proceeded at a fair paced walk. Conall also seemed to be looking about, trying to sense Fiona and Farley. From the height of Conall's back, Ciarán could see a fair distance and there were hardly any trees or hedges to block his vision. Then he noted, two figures far down the road, walking in the centre, between the muddy ruts. As he neared, he noted that one figure was carrying a bag and the other was definitely a solid, red grizzled terrier. They turned and waited for him.

"What are you doing here?" he demanded. "I've been looking for you! Why didn't you wait for me?"

"Wait?" Fiona let the question hang in the air.

"Yes, wait. Were you going to walk all the way to Ballybofey?"

"But I'm not going to Ballybofey."

Ciarán leaned towards her to look at her face.

"What do you mean you're not going to Ballybofey? You're coming to my uncle's with me, are you not?"

Fiona swallowed and looked at her dirty feet in the road.

"I don't know," she finally said. "Are you asking me to come with you?"

"Of course, I am. I thought you understood that. My uncle has stables and kennels. There would be all sorts of work you could do there. You'd be a boon to the place. And Liam, you know Liam – he'll be pleased to see you."

"Will he?" Her voice was faint, and she was as far away as if she had wandered into a faery knell.

"Why are you being like this?" he demanded.

Fiona still didn't look at him, she looked at Farley though, who gazed up at her, eyes limpid with compassion.

"You have a life there. Work, and a betrothed and family. You don't need me. Not anymore."

He was getting fed up with her. Now she was acting like a silly woman, like Gráinne or Kathleen, all emotions and hurt feelings and he just wanted his friend Fiona back.

"Fiona! It's not a question of need. I want you. You're my friend, and I owe you. You've saved my life. I can't leave you to walk the roads. Now come here and get up on this bloody horse!"

She crossed her arms and gave him an evil look.

"Acting the big man now. What am I your servant? Because I'm not. I don't belong to anyone and won't ever. You can't tell me what to do."

"Christ Fiona, if I have to get off this horse and throw you up here, I will but how I'll get back on is beyond me. Will you just take my hand and let me pull you up?" He reached down, begging her to comply. To his astonishment, Conall bowed low, making it simple for Fiona to throw a leg over his neck and slip in front of Ciarán, if she chose to. "Even Conall wants you to come along. Will you now? For his sake, if not mine."

"Oh, I'd do anything for Conall," Fiona relented. She never could say no to an animal. To Ciarán she remarked tartly, "Conall's a real gentleman." With that she threw her leg over the horse's neck and settled in front of the saddle.

Ciarán reached his arms around her to grip the reins.

"Thank you," he breathed into her ear. Farley gave one bark of confirmation and the quartet started on their way to Ballybofey.

They had not started early, and it would have been a long journey, even without a poorly leg so Ciarán knew he would have to find a place to stop for the night. He had chosen the road through the Blue Stack Mountains, as it was the road he and Liam always used, being more direct and less inhabited. They'd be lucky to find a cottier who'd let them use the stable. Just shy of Gaugin Mountain, he spotted a ramshackle cottage and turned Conall in that direction.

"We'll stop here to rest. I have some coins, maybe we can buy some food."

"I've got food," Fiona piped up. "Is it safe?"

"This is so far out, I'm sure they get very little news and if they do, they can't be bothered. A few coins will buy us a place to rest and maybe a hot drink, or something stronger. God knows, I need it. I'd no idea it would pain me this much to ride."

Turning around in the saddle, Fiona gave him a hard look.

"We should have stopped sooner then. You won't get better if you break your leg again."

"I'm sure you're right," Ciarán sighed. He was in no mood to argue. He ached all over and just wanted to slide out of the saddle into a bed of straw, feathers, or hard dirt. It didn't matter to him at all. "You go knock at the door. They'll be less likely to turn a young girl away." Fiona harrumphed but did not dissent. She tapped Conall gently on the neck and the horse leaned his head far forward, allowing Fiona to descend. "How

179

did you train him to do that?" Ciarán queried, but only rhetorically. As far as creatures were concerned, he had learned that Fiona had her own ways.

Feeling rather anxious, Fiona approached the doorway of the cottage, but the half door opened before she could knock. An elderly cottier stood at the split door eyeing her suspiciously. "What do you want?" he demanded, in a very unwelcoming tone of voice.

"Just leave to stop for the night. Me brother and I," Fiona hoped they could pass for brother and sister, though they had no looks whatsoever in common, "We are weary and just need a place to lay our heads and let the horse graze."

"I've no room here. Go onto somewhere else," the man began to shut the top half of the door.

"There is nowhere else," Fiona almost wailed. "We don't even need to come indoors. Just let us stop here." Silence ensued. "We have coin," Fiona remembered to add.

"Ah, well then, that is a different story. How much?"

Fiona fumbled. She was not good with money as she and Nan had rarely used it. Mostly they had bartered for what they needed.

"I'll have to ask me brother. It's himself with the money, not me." She turned to Ciarán, questioning.

"With that fine horse, I am sure he has plenty of coppers to spare," the avaricious cottier continued. At this, Conall showed his rather large teeth, causing the old one to step back a bit from his door. "Vicious one that."

"Maybe not so fine then," Fiona interjected. She was remembering how her nan had bargained, getting the best she could from their cheese or goat's milk.

The old one was getting into the spirit of the thing,

"I'll have a tuppence then, and you can use my fire to make some tea. You can even sleep indoors, but not the horse. He'll have to stay outside."

"A tuppence," Fiona crowed, "More like a farthing!"

Ciarán had tired of the exchange and threw a copper down into the road. "Give him this copper and help me off my friend here." The ancient gentleman seemed to lose years as he dashed out of the door, grabbing the coin in his gnarled fist. Fiona, in consternation, went to Conall and laid her hand on his shoulder, whispering to him in Gaelic. The horse slowly descended onto his knees, one by one, buckling down so that he was laying on his belly, making it as simple as possible for his rider to lean to one side and escape from the saddle.

"Thank you," Ciarán gasped, as he put weight on his damaged leg. The old man, still grasping his coin, looked impressed with Conall's contortions.

"You've got a Listener there I see," he nodded towards Fiona. "I haven't heard of one in this long time. Useful *cailín* to have around. He grinned lecherously at Ciarán, "Hardly your sister though. Listeners only throw the one sprog."

Ciarán glanced at Fiona, but she was busying herself with Conall's saddle.

"Fiona?" he asked.

"We're in the back-country Ciarán. People still tell the old stories out here. Go on inside and rest yourself. Maybe himself can even make you a cuppa. Though I'm sure he'll ask for another fee to go to that length." Tired, Ciarán decided not to engage in dispute and followed the old one indoors. He should worry about Fiona's honour, the man was accusing him of something immoral, but Fiona seemed undeterred and realised the old man hadn't many neighbours to gossip with. Surely, he could just go into the cottage and sit if the proprietor had such a thing as a chair? Please God he did.

When Conall's tack was removed, Fiona carried it indoors. The saddle was rather heavy, but she was like a pit pony – small and sinewy. The cabin was dim enough, but she could see that the fire was going and Ciarán was in the only chair. The ancient householder, who had by now introduced himself as Fergus O'Flanagan was pottering about with some leaves and a cup. It seemed he had only the one cup.

"Give us that," Fiona inserted, rather forcefully. She pinched out Fergus's leaves and dropped them in his palm. Rinsing the cup in the bucket of water by the fire, she pulled out her stock of leaves from her pocket and made Ciarán a cup of nettle and willow bark tea, with some wild liquorice added in to hide the bitter flavour. She hooked the kettle off its stand in the fire and poured the cup, handing it to Ciarán.

"Ah, a faery brew," Fergus cackled. Fiona was getting mightily sick of the decrepit git already.

"It's leaves I've picked in the fields. It'd be a lot easier if I were a faery and didn't have to go foraging and drying and all the other hard work."

"But you have the knowledge," Fergus continued adamantly.

182

"So does any decent housewife that knows her simples, now do shut up old man. I've some bread and cheese which we'll share with you if you can keep your gob closed."

"Fiona!" Ciarán corrected, but she ignored him. Ciarán did not need to be hearing these things. It would only remind him how quare she was. What if he decided she was too irregular to be taking to his uncle's house? It would be bad enough as it is. She had no idea how she would fit in if she could fit in at all. She had had so little contact with other people in the life she had lived with Nan. It had been just themselves and the goats, and Farley of course. These past weeks with Ciarán had been more social interaction than she'd had in her whole life together. Even going to his brother's kitchen to collect messages had been a revelation. She had always known that she and Nan were different, but to see the sneering glances and even the fingers under aprons, making the signs to ward off evil. She did not believe it was wrong to be a Listener, so had no desire to change who she was. She could hear what the animals were saying and in turn, they could hear her – where was the evil in that?

Angrily, she tore the loaf into bits and handed these in turn to Ciarán, Farley, and lastly Fergus. She kept back a small bit for herself. She crumbled the cheese into fragments, dispersing these as well. For a time, there was only the sound of hungry chewing. Then the aged fellow belched appreciatively and offered,

"I've got a wee drop of poteen if you have a thirst on you." He took Ciarán's cup and threw the leaves onto the fire, refilling the cup with clear liquid.

"I wouldn't drink that if I were you," Fiona advised. "It could make you go blind."

Fergus cackled again – it was beginning to be quite a grating habit.

"Never worry *cailín*, I've given the faeries their portion," and in demonstration, he took a long swig from a leather bag, offering it then to Fiona. She shook her head in distaste and went to Ciarán.

"I've some of the ointment here, do you want it for your leg?" Ciarán handed her the lone cup, which she rinsed again and made herself a cup of tea, using her own leaves of course, as anything in this cabin was likely to be mouldy or worse. She gave the jar of ointment to Ciarán, but he was at a loss as to how to apply it. "Go on," she said, "I'll turn around," not that she hadn't seen his bare leg many a time before, but with Fergus here it would be more appropriate to be discreet.

Ciarán dropped his trousers and began rubbing the liniment into his thigh. Fergus crept around the side of the chair and eyed the injury with interest. "Quite a scar you have there. How did you acquire such a thing?"

Ciarán grunted in pain, as he continued to massage the remedy into his leg.

"Horse threw me," he offered, feeling a pang of betrayal towards Conall, who had never thrown him, not since they had sorted out who was the leader – Conall of course. Pulling on his trousers he sat down wearily. Fiona, returned, pulling his cloak away as he sat and laying it over him.

"Get some sleep." Then wrapping her shawl around her, she crouched next to the fire, Farley leaning on her leg. "Good night Mr. O'Flanagan, thank you for your hospitality," she decided to add, trying to keep the sarcasm out of her voice.

184

Fergus snorted and went to his lice ridden pallet in the corner. He was welcome to it.

Curled up with Farley near the hearth, Fiona wasn't entirely comfortable. Her shawl wasn't giving that much warmth and the dirt floor was damp and hard. She had got used to the nest of blankets she had made back at their cabin. Sleeping lightly, she was able to hear Ciarán as he grunted and shifted in the chair.

"Can you not find ease?" she sat up, watching Ciarán rubbing his leg.

"Ach, no. I think I'd be better lying down then I could stretch it out fully. And me arse is that sore from riding. I'm not so used to it now." Fiona went to him and took his arm, boosting him to a standing position.

"You best stay by the hearth, it's warmest and Farley will keep the rats off you." She helped him manoeuvre himself onto the floor and then lay his cloak over him. "Will you be alright there?"

"I will so," he assented, shuffling about on the floor, trying to find a less lumpy spot. "Are you warm enough? If not, come over to me and we can share the cloak."

"Your man will have his opinions," but Fiona was already settling next to Ciarán. She was cold and cared very little for convention. There was no harm in trying to keep the chill at bay. Fergus could chortle suggestively all he wanted.

Farley alerted them to movement and they both sat up as Fergus moved towards the fire, stabbing it with a poker and throwing on a brick of peat. His snort of derision was duly noted, and Fiona stood up, reaching down to help lever Ciarán to his feet. He looked about for his stick but realised he had left it with their belongings. Surprisingly, Farley fetched it from the corner where they had left their bundle. Sometimes it seemed the dog could read his mind. It certainly understood anything Fiona asked of it, though Farley did not always choose to comply.

Stiff with the morning cool, Ciarán leaned heavily on the stick, making his way out of the door to relieve himself. Fergus handed her the bucket.

"Will you fill that *cailín*? There's a bit of a pond up behind the cabin." Reluctantly she took the bucket. It should have been filled last night. Then they could have had a hot cup of tea before wandering around in the wet grasses. Obviously, Fergus wasn't exactly an organised householder.

Ciarán and Fiona let Fergus have the cup first, as it was his and then quickly shared a hot cup of tea. Fiona would have preferred to give Ciarán some comfrey tea, but they were anxious to be on their way.

"Have you any more of that bread and cheese?" Fergus suggested but Fiona shook her head quickly. There was some, but not enough to share. She carried the saddle out to where Conall had rested in a sort of lean-to and Ciarán bore their bags over his shoulder. Neither of them had packed much so he could bear the weight. Farley killed a mouse that ran out of the lean-to as they entered and swallowed it perfunctorily. When she had saddled the horse, Ciarán took a small package from his bag and asked her to tuck it under her shawl. Ciarán mounted, as Conall graciously lowered himself and Fiona hopped on, behind him this time. They started out on the road, where Ciarán asked Fiona to open the package, have a scone and pass him one. She broke off a bit of hers and tossed it to Farley, trotting alongside them.

"Do you think he'll say anything to anyone?" Ciarán worried.

"I hardly think he'll see anyone," Fiona rejoined, "And if he does, it will be more about the faery Listener that stayed at his cabin and charmed a horse. There will be little mention of you at all I should think."

"Of course, there will! I've charmed one of the old ones and have my own captive Listener. How many men can boast of a friendship with one of the Tuatha Dé Danann?"

Fiona would have walked away if she weren't clinging to his waist, on top of a rather large stallion.

"I don't find that even a bit funny, you know!" She wanted to explain to him how being a Listener actually worked and how important it was to her. She had tried, but she knew it wasn't something she could completely explain. Perhaps Ciarán had an inkling of what she meant – she knew there was a strong bond with Conall but describing the images flashing back and forth between her and beast was beyond her words. She felt what the animal felt. Sometimes she could turn feelings and images into words, but that was translating from the original language, which was, what? An energy between her and the animal? Some psychic ability? She had no idea. She just knew that she had been taught this knowledge from a very young age and now it no longer required skill, it was a simple touch and the animal spoke to her. She looked down at Farley, keeping pace adequately as they were controlling Conall's speed in deference to Ciarán's leg. Except with Farley. With him, she did not even have to touch him. His mind and hers were intertwined. When he ate the mouse, she felt the bones crunching between her teeth and when she looked for Ciarán's stick, Farley collected it. This was because Farley was her acolyte. Without him, the world of the beasts would be silent to her. With him, they all spoke, some more easily than others, but she could hear even the birds, her least favourite of animals. Dogs, goats, horses, cows, farm animals spoke to her glibly but there were stuttered phrases from others. Farley was her conduit. Without him, she was just a homeless young lady with no real means of employment.

Ciarán was surprised by her sulky retort and pensive mood, so they continued the rest of the journey in silence. They stopped once to have a drink from a stream and let Ciarán stretch his leg. Conall wandered a bit, grazing calming and Farley lay down in the grass, crawling forward on his front legs to give his belly a good scratch. Fiona produced two apples from her apron pocket and she and Ciarán ate them, while watching Farley skirtle in the grass. Fiona bit off a chunk and threw the piece of apple to Farley, who pounced on it, chewed it twice and swallowed.

"Do you share everything you eat with him?"

"Pretty much everything. I did once give him some ale and he started a dog fight and bit a wee lad, so I don't think the drink agrees with him."

Ciarán nearly fell over laughing.

"Your dog can't take his drink!"

Offended Fiona retorted, "A lot of people have problems with liquor I hear."

"That is a fact," he conceded. "There's a bloke, what's his name, ah, James Cullen. He's after starting an organisation called the Pioneers. You see, you take a pledge never to take strong drink again and you get a special badge. He wants all the constables to take the pledge."

"And are you a member of this organisation?" she smiled.

"Not on your life. I'm afraid Farley will have to take the pledge on his own." They both looked at the dog, now lying on his side, trying to soak up some warmth from the weak sun. Farley let out a quiet pop, probably from eating the apple. "I think he just said, 'no'" Ciarán laughed.

It was approaching teatime when they arrived at William McGovern's not unsubstantial farm. He had been luckier than his brother, moving from wheat, barley, and potatoes to livestock and had been able to rent larger tracts of land. He had a few tenants under his care now and was one of the few Catholic landlords in the area, albeit on a farm that was miniscule compared to some of the estates of the absent English landlords.

As his brother John had died young, leaving his much smaller holding to his son John, there had been no place for Ciarán. McGovern had decided to take the young man under his wing, so to speak, and train him to be a decent agent. Then when McGovern's own son, William, or Liam as he insisted on calling himself, came into the land, he would have his agent there and ready, and it was all kept in the family. It suited them well. It was even better when Ciarán found the young lady of the neighbouring holding easy on the eye. An agreement was arranged and Ciarán would then have his own bit of land to manage once the marriage was consummated. It was all so terribly tidy; it warmed McGovern's heart.

Riding into the yard, a stable boy spotted them and called out a warning,

"The divil himself is back. Hope that stall door has been repaired since the last time he kicked it down."

"Hello Jamie," Ciarán carolled warmly. "I hope you've got a great stack of hay for my beast and some sweet straw." Fiona touched Conall's side, and the horse began to bow.

"Whaat!" Jamie jumped back in alarm.

"No worries, lad. Conall is helping me with this bum leg." Ciarán slipped off the saddle, then leaned heavily on the horse. Fiona hopped down afterwards, and searched in the bundles, procuring Ciarán's stick and handing it to him.

"You were hurt bad," the boy observed. Then his eyes fell on Fiona who had turned to Conall to thank him for the journey. "Who's she?"

Ciarán took Fiona's hand and pulled her forward.

"This is Fiona, and she has tamed the wild beast so respect her." Jamie stared with wide eyes at Fiona.

"Conall hasn't bit you?"

"Of course not! Why would he bite me? Conall is a sweetheart," Fiona was appalled. What a disrespectful child this boy was!

"Well, you best be taking your sweetheart to his stall then. Master Ciarán, they'll be glad to see you up at the house," and with that Jamie scuttled quickly out of the reach of Conall, who thought perhaps the insolent lad was due a quick nip.

Ciarán looked at Fiona, who suddenly seemed very young and frightened.

"Are you alright staying with Conall a bit, getting his saddle off and rubbing him down? There might be some oats as a special treat as well. He's had a long time of foraging." She stood staring at him. "I'm not asking you to be a servant

190

Fiona, it's just no one else can get near him without losing a hand and I'm just no good at it yet," he gestured with frustration at his leg.

She nodded,

"Of course. I'm sure he can show me the way." She took the reins over Conall's head with one hand and laid her other hand on his neck, asking him to take her to the stall. Hopefully, someone would show her where the oats were, and how much to give him. She'd never cared for a horse in a proper stable. It seemed he could do with a good grooming as well. Would the lad, Jamie, tell her where she could get a comb? She hoped so. The boy seemed a bit scatty but surely if he worked in the stables, he would know where things were kept. With a deep breath, she remembered that Conall was her friend and there was always Farley by her side.

As Ciarán limped towards the house, both his cousin and uncle came rushing out to meet him. Liam embraced him, nearly knocking Ciarán over and then encouraged Ciarán into the sitting room, where tea was called for. McGovern, Ciarán's uncle, pulled out a bottle of whiskey, which they added liberally to their teacups in celebration.

"It's that good to have you home," McGovern exclaimed, while slipping a biscuit to the somnolent wolfhound sprawled at his feet. A second wolfhound raised her head in mild interest, so a biscuit was tossed in her direction as well. The fire was crackling, the sofa was comfortable, and the drink was a tonic.

"And it's that good to be home," Ciarán settled back on the sofa, lifting his leg up onto an ottoman. He could feel the fire warming his bones and the whiskey warming his innards. He could sit there all night he thought. McGovern began to fill him in on the business of the farm. They were bringing in the sheep to the lower pastures and they would need to think about bringing in the cattle before the fields got too thick with mud. The new mare had taken from her breeding earlier in the year and McGovern had high hopes for the offspring. It was true, he had paid a bit too much for the mare but the legs on her were solid hunter's legs. The pack was not doing so well, seemed a lot of the dogs were suffering from an ear canker. With that, Ciarán remembered Fiona, left in the stables.

"Uncle, a young girl helped care for me when I was poorly. She's a right clever thing – knows all sorts of remedies, and sure she did me more good than the gormless git of a doctor." He looked to Liam for confirmation but wasn't encouraged by the rather dubious expression on his face. However, Liam nodded.

"A bit of a quare one but certainly capable," Liam managed to contribute. "Of course, Ciarán would sing the praises of anyone who took a fondness to that horrible beast of a horse he has."

McGovern put down his cup with a look of surprise,

"She took a shine to the devil incarnate?"

"Took a shine to him isn't the half of it," Liam was warming to the story, "Conall follows her around like a kitten and nibbles at her hair. She can even ride the thing."

"She must be some brawn *cailín* to ride a stallion!" McGovern leaned back and reached for a dog, to scratch behind its ear. One of the wolfhounds obliged by getting up and leaning against McGovern's chair, moaning in content as the right spot was located, just near the collar.

192

"She barely comes up to my waist," Ciarán said proudly, "She's trained Conall to bend down so she can clamber up, and it's well she did because I can't mount him without this trick, not at the moment."

"Well, I'm sorry to have missed this," McGovern was now rubbing the wolfhound's rump, who was enjoying the massage with relish.

"But you haven't, I've brought her home with me."

Liam sat up abruptly. "You did what?"

Ciarán was taken aback.

"Sure, I couldn't leave her to walk the roads looking for work. She saved my life." There was only stony silence from Liam, so Ciarán turned to his uncle. "She could be a great help here. Old Petesy is near crippled with age. You just said yourself that he's let the dogs go."

"Kennel work is a man's job," McGovern replied crisply. "We can't have some slip of a girl controlling a great pack of hounds."

"You've not met her, you've no idea what she can do," Ciarán pleaded.

Liam mumbled,

"He certainly doesn't have any idea, and nor do I." Ciarán shot him a quelling look, begging silence. Uncle William was not keen on the old ways and any mention of faery gifts or cunning women would turn him off completely. All McGovern wanted was to move forward into the 20th century and be accepted among the Protestant community.

"She's got a true gift with animals. Please uncle, I do owe her, just meet her."

"I don't need any more servants, I have too many as it is. I'm just too soft hearted," McGovern tossed another biscuit into the waiting jaws of the wolfhound leaning on his chair.

Liam was starting to feel guilty. Ciarán had a point. Fiona had helped them both out in a desperate situation and there was no denying she had a talent. Her skills made her a bit strange to have around, but Ciarán obviously didn't feel that way. Liam loved his cousin dearly and didn't want him to be distressed, not after all that he had been through. Ciarán was still thin and wasted looking and watching him still leaning on a stick to walk had been unpleasant. Hopefully, there would be no harm having the girl around, unless, he looked at Ciarán sharply, he hadn't fallen in love with the backward child? Ciarán did remember he had a fiancé, didn't he? But no, Ciarán was too aware of his penniless state. He needed Gráinne and he needed the goodwill of his uncle. Tampering with that match would destroy William McGovern's goodwill entirely. Ciarán was far too sensible for that. His cousin was just trying to do the honourable thing.

"Where is she now Ciarán?"

"In the stall with Conall."

"Shall I go fetch her then?" Liam turned to his uncle for a reply. The man nodded and sighed. He supposed he could find a place for her somewhere. It wouldn't cost him dearly; women didn't eat that much.

Liam found Fiona in Conall's stall, carefully combing out the mane of the stallion. As he approached Conall tossed his head and bared his teeth at Liam but with a whisper from Fiona he retracted his challenge immediately. Fiona looked up at Liam steadily. She was aware that Liam was not her best friend but didn't see why he found listening so unnerving. Maybe he was jealous.

194

"Is Ciarán settled alright?" she asked. This took Liam aback, but of course, she still saw Ciarán as her patient. Or did she? The problem could be the other way. Maybe the girl was lovesick and had begged to be taken along.

"He's fine. By the fire with a cuppa and his leg up on a stool."

"That's good then," she turned back to Conall's mane and began picking at a particularly stubborn tangle.

He decided to get right to the point,

"Why are you here?"

"Because he insisted." Liam looked doubtful.

"He did. I'd left hours before. He came looking for me." There was a long pause. "If I'm not wanted, I'll go. It's no bother to me."

"No bother really? And where will you go? Do you have other work arranged?" Fiona shrugged and continued to be occupied with the horse's grooming. Liam sighed. "Look Fiona, I don't mean to be ungrateful and I'm sure my father can find a place for you here. It's just you need to understand that Ciarán has a life here. He has work and family and a fiancé. You know that don't you?"

Fiona turned to him, hands on her hips. The horse noted her indignation and stamped a foot, the one on the opposite side from Fiona.

"I haven't asked for anything. You paid me well and I have some coin to go on. If you want me to leave, I'll leave." She turned to pick up her bag from the corner of the stall and Farley joined her at her heel. Stepping from the stall, she turned to Conall and laid a lingering hand along his muzzle, he blew softly into her hand, and she nodded. Marching past Liam, as if he weren't even there, she started for the door of the stables.

Liam hurried to join her and caught at her arm,

"Don't go. You've done us a great service and Ciarán probably still needs some of your healing." Fiona stood still, looking down at the floor and not responding. "Please," he added.

"Very well, and people say women are fickle," Fiona shook off his arm. "Where to now, or am I to sleep in the stall with Conall?"

"Well, first to meet my father. He needs to make an agreement with you. Then, I imagine you're hungry, or at least that dog of yours is."

"He's starving. So am I. Hopefully, this meeting won't take all evening." Farley barked in agreement.

Walking into the sitting room, Fiona became conscious of her dusty bare feet, her faded, stained skirt and unkept hair. Farley leaned against her leg as she stood in the doorway, reminding her of who they were together. She took in the scene – velvet covered sofa, upholstered chairs, large, blazing fire, even on a day that had not been so cold. There were opulent carpets, paintings, ornaments and two of the most handsome creatures she had ever seen in her life. Her heart reached out, and the two wolfhounds clambered onto their feet, walked sedately towards her, and stood, to attention before a Listener.

"This is Fiona," Liam started to say as his father, noting Farley, interrupted,

"Mind my dogs, they aren't always friendly with strangers!" but Fiona had fallen to her knees and put out both her hands. Each hound came up and ceremoniously licked her hands, then one lay his great head on her shoulder and groaned into her ear. The other hound sniffed Farley politely and then lay down before him, giving him the full respect due to an acolyte.

Finally, Fiona stood, tears shining in her eyes.

"Your dogs, Sir, are beyond words."

Turning to his nephew, McGovern had to agree,

"She certainly does have a way with animals."

It was decided that Fiona would help Petesy with the kennel work. The room attached to the kennels, that was currently Petesy's would be transferred to Fiona so that she could see to any night-time emergencies, such as whelping. Petesy instead, would be offered a labourer's cabin that had fallen derelict. The cabin would need a bit of work before Petesy could be moved into it. It would be presented to him as a reward for his long service. Meanwhile, Fiona would lodge with the kitchen maids in one of the attic rooms. Ciarán offered to take Fiona to the kitchen to introduce her to the housekeeper, Mrs. McGuire, a stout, middle-aged woman with a perpetually flushed face. He was hoping to cadge a snack for himself and Fiona since the apple and scone on the road had barely been adequate, and it was not yet time for supper.

Mrs. McGuire was all over Ciarán with pleasure at his return and concern over his injury. Tutting, she blamed it on all his wild horse and expressed the opinion that the dreadful thing should be shot. She fussed Ciarán onto a bench by the long table and then nodded to Fiona.

"And who is this one here? With a dog in me kitchen no less." Fiona moved protectively towards Farley. She had heard that there were people that didn't like dogs and she wasn't going to let this overbearing woman come after Farley with a broom.

"This is my good friend Fiona," Ciarán interjected. "She was a great help when I was poorly, and Uncle has just hired her to help out with the kennels." Mrs. McGuire examined the girl from head to food.

"Not much of her is there? What is she twelve, thirteen years?"

"I'm seventeen," declared Fiona, "and strong enough to do most jobs. Ask him," she jutted her head towards Ciarán. "I've been lifting and dragging him about these past weeks."

Mrs. McGuire raised her eyebrows, considering.

"It's true," Ciarán interposed. "Strong as a Pitbull terrier." Fiona wrinkled her nose at the description. Fighting dogs were not something she approved of, and she really didn't want to be compared to one of the poor creatures. "Though, a tad more bonny," Ciarán scrambled to say.

"Sit," Mrs. McGuire gestured. "I'm sure you're both famished." Calling over her shoulder she had one of the kitchen girls bring them bread and butter, along with large cups of tea. Mrs. McGuire noted Fiona breaking off a large piece of bread for Farley. "Would the wee dog like a bowl of bread and milk?

"Yes, please," Fiona requested. "More bread than milk please. If he drinks too much milk, he gets wind." Ciarán stifled a laugh.

"I'll remember that, is there anything else his lordship requires?"

"He's that fond of a good beef bone when you have one going," Fiona offered. Perhaps the housekeeper was teasing, but Fiona might as well make it clear that Farley was no ordinary dog and special treatment was to be expected.

Impertinent little snip mused Mrs. McGuire, but she continued the banter with,

"His needs will be taken into consideration."

Ciarán was getting a bit nervous at this exchange. The housekeeper wielded a great deal of power in the McGovern household. She could make Fiona's life quite unpleasant if she chose to do so.

"Uncle has asked if you can find Fiona a bed upstairs with one of the kitchen maids. She'll be moving to the kennels once we have a cabin sorted for old Petesy, but that may take a bit of time. Would that be alright Mrs. McGuire?" he requested in his most respectful tone.

Mrs. McGuire sighed heavily.

"I suppose she can share with Susan, but she'll need a wash and change of clothes first. I'm sure Mr. McGovern doesn't want any of his servants running around looking like beggars or tinkers. Do you have any shoes child?"

Fiona wasn't proud but she knew she wasn't particularly dirty. Certainly, her clothes were old and worn. Well, actually, they weren't even her clothes, but what her mother had left behind, so were far too big and ill fitting, Eala, having been of a much taller and severely slender build. Sullenly she retorted,

"I don't wear shoes."

"Well, you will wear shoes if you intend to serve here!" Mrs. McGuire was not used to girls who talked back. She had all the staff under her thumb, following her orders, as if she were the general of a small army against dirt and bad dinners.

Fiona stood up, smoothing down her travel-stained and threadbare skirt as if it were made of silk. She beckoned to Farley and turned towards Ciarán.

"I will be nobody's servant. That was not part of the agreement with your uncle. I will work for wages, and I will take the best care possible of his dogs. However, I do not bow and scrape. I don't come from that kind of people."

Puffing up like an adder, Mrs McGuire exploded,

"Well, aren't we a Miss La-di-da! How dare you come in here, putting on airs as if you weren't just poorhouse fodder."

"Mrs. McGuire, please," Ciarán stepped between them. "We're both tired and hungry from travelling. Fiona is shattered from looking after me this long time and she's not used to your ways. Just let her be to do her work in the kennels. You have no need to bother with her at all. She'll be managed by Petesy in the kennels and Brendan oversees all the out-building staff. If there are problems, let Brendan deal with it." Ciarán prayed that Brendan would be a bit more understanding of his short-tempered protégé. He imagined Brendan would be furious to have a girl in the midst of the stable lads but surely, he would be impressed with Fiona's ability to attend to Conall. None of the boys were able to get near Conall and Ciarán couldn't saddle and groom the horse himself right now. Brendan would realise that she was needed and accept her. He was a practical man. He might glower for a time, but he would come round. If any of the horses needed healing, he'd bet Fiona would be a help there as well. She didn't know horses, true, as she'd mostly worked with goats, but if she could listen to their complaints, that must be a boon. Couldn't any animal tell her where the pain was coming from. Didn't it work that way?

Mrs. McGuire pressed her lips together tightly, so many words just waiting to come flying out. The *cailín* needed taking down a peg, that was sure. It would happen though. Likely the girls themselves would do it. They didn't always take to newcomers and this strange one with her odd eyes and queer coloured hair was hardly likely to fit in. A bit of teasing could go a long way.

"I've some old uniform bits that might fit her in my cupboard. I'll bring them down and she can change. I'll burn those clothes she has on now. I won't have lice in the house." Ciarán laid a restraining arm on Fiona before she could confront the insult. Fiona threw off his arm and marched out of the kitchen, back towards the outbuildings. She and Farley would sniff out the kennels and meet the dogs – they would welcome her at least.

They walked into the kennel block, a row of kennels down one side of the building and an area for preparing food, a whelping box and other sundry equipment on the other side of the block. There were three to five dogs in each kennel, all lined with straw and a trough for water along the right side of the kennel. The doors were wooden, so Fiona had to look over them to see the dogs and was interested to find a different type of hound then usually observed in the British Isles. A rather bent old man came hobbling towards her. Fiona imagined that he could do with quite a bit of nettle lineament and wondered if he would accept her treatment.

"They're Basset Griffons," the gruff voice informed her.

"What lovely eyes they have, like the waters of a sacred well."

Petesy guffawed,

"Far too much mischief in them to be coming from any sacred well."

"Are they lively then?"

"Oh yes, if they get a scent, you can hear them hollering all over the county and they'll go for days. You could never call them back off a scent, not for anything, but gentle as your own mother. Don't even know how to growl."

Turning to Farley at her feet,

"Did you hear that Farley? No growling! I bet they don't nip either little man!" She tickled Farley under the chin affectionately.

"I see you've got a terrier there. Now that's a feisty bit of dog. Just as soon bite you as say hello."

"If you're a rat, that is so. He's a good friend to me though."

"Aye, well that can only be true. A dog will be a good friend, much more loyal than a man. My name is Petesy, by the way, and you're the young *cailín* Ciarán brought home with him."

"Right you are. My name is Fiona," she stuck out her hand in greeting and both gnarled hands held hers tightly. She looked up into the elderly man's eyes, blurred with cataracts and felt he had some knowledge similar to hers. "I think I'm to help you with the dogs. Will you mind that?"

"Depends on what sort of help. What experience do you have with dogs, besides your little terrier here?"

What could she say? I hear the things that Farley listens for, the rustles in the grass, the scream of a rabbit. His smells are my smells, I know when a bitch in season has passed this way,

I know when a dog won't share his territory. I know what it is to be a dog, but I am not a dog. None of this could be said of course.

"May I?" she asked as she opened a kennel door. She and the old man walked into the small box, where three hounds immediately jumped to their feet, barking with enthusiasm. One of the group leapt up, placing its paws on her shoulders. She put her hands on his head, taking both ears in her hands and looked into the dog's eyes. Normally, one would never do this with a strange dog as it is extremely rude, but the dog knew her for a Listener and had come to her with a message. "His ears are paining him something awful, especially the left one. Probably some sort of wee bug as he can hear a terrible chewing sound and it's driving him mad." She bit her bottom lip. Had she said too much? Should she have left out the bit about the chewing?

"The ears are a bother at the moment, but you can smell that. What makes you think there are wee beasties in his ear?" He was not doubting, just curious. All the same, she couldn't say, 'Because he told me.'

"It's the look in his eye," she fabricated, "I've seen it before. What are you using? Oil with a bit of garlic can help. If that doesn't work, I'd get some vinegar, water it down mind you, and clean the ears with that."

"I've used liquid paraffin, which can work well enough. But it keeps coming back and then they all get it and I've the divil of a time getting them all treated and then having to start back at the beginning. It's been going on for months and it just seems to get worse and worse."

She looked down at the straw bedding, which was not at its best.

"With two working at it, perhaps we can get a handle on it. Shall I start by cleaning out all the kennels, giving them a good scrub and some fresh straw?" If she offered to do the more menial chores, perhaps Petesy wouldn't feel as if she were taking over, though she saw that she would have to. He didn't have the physical ability to keep all these dogs in good nick. She was surprised Mr McGovern had not seen fit to hire another kennel man earlier. Maybe the McGovern's weren't as wealthy as she had assumed, or maybe they just liked the old man. She could see why they would.

Petesy grinned. She had a suspicion that he knew exactly what she was doing but didn't mind anyway.

"Sounds like a decent enough plan. I'll go make some tea for us while you start. There's an empty kennel at the end you can put this lot in while you clean them out. Will you need help moving them?"

"I'm all right, and a cup of tea would be lovely. I've been rushed here and there since I arrived and am nearly parched now." Petesy nodded and moved off towards his room just off the kennels. He probably had a small stove in there, a pallet and little else. That's where she would be living in time. It suited her perfectly, living alongside twenty dogs was a home she could get used to.

FIONA PROVES HER WORTH

Unfortunately, it took a week or so to organise Petesy's move to a cabin of his own and the instalment of Fiona in the kennel lean-to. In that time, she was supposed to be sharing with one of the house maids. Fiona was directed to wash her feet by Mrs. McGuire and then given into the care of Susan, who led Fiona upstairs. When they got to the top of the house, Susan opened the door to a stuffy, spare room with a slanted ceiling. A single bed was shoved up under each of the eaves and the girls were sharing, two to a bed. Susan had previously had the luxury of her own bed and was now forced to share with a backward kennel maid. It was intolerable really. She flung her hand out at the bed on the right side of the room, where a black patch of mould was creeping up the wall.

"That's my bed. You'll be sharing with me till they sort you out." Farley had followed them into the room and was quite taken with the bed, being more used to a pile of blankets. He jumped up on the quilt and began to circle, preparing himself for a comfortable nap. "Off! Off!" Susan screamed. She flapped her apron at Farley, who ignored her entirely. "He's not to be on the bed. He can't be in here at all. I won't sleep in a room with a filthy dog and all its fleas. Get him out now!"

Fiona picked up Farley and walked to the door. What was she going to do? She wasn't going to lock Farley out on their first night in their new home – if she could even call it that. It certainly didn't feel much like home. Suddenly, she was overcome with a wash of loss, thinking of Nan's tidy cabin and how the three of them, herself, Nan, and Farley would snuggle warm under the blankets at night, a hot brick at their feet. They would lay there in the dark and Nan would tell Fiona and Farley about the selkie wives in Scotland and the fox maidens in the far east. Sometimes there were tales of earlier Listeners and the great deeds they had accomplished. In the morning Nan had always managed to be up before her granddaughter and had the fire going with the kettle on, and a porridge bubbling.

Fiona turned to the housemaid, who stood, hands on her hips, glaring at her. "Good night then," Fiona said cordially and made her way down the stairs and back to the kitchen. The big door had already been locked for the night but Fiona was able to lift the wooden bar and slip out into the darkness. Using their sense of smell, she and Farley found the kennels and crept inside. There were a few inquisitive barks, but the dogs settled quickly and old Petesy was not disturbed. Fiona felt along the kennel block until she came to the stall where the dog Ambrose lived. She had met him earlier in the day and he had welcomed her with snuffling affection.

Ambrose was probably twice the size of Farley and had a great deal more coat. He was mostly white, with light brown patches and long, drooping ears. His muzzle was extensive, making him especially skilled at nose work, indeed he was well known for his ability to scent a rabbit or a fox at vast distances. He had the calm demeanour of a true leader, with no need to dominate. He led his pack by good example and innate confidence. He knew when to howl and when to curl up in a ball and sleep. In the field, he was instinctive and in the kennel he was reflective. His pack endeavoured to emulate his pacific behaviour so there were few squabbles for him to adjudicate. His tolerance of the young made him a popular godfather and his handsome physique endeared him to many a bitch. Ah, but when his nose went to the ground, he was a different dog. Then, the scent inflamed him, and he would bay to the wind, chasing madly at the odour that was calling to him. The pack would follow, thrilled at the pursuit, whether it be rabbit, fox, or a meat pie.

This evening, Ambrose was sharing with a dog and a bitch, however, they were happy to shuffle over on the straw and make room for Fiona and Farley. Ambrose was solicitous of the Listener and advised that the dogs surround her completely since she didn't have fur and might feel the cold. Snugly ensconced, Fiona fell asleep. feeling that perhaps this venture would work out after all. Ambrose lay his long nose over her shoulder and inhaled deeply.

When Petesy entered the kennels in the morning, Fiona woke along with the hounds. The venerable kennel man did not act surprised to see her, merely nodded and asked if she had eaten. She shook her head, so he led her into his lean-to and made her a bowl of porridge. Gesturing towards Farley, he remarked that he only had the one bowl. Fiona told him that she would finish quickly and then use her bowl for Farley's porridge. Petesy asked her to come over to the kennels when she was done but to make sure she had a cup of tea first. He pointed out his supply, and where he kept a mug. Mouth full, she nodded and then Petesy went off to his morning chores.

They were cleaning out the kennels of the old straw and sluicing them down with soapy water when Ciarán came in, looking for Fiona.

"I thought you'd be here," he said, obviously relieved. "Mrs. McGuire said you'd run off in the night and left the door ajar. She was checking through the silver to see if any had been nicked."

Petesy chuckled but made no comment.

"She can take her bloody silver and," Fiona began, but Ciarán held up his hand and interrupted the threat.

"I told her you'd no interest in that sort of thing. I was just worried because Susan said you'd not stayed with the servants upstairs."

"It was not as if I had any choice!" Fiona flared. "She wouldn't have Farley on the bed. She wouldn't even have him in the room. She called him flea bitten!" At this Petesy had to lean on his rake for laughing. Fiona turned on him. "What do you find so funny?"

"Ach *cailín*, you haven't learned the difference between house servants and us outdoors."

"Oh, I think I have," Fiona re-joined. "The one is priggish and full of herself, and the other knows how to do a proper job."

"Well, there you have it," Petesy agreed, wiping tears of mirth from his eyes. "You'll get on well here and in the stables. Just mind you keep away from the wee biddies indoors."

"Don't worry, I won't be having anything to do with them from now on."

Ciarán was not satisfied though.

"But where did you sleep last night?"

"With Ambrose," Fiona beamed at him, "Such a gentleman."

Startled for a moment, Ciarán calmed himself when he remembered that Ambrose was his uncle's prize hound.

208

"Fiona!" he admonished, "You can't sleep in the kennels."

She shrugged and turned back to her work.

"I'm sure I don't see the problem at all."

Ciarán turned to Petesy for support, but the old man just chuckled again and poured his bucket into one of the kennels. Fiona got down on her hands and knees and began to scrub the floor.

"She's a fine little worker. Very glad to have her help. Never you mind Master Ciarán. I'll look after her." Ciarán wanted to protest further but realised that he couldn't compete with both Fiona and Petesy, so he let the matter lie. People would say what they would. He might care, but Fiona certainly wasn't bothered.

The days fell into a comfortable schedule for Fiona and Farley. They moved into the lean-to next to the kennels and arose at dawn for a cup of tea with bread and butter, and if the cook was feeling generous, they might even have been given a pot of jam. Then it was off to the kennels to let the dogs out into the yard to relieve themselves. While the pack sniffed about and marked the yard, Farley mingled with them socially and discussed their upcoming breakfast. Fiona and Petesy began filling the bowls with dog biscuit made from vegetables, wheat, bran, and beef blood. Sometimes there were raw bones left over from the butchering of a lamb or hog, though the cook usually claimed the bones for soup. The kennels were swept out and sluiced if necessary and then the dogs were called in, each running to its assigned kennel, thrilled to be partaking in breakfast. Of course, Farley always helped himself to a second meal as he felt a touch peckish by this hour of the day. Petesy and Fiona would take a rest and have a cup of tea, discussing the chores that needed to be done that day – perhaps some of the dogs needed to be groomed: nails clipped, ears cleaned, coats de-matted. And if one of the dogs had an upset stomach, a concoction needed to be created to placate the turmoil. Worming was done regularly with Wormwood, but its bitter taste had to be disguised in a healthy dose of cheese. Once a week, the whole kennels were scrubbed clean so that disease would not percolate. Petesy had been a kennel boy from the age of eight and had learned, over the years, what kept the dogs in top form. Fiona had her husbandry experience with the goats and her listening skills; between the two of them, the pack was well cared for. Fiona was happy to take on the more vigorous chores, leaving Petesy to supervise from a comfortable chair that had been discarded by the McGovern household. Content to sit among his pack, Petesy sat stroking and chatting as dog after dog came up and lay their head on his lap, leaning against him or falling asleep over their carer's feet. Both Petesy and Fiona favoured Ambrose, the largest and most handsome of the hounds, who had a baritone voice that could have graced the opera houses of Europe. It was no secret to Petesy that Fiona frequently sneaked Ambrose into her lean-to, allowing the hound to share the pallet with Farley and herself. This was a totally inappropriate spoiling for a pack dog, but Petesy held back his correction. He was ever so fond of the young girl and if it made her happy to turn Ambrose into a house dog, he was not going to interfere. Besides, the dog was getting on in years and his days on the hunt would not last forever. It was Petesy's hope that Master McGovern would take the dog into the house as a pet and not dispose of him, as happened with most pack dogs when they could no longer work.

When Fiona wasn't busy with the dogs, she visited Conall in the stables and became friends with Jamie the stable boy, a youth of twelve years whose father was one of the farm labourers. Jamie worshiped Fiona as the 'tamer of the divil himself,' meaning Conall. She found this amusing and treated Jamie like a younger sibling with alternating indulgence and mock severity. She was pleased to see that the boy was learning to watch the horses carefully and learn their language. She would point out the carriage of their ears and when they grew tense around the eyes, and Jamie began to see the subtle signs that indicated fear so he could slow down before the horse became panicked.

Ciarán was often in the stables to take Conall out for a ride around the estate or to check the smooth running of the stables with the groom. Occasionally, Ciarán would help with the training of a younger horse and Fiona loved to watch these sessions, sitting on the arena fence as the horse was schooled in proper manners and taught to jump, in preparation for being a hunter. Jumping looked amazing and Fiona was determined to learn how. She asked Conall if he would teach her, but he was vague on the requirements for humans and suggested she ask Ciarán instead. Ciarán was flattered to be asked, thinking that Fiona knew far more about animals than he did. Lessons began one overcast afternoon, with rain falling softly on the arena. Ciarán had found a pony more appropriate to Fiona's size and hoped that Fiona's skills could overcome the pony's tendency to stubbornness. Fiona found the pony, a somewhat obese bay mare oddly named, 'Jenny,' to be insistently lazy. However, they came to an agreement that Jenny would jump if Fiona produced apples.

Riding side saddle was not an option that Fiona would consider, claiming that it was uncomfortable for the horse. Neither did she own a riding habit so riding astride, with skirts rucked up was her style. Ciarán remarked that this manner of dress was frowned upon in polite society, but Fiona just gave him a look. He determined to ask his aunt if she had an old habit that could be cut down to fit Fiona. Not only would it be seemlier to wear a habit, but it would also prevent chaffing during long rides. He had a feeling that Fiona was determined to be a horse woman and would be riding quite often.

Sitting astride the reluctant pony, Fiona attempted to press into her heels and lean along the neck of the pony, as she had been told that this was the appropriate jump position. Unfortunately, Jenny was not really in the mood to jump and refused the first time, unsettling, but not entirely unseating Fiona. A short discussion ensued, where the price of jumping was raised to two apples and Fiona again encouraged the pony towards the jump. This time, Jenny stepped over the low pole and then turned her head, requesting her payment. Fiona did not accept the performance though and dismounted, raising the pole to a height that made it impossible for the pony to do anything but jump. Annoyed, Jenny cantered up to the jump and then stopped abruptly, causing Fiona to go flying over the pony's head and into the mud on the other side of the jump.

"That was not the way I wanted to go over the jump!" Fiona admonished once she had got her breath back. Luckily, no one had seen her ungainly attempt as Ciarán had left her to practice stepping over poles, foolishly thinking that Fiona would do as she was told. Marching up to Jenny, Fiona took the pony by the bridle and stared into her eyes, a very rude and intimidating gesture in horse language. Jenny tried to toss her head free and stamped a foot in frustration. However, she got the message and when Fiona remounted, Jenny cantered into the jump, flew across it, and then trotted to a stop. Fiona produced two apples from her pocket and thanked the pony. The jump had been amazing – a moment of flight in a sedentary world. Yet, the likelihood of Jenny repeating the performance was slim. Fiona decided she needed a mount with a slightly more forward going disposition.

As Fiona didn't have permission to use any other horses than Conall and Jenny, her only choice could be Conall. She neglected to tell Ciarán as she had a strong suspicion that he would warn her off. She told him she had successfully practiced stepping over the poles with Jenny and when he had time, she would request a further lesson. She informed Conall that she had done her lessons on Jenny and was ready to jump properly with him. Conall sniffed derisively at the mention of Jenny, a fat pony with no athletic ability at all.

Early one Sunday morning, before anyone else had risen, Fiona surreptitiously led Conall out of the stables, doubling the stirrups twice so they would fit her, she mounted him in the yard. She told him to take her on a countryside tour, jumping any fences or hedges in his way. Conall was thrilled to stretch his legs in this manner, as too often he had to sedately ambulate around the estate when he and Ciarán were looking for fences that needed mending or casting about for lost sheep.

So, they flew, and it was all Fiona had imagined it would be. She felt some understanding of her mother now, who had chosen to become a creature of flight. With her fingers entwined in Conall's mane, Fiona moulded herself to his neck and lifted her seat; she and Conall becoming one as they cantered, galloped, and leapt. Her hair fell loose and was a ribbon of varied colour, streaming behind her. Farley ran alongside, barking with their joyous abandon.

Of course, she was still a beginner, and her tour was not without mishap. At one fence, the opposite ground was uneven and Conall stumbled, causing her to slip sideways into a bramble bush. She found herself bruised, scratched, and muck covered by the time she returned, but deemed her outing well worth the minor injuries. Ciarán was not as insouciant on her return. First of all, he had meant to ride Conall to mass and he was late, looking for his horse. When he saw the state of Fiona he exclaimed at her dishevelment and gave her a good shake. She wasn't strong enough to jump a horse like Conall and she could have been killed. Didn't she know that people broke their necks riding horses all the time. She just smiled and replied that if that had been the case, she would have died happy. Disgusted, Ciarán rode off to mass, getting himself into an even more foul mood when the priest remarked publicly on his tardiness.

Fiona was aware that she had missed mass as it was far too late to begin walking. She would get a telling off from the housekeeper, who was supposed to be in charge of her proper

214

development, but Fiona wasn't much bothered. She rarely even went into the chapel, standing on the porch with Farley and once, during inclement weather chose to miss the ritual altogether. Accepting that she would be told off by Mrs. McGuire, Fiona went into the kennels and found her favourite hound there, Ambrose. She and Farley curled up with Ambrose on the straw and told him about the ride. Ambrose knew the fields well from hunting and could relive their morning with them: pointing out spots that Farley could go back to for a decent rabbit hole, or places where he had run a fox to ground. Ambrose had never actually killed another creature, that was taken care of by terriers on the hunt or the wolfhounds. The hounds of the pack lived for the scent. There was nothing so wonderful to them as inhaling deep within a rabbit warren, absorbing all those delicious odours. Like a connoisseur of French cheese or fine wine, Ambrose described the scent of a particular field, redolent with badger, deer, rabbit, and fox. Farley remarked that they had certainly been in that field earlier in the day but at the speed he moved through it he hadn't had the opportunity to absorb the aroma. Ambrose promised to go back with him soon and point out the specific highlights. Farley looked forward to urinating on those areas of special interest. Exhausted, Fiona fell asleep between the two dogs as they continued their conversation on the finer points of scenting and marking.

Petesy found Fiona in the kennels and told her that Sunday dinner would be ready soon and that Mrs. McGuire was ready to tear a piece off her. Fiona shrugged and told Petesy about her adventures. He remarked that she might want to put some ointment on her scratches before they turned septic. Ambrose licked a long scratch on her arm in consternation. He couldn't bear it if his girl fell ill.

Investing in hounds had been something William McGovern could afford. He'd only had to buy the one pair and then pay a few stud fees for outcrossing, but horses were another story. Now that he was establishing himself as gentry, he really did need to develop a stable of horses that he had bred -that was one of the main reasons he had taken Ciarán under his wing. The boy was a rare hand with horses. He was like your man Sullivan, from Cork who whispered in the horses' ears. No wonder Ciarán got on with the wee kennel maid and her talking to the dogs all the time. McGovern planned to breed a few decent horses and make good use of Ciarán's skill in developing the stable. The lovely new mare McGovern had bought off a man in Strabane, was the start of a new breeding line, with Ciarán's stallion servicing her. McGovern hadn't been so sure about that, what with the stallion's temperament and all but Ciarán had assured him that Conall was only himself because he hadn't been gelded. Certainly, Conall was a decent piece of horseflesh, if not the most even-tempered ride; it was worth the gamble.

Now that the foal was nearly due, McGovern had become nervous. Conall was a big horse and though the mare was sturdy, she was a first-time dam. He had warned the groom and the stable lads to monitor the mare closely and to collect him at the first sign of her foaling. He knew that her teats had filled and that she could be ready at any time now. He wondered about asking a veterinarian. He had heard they could be useful fellows but had never consulted one before for any of his animals. He'd always hired knowledgeable men who could sort out the animals themselves and now he had the little kennel maid. She might be useful. He'd heard that she was mixing raspberry leaves into the mare's feed. At least, she had asked the groom first. All the staff knew how McGovern valued the mare, though he had kept the price to himself. His wife would go spare if she ever found out.

Ciarán was excited about the upcoming foaling. It had taken some convincing for his uncle to use Conall, though what choice he had otherwise wasn't clear. There weren't any other stallions in the stables and Ciarán knew for a fact that McGovern had spent far too much on the mare and didn't have the cash for a stud fee. Conall had been a gift from Ciarán's father, a leggy yearling with a nasty bite that John Gallagher had got cheap off a traveller. Travellers knew their horses though, you had to give them that much. Apparently, Conall had been nipping at the other horses, leaving marks that made them less valuable at the horse market. Ciarán had seen immediately that Conall needed special handling, and had spent hours not even touching the horse, just crooning to him, and only approaching when the horse invited him to join up by turning away and walking around the edge of the paddock. A teenage boy had a lot to say to a horse and Conall had listened. He was an extraordinary horse and now a line of his progeny would begin at the McGovern stables.

Fiona had never seen a foaling, though she had helped bring many a goat into the world. She imagined it was going to be quite a bit different and was curious. She often visited the mare, whose name was Collette, and asked her how the foal felt inside her. Colette was indeed a stunning horse, but not particularly intelligent. She told Fiona the foal felt heavy and that she would be glad to be rid of it. Looking at her bulging sides, Fiona figured that made a lot of sense.

Although the equine gestation period is protracted at eleven months, the birth is paradoxically quick, taking place within one hour or less. Colette had started circling her stall after tea one dank November afternoon. Jamie, the stable lad, had noticed and called the head groom, who went to the stall and watched the mare for a while. She was definitely looking that way. She hadn't started lying down and getting up again, but all the signs were there. He sent Jamie up to the house to notify Master McGovern. The boy went in through the kitchen, cap in hand and asked to be taken to the master. The housekeeper took one look at the child's filthy boots and forbade him from walking over her clean floors. Desperately, Jamie hopped from foot to foot, reporting that he was to collect the Master as soon as possible because the rare pricey mare was about to drop a foal. Mrs. McGuire snorted disparagingly but waddled off to the library to notify the master. McGovern, his son and Ciarán, were all poring over a ledger when she knocked and let herself into the library.

"There's a boy from the stables that says you have a horse about to foal. It's dripping rain and desperate cold out there. Will you be wanting your supper before you go?" But all three men leapt up and pushed past her, racing to the stables. Jamie satisfied that his request had been delivered took the long route back, by the kennels and leaned in over the half door to give Fiona the news. Excitedly, she left the dog whose coat she was combing out and followed Jamie to the centre of activity.

Jamie and Fiona slipped into the empty stall next to the mare and managed to use an old crate to stand on and watch the proceedings. The groom was in there with McGovern and Ciarán. Liam stood on the opposite side of the door so that not too many people were crowded in the stall. Collette had lain down on her side and then got up again. All mares are restless when foaling, but she seemed beside herself. Ciarán spotted Fiona over the edge of the stall, "Do you think you could come in here and calm her a bit?" Fiona hesitated and looked towards McGovern. He had not encouraged Fiona to help with the horses and she did not want to overstep her place. McGovern said nothing but the groom looked at Fiona and waved her in. He was confident enough that the girl had some skill, and he would take all the help he could get. They couldn't afford to lose either the mare or the foal.

Fiona slipped into the stall and waited while the mare circled again, tossing her head and snorting. Collette was clearly distressed. When she paused, Fiona went to her and placed her hands on the horse's lathered neck and waited. She was nearly overcome by a wash of fear and pain; this was Collette's first foal, and the poor horse wasn't sure what was happening. Fiona tried to reassure, sending a message that this was natural and would pass soon, and with the passing the pressure in the horse's abdomen would cease. Colette kicked at her flanks, like a horse in colic and the men jumped back to avoid contact with the hoof. Fiona held her place, asking the horse to breathe.

"Can we walk up and down?" Fiona asked the groom. He nodded and got a rope to attach to

Colette's head collar. Fiona handed the end of the rope to the groom and accompanied Collette as she walked up and down the length of the stables. They did this many times, until Fiona felt the horse relax a bit. She asked if Collette was ready and when the mare assented, Fiona and the groom led her back towards the stall. They were just able to unclip the rope when Collette threw herself down on the straw and began to roll, almost writhe. When she stood up, her waters broke and flooded the stall. There was a sigh of relief from the men and then words of encouragement as a tiny hoof appeared at the birth canal. After the hoof came the fetlock and then the knee joint, but it was only one leg. They waited. Collette strained, but not productively. They wiped the sweat from the mare's flanks and spoke soothingly but after ten minutes, there was no progress. The groom sighed and stepped outside of the stall to a bucket he had set there. He washed his arms, leaving the soap slippery on the right arm. When he returned to the stall, he asked Ciarán to hold the mare while he inserted his arm into the birth canal, feeling for the lie of the foal. After a few moments of reaching, he shook his head and pulled his arm free.

"It's a very bad position. Breech, with one leg pulled up. I tried to pull back the other leg but I'm afraid of damaging the mare." He looked at McGovern, the question was there - the mare or the foal? Most men would go with the mare as they'd no idea if the foal was of any quality or not, but it wasn't the groom's decision to make.

"We'll give her a bit more time," McGovern answered.

"We can't give her much more time," Ciarán reminded. Eventually the foal would die. Even so, the foal might die anyway. If they couldn't get it out, they would have to insert a wire and dissect the foal in the womb, pulling it out piece by piece. He'd seen the grisly business done once and did not care to see it again. He took Fiona's arm then and showed it to the groom.

"She's a good deal smaller than you, could she maybe sort the foal out?"

The groom shook his head.

"She's not strong enough."

Ciarán turned to his uncle,

"Surely, it's worth a try?" Then to Fiona, "Do you think you could manage?"

He had put her on the spot and in front of his uncle, a man that Fiona never felt comfortable with. She was angry. However, at the same time, the mare was suffering, and she had to do something to help if she could. She made a face at Ciarán but nodded and went to wash her arms outside the stall. Returning, she lay her hand on Collette and explained that she was trying to get her foal out. She asked Collette to listen to her and to push when asked. Collette tossed her head, froth foaming from her mouth. Fiona only hoped the mare would be able to listen.

Reaching inside the mare, Fiona made contact with the foal and to her surprise, connected with the consciousness of the foal – it was alive, alive and listening. Concentrating with all her might, Fiona asked the foal if it could move. The foal responded by pulling its leg back inside the birth canal. It took several minutes to familiarise herself with the anatomy of the foal – she had not done this before, and at first it was a jumble of hooves and gangling limbs. Initially, she had wanted the foal to turn himself, for she had discovered it was a him, but she realised that it was impossible in the cramped quarters of the womb. It would have to be a breech birth, risky but possible. Fiona knotted her forehead, trying to send a picture to the foal that it could understand. She wanted him to stretch both hindlegs out. If she could get hold of both hind hooves, they could pull, and if quick enough they could save the foal. Breathing deeply, she sent the image of a long stretch and felt the hooves come towards her. At the same time Collette squealed in pain as the foal pressed against the uterine walls, but the hooves appeared - both of them! Fiona stepped back, letting the groom and Ciarán grab the hooves and pull downwards, while Fiona went to Collette's abdomen and willed her to push with all the power the exhausted mare had left. In a whoosh, the rest of the foal appeared. Ciarán grabbed a handful of straw and wiped the muzzle clear while the groom vigorously rubbed the body. The creature took a gasping breath, and everyone let out a huge sigh of relief. Collette turned around, surprised to see her offspring, and gave a nicker of delight. McGovern clapped his hands in glee!

"Will you look at that! Now that's a pretty lad, isn't it?" And indeed, it was, the foal was a bay, like his dam, but with white stockings and a flash of white on the head and chest. He was big and looked sturdy enough to stand soon.

Fiona had never before communicated with a creature that had not yet breathed air. She had not known it was even possible. Yet, she had done it, and she gazed proudly at the handsome foal resting in the straw while his dam nuzzled him and licked away the dregs of birthing fluid. Then all went black.

Farley, who had been locked out of the stall, gave a short, sharp bark and the audience around the foal turned to see Fiona, prone in the straw. Ciarán rushed to her and patted her face. She was ever so pale. Maybe he had asked too much of her? Her eyelids fluttered and she moaned – Farley grew more insistent outside the stall.

"Will you shush that dog," McGovern commanded. "It will upset the mare."

"Can you not see that Fiona has fainted?" Ciarán snapped but McGovern made an impatient gesture towards Collette. The groom stepped over to Ciarán and Fiona.

"She did a grand job, the wee *cailín*. She's probably shattered. Let's get her out of here and a drop of whiskey in her and she'll be right." Helping Ciarán with the stall door, they got Fiona out, fending off Farley who was leaping about at their legs, and carried Fiona to her pallet in the lean-to by the kennels. Brendan, the groom, reached into his coat and pulled out a flask. "Here, give her a drop of that to get her strength back." Ciarán poured the whiskey into Fiona's mouth, and she sat up abruptly, spluttering and spitting.

"What are you – oh." She looked around her, seeing where she was and the two men leaning over her with concern.

"I'm fine," she said with a sigh. "Just destroyed entirely, let me sleep." With that, she rolled over, pulling her blanket around her.

"Are you sure?" asked Ciarán. Fiona rolled back and glared at him.

"Listening is one thing but talking to an unborn foal is altogether different," she said, pulling the blanket over her head and curling up into a ball, Farley already curled solid against her stomach.

There was much celebration that night, both in the main house and the stables. A large jug of cider had been sent to the stables and the groom, Brendan and his stable lads were drinking steadily, taking occasional forays over to the stable to admire the new foal. Petesy had joined in the festivities, and they asked him where Fiona was, but he just shrugged. She slept through it all, drained from her most challenging listening task to date.

In the main house, McGovern toasted Conall, Collette, the foal, Ciarán, the groom Brendan and with a prod from Ciarán, Fiona as well. They argued over names for the new addition, Cuchulainn? – no that means hound! Aengus? – No too soft, how about Fionn? He had defeated a dragon after all! Now that was a proper name for their new stallion. 'To Fionn!' They cheered and emptied their cups again. Mrs. McGovern soon grew tired of the talk about horses and left the men to their drinking. McGovern reminisced about his first horse, growing maudlin as he talked of riding out with his long dead sister. Liam cut him off before the evening grew doleful, and instead talked about the races that Ciarán and he had gone to in Kildare. Ciarán grew animated, recalling the gorgeous horseflesh and the excitement of the thundering hoofs, the shouts of the crowds, and the thrill of a wager. It had been one of the first times he and Liam had gone off on an adventure on their own, and they had felt themselves to be dashing men about town. They had gotten drunk, of course, and chatted up some ladies that turned out to be of the professional sort. Embarrassed, Ciarán had grown flustered, but Liam had the cash and proceeded with a transaction. The girl on Ciarán's lap, a young blonde lady with a bodice bursting forth with what looked like two ripe peaches, was furious to have wasted time on a penniless youth. She gave him a good shove as she got off his lap and spilled his beer. Ciarán had gone outside to escape her wrath and to wait for Liam, who appeared, flushed, and smiling an hour later. He described his encounter in detail to Ciarán so that he would 'know what to do when the time came.' Ciarán was tempted to punch Liam, but instead trudged back to their digs for the night and slept with his back turned to Liam, who continued to describe the delights of his young lady in detail.

Recalling that night Ciarán shifted restlessly on the sofa he had been sprawled on. He still had no real experience with women and yet he was to be married in the new year. He tried to imagine Gráinne sitting on his lap but instead thought of Fiona giving him that wicked look before agreeing to help with the foaling. Had she really communicated with the unborn creature? What an amazing gift she had. If only his uncle appreciated how precious the odd, little *cailín* really was.

A DOG GOES TO THE BALL

Kathleen had sent a frock to Fiona to thank her for her care of Ciarán. Ciarán tucked the package under his arm and struck out towards the kennels, pleased with his sister. She was a dab hand at sewing and she must be feeling well to be able to put together a gown. He was not sure it would fit Fiona as Kathleen had only his vague description to go by, 'short but not too thin.' Still, it would be lovely to have something to give to Fiona, especially a new outfit. She had only her work clothes and with the Christmas festivities coming up, she might want to spruce up a bit. He would tell her that all the house staff and labourers were invited into the parlour on Christmas day. There would be music, dancing, and plenty of food. Perhaps she'd like that, or at least Farley would.

He found Fiona holding a dog for Petesy while the old kennel man lifted an ear and took a whiff.

"Smells clean to me," he muttered, and Fiona released the dog with a fond rub to its backside. The dog gave a yodel of greeting and Petesy stood up slowly and touched his cap. Fiona popped up beside him and gave Ciarán a dazzling smile.

"The ear canker's all gone now! We've got it sorted!" Petesy clapped Fiona on the shoulder.

"This one's got it sorted. Right handy *cailín* you brought me Master Ciarán. I have to thank you for that."

"Not at all," Ciarán replied. It was a relief how Petesy had taken to Fiona. He could have felt threatened and begrudged Fiona her place but the two had got on like a matched brace. Ciarán supposed the work had got too heavy for Petesy and the old man was glad of a bit of help, but the fact that he listened to Fiona was a boon. Then again, Fiona could be pretty convincing when it came to animals. Even Uncle was almost impressed with her touch.

"I've a package for you," he said, handing Fiona the gift from Kathleen.

She looked bemused, "For me?"

"Aye, it's a wee thank you, from my sister," Ciarán added helpfully.

"But sure, she never even met me, and she was poorly herself, bless her."

Ciarán agreed

"She's well enough now and she does love a bit of sewing. I hope you like it," he added, feeling a bit self-conscious. Fiona wasn't really the fashion type. Maybe he had been wrong. Maybe she would have liked something more practical, or something for Farley.

Petesy shuffled off down the row of kennels, discreetly leaving Fiona and Ciarán to themselves. Fiona unwrapped the package carefully, being sure not to tear any of the brown waxed paper. It was useful for mending windows. Then she saw the dress. It was a calico print with small violet flowers, a simple bodice with a round neckline and long sleeves. There was a delicate trail of lace on the edge of each sleeve and around the collar. The waist nipped in, and skirt was not so full as to require several petticoats but gave the hint of a bell-shape to the dress.

Fiona lifted the dress and held it up to herself, it was only a smidge too long. She smelled the fabric.

"It's new!" she exclaimed.

"Do you like it?" Ciarán asked anxiously.

"I've never had anything new." She twirled around and then danced down the row of kennels. "Look, Petesy, I've got a new frock." The old man smiled at her and then looked at Ciarán, cocking his head in a curious, assessing gesture.

"It's a lovely thing, it is surely," Petesy congratulated her.

Fiona pranced back up to Ciarán.

"Will you tell your sister it's the loveliest frock I've ever seen. And it's terribly kind of her, though," she frowned. "I'm not sure when I will ever have need of such a beautiful dress."

"You can wear it to mass," Petesy instructed.

"Oh, yes, mass." Fiona wasn't over fond of attending church as she didn't like sitting still that long, especially in the draughty vestibule on a hard bench. Occasionally, she had been able to secrete Farley into the chapel under her cloak, but she was usually noticed, especially when he howled along with the hymns. After that, they were both told to observe the services from the foyer.

"Uncle holds a Christmas party for the servants every year. There's a big spread of food, and then we push the tables back and have music and dancing. You can wear your new dress to that."

Fiona pursed her lips,

"I've never been to a party before."

"It's grand," Petesy offered. "Lots of good grub. Your dog will be like a pig in shite." He reached down and tugged at Farley's tail which Farley withstood only out of courtesy to Petesy's age.

Ciarán laughed,

"It is good fun. I'm sure you'd enjoy it."

"I don't know any dance steps," Fiona worried.

"No worries," Ciarán reassured her, "I'll teach you." Petesy gave Ciarán another quizzical look.

"No offense lad, but can you manage to dance with your gammy leg?" Petesy queried.

"Well, I won't win any contests, but I can hop about a bit. I'm not that lame."

"Ah well, that will be grand then," Petesy said with very little conviction. Did the young man not know what he was playing at? The poor girl would go and get besotted with him, and then he would waltz off and marry that posh Miss on the next farm. Petesy sighed. Youngsters didn't have the sense they were born with. He hobbled over to his stool and sat down resignedly.

"Are you tired?" Fiona asked him with concern. "I'll just put away me frock and finish up in the kennels here, then I'll bring you a cup of tea."

Petesy reached out and grasped her hand as she began to run off,

"Sure, if I had me own daughter, she couldn't be better to me." Then he gave Ciarán a very hard look. Petesy would be keeping his eye on that boy. Fiona laughed and ran off to her lean-to.

Ciarán turned to the old man on the stool.

"It's only a gift from my sister to thank Fiona for nursing me. She was paid, Fiona was, but my sister felt that bad that she hadn't minded me herself." Petesy just lifted his bushy grey eyebrows at Ciarán. "Fiona can't go on everywhere in clothes that stink of dog."

"I think she likes the smell of dog," Petesy said evenly.

"Well, yes, I'm sure she does, but some people don't.

"You can't make her into something she isn't," Petesy warned.

Ciarán looked uncomfortable but continued,

"I just want her to be happy here."

"She's happy with the dogs, you can see that."

"Right," Ciarán said, "You're right there." He backed out the door, nodded a farewell at Petesy and left the kennels. He felt unfairly judged by Petesy and was not sure why the old kennel man had taken such aversion to a simple gift.

As a young, single man with good prospects, Liam was in much demand at holiday festivities and Ciarán was always invited along to participate in the craic. It was from one of these parties that the cousins were coming home on a crisp winter evening, the moon full in the sky. Ciarán breathed in the refreshing atmosphere, trying to recover from an over ingestion of port. Liam was singing an inappropriate ballad, and the horses were eager to return to their warm stables and a late dinner of hay and perhaps a few oats. As they grew nearer to the McGovern land, Ciarán saw a small figure across the fields, heading towards the loch. He thought he was seeing a ghost until he realized the apparition was being followed by a dog, bounding over the tussocks of grass. He had seen that particular movement pattern before and recognized Farley trying to avoid the tickly grass on his belly. He pulled up Conall and watched the duo as they reached the lochside. Liam also paused and looked to his cousin for the reason they had stopped.

"What is it? Are you going to be sick?"

Ciarán shook his head and pointed towards the loch. Leaning forward precariously, Liam stared into the distance.

"Is that Morrigan washing your clothes before battle?" he asked.

Snorting, Ciarán leaned over and pushed Liam back into his saddle before he capsized.

"No, not the Morrigan, just Fiona and her dread dog."

Sitting up straight, Liam looked again.

"Oh, aye, it is." Then, after a pause, "What is she doing?"

Ciarán shrugged,

"Lord knows why that *cailín* does anything," he replied. "You go along home Liam, can you manage? I'm going to make sure she gets back alright. It's late for a wee *girseach* to be out on her own."

Liam tried to act offended, belched loudly, and then assured Ciarán he was perfectly capable of finding his own way home before prodding his mount into a trot. Slipping dangerously once, he righted himself and continued down the road, breaking into an off-key bawdy song. When he had passed round a bend, Ciarán urged Conall over the stone fence and trotted down to the loch. He dismounted, and stood holding Conall's rein, waiting for Fiona to speak. She had not turned in surprise as he had approached. Doubtless, Farley had heard and smelled them both when he was chatting on the road with Liam.

She was seated on a broad stone, near the edge of the loch, just where the reeds were growing. She was staring at the reflection of the moon, glimmering across the regular waves moving over the water. Finally, she stood up and gazing at Ciarán, cocked her head in query, looking ever so like the terrier, seated beside her, also cocking his head to one side.

"Are you alright?" Ciarán asked, suddenly awkward and aware that he had been intruding.

"Of course," she replied and began walking the rise of the field back towards the road. Ciarán kept pace with her, Conall, plodding alongside.

"It's a cold night to be out and about," he remarked.

"You were out," she retorted.

He sighed.

"You are right there. I was at a supper party with Liam."

"Did you enjoy yourself?"

"Perhaps a bit too much," he admitted.

She laughed softly.

Maybe he shouldn't press, but he couldn't help himself.

"What were you doing Fiona?"

"Do you know what day it is?" she asked.

He was annoyed with her twist to the conversation.

"It's the 21st of December."

"The Winter Solstice," Fiona informed him.

"Aye." There was an extended silence.

"I was praying," Fiona explained. And tomorrow, "When the sun rises, I will give thanks that the shortest day has ended, and the light is beginning to return."

"The old ways," he interpreted.

"Yes, the old ways."

He reached out and caught her arm,

"Maybe it's best that not so many people know this."

She gave a curt nod which he hoped was an agreement.

"Let's ride home now Fiona. It's very late." He tapped Conall who paused for him but before he could lift Fiona into the saddle, she hissed at him to wait. They stood in the darkness and Ciarán heard a nearby owl hoot into the darkness. Embarrassingly, he felt a chill go down his spine, but Fiona turned to him, excited.

"He's calling for her. Let's see if she answers." Trying to be still so that the frost did not crunch under their feet, they listened. Then from several fields away, they heard the reply. The male called again and his mate, closer now, returned his cry. "They'll be together now," Fiona breathed, and he could hear the satisfaction in her voice. Not knowing what to say, he lifted her up onto the horse's back, feeling her weight, not much more than a child's. He put his foot in the stirrup and pulled himself up into the saddle.

"It will hardly be warm enough for you in the lean-to tonight. Not after getting yourself chilled like this."

He felt her vibrate against his chest with a giggle.

"There are plenty of dogs to keep me warm. I've got my Farley, and Ambrose usually joins us. I'll add on a few more dogs tonight, so, and I'll be grand."

He wanted to protest that she should stay in the house tonight but realised she would be happier with her pack. Only, unlike the pack, she could not be tamed.

Ciarán had been asked to attend Christmas Eve with Gráinne's family. There had been roast goose and half-way decent wine, a flaming pudding and then gifts were exchanged. He had given Gráinne a bracelet of small crystals, selected by his aunt. Gráinne had leapt up and hugged him.

233

She had given him some fine linen handkerchiefs with his initials stitched in the corner. Of course, she had done the work and it was lovely embroidery. Ciarán had a sudden memory of Fiona sewing up a wound in one of the hound's, pulling her needle through the flesh, simultaneously crooning to the hound, and cursing in Irish at the dullness of the needle. He took a flute of champagne and erased the vision from his mind. He couldn't compare the two. They were women from two different worlds.

In the morning he had gone to mass with Gráinne's family and then rode back along the icy roads to the McGovern farm. Gráinne was rather put out that he wasn't staying to have lunch with her family, but he told her that his uncle expected him to return. This was a lie, but best behaviour in front of Gráinne's people was getting exhausting. He needed to get drunk with Liam and have a dance at the holiday party. No one there would comment on his limp and wonder if he was worthy.

The cook had not stinted in her arrangements for the *céilidh*. There were two hams, potatoes, wheaten bread with plenty of butter, carrots, swede, Christmas cake that had been soaked in poteen for four months, and plenty of cream. Ale, cider, and punch had been made available. The punch was liberally spiked with poteen and was reported to be lethal. She had not approved of the mix but the men from the fields and stables had worked hard all year. Tomorrow would be no holiday for them either as the traditional hunt would be gathering at the McGovern farm, necessitating more food and drink preparation as well as setting up rooms for guests and stabling their horses. She sighed. No rest for the wicked. At least no one could complain about the spread, and she was looking forward to the music and dancing. A local fiddler was coming along and a few of the girls and maybe one or two of the men would share a song. It would be a bit of a change at any rate.

Fiona had bathed and put on her new frock. She decided to wear her hair down, something she didn't normally do as it would get in her way and annoy her, but she wasn't working today. Petesy had said he would sort out the hounds and it was only a light feed they would be getting anyway. With the hunt on tomorrow the hounds didn't need a heavy meal, and certainly no exercise. They needed to be raring to go when the horn sounded. Fiona gave a snort of disgust. Hunting was a ridiculous past time - a herd of humans and a pack of hounds chasing a single fox. Only people would invent such an unreasonable pursuit. Fiona picked through her hair with her fingers and tried to remove the last few tangles. She would like to get a brush someday. She had a bit of money now but hadn't been to a decent sized town in ages. Maybe she could ask Ciarán to get one for her and then blushed at the idea. Surely, Ciarán couldn't buy a woman's hairbrush – that would be too embarrassing, for both of them. Turning to Farley, she cleared some discharge from the corner of his eye and checked his beard for left over snacks. Neither of them had ever been to a party before and she was determined that they would not look scruffy. She promised Farley he too would have his own brush when she got one for herself.

Petesy had finished in the kennels and came to collect her. He was wearing a clean waistcoat and had slicked back the straggling bits of grey hair off his forehead. He looked Fiona up and down and then noticed her shoes.

"They need a bit of a polish *cailín.*"

Fiona wrinkled her nose. The housekeeper had found an old pair of boots that her granddaughter had outgrown and given them to Fiona. She was not used to wearing shoes, but the housekeeper had insisted she wear shoes to the *céilidh,* and Fiona didn't want to miss the festivities. Rummaging through a basket of supplies in the kennels, she found a strip of bandage. She spat on it and rubbed both shoes viciously. Petesy nodded and then took her arm. She adjusted her pace to his arthritic gait, and they went up to the house to join the festivities.

Petesy was happy to take a plate and sit on a bench that had been pushed against the wall in the dining room. He had taken several slices of the juicy ham, as he rarely had meat in his own cabin. The table had been pushed along to the other wall and that was where the feast rested. Farley decided to initially station himself under the serving table and then would work the room as people became careless and began to let morsels slip from their plates. Of course, he was served a large piece of ham on arrival as Fiona had progressed to the table and selected a choice slice for him. There were a few clucks of disapproval, but Fiona was good at ignoring the opinions of others. She chose some food for herself and took a glass of punch. She was relieved to see that goose had not been served. It was a little too close to swan for her comfort.

"You'll want to watch that punch," Petesy advised. "It's potent stuff and you're not so used to the drink."

"It's lovely and sweet," Fiona answered, blithely ignoring him, she was looking around the crowded room for Ciarán. She wanted him to see the dress that his sister had made but she did not feel comfortable wandering the room on her own, so she stood near Petesy. The housemaids had made it clear from day one that they thought Fiona was a dirty *culchie* and were disgusted by the fact that Fiona shared a bed with her dog. The stable lads were more friendly, mostly because they were in awe of her easy handling of Conall. Brendan, the groom, treated her respectfully enough as he and Petesy were old friends and Petesy did nothing but sing Fiona's praises. All told, it was best to stick to the male end of the bench. Farley had begun to work along the seating arrangements as people conversed and let their attention drift from their plates. Fiona reminded him to not overeat as the food was rich, but he only drew back his teeth and offered her a grimace of amusement. One of the house maids leapt away from him, shrieking that he was about to bite, which forced Farley to join Fiona at the male end of the room. This was a suitable placement as the men were less excitable, and already several were drunk and no longer responsible for their plates of food.

Fiona finally spotted Ciarán at the door. He had come in after the family, having had to unsaddle and wipe down Conall, wash and change before he could join the gathering. She watched him scan the room until his eyes met hers. She lifted the beaker of punch in greeting, surprised to find it empty already. Crossing the room, he took the glass from her and peered into it.

"I hope that was your first and last drink of the punch. This stuff would fell a grown man." Fiona giggled and Ciarán shook his head in admonishment. "Surely, Petesy, you told her to lay off the liquor?"

"Aye, I did so Master Ciarán, I did indeed," Petesy answered, "Just as I told that wee dog to lay off the victuals, and neither of them listening to me."

"Well, that won't do at all, will it Petesy? Foolish youngsters," Ciarán took a seat by Petesy. "Is there anything you want man? Fi, will you not go collect him a mug of cider? And one for myself?"

"I think you have me mistaken for one of the house maids," Fiona sniped back, but she went anyway, not minding serving her two favourite people. She returned with two mugs and then cocked her head at Ciarán, "I thought men were supposed to wait on the ladies at a party."

"Oh, I would," Ciarán retorted, "But this lady seems quite capable of helping herself." Fiona flounced off then and came back with a refilled beaker of punch. Petesy shook his head but kept his remark to himself. They all turned then as the fiddler started up a reel. The house maids tittered excitedly and pulled each other out onto the floor, where the rug had been pulled away, leaving a fine smooth surface for dancing. The stable lads shoved each other but none had the bravery to step onto the floor, so Liam led his mother out and they began the reel.

Fiona watched enchanted. She had seen dancing once when they had stayed late in Ardara after a market day, but she had never been to a dance herself. She tapped her foot in time to the music and considered entering the floor with Farley as a partner.

"Come on boys," Ciarán encouraged, yanking a few of the men onto the floor and pushing them towards a girl. Then he turned to Fiona and offered his hand.

"I haven't a clue what to do," Fiona admitted nervously.

"Don't worry, just follow me and avoid getting stepped on." He swung her out onto the floor, and they joined hands with other dancers, spinning and stepping to the speed of the fiddle. At first, she was self-conscious and tripped over her own feet repeatedly. Ciarán gave her a little shake and told her not to worry about the steps and just listen to the music. She lifted her head from where she was studying the floor and realised that no one was paying much attention to any sort of pattern. There was a lot of shoving and hilarity, with the odd man falling over and the girls giggling hysterically. No one was watching her at all.

Ciarán put his arm around her back and lifted his other hand over head. She copied with her own arms, barely able to reach his waist due to the height difference. He laughed as she struggled and then began to turn, smiling down into her face. His eyes were brown, like Farley's but had a different glint in them. She felt him pull her tighter to him, as they spun faster. She was breathless and laughing. They spun apart and she nearly whirled to the floor, but he caught her hands and lifted her up, drawing her in close to his chest. She could feel the warmth of him through the fabric of her new dress.

"That frock suits you very well, I think," he said smiling. It seemed he wanted to say more, but the music stopped, and he broke away from her; she reluctantly released his hands.

It was thirsty work, dancing, and a break for food and drink was essential. Then Mary, who helped the cook, had a word with the fiddler, who accompanied her with a ballad, *'The Sailor Who Courted a Farmer's Daughter,'* there was much applause, for she had a lovely voice, and her humorous choice of song was popular with the household. Encouraged, she went on to sing, *'You Silly Old Man,'* which proved even more well-liked as people joined in with the chorus of, *"To please a young woman is more than you can; It's not in your power you silly old man."* Mrs. McGovern looked less amused than her staff with this ribald song, and the cook had a quick word in Mary's ear.

Feeling a bit dizzy from the dancing, Fiona had slipped out through the kitchen, and was sitting on the back step breathing in the damp evening air. A light rain had started to fall, and she thought she must get up or her dress would get damp. Standing, she lost her balance and nearly fell off the step.

"Easy there," Dermot McNulty caught Fiona's arm and set her straight. Dermot was one of the house servants. It not being a very large house, Dermot served in a variety of roles, including a foot man and a valet. He had just been rebuffed by one of the house maids and had come outside to let her know that he wasn't playing her game of hard to get. He took a look at Fiona, hardly recognizing her in a proper dress and with her hair down. She was flushed from dancing and drink and, aside from her strange, huge eyes, almost looked pretty.

"You alright there *cailín?*" he asked with real interest.

Fiona went to shake her head but then stopped herself when it made the dizziness worse.

"I think I had too much of that punch."

He laughed,

240

"Is that right? Can't handle your drink?" He slipped his arm around her waist. "Looks like I'll have to help hold you up then." He pulled Fiona closer to him. She resisted, but not with much effort, feeling too queasy to do anything very energetic. "Now, why have I never noticed what a pretty little thing you are?" He reached out and brushed her hair off her face. Fiona felt like she should do something but wasn't sure what. Dermot reached for her chin and lifted it, considering what it would be like to kiss the kennel girl. That would show yon stuffy girls indoors. He bent forward, only to feel a hand gripping his shoulder and pushing him back hard against the wall.

"What do you think you're doing?" Ciarán demanded.

Dermot held up his hands in appeasement,

"Just stealing a wee Christmas kiss. No harm meant."

Ciarán raised a fist, intending to use it on Dermot's grinning face, but dropped it when he heard Fiona stagger away and begin to retch in a rosebush. He shook his fist warningly at Dermot who smirked at him and disappeared indoors, leaving Ciarán to rescue the sick girl collapsed at the edge of the garden.

Crouching next to Fiona, Ciarán lifted her up and began carrying her back towards the kennels.

"Didn't I tell you?" Fiona only groaned in reply. He got her to the lean- to and put her down momentarily to unlatch the door. She leaned her head against the wood and considered being sick again. Before she slipped down into the mud, he scooped her up and deposited her on her pallet, taking off her shoes, rolling her on her side and covering her with a blanket. He noticed that the new dress was crumpled and stained.

"Farley?" she asked.

"Oh Lord, I better collect him too, before he's as half cut as yourself." He placed a pot next to Fiona and lifted away a hank of her hair. "It was a sight to see your red grizzle hair rippling in the candlelight while we danced, but you'll have to wash the sick out tomorrow morning."

When Ciarán returned to the gathering, Liam came over to him and clapped him on the back.

"I thought we'd lost you, the party's just getting going. Mam and Da have gone upstairs and the fellows are starting to sing some proper rousing songs now."

"I'll be back with you in a minute. I just need to ..." he let his eyes roam the room and came upon Farley, sprawled on his side under the table. His belly had ballooned, and the dog was audibly groaning. "Jaysus, the dog's even worse than his mistress."

"What are you like Ciarán? Are you minding her dog as well? We all saw you dancing with her and Da asked if you were, you know, a bit too friendly with Fiona." He waited for Ciarán's reply but his cousin just gave him a stony look. "You know, he's put some effort into the match with Gráinne, he's trying to give you a step up in the world and he wasn't expecting you back today at all. He thought you were staying with them till the hunt tomorrow."

"And miss a Christmas jar with my favourite cousin?" Ciarán levered Liam to one side. "Let me just get that Farley out of here before he messes the place. He tucked the incapacitated canine under his arm, only to be rewarded with a resounding fart. A few men around the table guffawed and cheered. Ciarán grinned at them and gave his stomach a pat. Saluting his cousin, he again made the trek to the kennels. He found Fiona curled up in a foetal position looking as pale as eiderdown. He plopped Farley down at her feet and then sat down next to her on the pallet, rubbing her back in what he hopped was a comforting manner.

"We have all done this once. You'll live. You'll just have a shocking head in the morning, but you've got some remedy for head pain, I'm sure. I imagine you've got something for sick bellies as well." Prompted by a low moan from Farley, he asked, "Will I get you or Farley anything?" Fiona didn't answer him, only clutched at his free hand, and held it, surprisingly fiercely for someone who looked like she was completely destroyed.

"I'm sorry," she whimpered. "I should have listened to you. I wanted to dance again."

"And you will *cailín*. There will be plenty more gatherings and next time you won't be tasting the punch."

"But I'll never dance with you again. You'll be married then."

He took a sharp intake of breath. This was true. His life with Gráinne was just around the corner. Tentatively, he stroked Fiona's hair.

"Well, we had a good dance tonight anyway."

Her knees came up tighter to her chest and still she clung to his hand. He heard her begin to sob. Christ. What could he do? He shouldn't even be here with her alone, especially after what Liam had said. They'd all be talking tomorrow, that Fiona was his mistress, especially after he had threatened Dermot. That tale would already be all

243

around the servants. He had never meant things to come to this. It was just the easy way they had together, after all the time spent in each other's company when he was healing. They had a laugh together, he taught her about horses, and she taught him about listening. It was like his friendship with Liam or his bond with Kathleen, that's all it was.

Abruptly he said, "Look Fiona, it's the drink. It's made you maudlin. You'll be right in the morning. Now your Farley is here with you, and I'll have Petesy stop in on his way home to make sure you're alright. Quick dry your eyes and let me go." He disentangled his hand from hers and went to leave but impulse made him lean over and kiss her forehead. "It was a grand time, wasn't it, Fiona?"

A VERY SAD BOXING DAY

No one was feeling too well after the Christmas celebrations, but the St. Stephen's Day Hunt was a tradition, and this year the McGovern's were hosting it. William McGovern had taken his hounds and horses to the hunt from the very early days of his farm, back when he had only the one horse and two hounds. Now he had a full kennel of beautifully baying Basset Griffon Vendeens, the pride of the county. Other kennels had English Foxhounds or beagles, but McGovern had had the sense to buy two French hounds and had developed his distinctive pack. People came from far and wide to hunt with the rough-coated bassets. It was said that George the 2nd had enjoyed working with Basset Griffons. McGovern liked to drop this fact whenever he hunted with the Church of Ireland chaps. It inferred that McGovern was a royalist, helping keep him safe from being tarred with a Fenian brush.

The hunt began to gather in the morning and Christmas ale was shared all around. Fiona was still poorly from her night of sickness so felt even less like going on the hunt than she had previously. She had managed to drag herself out quite early in the morning, not to tend the hounds as she should have, but to pass messages to the wildlife in the fields. While she loved her hounds, she did not think it fair play for the whole pack to chase one fox. So, she had reached out to the hare, the deer, and the birds, hoping they would carry her message to the foxes. All were grateful for the warning, as they preferred to stay clear of the humans running rampant on excited horses with dogs screaming ecstatically. Leverets were

245

urged out of hollows in the field and moved to more remote locations, deer moved farther from the farm and the fox burrowed down in his hole, hoping he would not be dug out.

Fiona had originally refused to attend the hunt but was told it was necessary as sometimes a hound or horse was injured. She agreed that she would want to be there to tend her pack, though she discussed with them at length about tearing the fox to bits. She agreed that the scent was thrilling and hurling themselves, on masse, was a game too fun to resist but she knew them to be soft-mouthed creatures and was surprised at the desire to end it all with a blood thirsty attack. Most admitted they had no idea how it happened, things just went so fast and got out of control. Others blamed the terriers that ran along with the hunt. A terrier was always up for a fight and could easily be convinced that a fox was encroaching on his territory. Ambrose, the pack leader, blamed the humans. We are bred and fed to hunt, he explained to Fiona. If we do not do our task well, we are taken from this earth. Fear is a powerful motivator. Fiona, sitting next to Ambrose and carefully combing fleas out of his coat, leaned over, and kissed him on the top of the head. He was so wise. He licked her hand once, thanking her for removing the annoying parasites and for understanding him.

If she had to go, she would, but not in good spirits. Her transgressions at the ball had further depressed her and the hounds circled her uneasily, not used to a bad-tempered Fiona. Ambrose came up and pressed his huge wet nose into the palm of her hand and she regained herself momentarily, kneeling down next to him and fondling his ears. He looked into her eyes and promised her he would not incite violence and she believed him. With one last scratch behind his ear, Fiona left Ambrose and went to saddle the pony she had been given to follow along behind the hunt. She tucked a few bandages, a leather flask with water and a pinch of salt into her bag. Any further first aid could be done when they returned to the kennels. She led her pony out into the yard where the hunters were gathered. Ciarán was there, mounted tall on Conall. Fiona was embarrassed by her behaviour the previous evening and hoped he had put it down to inexperience with drink. She tried to sidle away from him, but he saw her and brought Conall up alongside Fiona's pony.

"Are you well today Fiona?" She scowled at him and did not bother with an answer. To further discomfit her, Gráinne joined Ciarán, barely controlling her delicate bay mount. Gráinne was not a skilled horse woman, and she rode side-saddle, a style that was uncomfortable for the horse unless the saddle fitted perfectly, and the rider had decent technique. Fiona had heard several horses complain that the practice hurt their backs and that the saddle rubbed uncomfortably. Too many women fell off in their precarious saddles, and then the horses were blamed for being flighty or unruly. It was unfair and stupid as far as Fiona was concerned and she certainly felt that Gráinne was incompetent and insensitive to her mount.

"Hello Fiona," Gráinne smiled at her. Fiona pretended to adjust the cinch on her saddle and only gave a curt nod in reply. "Is this your first hunt?" Gráinne continued.

"It is," Fiona replied bleakly.

"Aren't you excited?"

"About chasing after an innocent creature and killing it? Not particularly." Ciarán gave her a hard look, so Fiona grimaced at him, daring him to chastise her.

But Gráinne trilled with laughter.

"You are amusing! Why foxes are vermin, they aren't animals really. Not like sheep or horses." At this, Ciarán realised he better interfere before Fiona had a chance to open her mouth.

"Will Farley be joining us?" he asked, as innocently as he could.

"I don't think so," Fiona answered. Farley too had over indulged at the festivities and was suffering from a draining case of the shits. He had promised Fiona that he would try to trot about the countryside and continue the hunt warning. However, as the hunt would soon be making enough noise and destruction to herald the end of the world, Fiona relieved him of the responsibility. Instead, Farley would stay in the kennels on a bed of straw, drinking water and stepping outside to empty his bowels on frequent occasions.

Fiona drew away from the throng and when the horn was sounded, she was well behind the gentry as they took off on horseback. She trotted along on her pony, deciding to pretend she was on a trek in the countryside, enjoying the fresh air and the company of her steed. It would almost have been pleasant if she didn't have a pounding headache and lingering nausea. In the distance she heard the baying of the hounds and the thunder of hooves. She usually loved to hear the hounds in full song, and it was even better when the wolfhounds added their deep voices. Sometimes, in the evenings, she would encourage the Bassett Griffons to hold a howling, when the entire kennels would lift up their noses and sing to the night. Today, she realised that if the canine chorus didn't warn all and sundry into hiding, nothing would. Following in their wake, she could see how the horses had cut across farmland and even knocked a few stones loose on fences. Luckily, there were no crops in the field right now. The fences would be mended by the tenants - just more work for the farmers. McGovern might send a few men to help so as not to antagonize his neighbours entirely.

The yelp of pain carried even above the noise of the horses and hounds. Fiona felt it like a knife being driven into her ribs. It was one of her pack. She put her heels into the pony and galloped his short legs as hard as she could, jumping a wall she'd never have dared if not panicked. She saw a knot of men standing around a dog, laying in the field. One of the men, dismounting, kneeled next to the dog. As she drew closer, Fiona began to recognize the markings and her stomach juices rose into her mouth. Not him, not her dear friend.

Leaping from her mount, she ran across the field and threw herself down next to Ambrose. He whimpered and licked her hand hopefully. She took one look at his leg, he had stepped into a rabbit hole and moving at speed, his leg had twisted and broke clean though the skin. She stroked his head and murmured to him, all the while assessing what she could do here and what could be done later in the kennel. Even at a glance she could see what a severe fracture it was and with it being open through the skin, the chance of it going septic was almost certain.

Fiona realised the man kneeling next to Ambrose was William McGovern. When he spoke, there were tears in his voice,

"Finest hound I've ever had. What a shame. What a rotten shame." He patted Ambrose once on the head and then stood up, asking for his gun. It took a moment for Fiona to realise what was going on.

"I can fix it sir, I'm sure I can. It's a bad break but I'll do my very best. You can't shoot him sir, please!"

McGovern shook his head.

"He was bred to run girl. He'll never run again with a leg like that. He won't be able to do his job."

"I'll keep him as a pet then," Fiona begged, "I'll pay for his feed out of my wages. He's needed in the pack sir." For, what would the pack do without the quiet calmness of their leader? There was no other dog that could command the respect without aggression. And what would Fiona do without her good friend? He had trained her in her role as carer for the hounds. He had taught her the way of the McGovern farm. He had, next to Farley, been the best.

Ciarán came up and took Fiona by the elbow,

"It's a kindness Fiona. He's in so much pain and he'll never be right again."

Fiona turned on him, her brown eyes blazing with fury,

"Should we have shot you then? Sure, your leg was just as bad." Ciarán had the good sense to look abashed.

"There's a far difference between a man and a dog," McGovern decreed and lifted his rifle.

Fiona screamed, breaking away from Ciarán and throwing herself across the dog, who moaned softly telling her that he understood.

"For the love of God girl, I could have shot you!" McGovern didn't relish shooting his best hound and this silly girl was making things far worse. And the cheek of her behaving like this with all the county looking on. "Ciarán, get her out of here at once!"

"Come on Fiona," Ciarán tried gently, reaching for her but she struck him, her arm flying back and hitting him in the face. There was a collective intake of breath from the watching crowd, and a squeak of distress from Gráinne. A servant could not behave like this. Ciarán had no choice. He lifted Fiona and threw her over his shoulder, striding away from the scene as quickly as he could with a small woman battering his back with her fists and calling him every vile name she could think of.

The shot sounded out. McGovern gave orders to place Ambrose's body over the pony's back and instructed one of his men to dig a grave for the hound in the ground by the kennels that he had reserved for the burial of his favourite dogs. Being the hound that he was, Ambrose deserved a decent resting place. Maybe McGovern would even have a marker made for the grave. He had done that before with his house dogs. An eerie sound of hounds howling rose around them, underscored by the wolf hounds, sonorous and sorrowful. In the morning mist with the grey sky above them, the Boxing Day hunt had lost all remnants of festivity.

Fiona had gone limp hanging over Ciarán's shoulders. He slid her down to the ground, where she sank into a heap, sobbing. He tried to apologise, but she only glared at him and spat back,

"You didn't even try to help me save him."

Gráinne trotted up to Ciarán and Fiona, peering down at the scruffy woman, curled on the earth, keening.

"She's awful upset over a dog!" Gráinne exclaimed. "And Ciarán, you really shouldn't let her talk to you that way. It's disrespectful. If she were a servant in our house, she would be sent on her way without a reference. My father doesn't tolerate this kind of behaviour." Ciarán, torn between the two women, had an overwhelming desire to slap them both, but closed his mouth tightly over his gritted teeth.

"She takes her work seriously," he finally managed to say to Gráinne and then reached out to touch Fiona's shoulder, "Come on *cailín*, why don't you head back to the kennels?" Fiona leaped up from the ground then and gave him a look to kill,

"I hate you," she shrieked and turned and ran.

"Well, I never ..." Gráinne began but Ciarán put up a hand to stop her.

"She loved the hound, people say funny things when they're grieving," and do funny things when they're cowards he added to himself. Why hadn't he taken her part? Why always let Uncle William be right? Gráinne, tossed her head with annoyance and suggested they re-join the rest of the hunt. Tapping her whip to her mount, she cantered off and Ciarán could only follow her, though he felt some reluctance from Conall, who clearly wanted to pursue the Listener.

Fiona decided she was never going back. She hated Master McGovern for shooting Ambrose, and she hated Ciarán for not resisting him. She hated that stuck up, overdressed Gráinne, and she basically just hated everybody. She wanted Farley.

252

She ran in the direction of the kennels and was going to collect him and her things and take to the road. However, when she got back to the kennels, Petesy was sitting on his stool, offering some honey on a spoon to Farley. "It'll do his guts some good," Petesy muttered. Fiona realised if anyone would understand her, it would be Petesy. She knelt down on the floor by the stool and took Farley in her arms, probably hugging a bit too hard as his gas-filled abdomen gurgled in protest.

"Petesy," the old man wiped the spoon with the edge of his coat and tucked it away in one of his pockets. "Petesy," Fiona began again, "Ambrose broke his leg."

Petesy looked at her and she saw tears begin to fill his eyes,

"They shot him," he said hoarsely. She nodded. "He was a good dog, one of the best. A very good dog." He blew his nose into a crumpled cloth that may once have been a handkerchief.

"I tried to stop them. I said I could fix it, but no one would listen to me!"

"I'm sure you did *cailín*," Petesy lay a gnarled hand on Fiona's head, "But perhaps it was for the best. Maybe he wouldn't have been happy as a lame dog. He loved to run, that boy, he did." The hand patted her head roughly and Fiona let herself begin to cry again. Farley stood up, licked her face anxiously and then began a high-pitched howl. His keening was taken up by a bitch in whelp that had stayed at the kennels, and two pups that were due to be sold to a gentleman participating in the hunt. Their song carried out into the stables and the few horses left there whinnied in response. A stable lad went to the kennel and peering in saw the old man and the girl weeping. The lad shrugged and left. It was no business of his what their sadness was.

Fiona didn't make good on her plans to leave the farm. She couldn't leave Petesy or the pack when they were bereaved. Following Petesy to his cabin, and they shared a cup of tea and some brown bread, and the old kennel man told her all the stories he could remember about the great Ambrose. After the wake, Fiona returned to the kennels, knowing she would need to deal with the pack and help them find some peace. She heard the hunt return, the clamour of people shouting for stable lads and grooms to take the horses, and the excited barks of the hounds. It was their dinner time. She stood in the kennel door and whistled to them, they heard and came loping her way. Once the last one was in, she slammed the door and braced the stool against it, shutting out any human interference. The hounds were fed their supper, and each returned to their allotted kennel. She walked along the kennels, touching each dog, resting a hand on a head or along the spine, asking them how they were, if there were any scratches that needed attending or any thorns to extricate. A few had minor injuries which she bathed with salt water, and one had a thorn in his pad which was painful to remove. She soaked the foot in salt water and then dipped some wool in her jar of lavender and marigold oil, wrapping the wool onto the pad with a bit of linen. The hound nosed at the bandage, but she asked him to leave it be as long as he could bear it. He looked at her with sad eyes but agreed.

Tired and full from their meal, the pack was subdued. The emptiness, where Ambrose had been, was unsettling, and many felt the need to gnaw at their feet or the wood of the kennel doors before they could curl up to sleep. Fiona had no way to comfort them but decided to stay with them tonight rather than go to her lean-to. At least, she could be with the pack as they grew accustomed to a new pattern in their family. She piled some extra straw by the two pups and curled up alongside them, Farley resting at her feet. Inhaling the sweet aroma of puppy breath, she hoped the two young ones would be treated well in their new life. Later in the night, she heard someone try to open the kennels, but ignored it. Farley told her the smell was of Ciarán, but she would not speak with him. Tonight, she had no words for people.

AN UNWELCOME VISITOR

Lieutenant Distaff was looking forward to visiting the McGovern farm. It wasn't the wealthiest around, but he could be assured of a good dinner, a decent wine, and a comfortable bed. He was still ostensibly looking for the missing republicans, but he liked to tour the estates and larger farms in general to 'keep an eye on things' as he told the landowners. Most suspected that he was taking advantage of their hospitality, but they put up with his periodic visits in order to keep relations amicable with the local British officers. It was a small enough price to pay.

Distaff shifted uncomfortably in his saddle; the rash he was suffering from did not lead to a comfortable ride. Damn the crab-ridden whores of Londonderry. He wished there was somewhere else to go on leave but travelling back to London was both too expensive and too time consuming. He would have to put up with the bleak shipyards of the Northern coast and the young ladies that served the sailors for the foreseeable future. After a vicious scratch, he lifted his head and realised he could see the main house of the McGovern estate in the distance. It wouldn't be much longer now.

The two privates with Distaff were also looking forward to a night in a house instead of out-doors or in a barracks. They would not be invited to dine with the family but would still benefit from a hot meal of better quality than what they were used to. As they turned up the long drive to Ballyhoe, as the Mc Govern farm was called, the horses noted the improved mood of their riders and quickened their paces. A warm barn and oats might await them.

Although they had not been warned, word had got to the farm long before Distaff's party arrived. Mrs. McGovern had instructed the cook to put on an extra joint and William McGovern had ordered some of the lesser quality wine from the cellar. Fortuitously, they were well warned in the stables as well. Ciarán had run down but Fiona had already put a head collar on Conall and was leading him out of his box when Ciarán arrived.

"I'll take him up to the top field, no one will see him there," she assured him.

"Do the stable boys know why you are taking him out?"

"Ah, yes. I told them he has a hot fetlock and I'm going to bathe it in the stream. They're not bothered so long as they don't have to handle him."

Ciarán nodded.

"Are you sure the soldiers didn't see me at the cottage?" he asked nervously.

"Surely, you were wrapped up as if in a shroud and I told them you had the plague or some such disease. They wouldn't go near you. I guess they figured you were dying anyway so there was naught for them to do." She shrugged. "No worries. They're only looking for a young man on a grey stallion. As long as the stallion isn't here, the young man isn't either." Fiona laid her hand on Conall who bowed down so she could clamber on his back, and they trotted off, with all and sundry avoiding their path. Ciarán let out the breath he had been holding and tried to settle himself. Please God, it would be alright.

William McGovern did not actively enjoy the British army presence in his country, but he

257

tolerated them. He had decided long ago that it was safer and more profitable to be polite and accommodating and just get on with things. His theory was that if he left them alone, they'd leave him alone. McGovern did not share his son's Republican feelings and was sure that the boy would grow out of it, along with the ridiculous penchant of calling himself Liam instead of his God given name of William. As for his nephew Ciarán, the boy had been sent to him to settle him down and McGovern had every intention of doing so, if only for the memory of his dear sister. Even though his family was not Protestant, McGovern knew that if he minded his own business and stayed within the law, regardless of how unfair that law was, there would be no trouble for him.

So, the soldiers were offered rooms, a decent guest room for the Lieutenant and a smaller room for the two privates to share. The rooms were furnished with warm water for the soldiers to wash, and the men were told that dinner would begin at eight that evening. Their horses were led away to be unsaddled, rubbed down, and fed. Tea trays were brought to the soldiers' rooms, and it was all very civilized.

Liam and, especially, Ciarán, felt a good deal less civilized at the dinner table. McGovern introduced Distaff to the young men as the wine was being poured. Resplendent in his bright scarlet coat, Distaff began to imbibe with an enthusiasm that indicated his face would soon match the colour of his coat. Ciarán and Liam were nominally polite but let William McGovern carry on the conversation. It was harmless small talk – the weather, how crops were doing, how was the McGovern stable was coming along, and were they out with the hunt often. Distaff surely knew of the kennel's reputation, but dogs were no match for horses when it came to prestige. Everyone in Donegal knew that William McGovern had some of the finest hounds around and had ambitions to be master of the local hunt, so Distaff expressed an interest in seeing the stables and McGovern promised to show him the new colt. Ciarán nervously gulped his wine, hoping Conall didn't mind the night outdoors. He choked as he finished off his glass too rapidly, and then wondered what it would feel like choking at the end of a rope.

Mrs. McGovern eased the tension at the actual meal, chattering away about the local gossip, letting Distaff know that Ciarán was promised to the daughter of the adjoining landowner. Distaff was not particularly interested but did wonder why Liam hadn't been given that prize. Then he looked around the fine furnishings and realized that the patriarch was going for bigger things. Liam would be doing the rounds of Londonderry and Belfast balls, maybe even take a trip to London or Dublin for the season. Local gentry weren't quite good enough for this aspiring landowner. Ballyhoe wasn't quite an estate, but it was not far off. It was obvious how the cousin fitted into the plans, but what was the boy's story? He turned to Ciarán,

"And where do your family come from? Do they farm land nearby?"

Ciarán coughed, thinking rapidly but saw that there was no way to lie in front of the assembled.

"We're a bit farther west," he replied.

"Very far west," Mrs. McGovern intervened. "Ciarán's father saw fit to traipse off to the mountainy region of all places! He would have done well enough if he started with sheep farming

259

but no, he had to go with arable, wouldn't he Ciarán?" Ciarán nodded, pretending to have a mouth full of food, though it was only a huge lump in his throat. "As Ciarán's brother John, took over the farm, we thought we'd provide Ciarán with some opportunity here. My husband is training him on how to manage a farm properly and soon Ciarán will have some land of his own to sort out." Mrs. McGovern continued gallantly.

"The west coast," Distaff said sourly. I was posted there earlier in the year. "Terrible wind off the sea, even the trees were bent over. Miserable place, in my opinion. And there were some nasty characters that way too. I'm still looking for a few of them but at least one of them has been dealt with, thanks to our valiant soldiers, two who lost their lives in the process."

There was a moment of silence given in respect for the demise of the unfortunate men, though it was Donal that Ciarán thought of rather than the guards. 'Dealt with,' what a business -like way to describe the end of a life and the destruction of another life. Poor Kathleen. Ciarán glowered at his plate, but he felt Liam kick him under the table and kept his mouth shut.

Mrs. McGovern revived the conversation as soon as it was polite to do so. She hadn't sailed through the intricate politics of Ireland for all her years without learning a thing or two.

"We are so looking forward to the wedding, and it will be grand to have Ciarán stay close by us. He and William Junior are such good friends. They are practically like brothers." Distaff nodded politely while scrutinizing Ciarán over his glass of wine. This one was one of those lads that used a name in their unpronounceable language. You had to keep an eye on that sort. And it was interesting that Ciarán refused to meet his eye. Still, it was a family that had always toed the line and he was sure Mr. McGovern had no Republican sympathies. Yet, things could be happening on his land that McGovern knew nothing about. It might be worth a look around after dinner.

In an effort to assist his wife in keeping the conversation off politics, William McGovern returned the discourse to horses and started discussing his plans to expand the stables. Distaff remarked that he admired good horseflesh and that he hoped to build up a stable of his own when he retired from the army. They went into a deep discussion of what contributed to the aspects of a good hunter. Liam offered the odd opinion, but Ciarán remained silent.

"Come, Ciarán, you must have an opinion on the subject," his uncle coaxed. "You've such a fine hand with horses, seeing as how you can control that great beast of yours."

Ciarán started. Please God his uncle wouldn't say that Conall was a grey stallion.

"Um," he stuttered, "A fine hunter. Indeed. Er," anything to get away from the mention of Conall.

Liam leapt in,

"What my eloquent cousin is trying to say is that the main thing about any horse is his heart. If his heart is in it, then he will do anything for you. Isn't that so?" Ciarán gulped gratefully and nodded. Jesus, would this meal ever be over? Would it be possible to complain of a bad belly and leave the table?

But it dragged on interminably, the main, a significant roast that was greeted with enthusiasm by Distaff and then the pudding and then the men adjoined to the library for brandy and a smoke. As

William Senior was tamping down his pipe he looked carefully at his beloved wolfhound, Juliet.

"My Julie seems a bit lame Ciarán. Will you call your wee lassie to look at her?"

"Now?"

"Aye, if she's about." Ciarán nodded and slipped out of the room with a sigh of relief and headed for the kitchen. Perhaps the housekeeper would know if Fiona had come up to the house for a meal. What a reprieve, to be out from under the eyes of Distaff, even if only for a while. When he got to the kitchen, Fiona herself was seated at the table, sharing a saucer of tea with Farley. He rolled his eyes at her.

"It's a good job no one else is at table now. Sure, they'd be completely disgusted."

Fiona gave him a narrow look.

"He's a right to tea at the table if he wants it. He's as good as any person here." Ciarán smiled at her. As ever, she regarded dogs of a higher social calibre than people.

"Of course, he is. But not every person would agree with that. My uncle would like you to come to the library and check Julie's leg. She seems a bit lame on it." Fiona gulped the last of her tea and stood up. "The British soldier is with him. He's having a drink in the library with Uncle now."

"Well then," Fiona said, "I'll have to make sure to spit in his drink when I pass." She paused. "He hasn't asked any questions?"

"There was an awkward moment when Uncle mentioned Conall." Fiona's eyes went wide in alarm. "Not to worry, he didn't describe him. The lieutenant, his name is Distaff, did mention being in Donegal though."

"That's not good," Fiona frowned. "Well, no one ever saw you so you're safe enough. And they never saw Conall in Donegal, so really, we have nothing to worry about." She reached for Ciarán's hand to give it a squeeze and then stopped herself halfway. She shouldn't touch him in the house. She knew that. She jerked away and started towards the library. Best get it over with, and she didn't want Julie to be suffering after all.

Julie was laying in front of the fire, gently roasting her belly. Later she would do the other side but for the moment she was content. She had twisted her ankle chasing after her mate, Romie and it didn't really hurt that badly, but she wouldn't mind the ministrations of Fiona. Fiona would listen and do what was needed, as she always did. Romie rested his chin on Julie's back and sighed heavily. He didn't like the atmosphere in the room tonight. As a rule, he didn't like visitors. He felt he had to be on guard to a greater extent and it was exhausting. This visitor in particular bothered him more than average. There was something unpleasant about him and he needed careful watching. He was relieved to smell Farley entering the room with Fiona. Together they could figure out what was going on.

Farley went up to the wolfhounds and touched noses with them in greeting. Romie sat up and both he and Farley turned to the stranger, eyeing Distaff accusingly. Catching their gaze, Distaff gave McGovern a worried look.

"Gentle as can be, Lieutenant At least my Romie is. I can't speak for the lass's wee terrier, but I am sure she can control him. Now Fiona, my Julie seems a bit off on her left fore. Will you have a look at it? I don't want to be leaving her in pain through the night."

"No, we can't have Julie uncomfortable," Fiona agreed, forgetting to add 'Sir' or 'Master'. She had never been obsequious with him as the other servants were and he was a bit discomforted at her straightforward demeanour in front of the Lieutenant but could do nothing about it. The girl has made it clear from the start that she was not 'in service' and would come and go as it pleased her. She was insolent, brazen, and uncouth, but she was a damn fine hand with the animals.

Palpating the left foreleg gently and listening to Julie's tale of landing wrongly after jumping a ditch, Fiona came to a place of heat at the ankle bone and massaged it gently. Julie whimpered slightly and licked at Fiona's hand. Fiona agreed that it was sore and promised to make a poultice to ease the pain, advising Julie to rest in front of the fire for a few days. Julie had no problems with this prescription.

"She's strained it a bit Mr. McGovern. Probably stepped wrong out in the fields. I can make a poultice to ease her, and she should rest a few days," Fiona stood to go, as Mr McGovern nodded his assent. She passed by Distaff when he suddenly reached out and grabbed her arm. Instantly all three dogs were on their feet growling. Fiona removed her arm from Distaff with obvious disgust but gave no word to the dogs to desist. She could feel them standing on their toes, tails erect and the hair on their spines rising up. She couldn't help but grin at the fear in Distaff's eyes.

"My friends are very protective sir," she glowered at him.

"Call off your dogs' man!" Distaff spat out. Mr McGovern looked at Fiona who was standing, crossed arms, smiling with satisfaction at Distaff.

"Fiona," he said querulously. He suddenly felt rather frightened of the young girl. At this point, both wolfhounds were flanking her, and their teeth were obvious in their enormous, drooling jaws.

"Fi," Ciarán said quietly, "Ask them to settle please." Fiona shot him a glance of amusement and then laid her hand gently on the hounds. She didn't need to touch Farley. Romie and Julie, dropped their heads and stiffly walked back to the fire where they settled with a resounding flop, though they kept their attention on Distaff. Farley eyed the intruder speculatively, waiting for the next development.

Recovering himself, the Lieutenant sat back in his chair.

"Well young lady, you certainly have a way with animals. I'm sorry I startled your 'friends,' it was only that I believe we have met before."

Fiona said nothing. Just stood before Distaff, waiting for his next move. She knew him well enough. He had been with the party of men that had come to the cabin looking for Ciarán. She wasn't likely to forget that incident.

"The last time I saw you, you were in a cabin near Glenties. Were you not? Nursing your sick brother, you said. And how is he now?" Distaff smiled at her, as if genuinely interested.

"I have no brother, now," she replied.

"Oh, I am sorry to hear that."

"I was not aware you had a brother Fiona." McGovern was confused. He thought Fiona had been hired to nurse Ciarán. A brother had never been mentioned. In fact, Ciarán had said there was no family. He supposed there wasn't now if the brother was dead. It was odd he had never been mentioned though.

Fiona shrugged.

"I had a family once," she looked hard at Distaff, an uncomfortable glare that he found to be bordering on obnoxious. It was no fault of his that the Irish were too poor and dirty to keep themselves alive long.

She turned to leave the room, without a nod or curtsy, as was her habit. The girl had no manners whatsoever. Thank goodness she kept to the kennels most of the time. McGovern was deeply annoyed that he had asked her in here before company. Julie could have waited overnight. And he was annoyed at Ciarán as well. Why had he brought this backward girl home with him? Why hadn't he just paid her wages and sent her on her way? If she weren't so useful, he'd be rid of her in a minute.

The next morning Fiona went out to check on Conall in the far field. She knew it was too risky for Ciarán to go up that way. It was an overcast day and the mist lay so solid on the ground it looked as though she'd have to kick it out of her way. She could feel her skirts getting soggy and made a grumbled curse at the inconvenience the lieutenant's visit had caused her, but upon spying Conall, her spirits lifted. He snickered in greeting and came to rub his muzzle against her hair. She laughed as she felt him blow warm air down her neck and reached up to tickle him behind the ears. Farley gave a short bark in greeting and then wandered off to check for rabbit holes. Conall reported that he had spent a fine evening, although a tad chilly. Fiona leaned into his bulk and told him of the interaction with Distaff. If a horse could chuckle, Conall would have done, instead, snorting in amusement. She promised to send Farley as soon as the Lieutenant left and then turned back towards the kennels to begin her day's work. Farley was snuffling in the underbrush and left Fiona to her own devices. She needed no monitoring in the kennels.

Stepping into the darkness of the stables, Fiona savoured the warmth of the horses and their straw beds before proceeding through to the kennels, but she was stopped en route by a hand on her arm. She looked up to the florid face of Lieutenant Distaff.

"The girl herself! I was looking for you," he smiled, rather like a crocodile.

Fiona didn't deign to reply. She stood very still and waited.

"And where have you been this morning, young lady? Obviously out walking, you're soaked."

Fiona shrugged, trying to disentangle her arm, but Distaff held it firmly.

"I've work to do," she insisted stiffly.

"I wanted to talk with your more about your brother. Did he ever own a grey stallion?"

"We weren't the sort of family that owned horses, Sir." Could he hear the sarcasm in her use of 'sir?' She hoped so. "I've got to go now, if you don't mind," jerking free her arm, she made off as quickly as she could, relieved Conall was well hidden from this unpleasant man. To her astonishment, the Lieutenant followed her, all the way to the kennels. She decided it was best to ignore him so picked up her pace slightly and kept going. When she reached the kennels, she put her hand on the latch, but he grabbed her shoulder and turned her around abruptly.

"You have no manners at all. I can't believe your master hasn't taught you a lesson."

Fiona narrowed her eyes and reached into her pocket for her foraging knife.

"I have no master."

No master? How would you feed and clothe yourself without the goodness of the McGovern family? Sell your body? I imagine your type wouldn't find that difficult." He pressed against her, pushing through into the kennel and kicking the door closed behind him. The dogs inside started at the noise and began to bark. "Are you going to loose your hounds to protect you now? I don't think so!" He grabbed her arms roughly and turned her to face the door, forcing her forwards and separating her legs with his knee. Fiona struggled to get her hands free so that she could use her knife.

"*Cabhru*," she called, reverting to Gaelic in her cry for help. The dogs began to howl and jump in their kennels. Distaff, let go of one of her hands to release his belt, allowing Fiona to pull an arm loose and slash the knife, back and down. At that angle, there was little force behind the knife, but she managed to incise the man's thigh.

"Bitch," he roared, smashing the side of her head, the shock forcing her to the floor. The chaos of the dogs became overwhelming. Could no one hear it? She was going to be raped by this ogre, here in a place that she had always thought of as sanctuary. She could feel bile rising into her mouth and wanted to vomit in fear.

As Fiona had fallen away from the door, it swung on its hinges, allowing a small being to fly through the air and attach its teeth into Distaff's buttock. With all the terrier tenacity in him, Farley clung on, jaws clamped tight on the exposed flesh. Distaff yelled and tried to dislodge the intruder, but he had no hope against a terrier hold.

And then Ciarán was there, roughly taking hold of Distaff.

"Get out of here you feckin' Gobshite! And take your bloody friends with you!" Ciarán pulled Fiona to him and held her tightly. "Go I said," he bellowed at Distaff.

"Are you alright *mo mhuirín*?" Fiona nodded and buried her head in his chest, relief flooding through her. He'd heard, and he'd come to her rescue with Farley. She was safe.

At this point, the heroic dog casually released his grip and dropped to the ground behind the Lieutenant. Nonchalantly, Farley lifted his leg and pissed on Distaff before sauntering off to a corner to sit back and watch the proceedings.

Managing to fasten his trousers, Distaff pulled himself up to a soldier's stance.

"So, it's like that is it?" He sneered at Ciarán, "Not keen on sharing your little whore." Ciarán raised his hand to strike Distaff, but Fiona held his arm.

"Let the dogs do it Ciarán, he'll only make trouble for you."

"Oh, I will make trouble for you," Distaff snapped, "But first I'll have this bitch arrested for stabbing me, and that rabid dog of hers should be shot."

"My uncle doesn't take kindly to rapists, Lieutenant and he'll be well proud that Fiona, and the dog, defended her honour. It's best you leave, and now."

Distaff snorted, but turned, straightened his jacket, and set back across the yard, through the stables, to the house.

Ciarán held Fiona away from him and looked at her. "He's hit you. Are you sure you're alright? And what do you mean about the dogs? If you set the wolfhounds on him, they will be killed. Uncle would be destroyed if he lost Romie and Julie."

Fiona shook her head. "I'm fine. No worries for the wolfhounds. It will be sorted without them." Ciarán looked at her doubtfully. "Please, I need to be with the hounds." She slid the latch on the nearest kennel door and entered the mass of squirming dogs, all anxious to sniff her and see that she was well. She sank to the floor, and they crawled into her lap, nuzzling her face, and licking her ears, pressing wet muzzles into her skirt, and snuffling the top of her head. She closed her eyes and let them press against her, their bodies promising the care of the pack. She sighed in relief and felt the pieces of herself come back together. When Farley entered the kennel, the hounds moved back, allowing him passage to Fiona. He crawled into her lap, turned around once and with a grunt settled himself in a comfortable heap.

It was only then that Ciarán felt he was welcome and stepped in, sitting beside Fiona, and taking her hand. Opening her eyes, she turned and smiled at him.

"We'll be alright now," she assured him.

"I can't bear to have another man touching you," Ciarán said in a strangled voice. "I can't bear it. You're mine!" With a sharp intake of breath Fiona looked at him and then shook her head sadly. "Yes," he insisted and pulled her close. They sat in silence for several minutes, murmuring, "I wish I could hold you like this forever and keep you safe. Do you remember that night in the cottage when you fell asleep in my arms? I've wanted to clasp you close ever since. I lay awake at night, wanting to hold you."

Pulling herself away, Fiona took one of his hands in hers and said nothing for a time. Then, "If I didn't have the dogs, I think my heart would break."

"My heart is breaking," Ciarán insisted. She bowed her head. "You've made your choice Ciarán. There is nothing I can do to help you with that. You know I wouldn't be your mistress."

"I know, and I wouldn't ask you, but would you be my wife?"

Shocked, she dropped Ciarán's hand and gave him a hard look.

"Are you mad? She's got a dowry, and a piece of land. You can't give up that, not to mention that your uncle would be beside himself and would have nothing more to do with you."

Ciarán took back her hand and then reached up to brush a strand of hair out of her face. Gently he stroked the growing bruise where Distaff had hit her and then leaned forward and kissed her softly on the lips.

"But I love you Fiona, strange wee thing that you are, I don't think I can go through the rest of my life without you." Fiona pushed away from him enough to look up into his face.

"You know that cannot be. You are promised to Gráinne, and I have nothing to give you."

"And I have nothing to give you," Ciarán rejoined. "But I want you, more than I have ever wanted anything. I will figure something out regarding Gráinne. Don't worry about that now."

"But you don't know about me," Fiona exclaimed, trying to pull away from him.

"We lived in a cabin together for weeks on end. You've nursed me through injury and fever. We've worked side by side here on the farm. I know you enough to know I want to be with you."

Fiona felt the tears spill over and run down her cheeks.

"But you don't really know who I am," she whispered. "Do you remember the story I told you about my mother?" Ciarán nodded, "She drowned. I'm sorry."

Fiona shook her head. "I never said she drowned. I said she went down to the lake and never came back. She didn't drown. She turned into a swan," Fiona blurted out. Ciarán scanned her face, waiting for an explanation. When none came, he demanded,

"What are you trying to tell me?" his voice rising in alarm.

"I'm telling you my mother became a swan." Her voice was flat and faraway.

"You're making no sense at all," Ciarán insisted, grabbing her arm, and trying to pull her back to him. "How? What? She was a shapeshifter? Are you going to become some creature as well?" She sat, unresponsive. He stood up suddenly and walked away from Fiona, pacing down the length of the kennel and then turning to her, still huddled on the floor, dogs scattered about her.

Fiona felt tears running down her cheeks and scrubbed them away impatiently.

"I am a Listener. I've told you that this long time. I can shapeshift," then hurriedly, "But I don't want to!" Ciarán just stared at her.

Finally, he said quietly,

"Try to explain it to me."

Fiona sniffed loudly.

"The Listeners are given the task of caring for the creatures. We take a vow as a child and then practice our skill through our lives." Ciarán made an impatient gesture – he knew all this.

Fiona ignored him and continued, "My grandmother could listen to many types of animals and in a manner, speak back to them. She was one of the most gifted Listeners ever. My mother was not. She had her swan and their conversation, but she had no interest in learning more." She paused, risking a glance at Ciarán, but his face remained immobile. "You know I'm a bastard. My mother never married. She had no time for the fellas. I think maybe she was raped once when she stayed by the loch too late one evening. She could have got rid of me; me nan had the herbs for that. But maybe me mam thought she wanted a child. I don't know, but I don't think she cared for me too much when I was born. She only ever cared for her swan. And then one day, she decided to be with him. And once you change, you can't change back. She knew that, so she left me, on the shores of the loch, on me own." Abruptly Fiona stood up and began gathering the dogs' bowls for cleaning and refilling. "I won't let you ruin your life on my account. She's a very pretty girl, your Gráinne. I am sure you'll be very happy and have darling children. Now, get going and let me get on with my work."

Ciarán was not ready to end the conversation so suddenly,

"So, you could change into a dog?" he ventured. Fiona nodded. "But your grandmother, she never changed, did she?"

"No. You can do better for the creatures if you stay human, which is why I won't change either. I have to stand in both worlds to make their world better."

Ciarán sighed.

"Well, I could tell you were a bit unusual when I met you." He walked up to her slowly and took the dog bowls from her, placing them on the ground, where Farley sniffed them hopefully. Ciarán took Fiona's face between his two hands and held her there, staring into her large brown eyes, irises far too wide to be normal, almost no white left at all. He fingered her oddly coloured hair, a bit of tan, a bit of black, a bit of brown – red grizzle she called it, same as Farley's.

"It doesn't matter lass," he decided. He drew her into his arms and kissed her for a very long time. Farley cocked his head, watching and then trotted off. He wasn't needed at the moment and breakfast wouldn't be coming for a while.

Distaff and his men departed the farm as soon as they had broken their fast. He was curt with his host and complained about the rudeness of the staff. Worriedly, McGovern offered to show him the kennels and the new foal in the stables, but Distaff said he was no longer interested in spending more time on such a poorly run holding. McGovern wanted to know which servant had offended, and Distaff was happy to complain that the kennel lass had thrown herself at him last night and then tried to pick his pocket. McGovern apologized profusely but Distaff would not be dissuaded and took to the road promptly.

Shortly after his departure, Ciarán appeared in his uncle's library and reported the assault on Fiona. McGovern was in a quandary. He didn't like to think of his nephew as being liberal with the truth, but he knew the boy was infatuated with the girl. It really had to end. He would concoct some errand away from the farm and send both Ciarán and Liam away for a few days. He wasn't sure what he would do about Fiona during their absence. Something, but he didn't know what yet.

The next morning, Ciarán woke with a smile on his face. He had been dreaming and he was glad no one could see his face as he relived the dream. Fiona was his, in his arms, and – well, the rest was private. He got up and rapidly threw on his clothes. Not waiting for breakfast in the dining room with the family, he rushed into the kitchen. Sometimes he had caught her there, sharing her porridge with Farley, much to the disgust of the cook. Today there was no sign of her.

"Master Ciarán, you aren't running out without a bite to eat? If you can't wait to be served in the dining room, at least have a cup of tea and a bite of toast will you," Mrs. McGuire admonished. "Where are you going in such a hurry anyway? There's nothing so important that you don't have time to get a hot meal in you first."

Ciarán laughed and grabbed some bread that one of the house maids had just sliced. Mrs. McGuire, grabbed it back from him and buttered it thickly before handing it back to Ciarán with an audible, 'Hmph.' Bowing ostentatiously to her, Ciarán was out the door and on his way to the kennels. They will think he had some business with the horses. That was best for now.

He found her hauling two buckets of water from the well and quickly took them off her.

"Why don't you get the stable lads to haul the water for you?"

"Them lazy lads? I'd be waiting till next week. And I'd never hear the end of how a weak wee girl should be in the house and not working with the animals. What are you doing out here at this time of day?"

Ciarán bent over and planted a kiss on her cheek.

"That's why." Fiona blushed and shook her head.

"Someone will see us!"

"Surely you know that they already think you share my bed?"

"Do they now?" Fiona shrugged. "Well, they can think what they like I suppose. It's no matter to me."

"Do you really not care?"

Fiona cocked her head to examine him, just as Farley did when he was trying to figure out what a person was saying.

"Surely, what people do in private is no business of anyone else."

"But your reputation."

Fiona snorted.

"My sort don't worry about things like that! As long as I listen to the creatures that speak to me, I'm doing what I'm supposed to be doing."

"Then you wouldn't mind to be my mistress?"

"I would mind to share you. If you're mine, you're mine. I won't let another woman in my den."

"So, you're jealous then? I never would have thought."

She gave Ciarán a good shove and nearly spilt the water.

"Steady on, I'll be drenched in a minute."

Fiona tossed her head and marched on ahead of him.

"I need the water for the drinking troughs, and some left over for cleaning out the middle kennel."

"Yes, ma'am!"

When they got to the kennels, Fiona lifted one of the buckets and started towards the middle kennel. Ciarán took the bucket from her, putting it aside and then encircled her with his arms, pulling her into his warmth and beamed down into her face.

"Now I've run out without breakfast just to get a chance for a wee cuddle. You won't deprive me of that, will you?" He stroked the hair from her face and bent to kiss her, long and sweet. She sighed and leaned against him, resting her head on his chest.

"I could stay here all day."

"Soon, we'll be able to," he whispered into her hair. "I'll let the palaver over the Lieutenant settle down and then I'll speak to my uncle. He's sending me over to Strabane at the end of the week to see some horses there. Liam and I will be gone for a few days but once I'm back I will speak directly to uncle and tell him our intentions."

"And Gráinne?"

"Oh, aye, I'll speak to her as well. But uncle first. I think he'll be more upset. He was so looking forward to that land being joined up with his."

"So why doesn't Liam marry her?"

"He's set for bigger things, Liam is. No country lass for him. He'll have to have a great lady from Derry or Belfast."

"Do you think Gráinne will be upset?"

"To be sure, she'll be a bit cross. It will be humiliating you see. But I don't believe she'll be broken hearted. I can't say that either of us were ever in love."

"So, you were going to marry her, when you had no feelings for her?"

Ciarán stepped away, a bit uncomfortably.

"Sure, I had feelings for her. Any man would. She's a lovely lass, quite easy on the eye. But not love type feelings, more like ..."

"Lust?" Fiona queried, lifting her eyebrow in appraisal. Ciarán ran his hand nervously through his hair.

"Well ... I am a young man. I can't help that, can I?"

"And how do I know that that's not all you feel for me? It certainly seems like that's what's on your mind this morning."

He took her hand and held it gently.

"We know each other, Fiona. We've lived together, in the cottage when I was ill. You've seen the worst of me and didn't run. And besides, Farley is ever so fond of me."

Laughing, Fiona fell into his arms again and pressed herself close against him. She felt his leg come between hers and as he reached his tongue into her mouth, he cupped her buttocks and drew her even closer. The desire to be one with him was overwhelming and she reached her hands under his shirt and felt for the flesh that she had only touched before as a nurse. Now she was his lover and there could be no more reason for embarrassment. She wanted him to lay her in the straw and join with her right there, among the dogs but he grabbed her wrist and pushed her away from him.

"No Fiona!" he gasped, breathless from his efforts to separate himself from her.

Startled, she stepped back from him and felt the heat rising into her face.

"What," she stammered, "What have I done wrong?"

He looked up at the ceiling and took a deep breath.

"You've done nothing wrong *acushla* it's just that if you let me go any farther, I won't be able to stop myself."

"But I don't want you to stop." She was confused. They both wanted each other. At least she thought he wanted her, and she certainly wanted him. Why should they stop?

"We're not married yet my little heathen. We have to wait till we're married." He released her wrists, which he realised he was gripping too tightly. Fiona rubbed at the marks he had created. She was ashamed and would not meet his gaze. There was nothing wrong with coupling in the world she had known. Obviously, things were different for Ciarán. But he had come looking for her! He had asked for 'a cuddle.' Sometimes humans were so confusing.

"Well then, you best be off on your journey," she turned from him and began gathering the food bowls in order to feed the dogs, who were now getting quite anxious for their morning meal.

"Ah, don't be that way Fiona," Ciarán reached for her shoulder, but she pulled away. She heard him sigh behind her but continued with her work. "I'll have this visit to Strabane over soon, my love, and then I will sort out the mess I've created, and we'll be married. Fiona?" She stopped then, her back still turned, but unable to move. Ciarán stepped behind her and wrapped his arms around her, leaning over to kiss her neck, he whispered in her ear. "I love you Fiona, make sure you are still here when I get back from Strabane." And then he was gone, and she was alone with the dogs.

DISTAFF'S REVENGE

Ciarán knew that he and Fiona had to keep their affection as private as possible, but now that he had declared himself to her, he found it almost impossible not to touch her. Passing her in the stables, he would reach out and tug her plait. Standing watching the horses in the paddock, his hand would find hers and they could only hope no one was watching – if only that had been possible. Ciarán was yet to figure out what he was going to do about his uncle and breaking his betrothal to Gráinne. He imagined he would be sent away in disgrace, and he would need to find employment elsewhere, possibly as a groom, nothing higher as he could hardly rely on a letter of introduction from his uncle.

The third day after Distaff had left, McGovern called Liam and Ciarán to him in the library to discuss the journey to Strabane. He wanted them to return to the stables where he had purchased Colette, but he needed them to bargain the agent down on his prices. McGovern wanted a colt or a stallion this time, as he was not keen to continue using Conall to service his mares because the stallion was a bit too coarse for the type of stock McGovern hoped to breed, and his temperament was not exactly reliable. However, a decent stud horse was not going to be cheap. The young men were excited about the trip as examining fine horses was far preferable to the routine labours of running the farm and helping McGovern with the ledgers. Yet, Ciarán was reluctant to leave Fiona for the two or three days the possible purchase would take, but it was only a few days he reassured himself.

He and Liam planned to leave early the next morning. Ciarán knew Fiona would be busy with the hounds in the morning, so he slipped out of the house after supper and sought out Fiona in her lean-to next to the kennels. She was wrapped up in a quilt and sitting by the small stove she had for heat in the dwelling, a fireplace being far too dangerous near the combustibles found in the kennels and stables. She had been reading a recipe for foot poultices in her nan's book. The hounds were forever getting thorns in their feet or splitting a pad. The abscesses that followed were both painful and debilitating. Fiona had tried a variety of recipes with both success and failure. She wanted to find something a bit more dependable. She thought coltsfoot would be a good option, but it wasn't found anywhere near Balleybofey, though she remembered gathering it back home in Maghera. It was a plant that preferred the sea cliffs. Sighing with frustration, she thrust the book aside. Chickweed maybe? But she should start trying combinations. Nan had been good with that. Fiona pressed her hands to her forehead trying to remember. Had it been chickweed with cleavers and what else? Oats and another ingredient. It escaped her now, but she could see them placing the poultice on the sweet little nanny they had called Deirdre. The nanny had slipped climbing over a wet rock wall and had a nasty wound on her belly. She had been ever so good about coming for her poultice twice daily and had healed marvellously. Maybe the ingredients were in the book somewhere, but Fiona was too tired to read anymore. She stood and stretched when she heard a muffled knock on her door. Probably, the stable boy Jamie, he always came running to her when anything went awry in the stables. He should have gone to the head groom but was too frightened of getting a wallop on the side of his head. Keeping the quilt wrapped around her she opened the door a crack to keep the cold out. Ciarán pushed the door open farther and slipped in quickly.

She smiled to herself, not really surprised to see him. It had been the talk of the stables that Ciarán and Liam were going to look at a horse in Strabane on the morrow. She thought he'd come and say goodbye to her. Reaching his cold hands under the quilt, he embraced her and kissed her.

"You're all cold!" she gave a little shriek and jumped back from him.

"Well, then I need you to warm me up," he reached for her and pulled her close again and began to kiss her neck, pressing his icy nose into the warm spot beneath her ear. She leaned into him, feeling as if her legs were sliding out from underneath her. He lifted her then and she wrapped her legs around his waist. Ciarán gazed into her eyes for a moment and then carried her over to the pallet and lay her down on the narrow bed. He began to kiss her again, his body pressing against hers and hers arching up to meet him. His hand ran up under her skirt, feeling the hard, tight muscles of her thighs. Then he pulled himself back and raised himself up on his elbows above her.

"You would let me." It was a statement not a question.

"Only you," she promised. Breathing hard, she waited.

"I won't," he said suddenly and got up off the pallet. Her hand reached for him, but he pushed it away. He felt himself trembling with the effort and had to move over to the stove. Farley, warming himself, lifted his head and observed Ciarán noncommittally. "I need to break the betrothal first. Otherwise, it wouldn't be right."

Fiona didn't say anything. She was sitting up on the pallet, her knees pulled into her chest. This felt like a repeat of the other morning, and she was getting both frustrated and annoyed. Ciarán needed to make his bloody mind up.

"I'll speak to Uncle when I get back from Strabane," he looked at Fiona, waiting for a reply, but still she remained silent.

"That's a promise," he added.

Without looking at him, she replied,

"I've not asked anything of you. You need to make your own decisions."

"I have," and then he was holding her again and kissed her hard. "I have to go now. I can't trust myself," he stroked a loose strand of hair behind her ear. "I'll be home soon, my *acushla*."

It seemed an odd coincidence that Distaff, and two privates appeared a few hours after Ciarán, and Liam had left for Strabane. McGovern greeted them civilly and agreed that yes, an assault had occurred on an officer of the British army, and it was appropriate to take the suspect into custody. The soldiers were escorted to the kennels where Fiona was mucking out the dirty straw and chatting with Petesy, resting on a stool near the end kennel. When Distaff's party entered, Farley immediately began an alarm bark, interspersed with savage growling. Fiona picked up her snarling beast and landed him in Petesy's lap. "For the love of God and St. Francis, promise me you'll keep him safe." Petesy clamped his arms around the writhing terrier and nodded his assurance. The two privates grabbed Fiona by each arm and Distaff read out her crime of assault against an officer. McGovern stood by quietly, his eyes averted from the malevolent glance given by Petesy. Fiona said nothing, only locking her eyes on Farley and begging him not to follow her. They dragged her away, the boys coming out from the stables to watch in horror and the girls in the kitchen folding their arms in approbation. It was as they expected from a backward *culchie* girl.

"*Bad Cess* to you," Petesy hissed as he made his way past his master towards the stables. McGovern looked up at him in alarm and was even more shocked to see that the old man was making the sign to ward off evil, the index and smallest fingers of the arthritic hand pointing out at him. McGovern crossed himself and started to say something, but Petesy pushed past him, calling for Jamie, one of the stable lads. With the boy's help, Petesy managed to lock the frantic terrier in the most secure place they could find – Conall's stable. Farley leapt at the walls, his high- pitched cries of agony piercing their ears. "You'll want to get some bread and milk in there for the poor creature. He won't take it, I'm sure, but we'll try." Jamie nodded seriously at the instruction.

"Master Ciarán will be back tomorrow or the next day," he said hopefully.

"And there'll be a *stramash* then," Petesy added.

Fiona's hands were tied behind her back, and she was thrown into the back of a cart being pulled by a very tired nag. She tried to speak to the horse, but it had been so whipped and mistreated that the poor creature shied away from the nudging at her mind. Fiona had to brace her feet against the floor of the cart to prevent from being knocked about each time the cart hit a rut in the road. The rope dug into her thin wrists, and she felt panic rising in her throat at the feeling of being so completely trapped. She closed her eyes and focused all her thought on Farley. He was safe. Her acolyte was safe. For, as long as he lived, she lived. She thought of his liquid brown eyes, his velvet ears, his tail wagging when he had his head down a rabbit hole. Just keep thinking of Farley she told herself. She would not think of Ciarán. She knew full well that he why she was here, bound and on her way to gaol. McGovern had guessed or been told about herself and Ciarán and would have none of it. If she were to survive, she would have to put that dream out of her head. All she needed was to be reunited with Farley, but not while she was in Distaff's hands. He would kill the dog. There was no doubt about that. Fiona allowed a short fantasy of the wolfhounds Romie and Julie chasing after the cart and pulling Distaff from his horse, shredding him to pieces, but was sure that McGovern had locked up the wolfhounds for just that reason. There was no one to rescue her. She would have to find her own escape.

Even starting late in the day, they could have made it back to Letterkenny by nightfall, but Distaff seemed in no hurry. Late in the afternoon, he pulled his horse off the road and signalled to his men that they would make camp for the night. The men were not best pleased, preferring to return to the town with its pubs, hot food, and barracks, easier to rest in than the open road. However, they were under orders, so set up a tent and started a fire in a field behind a stone wall.

Meanwhile, Distaff hauled the prisoner from the cart, not worrying as she fell, unable to balance herself with her bound hands.

"Did you really think you could get away with stabbing a British officer?"

"Is that what you called the wee scratch I gave you?" Fiona answered, immediately realising how stupid it had been to reply. Distaff's fist smashed into the side of her face and again she stumbled. He grabbed her by the elbow, just before she fell and yanked her to her feet.

"You need to be taught respect," he snarled in her face. "And that's just what I intend to do," dragging her away from the camp, he threw her down in the grass and undid his breeches. When she tried to get up, he kicked her legs out from under her and stood on one, to hold her in place. She screamed, and he cuffed her head till she saw stars. "Every time you scream, I'll hit you that bit harder," he spat into her face. But still she screamed and tried to wrest her leg free.

The other two soldiers had been drawn by the commotion but turned to go when they saw their commanding officer half-unclothed. Distaff leered at them and motioned them over.

"Hold her down boys and then you can have a turn as well." One of the privates hesitated but his comrade laughed at him and gave him a shove, insisting he join in the fun.

As they held her arms and Distaff spread her legs, Fiona closed her eyes. She thought of Farley. She thought of the day she first rode Conall, the wind pulling her hair loose and her cry of joy, accompanied by Farley's barks of excitement. The searing pain ripped through her, one man after the other. She was dimly aware of the tears seeping out of her tightly closed eyes as she tried not to smell the fetid breath on her or feel the weight of their bodies as they thrust into her. She had to stay in the fields with Conall and Farley, the two creatures in the world she could trust.

The next morning a runty woman, barely more than a girl, with a black eye and dried blood on her face and down the back of her skirt, was thrown into a cell in Letterkenny gaol. The trial would be tomorrow. She had committed a grievous crime, but the judges weren't hanging that often these days and even transportation had fallen out of favour. She would probably just rot in prison. The gaoler had untied her hands, already weeping from the abrasion, so she could eat but Fiona did not thank him. She sank onto the floor of rotting straw, a rat, rustling away from where she had fallen. She paid no attention to the hunk of bread and cup of water placed inside the cell. She curled up into a tight ball and lay immobile. The rat crept back, unafraid, and began to gnaw at the bread.

TRIAL AND PUNISHMENT

Ciarán dismounted and taking Conall lightly by the reins he led the horse towards his stall. An almighty barking started in, followed by hysterical yipping. Jamie, the stable lad, ran forward and stopped Ciarán.

"You can't open the stall door Sir. We've got the lass's dog trapped in there. We can't let him out. She made me promise." Ciarán tried to make sense out of the boy's anxious warning.

"What dog? Farley?"

"Yes sir, it's Farley dog in there. The kennel doors were too low to keep him. He was only safe here in Conall's stall. She said he mustn't get away or the soldiers would kill him, so I locked him there myself. I've been giving him food, but he won't eat. I don't know what to do. I'm so glad you're back Master Ciarán. If the wee dog won't eat it will die and then what will Fiona say?"

Taking the boy by his shoulders and giving him a little shake Ciarán made Jamie stop and look at him.

"What has happened? Where is Fiona?"

In horror, the boy stepped back.

"Did your uncle not tell you?"

"Tell me what?" Ciarán bellowed as he tried to figure out what exactly was going on.

In a near whisper the boy admitted,

"The soldiers came and took her away, the same ones that were here last week."

"But why? This makes no sense," Ciarán turned to his horse, who was by now quite aware there was an emergency and was stomping and blowing. "This horse has to be put in a stall, groomed and fed," unthinking he handed the reins to the petrified lad. Conall attempted to rear and to his credit Jamie hung on, which was just as well as Ciarán ignored them both and ran towards the house to get the full story from his uncle.

He found McGovern in his study, going over his farm ledgers. He looked up when Ciarán stormed in and assumed a neutral expression.

"Ah, you and Liam are back then. How was business?"

"Never mind business," Ciarán slammed his fist on the desk making the ledgers jump, "Where is Fiona?"

"The kennel maid?" McGovern, scratched his head, feigning slow recollection, which did very little for Ciarán's temper.

"Yes, I mean Fiona! Where is she? What happened while I was gone?"

McGovern moved the ledgers out of the range of Ciarán's fist and sat back in his chair, meticulously crossing his hands over his waist, where the roast beef and pudding from his dinner rested.

"You seem quite concerned about the lass. Rather a bit too concerned over a mere kennel maid."

Ciarán ground his teeth, the muscles in his jaw bulging out visibly.

Flicking a hand out to the side, McGovern remarked,

"She was arrested. Apparently, she had an altercation with the Lieutenant. Tried to pinch something off him and when he apprehended her, she stabbed him and ran off! If I had any idea that she was that sort of character, I would never have allowed her to work here."

"You know that's not true Uncle! I told you he was a bit forward with Fiona and she was just defending herself. I told you all this before I left! She hasn't done anything wrong. She shouldn't have been arrested if anything that *gombeen* lieutenant should be in gaol!"

McGovern put up his hand to stop Ciarán's tirade,

"It's his word against hers."

"No, it isn't! I was there!" Ciarán began to pace the room. His uncle stood and stopped him, taking him by the shoulders and looking, not unkindly, in his nephew's face.

"You need to let her go lad. You have a bright future ahead of you. You can't jeopardize it all for a kennel maid. Listen to me Ciarán. This is for your own good. You need to forget the lass and remember you have a fiancé, a proper lady, with a small inheritance."

Ciarán threw his uncle's arms from his shoulders and stepped away from him.

"Land. That's all that matters to you. Land. Well, I have a heart too Uncle." McGovern reached for Ciarán, but it was too late, his nephew had stormed from the library, slamming the door behind him.

Liam, waiting outside the library, nearly collided with Ciarán. "Cousin," he grabbed at Ciarán's coat.

Ciarán turned on him, snarling,

"I suppose you think I should let her rot in gaol as well."

Liam held up both hands in defence,

"I'm only just here myself. Brendan told me in the stables."

"Fine, so you've heard," Ciarán turned to go.

"Wait Ciarán!" Ciarán looked as if he was going to take a swing at Liam, who quickly held out his purse. "Money, Ciarán, you'll need it for bribes and what have you. It's all I've got but I can find you more if you need it. Get going and I'll follow you as soon as I can get away." Ciarán's face melted.

"You're not going to try to stop me?"

"Now that would be a foolish thing! You've been in love with the lass since she put maggots in your leg. I can't say Fiona is my favourite person in the world but she's obviously yours. Now, take my purse and see what you can sort out. I'll be in Letterkenny by tomorrow at the latest."

Ciarán grabbed the purse and stuffed it into his coat pocket.

"Thank you, Liam. You're a better man than your father."

During the interview, Conall had been given some feed and had a quick rub down. The tack hadn't been cleaned but there was no help for it. Ciarán signalled to Jamie to re-saddle Conall and then he took a rope and looped it around Farley's neck. He slowly opened the stall door and then the ball of fur flew at him, scrabbling at Ciarán's arms and barking repeatedly. Ciarán scooped up the writhing creature and buttoned him into his coat. "Off we go mate," he informed Farley as they mounted Conall and galloped towards Londonderry.

The gaol was on a street behind an assembly building. It was a squat, brick building with a sagging roof. The smell of stale urine and long unwashed bodies accosted Ciarán's nostrils as he tied up Conall outside. Farley wriggled in his coat, prompting Ciarán to coax him to hold still for a bit longer. Exhausted from the frantic journey as well as the earlier travel from Strabane, Ciarán had to lean against Conall for a moment before he climbed the steps to knock fiercely on the entrance door.

After an unreasonable length of time, a very well-fed middle-aged man arrived at the door, wiping the grease of his dinner from his chin. The gaol keeper viewed Ciarán with his mud-spattered coat and dishevelled appearance.

"What do you want?"

"I want to know if you hold a young girl here." The gaol keeper leered, "I wish I did hold a young lassie right now. Come back tomorrow man. It's late and I'm having my dinner," but Ciarán had pushed the door open now and the gaol keeper was forced into the hallway, "Hey, you can't just -" Ciarán held up the purse.

"A shilling to answer my question."

The gaoler rubbed his gleaming chin.

"There may have been a lass brought in yesterday. Hard to tell her age. She was in a bit of state. At this point, the gaoler found himself pressed against the wall, a large hand at his throat. "Ach, man, take care. I only work here."

"I need to see her. *Now!*" Ciarán hadn't released his hold yet and the words, hissing between his teeth, spattered saliva at the gaoler's face. All the same, the gaoler took a moment, weighing his options.

"It will cost you."

"Another six pence."

"A shilling," but the hand around his neck tightened. "Alright then, one and six and I'll say not a word to anyone."

Ciarán counted out the coins and waited expectantly.

"I did say now," he growled. Farley decided to join in to add to the request. The gaoler gave an odd look at Ciarán's rumbling chest but merely nodded and pointed down the hallway.

"That way sir."

The walls were damp with condensation and as they approached the back of the structure, and the odour of rotting filth was increasing. Farley sneezed in disgust. The gaoler pulled a set of keys out of his pocket and fiddled with a lock on a warped wooden door. With some manoeuvring, he managed to yank open the door and ushered Ciarán in.

"It's a wee bit dark. Perhaps I'll just fetch a candle," Ciarán gripped his arm before the gaoler could scuttle off.

"Leave the keys with me."

"Oh, I can't do that," the gaoler fussed. "It would be my job's worth."

"I don't trust you not to lock me in," Ciarán remarked, twisting the gaoler's wrist, until the keys dropped on the floor. Ciarán placed his foot over the keys. "A candle now, please."

Farley didn't need a candle, leaping from Ciarán's coat, he made his way to the first cell on the left and began to scratch at the bars, keening with a high-pitched whine. Ciarán rushed towards the sound, praising Farley's efforts.

"Fiona, love, are you in there? Fi, can you answer me?"

Something moved on the floor, a rat scampering by. Farley barked at it, infuriated and then, what looked like a pile of clothing heaped on the floor, stirred. A hand stretched forward, reaching vaguely. "Farley?" it whimpered. Ciarán was on the floor beside the dog, reaching through the bars.

"Fiona, we're here. Farley and I are here. We're going to get you out of this place. Can you hear me *mavoureen*?"

"Farley," the figure began to crawl towards the cell door, inch by inch, till the hand slipped through the bars and the dog fell upon it, licking frantically. Ciarán wanted to take the hand and kiss it also, but he dare not interfere. Whatever had happened to her, Fiona needed her dog now.

The gaoler appeared with the candle and illuminated the scene. "No dogs allowed in here," he offered hopefully.

Ciarán stood up with a roar, "I'll not give you another penny! Look at the state of this place! It reeks, rats running everywhere. Have you fed her? Have you called a doctor? You can see that she's hurt. You'll be lucky if I don't have you reported, much less give you more money."

The gaoler moved out of punching range and absolved himself, "She only came in last night. I wasn't told to fetch a doctor and I have put food in, though she's not touched it. No matter, she's going to trial tomorrow and then she'll be no business of mine then. We don't keep long-term prisoners here."

"Tomorrow?" Ciarán hadn't anticipated things happening that quickly. He crouched down again, and this time managed to catch hold of Fiona's hand. "*Acushla,* I'll speak to the court tomorrow and tell them what really happened. This will all be over. You and Farley will be together tomorrow. Fi, please, I need you to stay with us till then."

Her face turned towards him, he could see one eye swollen shut, her lips split and bleeding, a bruise swelling on her left cheek. He swallowed hard to prevent himself from swearing. The one open eye stared at him, blankly.

"Fiona?"

"Tomorrow?" she asked it as if it were a concept beyond her, a day that could never come.

"It's late already, Fi. Only a few more hours. You can do that," he squeezed her hand and tried to get her to see him, but she slipped out of his grasp and lay her head back down on the floor. Ciarán couldn't bear to leave her in this state, but he had to prepare himself for the court tomorrow. He had to go in looking like a country squire and have an indisputable story. He also had to get leave to speak. Abruptly, he took in the gaoler,

"Who is sitting court tomorrow?"

Rocking back on his heels considering, the gaoler, began to count on his finger.

"Let's see, last week it was Johnson, so this is the second week of the month so it must be, ah yes, tomorrow is Cruise, Lord Cruise I believe."

Ciarán let his head drop in relief. This was the best piece of luck possible. Lord Cruise had occasionally hunted with Ciarán's uncle. Why, he may have even seen Fiona working with the hounds. Please God he hadn't been there the day Ambrose had been shot. It was in their favour; It had to be in their favour. He dug in his pocket and handed the gaoler another shilling.

"I want her washed and made presentable. I'm sure you have a wife, or some woman that can help her. Clean clothes would be desirable, and, gaoler, if she's dead in the morning, you can expect the same fate yourself." With that he scooped up Farley and stood next to the bars, "Fiona, I'll be here tomorrow and then I'll take you home with me, back to Glenties. Get yourself ready

295

lass. Farley will be waiting for you." But the heap in the centre of the cell did not respond.

Ciarán secured himself a room at an inn and made sure Conall was well stabled, fed and properly rested. Farley was fed a sumptuous meal as Ciarán had only picked at his supper. Alarmingly, Farley didn't show much of an appetite either, so the inn dog did quite well on scraps that night. Unable to sleep, Ciarán planned out his testimony and counted the cash. He would probably have to bribe someone to allow him to speak, or could he just stand up in court and declare himself a witness? He had only ever observed cases regarding land disputes, nothing of a criminal nature. However, he did know he had to look like a person of property in order to be listened to, that he had to be fully the nephew of William McGovern. He sent for some hot water and a clothes brush and managed to tidy both himself, and his clothes. He polished his boots and then waited.

He was at the courthouse before anyone else. Farley had accompanied Ciarán but then slipped off to make a quick circuit of the neighbourhood. Ciarán was not worried about the dog; he knew Farley would return for Fiona. When the first clerk arrived, keys in hand to open the courthouse, Ciarán intercepted him.

"Is the case of Lieutenant Distaff being heard today?" The clerk sighed and shuffled his papers.

"It is," he returned to the door, but Ciarán grabbed at the sleeve of his coat.

"I was a witness to the crime. I need to make a statement," Ciarán felt in his pocket for a coin. Would a bribe be required here?

"That is up to the magistrate to decide," the clerk intoned, pulling his sleeve away from Ciarán.

"But you can tell him there is a witness that would like to make a statement?" Ciarán followed the clerk as he tried to move away. He realised he was quite a bit taller than the clerk and hopefully, just a bit intimidating.

"I can," the clerk looked to Ciarán's pocket.

Ciarán dropped a shilling in the clerk's own pocket. The money was going fast.

"I would be most grateful," he added.

The clerk nodded and turned to go, adding over his shoulder.

"You may wait inside. The judge won't be here for some time, but you are welcome." This encouraged Ciarán greatly. Following the clerk, he looked around for Farley but there was no sign of him. Surely the dog would reappear when needed.

The court was called to session at eleven o'clock, giving Ciarán plenty of time to review his speech and worry over each word. It would now be his word against the Lieutenant's. He knew the magistrate distantly but perhaps the magistrate was a drinking companion of Distaff's; perhaps they played cards together? No, Ciarán thought, Distaff was too crude for Lord Cruise. Cruise was a cultured man who preferred the company of intellectuals. He was a Protestant though. That would stand in Distaff's favour. Ciarán would have to begin by introducing himself as William McGovern's nephew and rely on the fact that Lord Cruise had enjoyed hunts with McGovern and had admired the distinctive hounds of the McGovern pack. Hadn't Lord Cruise even asked for a breeding pair? Surely the girl who cared for those hounds had to have some value.

Having arrived early, Ciarán was in the front row of benches, so it would be easy enough to stand and ask permission to speak. The room had begun to fill around half-ten as there were other cases to be heard first, land disputes, quarrels over cattle ownership, even dissension over dowries. Lord Cruise was obviously bored and at around one o'clock called a recess. Ciarán ground his teeth in frustration. He would not leave the court and lose his prime location, so he returned to his seat after all had risen on the magistrate's departure. As the crowd cleared for refreshment and to stretch their legs, a figure slipped into the seat next to Ciarán.

"I saw the dog waiting out front, so I knew you were here," Liam said. "Have you seen her?"

Ciarán nodded grimly.

"I got into the gaol last night. Thank you for the coin. It has proved useful."

"How is she?"

"Poorly used." His lips set in a firm line and Liam knew to ask no more.

"We know Lord Cruise; he rides at the hunt with us from time to time." Ciarán nodded in agreement. "That will help surely. Shall I testify as well?"

Ciarán gripped his cousin's arm in gratitude.

"That is good of you Liam, but it would anger your father to no end, and you didn't actually see what happened."

"Did you?"

"I saw enough. I saw enough to make me want to gut the man. He won't get away with this, one way or the other."

"Be careful cousin. We haven't had much success in our encounters with the army." Liam instantly regretted the remark. It wouldn't do to remind Ciarán of Donal's death and Kathleen's descent into grief.

Ciarán swore under his breath.

"This time is different. Thank you for your help Liam, but it is probably best if you aren't seen here – the less you have to explain to your father the better."

Liam handed Ciarán a package.

"These are her things. I went to her room by the kennels. There wasn't much there but the book looked important. I haven't any bank notes, but you can have this," he slipped a gold ring from his little finger and handed it to Ciarán.

"Your signet ring?"

"I'm not too proud of my family right now. Get it pawned. I'll retrieve it someday. Good luck Ciarán. Send me word when all is well." He stood up and Ciarán rose as well. The cousins embraced and then Liam left the court, hoping he would not need to return to see his cousin before a magistrate as well.

At half-three, sated from a roast lamb dinner and a rather fine Bordeaux, Lord Cruise settled heavily into his chair. The courthouse was now full, as criminal cases were good entertainment. Ciarán had observed Distaff striding down the aisle to take a front seat, oblivious to Ciarán's presence, which was all for the better. Distaff was seated with another soldier and the two seemed in a jovial mood. Ciarán thought he might be fracturing a molar as he struggled to keep from confronting Distaff directly.

Lord Cruise knocked with his gavel on his desk and sleepily murmured, "Bring the accused forward." From a back room, there was the rattle of metal and Fiona was dragged forward, her hands in chains. Someone had brushed her hair and plaited it and there was a sense that her face had been perhaps wiped with a wet cloth. She was wearing a clean apron over her torn and stained dress but there was no hiding the bruising to her face and the swollen eye. She was deposited in the witness stand. Ciarán risked a glance at Distaff. He was pleased to see the Lieutenant looking a bit uneasy. Didn't realise his handiwork would have such an effect, did he? Fiona looked forlorn and lost, a beaten creature, not a homicidal whore.

The bible was brought forward, and Fiona asked to swear on it. The judge had to ask her to speak up as her weak responses were inaudible. Ciarán wondered if she had lost a tooth, as he thought he heard an unfamiliar sibilance in her speech. He leaned forward, urging her to put some energy into her self-defence.

The magistrate consulted his notes.

"Your name is Fiona," there was a brief hesitation, "*Madra*?" That is an unusual surname. *Madra* – Irish for dog; Ciarán had never known Fiona's surname, or if she even had one. It seemed Listeners chose the species of their acolyte as a surname. It made sense to Ciarán, if not to Lord Cruise.

"And you were employed by William McGovern as his kennel maid?" Fiona nodded.

"You must answer verbally young lady," the judge commanded.

Fiona coughed and a small voice managed, "Yes."

"Were you working there last week, on Wednesday the 16th of April?" Fiona started to nod but corrected herself.

"I was in the kennels then."

"Lieutenant Distaff says that you had arranged to meet him there. When your 'tryst' was

300

enacted, you attempted to pick his pocket and when he discovered your attempt, you stabbed him with a knife you had kept especially about your person."

That's not what happened!" This was the first spark of life Ciarán had seen and inwardly he cheered Fiona on.

"Can you tell us what happened then? Remember Miss *Madra*, that it is your word against a respected Lieutenant of the British army." Ciarán dearly wanted to spit but kept control.

Fiona finally lifted her head and turned her battered face on Distaff. She stared at him for a discomfiting long time. If anyone believed in witches, they would surely believe she was laying a curse on him now.

"I was going into to clean the kennels," she spoke directly to the magistrate, "for those hounds you so admired." Ah, she had recognized the Lord Cruise and now he would have to take that into account. "The Lieutenant," she disdained to say his name, "came into the kennel and grabbed hold of me in a ..." there was a long pause and then in a cracked voice, "in an unwholesome way." She paused and the court hung on her words, willing her to sob. It was great drama. "I carry a knife for me work. It was in me pocket as always and I used it because I was afraid."

The magistrate turned to Distaff, "What do you have to say to this Lieutenant?"

Distaff waved his hand dismissively,

"All lies of course. She's a dirty, country whore. What do you expect?"

The magistrate examined Fiona, considering her bruises.

"Why has the girl been beaten Lieutenant Distaff?" he raised his eyebrows in interest.

Distaff had the intelligence to look slightly embarrassed. He cleared his throat,

"Resisting arrest, your honour."

The magistrate furrowed his brow.

"Can you stand up Distaff?" The loss of title was duly noted by Ciarán. Distaff stood cautiously, not sure what the magistrate had in mind. "You're a big man, Lieutenant, and you had other men with you?" The magistrate looked at his papers. "Yes, two privates. So, it took three grown men to subdue this young lady? She must be quite a fighter."

Distaff had regained his composure.

"Which is why I have arrested her. She is a dangerous person and does not belong in the household of a fine gentleman like Mr. McGovern." It was at this point that Ciarán chose to stand and make his case.

"If you'll excuse me, your honour," all eyes turned to Ciarán, and Distaff cursed, not quite softly enough. "I am from the McGovern household. Mr. William McGovern is my uncle, and I am representing his interests in court today. You see, your honour, this 'dirty, country,' girl is a valuable member of the household, and we are quite sorry to see her abused in this fashion." Distaff went to interrupt, knowing that William McGovern had no problem with Fiona's presence in court, but Ciarán raised his voice and talked over him. "As a matter of fact, your honour, I was witness to the event being referred to, luckily arriving in time to extricate the poor lass from the grasp of Lieutenant Distaff. The Lieutenant, having his trousers around his ankles ..." there was a gasp from the assembled, "was at a disadvantage

302

and did not realise I had entered the kennels. I was fortunate to arrive before any real harm had been done. Lieutenant Distaff, was then invited to leave the premises."

Lord Cruise struggled to hide a smile.

"This is most interesting. And the knife, Mr, sorry, did you say your name sir?"

Ciarán was thankful that he had scrubbed up enough to be considered a 'sir.'

"Ciarán Gallagher, at your service," he nodded respectfully to the magistrate.

"Did you see the knife wound then, Mr. Gallagher?"

"I noticed a scratch sir. The lass, Fiona, does carry a small work knife, for cutting herbs. She does some simple remedies for the dogs."

"Not quite a murder weapon then?" Chuckled the magistrate, ceasing to hide his amusement.

"Only for a dandelion, your honour," at this point, the whole courthouse broke out in unstifled laughter.

The magistrate pointed his gavel at Distaff and admonished,

"You have wasted my time soldier. If you have need of a woman, there are plenty to hire. Now, drop this business before I have you prosecuted for contempt of court and perjury." Guffawing, he added in an undertone that was still loud enough for most to hear, "Turned down by a country whore. That must hurt his pride!" The magistrate waved at the bailiff. "Release the prisoner to Mr. Gallagher. He can be responsible for the dandelion killer." With a further chuckle, the magistrate slammed down his gavel, 'Court adjourned,' was announced and the assembled rose as the honourable Lord Cruise left the room.

There was a clang, as the manacles hit the floor and Ciarán stepped forward to take Fiona from the witness stand. She clung to his arm but when she looked up into his face, it was Farley she asked for.

"He's waiting for you, out front."

Fiona squeezed his arm,

"We must hurry."

"Why? All is well, you are free."

"Please Ciarán, we must hurry." He didn't understand but half leading her, half carrying her he moved down the aisle with her to the door. The knot of people was starting to clear but Distaff stood at the front of the building, loudly declaiming the injustice he had endured. Farley was smart enough to remain hidden from the Lieutenant, but Fiona could feel the growling reverberating through her entire frame. She tried to quicken her step and push through the assemblage. Then Farley was at her feet, leaping up to lick her hand and she crouched down to squeeze him tightly against her chest. Lifting him, with what little strength she had left, she urged Ciarán to leave the crowd.

It was then that the onlookers began to hear the growling as well. Dogs seemed to appear from everywhere, side streets, back gardens, open doorways, stalking straight towards their prey, Lieutenant Distaff. Fiona pulled at Ciarán, "Can't you see? Farley has told them. We have to go, or they will think I made this happen. I didn't. I swear I didn't. I was too weak to call them." Ciarán thought she must be feverish from her ordeal. What was Fiona talking about? Until the first dog attached, and then it became clear. The dogs, poor dumb animals, with no voice of their own, valued a Listener. A Listener was precious and must be protected and revenged. But the citizenry would blame Fiona, labelling her a witch and she would be tried as a murderer, for surely Distaff was in the process of being torn to bits by a pack of very angry dogs. Ciarán scooped up Fiona and they ran, Farley following. It wasn't far to Conall's stable and from there they would flee.

Farley was wrapped into Fiona's shawl, and her small packet of belongings was tied onto the saddle.

"Are you able to hold on or are you better sitting in front of me?" Ciarán wasn't sure when Fiona had last eaten and beneath the bruises, her colour was worrisome. There was no time now, but he would have to get her to an inn and get some food in her, maybe a warm bath and some clean clothes.

"Maybe in front today," she had to admit and then winced as Ciarán hoisted her into the saddle.

She had always ridden astride – it was safer, but today it was painful, and a horrible reminder of what had been done to her. She leaned forward onto Conall's neck, asking the horse for some of his strength. Conall whinnied in distress and Farley growled. Farley desperately wished he could have joined in with the pack to rip his revenge from Distaff's skin, but his duty was with Fiona now. He had to see her safe.

"What's wrong Fiona," Ciarán touched her leg lightly and she recoiled. "I'm sorry, love, what's wrong?"

Fiona just shook her head,

"I'm fine," she gasped. "Let's go, please. I have to get away from here." Clearly, she wasn't fine, but Ciarán could understand her desire to put distance between herself and all that

305

happened to her – whatever had happened. He could see that she had been beaten but that alone could not be responsible for the broken spirit in his terrier-like lass. He mounted Conall and carefully placed his arms around Fiona as he reached for the reins.

"Is that alright?" he asked. He didn't know if it was hurting her physically or mentally. He could feel her stiffening at his touch and was beginning to suspect that Distaff had hurt her in more ways than with his fist. The thought made bile rush into his mouth, and he had to swallow quickly to prevent retching. "Would you rather hold the reins Fi?"

Again, she shook her head, then managed a reply,

"I'm holding Farley."

"Of course, you are and he's well glad of that. The poor wee fella nearly went mad with missing you."

"Thank you," Fiona croaked.

"No need love. Couldn't keep him yipping and barking forever. Now, you tell me when you've had enough. I'll try to get some miles away, but I'd like to find an inn for you to get some food and a rest before it gets too late."

"Just go please!" Fiona insisted again. "Ride all night. Just get me away from here!" So, Ciarán pressed his heels into Conall's side and off they went at a brisk trot. As soon as they were clear of the town, Conall broke into a gallop, only slowing to a canter when Letterkenny was beyond their sight.

It was not possible to travel all night as Fiona fainted after a few hours of riding. Ciarán felt her slipping at the same time as Conall and did not need to direct the horse to stop. He shook her lightly, but she only came to semi-consciousness, groggily insisting that they continue their journey, but Ciarán could not hold the girl up right and navigate the dark roads. He reached for Farley, motioning to Conall to bow, and slipped Farley onto the ground so he could not fall from the full height of the horse. Proceeding at a walk, Ciarán began to look for any sort of habitation where they could rest till morning. He was not sure if Fiona needed a doctor or just food and a bed, but he knew they could not continue any further.

After another thirty minutes or so along the road he saw the light of a dwelling and turned up a dirt track towards a cabin. As they approached, a farm dog came barking in protest but a quick retort from Farley quieted the other dog. Ciarán was afraid to leave Fiona on Conall so lifted her down as soon as he had dismounted himself. He carried her to the cabin door, which, in response to the dog barking, had opened a crack.

"Please," Ciarán begged, "My sister has taken ill, and we are too far from home to get there tonight."

The man at the door began to press it shut,

"I'll have no fever in my house, I have children here that could take sick," but Ciarán had pressed his boot into the doorway.

"It's not fever! She fell from the horse," that would at least explain the bruises, "I think she must have taken a knock to the head. Please sir, I just need a place for her to rest till morning." By this time, a woman, wrapped in her shawl against the chill of the night had appeared at the door alongside her husband. She had a candle in her hand and got a glimpse of Fiona's face.

"Oh, for the love of God, look at the state of the poor child! Come in out of the cold now," she elbowed her husband out of the way with a well-practiced movement and led Ciarán indoors. "Now you put her there on our bed. The husband can sit by the fire, and I'll take the bench tonight, though I don't know what we'll do with you. I suppose if you're her brother you can share a bed this one night." She eyed Ciarán, with his height and dark hair compared to the small stature of Fiona and her reddish plait. "You are sure you're her brother?" she narrowed her eyes at Ciarán.

Ciarán cleared his throat,

"Different mothers."

The woman of the house nodded, only somewhat mollified.

"Well, it's neither here nor there at the moment. Put her on the bed and I'll sort her out while you're settling the horse. There's a bit of a stable around the back." Two small boys had by now slipped out of their trundle bed and were viewing the evening's entertainment with interest. Without turning, the woman hissed at them and had them scuttling back to bed. Ciarán offered his gratitude and went towards the door.

"The dog," he pointed to Farley, "Stays with her at all times. Don't try to interfere with him. He knows what's best for her." He got a look of alarm from the good wife, but he did not elaborate. She could think what she wanted. He couldn't separate the dog and girl at this point.

When Ciarán returned, he found that the woman of the house, now introduced as Mrs. Boylan had removed Fiona's outer clothes and wrapped her in what few blankets were available in the house. She had broth that she was trying to spoon into Fiona's mouth but most of it was dribbling out of slack lips. Ciarán received a hard look.

"She's near delirious. Are you sure it's not a fever? She feels well hot to me." Ciarán sunk down on the floor beside Fiona and took the unresponsive girl's hand.

"I don't know what ails her," Ciarán whispered. He noted Farley, sitting at Fiona's feet. "Do you know mate?" Mrs. Friel shook her head. The lad was obviously touched in the head, talking to a dog like that.

"Have some soup and get some rest, it's late." She handed him the bowl from which she had been trying to feed Fiona. "You can send for the doctor in the morning if need be." She kicked her husband's booted foot aside and pulled a bench closer to the fire. "I'm right here if you need me." She heard rustling from the two boys, as they sat up to watch their mother arranging the bench to her satisfaction, "And I've my eye on you lot," she warned.

Ciarán had fallen asleep next to the bed that Fiona and Farley had slept on. He hadn't dared get in it during the night as he was well aware of Mrs. Friel's disapproval and didn't want to startle Fiona. As a result, he was very stiff in the morning and was only slowly able to get to his feet, while rubbing his twisted neck. Fiona opened her eyes, looked at him for a moment and then reached for Farley, who crawled up to the top of the bed and lay across her chest. Ciarán could hear the rest of the household rising – the fire being stoked, and the sound of the bench being pushed back into place. In a moment, Mrs. Friel had lit a candle and appeared at the bedside.

"Well, she's not dead then," she remarked. "Will you take a cup of tea lass?" The boys were up now as well and peering at the strangers. Their mother cuffed one fondly and told him to go fetch some water. "We haven't got much in, but you are welcome to what we have," she encouraged Ciarán to take a seat at the bench by the table and went to a cupboard for a half loaf of bread and a few smears of butter. "There's jam as well," she offered, producing another chipped bowl with what looked like a spoonful left of jam."

"I wouldn't take food from your children," though his stomach rumbled, Ciarán was aware that there might not be anything else in Mrs. Friel's kitchen. "A cup of tea would do us rightly, I'm sure."

Mrs. Friel shrugged and hung the kettle over the fire, shoved her husband, still snoring in his chair,

"Will you ever get up and milk the cow?" she addressed her beloved. Mr. Friel wiped his face with his hand, as if trying to erase whatever dreams had beguiled him in the night. It was another morning of reality and chores beckoned.

Nodding at Fiona, who was struggling to sit up, Mrs Friel asked,

"What are you going to do about that one?"

"Get her home. It's not far now. She'll be well enough to travel the distance." Ciarán wasn't sure this was true but if he took Conall at a walk, he could hold tight to Fiona. Farley would have to travel on the ground but could easily keep up with a walking pace. Mrs. Friel snorted at his reply but did not attempt to dissuade him. She was a generous woman, but there was very little she had to give. Strangers could lead to trouble as well. Best they were out of her home as soon as possible.

Fiona did manage to get to the table and murmur some thanks to Mrs. Friel. The milk was brought in and the tea wet. There were only three cups, two of which were offered to the guests. Mrs. Friel took the other, ostensibly to share with her husband but he seemed unconcerned and taking his slice of loaf, slightly buttered, went to sit by the fire. The two boys shared the rest of the loaf and jam and when Mrs. Friel's cup was free, she filled it with milk for the two boys to share. Throughout their meals, they stared intently at Ciarán and Fiona.

"You have a big white horse sir," the elder of the lads finally piped up.

Ciarán smiled at him.

"Aye, I do. His name is Conall, and he is quite fierce. I hope you did not go too near him. He likes to bite off the nose from wee lads." The younger boy looked horrified, but the elder was slightly sceptical.

"I'd be too fast for him," he boasted.

"Oh, I don't know about that. Conall is very fast. But I don't think he will bite your nose off today. You have done Fiona here a kindness and Conall is ever so fond of Fiona."

The boys turned their attention to Fiona, who really was much less interesting than the tall, young man, dressed as a gentleman.

"She's too small to ride that big horse," the youngest finally declaimed. "She can't get up that high."

"This is true," Ciarán agreed, "But Conall loves her so much, he will kneel down so that she can reach up and climb into the saddle."

"Really?" breathed the boys in unison. "How does she make him do that? Is she a *Cailleach*?"

311

Mrs. Friel interrupted then, smacking the nearest boy with the back of her hand,

"Such a thing to say! And to a guest! Apologise right now, the both of you and then clear off out of my way before I tan your backsides." She turned to Ciarán, red enough in the face with embarrassment that he realised she had the same thought as her boys.

Fiona stood up slowly,

"I am no *Cailleach*. I am no witch. I listen. There is no evil in that. The animals tell me their stories and I listen." Mrs. Friel nodded.

"I have heard of such women. That is why you have the dog. A Listener is a grand thing to have about. Your lot have saved many a family by curing their cow or sheep. I am glad that we were able to help you this last night."

And now you would like us to leave Ciarán heard in the woman's voice. It was one thing to have a cunning woman give you a remedy, another to have her stay in your home. The supernatural was something powerful, and therefore something fearful. Mrs. Friel would like it well away from her lads.

"We thank you for your help in our time of need," Ciarán put a few coppers on the table to show his appreciation.

"There is no need, Sir!" Mrs Friel exclaimed, while simultaneously sliding the coins into her apron pocket. "The Lord has asked us to never turn away a stranger in need."

There was nothing more to be said so Ciarán gathered their few belongings and took Fiona's arm. Conall was waiting impatiently in the stall. Fiona rested in the straw while Ciarán saddled and bridled Conall, then, as predicted, Conall bowed low so that Fiona could mount, followed by Ciarán.

The boys had watched this demonstration from afar and were duly impressed. Ciarán raised his hand to them, and the two children waved warily, hoping their mother did not see them.

Weakened by both lack of food and her incarceration, Fiona leaned heavily on Ciarán, and it was hard work to keep her upright in the saddle. He wanted to stop for food but also felt compelled to get to his brother's house and a permanent stopping place as soon as possible. His own overwhelming hunger finally forced him to stop at a farmhouse where he purchased an insubstantial pie which he split between himself and Farley, Fiona saying she was unable to eat. She had always had a healthy appetite, so this behaviour alarmed him even further. The girl felt feverish but there was more to her malaise. He hoped Kathleen and Maire would be able to discern the problem. He wasn't even sure he would be welcome at home but at the moment, he could not think of anything beyond begging for their help.

Part Three: Water

Power of river, lake, and sea,

Cleanse and nourish me.

Glenties, County Donegal

Once Ciarán had placed Fiona's body on the bed, they shoved him out of the room and went to work.

"First we'll be rid of these clothes. They smell like the devil, and I imagine they are crawling with lice," Maire declared as she began to unwind the ragged shawl and undo the bodice of Fiona's dress. She was startled by a low growl from the floor and then Farley leapt on the bed and stood over Fiona's body, teeth flashing impressively.

"Dear God! Where did this creature come from? Ciarán! Come back here this minute!" Ciarán, who was only standing by the door, leaning against the wall, was back in the room immediately.

"Ah, that's Farley. No worries. He's just protecting her." Farley relaxed slightly but stood his ground. "It's no use Maire, I'll have to stay. He doesn't know you."

"You will not stay! We have to undress her! Just take that varmint out of here now!"

Ciarán shook his head.

"I can't. She needs him. I'm sure she'd sicken more if she couldn't feel him beside her. Besides, I'd lose a few fingers if I tried to budge the creature. Go on with your work. I'll avert my eyes. Though, remember, I shared a cabin with this *cailín*. It's not like she had it very private then."

There was a sharp intake of breath from Maire and a weak smile from Kathleen.

"That was different," Maire insisted. "You were an invalid, and she was acting as a servant."

Ciarán shrugged tiredly.

"Nevertheless, I'm not able to move the dog and he won't let you near Fiona unless I'm here to mind him. Please, just do something for her now." He sank down on the bed next to Fiona and Farley and took Fiona's hand in his. With the other hand, he reached out to Farley in what Ciarán hoped was a pacifying gesture.

The clothes were eventually bustled off and being, accurately described as crawling, were thrown in the fire downstairs. Kathleen returned with a bowl of warm water and soap and the two women gently bathed Fiona, combed the nits out of her hair and dressing her in a clean nightgown. Ciarán had retreated to a chair in the corner of the room and had begun to doze off. Farley having agreed to sit in Ciarán's lap, sat up straight and kept an eye on the proceedings.

"The blood," Kathleen whispered. Maire nodded, tight lipped. "Could it have been her courses?"

"With the scratches and bruises as well? The poor child has been raped."

"Not by Ciarán!"

"Of course not, you eejit! He's a fool and a *gombeen* but he's not wicked. We don't know what happened to the poor thing. We'll have to ask your man when he's awake. I'll get some tea for the fever and a bone for the dog. Maybe if he's gnawing on a bone, he'll look less like taking a bite out of one of us."

"What are you going to tell John?"

"As little as possible. We certainly can't turn them away this time. There're no soldiers involved, as far as we know, and we do owe the girl. She cared for Ciarán when he was poorly and did the job well enough. Now, get a room ready for your

320

brother and we'll feed him and put him to bed as well. Off you go."

Kathleen gave a long look to the bruised body lying on the bed and then to the dog, taunt with protection. Farley lifted his eyes to Kathleen and the intense stare was both unnerving and exciting. She felt the dog reading her, as another human might.

"Don't worry doggy," she chirped nervously, "We'll look after your mistress," and then felt abashed. This wasn't a 'doggy' she was addressing.

John was not pleased when he heard the whole story.

"But she was cleared John!" Ciarán shouted. "The judge declared her innocent and told the Lieutenant to mind his manners." Maire and Kathleen exchanged looks. Did Ciarán know all of what had happened to Fiona? Kathleen stood up from the table.

"I'll just go up and sit with her. I only came down to get a bite to eat."

"You can stay put Kathleen. I'll sit with her," Ciarán pushed himself angrily away from the table and turned to go.

"You will do no such thing!" John bellowed. "Go on Kathleen. Your brother and I have somethings to discuss."

"Well then," I'll help Betty with clearing away the dinner things," Maire offered and, gathering some plates, hurried from the room.

The two brothers glowered at each other.

"Where is the Lieutenant now?" John finally asked.

"As always, just worried where you stand with the militia," Ciarán sneered.

"I don't share your disregard for the safety and wellbeing of our family."

"Well, you've no worries regarding Lieutenant Distaff. He's dead."

"What?"

"He's dead," Ciarán said brightly, "And it wasn't a very pleasant death either from what I saw of it." Nonchalantly, Ciarán reached for another slice of bread and carefully buttered it.

John reached across the table and gripped Ciarán's wrist hard enough to make the bread fall back to the plate.

"Did you have anything to do with it?" he demanded.

Ciarán sighed.

"No brother, much as I would have liked to, I had nothing whatsoever to do with it. The man was attacked by a pack of dogs and torn to pieces. A fitting end in my opinion."

"And you saw this?"

"Oh yes. As we were leaving the trial, the demon himself was right behind us, muttering how he'd see to Fiona by and by and then he stepped off into the street and dogs started appearing from every corner and crevice, behind buildings, under stairs, even one out a window and they just set upon him. Someone fired a gun to break up the pack, but the dogs took no notice. Fiona asked me to leave then as she was afraid, she'd be blamed for the dogs' attack, though it was no doing of hers of course. She'd been in gaol the whole time."

"And why would she be blamed?" asked John, finally releasing his brother but still eyeing him suspiciously.

"You know she has a way with animals. You heard how she was with Conall. Why, he's like a kitten with her. She has a gift," Ciarán drew back from his brother, leaning his chair away from the table. "She's a special *cailín*," he shrugged and half-smiled.

John slammed the table with his fist,

"You bloody eejit! You're smitten with her! A back-country girl with no training, no manners, and no money! What about Gráinne? Please God don't tell me you've broken it off with her? You can go back to Uncle right now and let her know that all is well. Does she know you've run after this *culchie* and sprung her from gaol?"

"I imagine, they all know at Ballybofey. She was only taken to Letterkenny, not Londonderry. As for Gráinne, I have said nothing to her and have nothing to say to her. I never loved her. You know it was all arranged by Uncle so he could get control over the bit of property adjoining his."

"And so, you could get some property and some land to work! Without that, you have nothing. How ridiculous can you be? Are you really going to throw away any chance at getting on in the world for a strange girl just down from the hills? And she's damaged goods you know. She's been raped, Maire says."

Ciarán felt all the breath leave his body. Raped. Of course. Lieutenant Distaff. No wonder Fiona was so fragile when he found her in the gaol. And now so ill. If Distaff were still alive, he'd fight off the dogs so he could tear the man apart himself.

Ciarán stood up, stiff with tension and deaf to his brother's insistence that he return. He felt as if he was no longer in his body, watching it move from hall to stairs. Slowly, he climbed the steps to the room where Fiona lay. When he entered, Farley was laying at the foot of the bed; Kathleen was doing some crocheting in the chair by the window, a single candle sitting on the sill.

It was long moments before he found his voice,

"Kathleen, let me sit with her a bit."

Gathering her things, Kathleen looked into her brother's stricken face.

"Bloody John! Maire shouldn't have told him." She laid her hand on Ciarán's arm. "She's quite settled now, and I think the fever is dropping. We'll get her well in body. You and that beast, she nodded at Farley, will have to see to her soul."

Slipping out of the room, she heard her brother kneel by the bed and begin to sob. She shut the door softly.

Fiona gave into the fever and travelled with the delirium back in time. She was with Nan, curled by the fire and Nan was telling her the story of the twelve brothers that were turned into wild geese, but their sister turned them back by knitting each brother a jumper made from bog-down. Then she was by the loch, holding her mother's hand and waving good-bye to Ban. She was in the Nugent barn, meeting Farley for first time; she was riding Conall, fast and furious over the fields and leaping high over the stone fences. She was in Ciarán's arms, dancing at the Christmas Ball and then, even in the fever she remembered that Ciarán would never want her again. She turned towards the dark, and moved down the long tunnel, deeper and deeper, and Ciarán sitting by her bed heard her breath become weaker and weaker.

Suddenly, Farley leapt from the bottom of the bed onto Fiona's chest and began licking her face furiously. Ciarán rushed to remove him, thinking the weight of the dog would make it entirely impossible for her to breathe but Farley snarled at him. Pawing at Fiona's face, Farley called to her, finally leaning over, and nipping her ear, hard enough to draw blood. There was a gasp from Fiona and Farley stepped off her chest and then lay pressed, tight against her side. From far away, Fiona felt the warmth of him squeezed alongside her and she let him pull her back up the tunnel, up and into the light.

Fiona woke in the morning to find Ciarán sitting beside the bed, her hand in his. She made a move to retract her hand, but he gripped her tightly, preventing escape. She just wanted to roll over and wrap herself around Farley, leaving Ciarán till she felt stronger. She had had to rely on Ciarán to get her free from gaol, but she should no longer detain him. She could go up to the hills above Maghera and see if any of the goat herd were still about. Maybe Nan's cabin would still be empty. She would go home and pretend that nothing in the last year had ever happened.

Finally, feeling her insistent tug away, Ciarán released her hand. She rolled onto her side, turning her back to him. As soon as she was well enough, she would leave. It would be best for both of them. Ciarán could go back to Ballybofey and marry Gráinne. He would have some land and a future. She would go back to where she came from. She might even visit the loch and look for her mother. If wild geese could turn back into brothers, maybe a swan could become her mother again.

She felt Ciarán lay his hand on her shoulder and begin to tenderly rub her back. She pulled her knees up to her chest and made herself as small as possible. He needed to leave her alone. She couldn't bear him being kind to her. Not after what had happened. He would be disgusted if he knew.

325

"It's alright *cailín*. I know what happened to you," the voice came out, cracked and broken with a night of tears. She clenched her fists tightly and pressed her nails into her palms, pulling herself into an even tighter ball. Farley grunted and stood up, tail quivering in anxiety.

Ciarán reached to stroke her hair. Kathleen had unplaited it to comb out the lice. He threaded his fingers between the strands and held a hank of Fiona's hair in his palm.

"I've always loved your hair. So many colours and so unusual. Just like you. *Mo mhirín di'lis*, my one true love."

She started to cry then, tears running down her cheeks, first silently then in weak, gasping sobs. He continued to stroke her hair, murmuring softly, as if soothing a nervous filly.

"I won't leave you. You will not have to do this alone. I'm here. I'm so sorry I wasn't there to protect you. I should have known he would come back. I should have been there, but I am here now, and I am not going to leave you again."

She could not turn back to him. She wept until exhausted and slept again.

The next time Fiona woke, Kathleen was there, with a steaming bowl of broth. She placed a tray on a cabinet beside the bed, plumped up the pillows and encouraged Fiona to sit up. Gingerly, Fiona moved herself into a sitting position, but the room swam, and she had to close her eyes to prevent a wave of nausea.

"Here," Kathleen slid her arm behind Fiona's back and supported her. "Let me help you. I'm Kathleen by the way, Ciarán's sister." Kathleen got Fiona propped up and then lifted the bowl, filling a spoon and offering it to Fiona. "Try to take a wee bit *girseach*, you need some food in you to get better."

Opening her mouth like a young bird, Fiona allowed Kathleen to spoon in the broth but only managed a few mouthfuls, then raised her hand in a gesture begging Kathleen to stop. Kathleen acquiesced, setting aside the bowl and then re-settling Fiona in a prone position.

"You rest now. I'll be sitting over by the window so I can see to do my crocheting. If you need me at all, I'll be right there. You don't need the pot or anything now, do you?" Fiona shook her head weakly and Kathleen pulled the chair over to the window. "Ciarán will be up in a bit. He's going to take your wee dog outside. It won't leave the room otherwise. Will I give the dog this broth?" The figure on the bed whispered 'yes' almost inaudibly. Kathleen placed the bowl on the floor, much to Farley's pleasure. He jumped off the bed and polished off the remains of the meal. Then he walked up to Kathleen and licked her hands once in thanks. He hadn't had a hot meal in days.

Kathleen gave a startled laugh and then reached out to the dog. He allowed her to find the spot behind his ears and scratch it thoroughly.

"Ah, you're a lovely lad, aren't you? A great comfort to your mistress, I'm sure." Kathleen noticed Fiona opening her eyes and watching her, so she continued. "And you helped her take care of my brother Ciarán, didn't you, when he was poorly? I thank you for that wee man. Ciarán's my baby brother and I do love him dearly. I'm very grateful that you helped care for him. So grateful, I'm going to ask Betty to save you some bones. I will so. Would you like that pup?"

"His name is Farley," Fiona spoke from the bed. Kathleen sat up, turning her attention from the dog to her patient.

"Is that so? It's '*Faircheallaigh*' in Irish, isn't it? She saw Fiona nod slightly. "What made you choose the name Farley?"

"Me nan chose it. She said she'd a good nanny goat from a bloke called Farley and she had always liked the sound of the name." She paused. "The English is easier to call out over the fields than the Irish."

"True enough," Kathleen agreed. "Oh, I almost forgot," Kathleen jumped up and pulled out a bundle from the cabinet by the bed. "Your things are here. Is there anything you want me to get out for you?" Fiona reached for the bag and felt for Nan's book. She pulled it out and smoothed the cover with her hand and then clutched the book to her chest. Would Nan have known a remedy for the pain she felt now?

Kathleen patted the hand gripping the book.

"What's in your book Fiona?"

"It's me nan's. Her recipe book."

"Recipe? Oh yes, her healing book. Do you want me to look for something to help you now?"

Fiona shook her head.

"I don't think she made a recipe for this."

"For pain?" Kathleen sat back in the chair and sighed. "There's plenty for physical pain but not much for heart pain. I know that well."

Fiona remembered Kathleen's loss and felt abashed. She was not the only one suffering.

Kathleen's voice came, brittle with anguish.

"You will survive. Each day you will wake up, surprised you can still put one foot in front of another, but you do. You go on. You live your life. You are a different person, but you do survive."

"I'm sorry," Fiona squeaked.

Kathleen looked out the window for a long time. She watched a magpie gripping a branch as the wind whipped it.

"Sure, we both are Fiona," she said.

A LISTENER IS A PRECIOUS THING

Kathleen had taken on the convalescence of Fiona as a personal mission and tended to the girl assiduously. Every morning she went into the room she had given over to Fiona and helped the girl wash and encouraged her to eat as much porridge as possible, generously offering a bowl to Farley as well. Ciarán would sit with Fiona a bit after breakfast, and then take Farley out for some fresh air before going onto his farm chores. Farley was required to return to the room as he did not have the gift for herding and preferred to jump up and hang off the woolly necks of the sheep. Ciarán was just grateful none of the flock had been fleeced yet or Farley would have killed at least three of them.

In the invalid's chamber, Kathleen sat and crocheted or sewed. She enjoyed the peace of the room, away from the shouting children and the bustle of the kitchen. She kept the fire going and offered Fiona cups of tea whenever she fancied one herself. At first, Fiona lay quietly in the bed, stroking Farley and saying very little. Kathleen was content to wait. Occasionally Kathleen chatted about the farm, or the baking that was being done that day, or how she hated washing day as the work was cold and lugging about the damp clothing and sheets made her arms ache. Now and again, she read to Fiona, but this was usually Ciarán's task when he came in from his chores of an evening. It was clear to Kathleen that Fiona was recovering her physical strength quickly, but that mentally she was only beginning to mend.

One day, when Kathleen was talking about one of the sheepdogs and how clever he was, Fiona volunteered that she'd like to meet the dog, although Farley snorted in disdain. He had already conversed with said sheepdog and found his one-track mind entirely boring. Kathleen explained that the sheepdogs weren't allowed in the house, but she was sure Fiona would be up and about soon and could introduce herself to the farm dogs. It was then that Fiona asked why they kept sheep and not goats. Encouraged that Fiona was engaging, Kathleen said she knew very little about goats and asked if Fiona could enlighten her. Hesitantly, Fiona began to talk of Billy and his herd, the big nannies, Jenny and Roisin, the way the kids leapt about and how much mischief they got into. She told Kathleen that she had to corral the kids away from the nannies when they were milked, or all the buckets would be turned over. She described how a weak kid would be taken into the cabin and fed milk sucked off a piece of cloth. They would wrap the kid in a blanket and put it in a box next to the fire trying to keep it warm. They were able to save many of them. One little kid, Fiona had named her Siobhán, had been terribly spoiled by living indoors and was always trying to butt her way back into the cabin. Fiona paused then. Kathleen cocked her head and encouraged Fiona to go on.

When they were playing up on the cliffs above the sea. Fiona would run up to the group of kids and then abruptly turn, so that the kids would pursue her. The young goats took the game so seriously, lowering their tiny heads with their budding horns and charging at her like miniature bulls. Farley was barking and the sea birds were shrieking overhead, and Fiona was laughing so hard her sides hurt. It was windy on top of the cliff and her hair flew all about her, blinding her from time to time but she swiped it out of her eyes and continued to race about. She could see their little cabin and the byre, Billy standing proud on the hill and looking out for Nan as she was foraging farther down towards the loch. She ran towards the kids again and then stopped abruptly; her skirts snagged in Farley's jaws as he pulled her away from the edge. Agile creatures, the kids were able to twist their lithe bodies away from the edge and trotted daintily towards safety, all except Siobhán. She had been nudged by one of her playmates as he turned, and she had slipped. She was gone. Fiona stood frozen, horrified, and then crept to the edge. There on the rocks lay the small body, crumpled into lifelessness. Fiona, a Listener, born to help animals had killed one of her charges out of her own carelessness. She could only imagine what Nan would say to her.

Fiona had been telling her tale with her head down, her fingers working the blanket on the bed. She looked up into Kathleen's face then.

"She was such a wee thing to hold something so big as death."

"I know," Kathleen said. She put aside her sewing and sat on the bed next to Fiona. "I know exactly." She put her arm around Fiona and pulled the girl's head to her shoulder. She felt Fiona shaking with silent sobs and let her own tears fall. She remembered the poem that Ciarán had learned to recite, "For the world's more full of weeping than you can understand," Kathleen murmured. Fiona gulped.

"Ciarán told me that poem."

Kathleen nodded.

"He learned it for school. I tell it to myself sometimes when I think of my baby. It's a comfort."

"Here I am making you cry!" Fiona exclaimed. "I'm ever so sorry."

"It's alright," Kathleen sighed, "tell me about keeping goats. I need some business of my own besides my sewing. I'd like to keep my own house again someday."

Fiona actually sat up all the way then and started telling Kathleen how easy goats were compared to sheep and that they were much more clever, and she could teach Kathleen how to milk them and make cheese. Kathleen vowed to start looking for a good nanny as soon as she sold some more crocheting and had a bit more money set by. Fiona promised to go with her to pick out a good milker. This is what Fiona needed, Kathleen realised, she needed to have something to look forward to, and it wouldn't do Kathleen any harm either.

It did not take much longer for Fiona to make her way downstairs and start to participate in the household. First, she was shy at meals, but Kathleen always asked her opinion and included her in discussions. There was much argument with John about bringing goats onto the farm. He felt he was busy enough with the sheep and Maire had her chickens. Kathleen explained that the goats would be her business, then Maire said Kathleen had enough to do with her sewing and helping with the children. Fiona almost volunteered to help with the goats but bit her tongue. She was only there till she was well enough to move on. She wasn't part of this family.

The children were curious about Fiona and fascinated by her relationship with the rough terrier that always seemed to be at her side. They asked her if her dog could do tricks and she told them he could do many tricks, but he was rarely in the mood. Seeing their disappointment, she called Farley to her and had him crawl across the floor on his belly. He enjoyed this activity as it scratched his tummy nicely, so he was not resistant to the performance. He looked so unusual though, crawling across the floor that the children dissolved into laughter and begged, 'Again, Again,' till Farley was tired and had to roll onto his side with a grunt.

Maire tried to involve Fiona in the household chores but found her an indifferent cleaner. Fiona had never ironed anything in her life and didn't see the point. As she gained strength, she was able to help with the washing, but as for cooking, it became patently clear that Fiona had very little skill in the kitchen as she spent half the time letting Farley taste the ingredients. Maire had hoped to train the young girl to be a decent wife for Ciarán, as he was obviously dead set on marriage to the odd young lady. However, Maire soon realized she did not have the patience or time to remodel Fiona into a housewife.

It was decided that Fiona should accompany Ciarán to help him with the farm work. She was content with this arrangement as she needed some time alone with Ciarán to sort things out. They went to one of the upper fields to check on the sheep. Many of them were in need of dagging and it was always a good idea to check for foot rot as well. The lambs had already been separated from their ewes and some had been sent to market, others being saved to augment the flock. Ciarán thought the work would be much easier with Fiona's help, hoping she could calm the sheep, skittish creatures at best, plain stupid at worst. Farley was a less welcome figure, the sheep being clearly frightened of a terrier but Bess, the family sheepdog was firm with the flock and had begun to round them into a smaller pen for examination.

It had rained earlier so the grass was wet and soon Fiona's skirts were damp. She wore no shoes and her feet reddened with the cold. There was a grey cloud cover that promised more rain later, with very little hope of seeing the sun. Still, you could hear a lapwing trilling across the grass, and the wind wasn't as cutting as it could be. There were worse days to be working outdoors.

Fiona could communicate with the sheep, though she found their conversation bordering on inane. She was used to the far superior intellect of goats and frequently made disparaging comments to Ciarán about the keeping of sheep.

"They are useful for wool," Ciarán remarked complacently. He wasn't bothered much either way, not being that interested in grazing livestock. It was horses he cared for. This was his brother's farm anyway, so any opinion Ciarán had was irrelevant. As soon as Fiona was well enough, they would marry, and she and Ciarán would go find work elsewhere. Being under his brother's yoke was not something Ciarán cared to continue indefinitely. Ciarán lifted an ewe up, presenting its backside to Fiona and with the heavy shearing scissors she hacked away at the matted wool, clotted with faeces and the occasional maggot.

"We got that one just in time," Ciarán remarked, "Check that there are no more maggots."

"I know that!" Fiona tossed back, reaching along the inside of the ewe's legs, and lifting the tail. "Clean." She wiped the shears on the grass and waited for the next ewe.

"Are you not feeling well?" Ciarán asked.

"I'm fine," Fiona retorted.

"Well, your temper's not."

Fiona put her hands on her hips and glared at Ciarán.

"Kathleen says that you've had the banns announced in the church."

"Aye, I have. They have to be announced three times before we can marry."

"What makes you think I want to get married?"

Ciarán slowly released the ewe he was holding and had the good sense to look embarrassed. He wiped his hands on his trousers and then tried a jocular tone.

"Well, my sister would like her room back to herself and we'd have to be married if we're to share a bed." Fiona continued to glare at him.
"I should have asked you first, I know, but I thought ... "

"You thought about what you wanted," she flared. "I never said anything about getting married."

"We had an understanding, before the arrest. Surely, that meant something to you!"

"That was before, everything is different now."

Ciarán shook his head and felt the muscle in his jaw leap as he ground his teeth together.

"Nothing is different. I still love you and you still love me."

"I'm different," Fiona said evenly.

Ciarán took a deep breath and walked over to the stone wall. He wanted to kick it but was able to resist that foolish act. Instead, He took a small stone off the top of the wall and threw it as far as he could, but it didn't help.

"I've given up everything to be with you. I had a position, I had land coming to me. My whole future was planned out and I put it all aside to chase after a girl with nothing! You didn't even own the clothes on your back. The only thing you have in the world is that dog," he flung out his arm at Farley, "Which I know you love much more than me, if you even love me at all. Why you're not even grateful to me for rescuing you! You're not happy to see me, you won't let me touch you. I did it all for nothing."

Fiona's mouth had dropped open but now she closed it tightly. She fisted her hands against her sides and shook with the contraction of her muscles. When she spoke, her voice was acid,

"I'm sorry to have gotten in the way of your plans. I never asked anything of you. I am grateful for the things you have done for me, but I never asked for any of it." With that, she ran to the gate and pulled it open, ignoring the rush of ewes behind her and the barking of the farm dog. Farley followed her and they ran down the hill, out of sight.

Ciarán thought about following her but then decided to let her go off and be with her dog, as that was obviously what she wanted. Roughly, he took hold of a nearby ewe and checked its feet and then under its tail. Damn, he couldn't do this job on his own. He'd have to get Kathleen to come up and cut away the matted bits under the ewe's tails. Calling the sheepdog, he stomped back to the house to collect his sister, who had the good sense not to question the reason for his foul mood. They worked steadily throughout the afternoon, Kathleen remarking that Fiona had mentioned goats as a good prospect for the farm. Ciarán's sullen answer was that Fiona didn't know everything about animals.

When they sat down to supper, Maire looked around and asked where Fiona was. Ciarán shrugged and reached for the mash. Kathleen slapped at his hands and whispered, "Grace," which John mumbled quickly so the men could begin eating. Maire was not satisfied though.

"Was she not working with you up at the sheep pasture Ciarán?" He shook his head, mouth full of the warm potatoes and butter. He gestured with his chin towards Kathleen, who looked perplexed. She hadn't realised she had been replacing Fiona.

"Do you have no idea where she is?" Maire continued, "She's still not strong. She needs to come eat her supper and be in the warm. I hope she's not in the barn with some sick animal while you're sitting here filling your gob."

"When did you become so fond of Fiona?" Ciarán countered. "I thought you figured her a quare, backward thing that was best out of your home as soon as possible."

Kathleen placed a restraining hand on his arm,

"That's not fair Ciarán. We just needed to get to know her. Now that we are more familiar, we love her like a sister, isn't that right?" Kathleen turned to the family gathered at the table. The children looked uneasily at their father, who grunted and avoided his wife's eyes. Maire did surprise Ciarán though.

"I've got a lot of respect for the girl. She hasn't had an easy time of it and has done her best to make her way in the world. She's clever, that's true and does have a fine skill with the animals, something a farmer can't dismiss," she gave her husband an admonishing glance. "More to the point, she's homeless and not well, and we should remember that Jesus said caring for the poor and sick is like caring for him."

"When you care for the least of my brothers, that you do unto me," one of the children, Danny, piped up.

"Very good Danny. Father O'Rourke will be glad to know you're learning your catechism." Danny beamed and waited to hear if his mother had any special reward for his good memory, perhaps an extra helping of potatoes. However, she turned her attention back to Ciarán, "You get up from this table and go find her and bring her home right now, before you take another bite of my food."

Ciarán, slammed down the spoon he had been using to scoop up the mash and stood.

"I've no idea where she's gone. She just ran off. How am I supposed to find her?" Thinking at the same time that Maire and John hadn't remembered Jesus' recommendations when he was ill.

"You can start by getting on that useless beast of yours and go looking for her."

"It's gone dark now!"

"All the more reason to find her and get her indoors." They stood glaring at each other for a moment, "Now! Go!" Maire pointed towards the door. Ciarán made sure to slam it as he left.

Conall was not best pleased to be disturbed in his warm stall but tolerated being tacked up. As he registered the mood of his rider, he became more agitated, swishing his tail and stomping. He even went so far to offer his teeth to Ciarán, who shoved the horse's head away from his face, with a mild curse. Ciarán decided to take the road towards Ardara, as Fiona might head back to her former home near Maghera. It was dark enough but at least it wasn't pissing with rain.

He let Conall set the pace, and eventually just sat back in the saddle and let Conall follow his own direction. It was in this manner that they stopped at a field, Conall swivelling his ears, listening intently. Then without warning, Conall jumped the low stone wall, nearly losing Ciarán in the process. Ciarán swore profusely but as he hadn't been paying attention, figured it was his own fault. It is never wise to fall asleep on a stallion.

Conall made his way determinedly across the field and stopped at a section of hedge, which had grown over a hollow in the ground, the sort of place where the old hedge schools had been held. Trust Fiona to find shelter even in this remote part of the country. Slipping from the saddle, Ciarán made his way over to the hedge. There was some light from the moon, but not enough for sure footing. He got as close as he dared and shouted,

"Sure, I know you're in there. Conall sniffed you out. The bloody horse has spent too much time with your dog."

"I know I'm here," Fiona replied crossly, "But why are you here?"

Ciarán sighed and hunkered down to the damp earth. He was tired of the cold and the dark. He wanted to be home, with a hot drink and maybe a whiskey. His temper had dissipated with the night-time journey, and he just wanted Fiona to come home. Surely, they could continue their argument indoors.

"Will you not come out and talk to me?" he entreated.

There was an extended silence and then Ciarán heard rustling. First Farley appeared through the hedge and then Fiona, pulling her cloak tightly about her. She stood over him but said nothing. He waited a moment and then took her hand.

"Sit down with me here, will you?" She resisted a moment, but he did not let go and she eventually succumbed. They sat side by side at the edge of the field and listened to the movement of small things in the grass, under a half-moon surrounded by the few stars that had pierced the clouds.

"I'm sorry," Ciarán admitted, "I should have asked you properly before I had the banns announced. I didn't realise that things had changed."

"How could they not change?" Fiona pulled her hand away and tore up a stalk of grass, shredding it to bits while she waited for his answer. Ciarán didn't know what to say. He tried to take her hand again, but she resisted, "Do you need the graphic details?" she spat out.

Ciarán's voice was low,

"I know he hurt you," was all he could manage.

"Do you know all three of them had a go?" She jutted out her chin and waited for the boldness of the comment to wound him. It did. He reached for her, but she stood up and moved away from him. He found he was shaking and fisted his hands to steady himself, grinding his teeth with the effort. He punched the soil and stood up, going to her, and touching her shoulder lightly, turning her to face him.

"That doesn't make you any less in my eyes. Whatever those bastards did, they could not take away what I feel for you."

She tried to see his face in the dim light, but it was all shadows.

"Then why are you mourning the life you were to lead with Gráinne? I'm sure if you went back and explained yourself you could have it all back. Maybe even your uncle would forgive you. You don't want me anymore. I'm spoiled goods!" She began to run away but Ciarán's legs were longer, and he soon overtook her, grabbing her arm and pulling her roughly back towards him.

"It's you that doesn't want me! You cringe when I touch you, you barely talk to me and now you've run away! What am I supposed to do?"

"Let me go. Just let me go and get on with your own life," she tried to pull away, but he was stronger. He grabbed both her forearms and pulled her close to him, face to face.

"You are my life, you and your nasty, wee dog. I have chosen you. If I could shake the sense into your head, I would but it's useless. Just listen to me for once."

"You're hurting me."

He let go, expecting her to run again but she stood still. He could hear the wind blowing up from the sea and an owl hooted in the distance, answered by its mate. And then he could hear her weeping, ever so softly. He could see her shoulders shaking and she wiped her nose on her sleeve. He did nothing. He just watched until she finished, dashing the tears from her cheeks, she looked up at him. He had thought of her as so powerful, with her amazing ability to hear the animals. But that is not what she thought of herself. She was just a frightened girl.

"I'm afraid," she whispered. He waited. Then slowly reached out one hand, cupping her face with one hand. With the other, he cautiously drew

Fiona towards him. He let his arms reach around her and hold her body, still frail from her illness, against his chest. Wrapping her in his warmth, he let his chin rest in her hair.

"I won't hurt you *cailín*. That could never be." He felt her relax, little by little and her heartbeat, against his embrace, begin to slow. He thought again how like a nervous horse she was. Finally, she turned into him, and her arms came around his back, hugging him tightly. He kissed her gently on the top of the head, stepped back, kneeled on the ground, and asked, "Will you marry me Fiona *Madra*, Listener to the beasts?" She tried to smile through her tears and then nodded, stepping into the comfort of his arms. She felt at home there, safe, with his solid flesh enveloping her, shielding her.

As the wedding was going forth, Kathleen decided they should go into Glenties and see if they could find some fabric to make a wedding dress for Fiona. Fiona herself was not that bothered with attire but agreed to Kathleen's demands as she had grown fond of Ciarán's sister and wasn't averse to keeping her happy. Kathleen had had little joy in her life after all her losses. If a wedding served as a happy distraction for Kathleen, Fiona was content to offer her services.

Glenties was one of the larger towns in Donegal, so there were a fair few shops to visit. They had other messages to collect for Maire, so they had come with the pony and cart. It was not a long journey back to the farm but with packages it would have proved cumbersome. Farley was at first a bit perturbed about the cart but when he settled into the rhythm of it, he decided it was quite an appropriate means of travel for a dog of his distinction.

Once they were in town, they left the pony and cart at a livery stable and began trawling the shops. Kathleen thought a sturdy navy fabric would look stylish, suit Fiona's unusual hair colour and be quite serviceable for a variety of occasions. She would decorate the collar and cuffs with some lace she had tatted herself, thus giving the dress a touch of finery, which would lift it into the category of a wedding gown. She thought she might be able to afford a few pearl buttons as well. There wasn't much money going, but John had reluctantly agreed to put some finances towards the wedding. He figured it was best that his younger brother was married before he strayed into any more trouble.

Fiona and Farley dutifully followed Kathleen, rather in a state of awe. They had not been in a market town for some time and there was certainly a lot to see and smell. Farley sneezed at the dank scent of ale passing the pubs but brightened considerably when the scent of meat pies wafted his way. Fiona asked him to stay nearby as the town was crowded and she didn't want him to get trodden upon. Being a market day there was cattle in the main street and the odd gentleman on horseback. Donkeys pulled rattling carts and children darted about, some begging, some picking pockets, with only a few actually behaving. Farley grudgingly agreed to stay by her side, she did need a bodyguard after all, but he had hoped to filch the odd morsel, and maybe meet up with a bitch in season. He sighed with the heavy duty of being an acolyte.

Kathleen had visited three shops, pulling down fabric and holding it up to Fiona's face before she found a shade that she was happy with. It was a lighter blue than she had intended to work with, more like the colour of the sea than the severe navy she had been looking for, but it suited Fiona's dark eyes better. She made her purchase and then told Fiona she needed to get some salt and a few other staples for Maire. She gave Fiona a coin and pointed out a shop that had fare that Farley might like to sample.

Fiona paused before crossing the street as it was now filled with muck from the cattle, as well as a heavy traffic of humanity. Kathleen had hurried on and was going to meet them back at this same spot so there was no need to rush. Fiona wished she had some money so that she could buy a small gift for Kathleen - the woman had been so kind to her. She pressed her face against the glass of a shop that displayed bonnets in the window, but the proprietor came out and asked her to move along. Of course, Fiona realised, she looked like a beggar and might drive off actual customers. Fiona had just started to cross the street when she heard the high-pitched neigh of a horse in distress. This was followed by a string of curses in a British accent and the thwack of a whip on horse flesh. Down the road, a beautiful skewbald had begun to rear, and her rider was dragging on the reins and employing the whip assiduously. Looking up, Fiona could see that a sheet, hung out from one of the upper story windows, was flapping in the breeze. The horse was frightened. It could be soothed and would walk on. She hurried to the horse's side and then slowly and gently reached out to lay her hand just below the skewbald's withers.

"What are you doing?" shouted the soldier and lifting his whip, whacked away Fiona's hand. "Trying to steal my horse, you are! Thief!" he spat out, whacking her again, this time across the face.

Fiona reached up and felt the blood from the slash begin to drip down her cheek.

"I'm trying to help," she shouted back. "Your horse is afraid of that laundry. I can calm it!" but it was hard to make herself heard because Farley had started to bark, single bursts of alarm, repeated again and again. Fiona turned to Farley. She'd heard that sequence of barks before. "No Farley," she begged, but it was too late. The dogs were starting to come to his call, appearing out of shop doors, from under stairs, from their farmers' sides.

"Get away from my horse, you filthy brat!" Private Lennox, the insensitive horseman, ordered. He gave his mount a furious kick in the sides and the horse, unable to move forward due to the terror of the flapping bedclothes could only respond to the prompt by rearing, which deposited the soldier onto the roadside. "Now look what you've done," he roared, again lifting his whip, and coming at Fiona, but he was stopped, as three dogs took him down and then four more leaped on the Private, tearing at his coat and making contact with his flesh.

British soldiers were not terribly popular in Glenties, so no great effort was made to assist the man. A few half-hearted, 'Whist with you,' were shouted at the dogs and one child went so far as to throw a few rocks but it wasn't sure if the missiles were meant for the dogs or Private Lennox. Fiona stood stock still, unable to approach the furious pack. Farley was ignoring her requests to desist, although he was only orchestrating the event and was not personally involved in the mayhem. She could feel Farley's barks coursing through her, his anger beat at her pulse. She was so consumed with the experience of his feelings, that she was

346

unaware she was standing in the middle of the watching crowd that had assembled. It was not a good place to be.

"Ah there you are," Kathleen remarked, as if bumping into Fiona casually. "I've been looking all over for you," with a friendly nod to a few faces she knew in the crowd, Kathleen took Fiona's arm and tucked it into hers. "We must be going now. Our packages aren't going to walk themselves home," she said loud enough for the general crowd to hear, not looking at the man on the ground or the dogs, now beginning to break away as their quarry lay still. A young man had taken hold of the horse and handed the reins to his companion. He went over to the soldier and checked on his status.

"I think he's popped his clogs," the youth said matter-of-factly. "He's certainly shat himself." There was an embarrassed titter from the crowd.

Kathleen tugged at Fiona and leaned close to speak into her ear,

"Walk now, quickly, but don't run. We're going to get in the cart and go home. If we're lucky, nothing will be said of this. We don't want words about you being in the middle of them dogs or anything like that." Fiona said nothing and let herself be led away. The cart was readied, and Kathleen urged the horse on briskly. After a mile or two Fiona was able to speak.

"Someone will talk."

Kathleen nodded but kept her eye on the road ahead of her.

"Aye. People will talk but it's what they'll say that matters. Your man there that fell off his horse was not well liked. He got a girl in the family way last year and made no amends to either her or her family. The poor girl ended up running off to Derry, and it's said she had to take to the streets to support herself and her bastard child. There's no one that will mourn a man that did that to one of us."

"I didn't call the dogs," Fiona defended herself. "It just happens that way. I mean," she struggled to explain to Kathleen without explaining what her role as a Listener meant to the dogs, or the horse for that matter.

Kathleen reached over and patted Fiona's knee,

"Your wee dog is very careful of you after your being hurt and all the credit to him for looking after you. You've a terrible gash there on your face, not what we want to see in a bride." She tutted and shook her head.

"I didn't want him killed. I just wanted him to stop beating the horse. It had only taken a fright at some laundry flapping."

"Of course, you were only trying to help, and he wasn't much of a horse man. It was always going to be a fall from a horse that killed him."

"But ..."

"Now *girseach*, it was the fall that killed him. Sure, John has seen the fellow ride and knows full well that the man couldn't sit a horse if Jesus himself held him in the saddle. No worries now. We just need to get that face of yours cleaned before your intended sees it and has me head off for not looking after you properly."

When they got back to the farm Danny, John's lad helped them unhitch the pony and put her out in the pasture. He looked with interest at Fiona's face, but Kathleen shooed him off.

"Go straight up to our room and clean yourself up," she ordered Fiona.

Fiona acquiesced, asking that Kathleen bring her a pinch of salt and a spoon of honey.

348

Kathleen left Maire's packages in the kitchen and collecting the remedies, took the stairs up to her room. She watched while Fiona mixed the salt into a washbowl of water and taking a cloth, Fiona dabbed at her face. She glanced in the mirror to make sure the dried blood had been washed away and the cut was cleansed. Then she spread some honey onto the wound.

"I dare say it will heal well enough but for now you look a state," Kathleen decided. "We'll have to give Ciarán some sort of story. I mean, it's not as if he can hunt the villain down and take his revenge for you but it's best that he doesn't know you were involved at all."

Sitting next to each other on the bed they decided to say that Fiona had been trying on a hat and a pin had got caught in her hair and when she tried to pull it out it had scratched her face.

"Sure, a hat pin could never do this much damage," Fiona worried, gesturing at her wound.

"Oh, but it could! They're evil wee things, hat pins are. I heard tell of a woman who put a man's eye out with a hat pin. That's half the reason women wear hats, to keep the pins about them. Fair, decent weapon they are." Fiona wasn't sure if there was any truth in Kathleen's tale, but she had to agree that it was the only good reason she could think of to wear a hat.

Ciarán was alarmed when he came in for dinner and grasped Fiona's chin, asking her what she had done to herself. She gave the story of the hat pin, only glancing at Kathleen once for encouragement. She wasn't sure how convincing her performance had been, but she was not questioned further, and Maire only tutted about young girls with their heads full of weddings and not paying attention to what they were doing.

Farley, quite hungry since he'd never got the snacks he'd been promised sat solidly on Fiona's foot, demanding some of her mutton. She was that cross with him that she almost didn't share but then again, he was only doing his duty. She slipped him a large chunk of meat. Maire, who never missed a thing, rolled her eyes at Fiona but chose, uncharacteristically, to keep her mouth shut.

A WEDDING

The weeks leading up to the wedding were not without incident. John had, of course, heard about the catastrophe with Private Lennox and quizzed Kathleen thoroughly, as the two women had been in town that day. He was not ignorant of the canine involvement and the presence of Fiona had been mentioned by a fair few folks. However, there were no direct accusations, and Kathleen's story that they had just seen the man fall and heard the dogs barking could not be disproven. Still, he watched Fiona whenever she was by, and wished for all the world that his brother had chosen to stay in Ballybofey and married the simple, but landed, Gráinne.

Children do play with *weans* from other families and kitchen maids enjoy the gossip after mass. Word got round that Ciarán Gallagher's intended was followed at all times by a small dog, which was probably her familiar and that she had tamed the young man's wild horse so that it bowed and did tricks for her. It was suspected that she had enchanted Ciarán himself, but there was no denying that a woman who had a way with animals could be rather useful. When a nearby cottier found his only cow dry up, he sent his son to the big house to ask for Fiona's assistance.

A young lad of about ten stood at Maire's kitchen door. His feet were bare and dirty, and he lifted one, to rub an itch on his alternate shin. Maire herself had opened the door and stood there, arms akimbo, "Well?" she said, with an upward twitch of her eyebrows.

"Please Mrs. Is the faery girl in? Me dad needs her to see to our cow"

"I've no faery girls in my house! Whatever are you on about?" The child stepped back from the door, just out of reach of Maire's arm, in case she decided to treat him with a cuff about the ears. He cowered before her outrage but knew a remedy was needed desperately, and if he went home without the healer his father would beat him.

"Is she a cunning woman then?" he ventured.

Maire gave an enormous humph and then called over her shoulder.

"Betty, will you run down to the stables and tell Miss Fiona there's a lad here to see her." Betty looked up in surprise, never having heard Maire give Fiona the title, 'Miss,' but she left her scrubbing and wiping her hands on her apron agreed to her mistress' bidding.

Fiona came up from the stables where she had been cleaning hooves to see the lad, nervously hopping from foot to foot outside the kitchen door. She smiled at him, seeing a child who had grown up in a cabin as she had, dirty, malnourished, and rather intimidated by the big house.

"Is it you who's come to see me then?" she asked the boy. He nodded but seemed unable to speak.

Fiona cocked her head, wondering why the child was afraid, but then remembered the incident of the dogs in the town. She tried to think of a way to set him at ease.

"Do you like dogs lad?" she asked. The boy went pale and shook his head in the negative. "This is my dog," Fiona said, crouching down and scratching Farley behind his ear. Farley leaned into the attention, and nearly lost his balance in the ecstasy of a good scratch. The boy giggled as

Farley regained his balance, recovering his dignity with aplomb. "Ach, sure, he's a silly old thing but he keeps me company. Would you like to meet him?" The boy looked unsure, so Fiona beckoned encouragingly. "Just reach your hand out, he won't bite, I promise." Farley licked the proffered fingers, and as they were filthy and quite interesting, he continued to lick. The boy wriggled and laughed, smiling up at Fiona. "You see," Fiona said, "He's only a daft old thing. Now, was there something you needed to ask me?"

So, Fiona accompanied the boy back to the cabin and the excuse for a stable that stood behind it. There was too much muck in the stable and the flies swirled in the air, barely put off by the cow's flicking tail and twitching ears. The boy's father appeared, a lean man, probably in his thirties, though he could be sixty. His trousers were held up by a piece of twine, and his worn shirt had been washed to the point of no colour at all. He wore a jacket which was shredded at the wrists. "Well," he said when Fiona appeared with his son and Farley.

Farley nosed through the manure and snapped at a few flies while Fiona went up to the cow. She didn't really need to listen, as she could see the swollen red teats and knew the cow had mastitis. However, she laid her hand on the cow and enquired as to the conditions, and if they had always been this way. The cow told her that a woman had milked her before and kept the stall clean but had not been seen in some time; that explained things.

"Do you have a wife?" Fiona asked the dour man, standing at her elbow now and smelling no better than the cow's byre.

"Dead, this last month now." He gave no more details. Fiona glanced over at the boy, who was running his toe through the mud at the edge of the stable. "What has that to do with yon cow going dry?"

"Well," Fiona began, "Your wife kept the stable tidy and the cow's teats clean."

The lad squeaked,

"Did our cow tell you all that?" His eyes were huge with admiration.

"She did and she didn't," Fiona admitted. "Now you lad," she pointed at him, "Are going to have to do your mammy's jobs. This stable needs to be scrubbed clean. I'll wash the cow's teats and make a poultice for you to put on them twice daily till the redness is gone." She turned to the farmer. "Can you get yourself some seaweed?"

He nodded,

"It's free enough at the shore."

"Then get some and dry it as well as you can and mix it into her feed."

"We've not much hay, I just usually let her graze up in the field." That was a problem. Fiona bit her lip, trying to think of a solution.

"The thing is, if she's not fed, she can't feed you," Fiona explained.

"I'm not an eejit. I know that but ..." the cottier didn't bother finishing the sentence. His poverty was all too obvious.

Fiona decided to take a risk,

"I'll ask me brother-in-law," (well, he would be shortly) "If he has any odd jobs that need doing. He'd maybe make an exchange for some feed. In the meantime, let's get your old cow cleaned up and find her some seaweed to build her up a bit." Fiona sent the boy for a bucket of well water and began gently wiping at the swollen teats, allowing

354

the coolness of the water to ease the pain. Then she took some mint leaves and garlic from her remedy bag and mixed them with a water into a paste. She applied the poultice and reassured the cow that she would be back again to minister to her needs.

"We'll need to strip out the teats, but it would be too painful right now. I'll let the poultice set over night and then check her again tomorrow morning." She turned to the lad, "This stable will be shining by then," she informed him, and he could only agree.

Surprisingly, John did not complain about the offer Fiona had made to the farmer and assured her an exchange would be made. In the meantime, he sent over a wagon with a bundle of hay. He knew of the family's loss, not only the wife had died but two girls, younger siblings of the boy. There had been no money for a doctor and even less for veterinary help. When the boy offered Fiona an egg for her efforts, she refused, saying that her bill would be included in with the work due for the hay. She had originally meant to admonish the farmer for the state he'd left his cow in. After all, her job was to be the animal's advocate. Yet, she knew the paralysis of grief and remembered opening the gate, letting all of Nan's goats go to the wild. The lad had the resilience of youth. Perhaps he could manage the change which had defeated the father.

Word of her 'miraculous cure' of a near dead cow (although it had only been mastitis) passed from farm to farm, and any whispers about inciting dogs to riot became less important. Cottiers stopped by asking for help with egg bound chickens, an infected eye in a dog, and a donkey that was 'as stubborn as the day was long.' Fiona was able to help mostly by giving advice on improving husbandry (the chicken had been quite vociferous in her complaints regarding the state of the henhouse and the lack of meat in the scraps she was given). Fiona had recommended that a frog be caught for the chicken, and the hen had devoured it with gusto. This act was met with both alarm and amusement and the local frog population declined rapidly. The dog's eye was washed with salt water three times daily and a tincture of eyebright applied. It had been scratched by a thorn and the resultant ulcer was painful, leading to rubbing and then infection. Fiona was able to heal the infection, but the ulcer remained angry, and the dog couldn't keep himself from scratching, despite Fiona's strict instructions to control himself. In a last-ditch attempt, she stitched the eye closed for a period of time (the dog refusing to wear an eye patch for fear of ridicule), and this final procedure seemed to do the trick.

Fiona had a long discussion with the donkey, who seemed to be suffering from the sin of pride, considering himself as lordly as a horse and wishing to be addressed in the same fashion. Fiona advised the owner, a gnarled old woman that reminded her a lot of Nan, that the donkey would like to be addressed in a formal manner. There were several replies to the effect of, 'his lordship can kiss me arse,' but Fiona suggested it might be worth a try. She later heard that the woman was heard walking to market asking, "Mr. Horse's Arse, will you step this way please, ever so kindly, if you don't mind," and the donkey was even seen wearing a garland of daises one afternoon. All this activity kept Fiona busy, and she had little time to worry about her upcoming nuptials.

Kathleen had finished the dress, having forced Fiona through a number of fittings, which had annoyed Fiona to no end. Kathleen had even set aside some blue ribbon, nearly matching the dress to tie around Farley's neck in a rather dapper bow. They usually walked as a household to mass as the cart could hardly hold them all, especially with the addition of Cousin Liam who had come for the wedding. The couple were given the cart in order to protect the dress and Fiona's new boots, which she detested but had agreed to on the family's insistence. They would not have a barefoot bride come into their family. It would be too degrading. Farley decided to join them in the cart and jumped up onto Fiona's lap, tracking a bit of mud onto the skirt and wrinkling it noticeably. Kathleen sighed. She had tried.

Mass was to be said first and then the wedding would follow. Any of the congregation that cared to stay for the ceremony were welcome and Maire had prepared some ale and cakes to be distributed to anyone that came to the house. There would be a formal wedding breakfast for the couple and family when they returned home. Farley was not allowed inside the church, so he waited on the porch, Fiona longing to stay with him. However, she followed Ciarán into mass and sat in the family pew, part way down the church, behind the community members of a higher class. Without Farley to hold onto, Fiona felt her nerves go wild, her stomach twisting into a thousand shapes, and her blood draining down into her new boots. Looking down the pew at her, Kathleen was afraid Fiona would faint and elbowed Maire sitting next to her. Maire eyed the girl and pressed her lips together in annoyance. There was nothing to be done about it now. If Fiona fainted in the middle of mass, she wouldn't be the first one. Fasting before communion often brought on fainting. The priest would just assume the girl was hungry.

When Fiona began to shake, Ciarán took her hand, although physical signs of affection were frowned on by the priest. He interlaced his fingers with Fiona's and squeezed tightly. She managed a weak smile at him, and he continued to hold her together.

The sermon was short, as the priest was very conscious that the wedding would add to the time he would have to wait for his dinner, and he was no great fan of fasting himself. Of course, one couldn't eat before touching the holy eucharist but an eight o'clock mass would be preferable to him. Then there would be plenty of time for both breakfast and dinner. These country folks were terrible for time though and would never appear at eight in the morning. He needed the numbers to keep the collection plate full, so he was forced to endure the later mass. When he finished rapidly intoning,

"May the peace of Christ be with you," and the congregation had replied, "And also with you," Father Martin rushed right into the wedding. "Can I have Ciarán Gallagher and Fiona," he stared at the second name, *Madra*, Irish for dog! What kind of name was that? "Fiona *Madra*," he continued with a wince, "Come up to the altar."

Kathleen gave Fiona an encouraging smile, but Fiona was frozen. Ciarán whispered to her to stand up and gently levered her into position, half-carrying her, half dragging her down the aisle. She did not look the willing bride and Ciarán was not best pleased when he looked at his bride, not blushing, but turning an unpleasant shade of green.

"Please Father," Ciarán begged the priest, "She's going to be sick, she's that nervous. Let me go get her dog and she'll be fine." Father Martin was not one to bend the rules but as he took a look at the girl's face, he envisioned vomit splashing his embroidered Sunday robes and gave a curt nod of agreement. Ciarán bounded down the aisle and let open the door, allowing Farley to rush up the aisle and sit on Fiona's foot. She bent down and hugged the dog tightly, took a deep breath and stood up. She could do this.

The entrance of the beribboned terrier, who gave a nod of acknowledgement to the congregation after Fiona hugged him, amused the worshippers and the mood lightened. Ciarán and Fiona stumbled through their vows, Fiona barely whispering and Ciarán gripping her tightly in fear that she might bolt, but they made it to the end. Liam, as best man, produced a ring and handed it to Ciarán. It was a silver Claddagh ring, typically used as a wedding ring in Ireland. It was neither expensive nor unique, but it was the first piece of jewellery Fiona had ever worn and she looked at her finger in astonishment. Then she smiled shyly and lifted her face up to Ciarán, who gently kissed her lips. It was done. They were man and wife, or as Farley referred to them, Rider and Listener.

Far too many people followed the family to the house and Maire had to open an extra barrel of cider. The whiskey was kept for the men of the family. The women had outdone themselves cooking up sausages, blood pudding, fried bread, fried potatoes and sultana scones with cream and jam for afterwards. Liam had brought a bottle of whiskey from his uncle, (though not his blessing –

he was still furious with Ciarán) and the men were able to celebrate without restraint. Kathleen got out her tin whistle and both Maire and Liam sang romantic ballads. The children danced and even some of the adults began to dance, with the dining table pushed to the wall, there was just enough room for three couples to populate the floor. Fiona and Ciarán were urged to share a 'first dance' and Farley barked at their heels as they whirled around the room in waltz step, more or less. They broke apart laughing at their ineptitude and then John and Maire danced, along with Liam and Kathleen. The youngest Gallager, Janey, dragged her elder brother Danny onto the floor for an impromptu jig. The adults attempted to avoid stumbling over the children, and the children did their best to trip up the adults.

As the night drew in, the festivities quieted, and Maire made sure the fires were lit in the bedrooms. She put a warming pan in the bed that the couple would share and sought out Kathleen.

"Will we shut the dog out?" she suggested. Kathleen made a face of disapproval.

"I don't think that will be a popular idea. Sure, just let him go up in the room with them."

"But it's their wedding night!" Maire deplored.

"And she's as jumpy as a cat – look at the poor thing! Do you think she's eaten anything at all today?"

"No, but that eejit dog has eaten the best part of three sausages and the Lord knows how much blood pudding and fried bread. I'm surprised he hasn't been sick."

"He has," Kathleen admitted, "Behind the sofa. I had Betty clear it up. She wasn't thrilled. I think she will want an extra coin after all the cooking and cleaning we've been doing."

"Have you tried giving Fiona any whiskey?" Maire queried. Kathleen shook her head. "Right then, I'll get a wee drop down her and that will set her at ease. Best thing for a young bride."

"I never got lashed at my wedding," Kathleen protested.

"That was different," Maire replied. "You had decided to marry Donal when you were eight years old and I'm entirely sure that baby of yours wasn't conceived in holy wedlock."

Kathleen looked away, red in the face. Maire was a wise one. It was good to be able to talk about Donal now and the child she had lost. It kept them alive to talk of them, and she was able now to speak of them without wailing. Maire gave her an affectionate squeeze on the arm.

"Come on girl, let's go get your new sister-in-law bladdered."

Despite the whiskey, Fiona still felt icy with fright. Ciarán had not pushed her since the night she had tried to run away but she knew she had duties as a wife. She just didn't know if she could fulfil them. Kathleen helped her into a new nightgown and tucked her into bed. Farley leapt up on the bed, located the warming pan and settled on the blankets covering the hot spot.

"Ciarán will be up in a minute love. He's roaring drunk though so it's likely he'll just fall asleep." Fiona just nodded, too frightened to speak. "You know, it won't be like what happened to you Fiona," Kathleen took her hand and sat on the side of the bed. "When someone loves you, they touch you with tenderness and all you feel is warmth and safety. Those men, they touched you with hate and they meant to hurt you. It's a very different act – universes apart. One is love making and the other is rape. You've nothing to be afraid of." She patted Fiona's hand and got up to leave.

"But I am afraid," Fiona called her back. "I'm afraid I'll pull away, or even fight him. I don't want to hurt him. What if I just can't help myself and push him off of me?" Kathleen bit her lip and then offered an answer.

"Tell him what you are afraid of. Tell him, you're not afraid of him, but of your own fear. He's a good man, he should understand."

"Even if he's stocious?"

"Oh, if he's that bad from the drink, give him a smack on the side of the head and tell him to sleep it off." Fiona giggled and snuggled deeper under the blankets. Kathleen waved to her from the door and then shut it behind her.

Fiona had almost begun to drift off when Ciarán came into the room. She heard him struggling to undress in the dark, tripping over his trousers, cursing, and then falling onto the bed heavily. Farley growled at being disturbed but did not move from the comfort nest he had made for himself. For a long time, the couple lay side by side. Fiona thought Ciarán had fallen asleep, though his breathing wasn't even yet. Still, he was well drunk so it would be hard to tell.

Ciarán rolled over onto his side and tried to focus on his bride, the blankets pulled up to her chin and her knees pulled up nearly as high.

"Is it all right if I come in, under the blankets with you? It's getting bloody cold out here."

"Yes," Fiona consented. Ciarán yanked the bedclothes here and there and finally managed to get himself under the covers, he reached his cold feet down towards the warming pan but was warned off by Farley.

"My feet are freezing, and your dog is hogging all the warmth."

"He's a wee pig," Fiona agreed. She stretched her own toes down towards the pan and Farley opened one eye, sighed tragically, and moved farther down the bed. "He's moved now," she advised Ciarán, who stretched again, brushing his feet up against Fiona. She shrieked. "You're like a block of ice!" she admonished.

"I told you I was cold, but you're not love. Come and warm me up a bit, will you?" He reached for Fiona but let her make the decision to move towards him. She hesitated for a moment but then decided she would rather be warm too. Finally, he held her close and murmured, "That's better. We'll be right in no time."

Strabane, Londonderry

Ulster

(Northern Ireland)

SEEKING THEIR FORTUNE IN STRABANE

Ciarán looked at the advertisement Liam had given him at the wedding. There was a job for a manager's assistant at an estate near Strabane. It wasn't as much horse work as he would have liked but there were some duties with a stable of hunters and then the general tasks of running a plantation. It was what Ciarán had been trained to do with Uncle William. It was unlikely he would get the job, as he was not mature and experienced enough but Liam said he had written a letter of reference for him. It occurred to Ciarán that Liam felt guilty for being well off, due to inherit his father's holding and likely to marry well, while Ciarán was penniless and had no prospects. They had started out their young adulthood together with big dreams and now Ciarán was trapped on his brother's holding, working as a farm labourer. There was a suspicion that Liam felt that Fiona had ensnared Ciarán, and Liam had to take the responsibility for that, having engaged Fiona to be his cousin's nurse He had never warmed to her, stemming from their first encounter where Fiona interacted with the fractious Conall so easily while Liam jumped away in fear of the horse. Liam felt that Fiona was laughing at him, and in a way she had been.

Strabane was not a place Ciarán would have chosen to live. It was mainly Scottish Presbyterian and was part of the Northern six counties. Only miles away from Donegal, it was still a different country. He knew he would feel uneasy, and Fiona would be even more of an anomaly. However, a job was a job, and he knew they weren't welcome with John. They never had been, but after the business of the dogs attacking a soldier while Fiona was in town, the need to depart was pressing.

He would discuss it with Fiona of course. Still, it was unlikely that the job would be offered to him. Nevertheless, he wrote an application and enclosed Liam's letter of reference, noting that Liam had chosen to use the English version of his name, William and had not signed himself as 'Junior.' It would be easy to misconstrue the letter as being from William Senior, but it wasn't out and out fabrication.

Fiona had never visited the North, so she had no prejudice against it. Ciarán explained that, as Catholics they would be treated as second class citizens. She laughed at that, whenever had she been treated as anything more? She had a point there. He assumed that he would find it harder than she would.

It was a surprise to receive a letter offering Ciarán an interview. He rode off early one morning, leaving Fiona at home. She was not best pleased at this arrangement, but Ciarán explained it would look unprofessional if he showed up with his wife. Fiona lifted her chin and gave him a long look. He had to further elaborate – any wife, not just this one. Taking her waist, he pulled her to him and gave her a lingering kiss.

"I'm proud to have you as my wife. You know that don't you?" She smiled but didn't answer. "Fiona?" he asked, impatient for an answer but she slipped out of his hands and walked away, asking him over her shoulder to check that the animals were treated kindly where he was going.

The land manager met Ciarán as he rode up the drive to the stately home. Ciarán had seen manor houses before, but this was stunning, with Grecian columns and large bay windows. There must have been at least twenty rooms in the residence. He dismounted, staring up at the mansion. Mr. Bennett, the manager, followed Ciarán's gaze.

"It is impressive by this country's standards but it's really just a summer house. The Viscount only visits in August, if he comes at all. It stands empty most of the year, with the maids wandering about rearranging dust sheets. It's occupied at the moment though." Ciarán looked quizzically at the manager's grim tone during his last sentence.

Mr. Bennett had no intention of enlightening Ciarán yet. He guided his applicant to the stables and pointed towards an empty stall for Conall, remarking on the stallion's fine physique. Ciarán gave the horse an affectionate slap and remarked that Conall wasn't bad for a devil horse. A stable boy came up to rub down the horse and offer hay and water, but Ciarán replied that he would have to do the chores himself, the stallion not taking kindly to strangers.

When Conall was sorted, Ciarán was ushered into a large room, well-lit by a vast glass window overlooking a lawn that descended to an ornamental lake. The room was warmed by a small fire and Mr. Bennett gestured to a chair near the discreet blaze. Ciarán sat, admiring the portraits of dogs and horses decorating the room.

"My wife would be most impressed with the artwork."

"Is your wife interested in art?" Mr. Bennet asked, surprised.

"Not at all," Ciarán replied. "Her passion is dogs and horses and, well, animals in general."

Mr. Bennett raised his eyebrows,

"How unusual. I hope this doesn't interfere with her household duties." Ciarán gave an uneasy laugh. He still hadn't worked out how they would eat once they left the gifts of Maire's kitchen. To his knowledge, Fiona could manage stir-about, stew and toast. He had a sneaking suspicion that baking was beyond her limited repertoire.

But the manager had moved on, selecting Ciarán's and Liam's letters from a pile of post on his desk. Liam had written in extravagant praise of Ciarán's work on the estate and omitting to use his full title, hoped that McGovern Senior's small reputation was worth assuming.

"I understand that you worked as an assistant manager on a farm in Donegal. Agricultural, pastoral, and equine work. Is that correct? Oh, and I see a hunt kennel was in operation there as well. Quite substantial for an Irish farm." The astonishment at his uncle's endeavours was not lost on Ciarán but he chose to ignore the slur. He nodded in agreement and added,

"It was not nearly as large as this estate of course, but it was sizeable enough for Donegal." Bennet approved of the retiring assessment. Ciarán swallowed his resentment and focussed on the fact that he needed a job. He was married now and had a wife to support. He realized he was not qualified for this situation and the false pretences were a further risk, however, the landlord only visited this property once a year and surely, would never cross paths with McGovern Senior.

"I don't really need an assistant," Bennet suddenly said, and Ciarán's heart sank. "However, the landlord's son is currently in residence and his ..." there was a deliberate throat cleaning. "His Honour Hayes Junior requires a bit of my time."

Hayes Junior had been sent to Ireland after some sort of disgrace with a married woman in

England. Young Wilfred Hayes found Ireland dull and backward and was not worried about sharing his opinion liberally. Aside from his apparent disgust with the Irish and their island, he was a thoroughly unpleasant young man. He had been endlessly indulged by his mother and felt he could have whatever he wanted, including whichever housemaid he took a fancy to. He didn't tolerate dissension and expected everyone to fall in with his wishes unquestionably, this included animals. Horses that did not anticipate his every wish got their bits yanked into the tender flesh of their mouths or their flanks kicked forcefully. Dogs slunk out of his way when they saw him coming as he would pat the head and then pinch an ear, laughing as the dog yelped and pulled away. In short, Willie Hayes was a spoiled brat and a bully.

Ciarán raised his eyebrows enquiringly. He waited for further details. Mr. Bennet gave a deprecating laugh,

"He's a young man, used to the excitement of city life in London. Of course, he finds things a bit tiresome here and needs to create some enjoyment for himself."

"Then why is he here?"

The manager returned to the desk and shuffled some papers. Coming to a decision, he crossed over to Ciarán and sat opposite him by the fire.

"The boy got into a bit of trouble over in England and Viscount Hayes thought it better for his son to cool his heels over here for a while." Ciarán considered. It all sounded a bit complicated, and he wasn't sure he wanted to get involved.

"Can I ask what sort of trouble?"

"Ah yes, well, it was a bit of an incident with a married woman."

Ciarán nodded and looked into the fire. This probably wasn't the right position for him with his Fiona. He scratched his chin and considered. Would she ever have to see the fellow?

"Can I ask you where you would have myself and my wife stay?"

Mr. Bennett sighed with relief. He might have got this one. There weren't many people that could tolerate working in the same vicinity as Wilfred Hayes Junior, but Ciarán was obviously desperate for work, and not familiar with the juvenile Viscount's reputation.

"There's a cottage down near the gates. It's well away from the house and a bit of a walk to the stables, so you'd have some privacy but not be too far away, and, before you ask, the wages are commensurate with the position."

Ciarán knew there was something wrong. The bloke was nearly offering him the job here and now. It would do well to find out more about this Hayes Junior, ask about the town maybe. On the other hand, he needed a job. He needed to get out of John's house and he and Fiona needed to start their life together. Surely, this position could tide them over till they found something more comfortable. It would just be a step on the ladder.

He slapped both hands onto his thighs decisively.

"Are you offering me the job then, Mr Bennett?"

The two men shook hands on it and arranged for Ciarán to move his wife and belongings, (what little they had) into the cottage within a week's time. Pushing the niggling doubt to the back of his mind, Conall rode home the next

372

morning with the good news and was congratulated by his family. All except Farley, who eyed him long and hard, smelling something that was not quite right.

They were going to borrow a wagon from John, but once they gathered their meagre belongings together, it seemed it could all be packed into saddle bags. They may have to take turns riding Conall but could make the journey in a few days, stopping at inns or begging a bed from a cottier. John gave a loan of money for travelling expenses and Ciarán promised he would be repaid when his first pay packet was delivered. Kathleen clung to Fiona and begged her to write. Fiona assured her that she would try, although she was not so clever with a pen. Maire packed their bags with provisions for the journey and gave them each a peck on the cheek. She was looking forward to running her household as normal with a slightly less irritable husband.

They started their journey with Fiona riding Conall and Ciarán striding alongside. He told Fiona of the cottage they had been allotted – he had stayed in it the night he had waited over at the estate. It had a separate bedroom and a large hearth for both cooking and warmth. There was a table, chairs, and kitchen press. In the second room there was a bed and a wardrobe. The walls were stone, although the floor was still mud-packed and as far as he could tell, the thatch was in good repair, though, he supposed they'd find out in the first decent rainstorm. The manor house was described in all its grandeur, three stories, with the servants' quarters at the top. There were so many windows, with no thought for the expense of glass. Ciarán hadn't seen any rooms other than the library and the kitchen, where he had taken meals with the household staff, but he was sure the place was stuffed with artwork, chandeliers and what have you. He did not elaborate on his interaction with the household staff. They had looked at him darkly when he mentioned he was newly married, and one of the maids had warned him to keep his wife safe away from the young Master Hayes.

"He's got terrible wandering hands that one!" she remarked, at which point, the other maid jumped up and ran out of the kitchen crying. The cook had kicked at the first girl and hissed at her for setting her friend off again. When Ciarán had asked about the Viscount Hayes Senior, the staff had remarked that he was fair enough, as landlords go but that the son was not an easy man and best avoided. After what she had been through, he knew it wasn't wise to bring Fiona into this situation, but he had to work. She could be kept safe at the cottage. He would tell her to mind herself. Maybe he could get her another dog – a really big one.

Fiona, for her part, was happy to be leaving the house where every word must be watched, and where she was sure she was considered to be Ciarán's downfall. They were off to start their own life together, and in a cottage that sounded palatial compared to what she had been used to in her younger years. There were stables there so she would find a place for herself among the horses, and she could learn to be a good wife to Ciarán, although, she doubted she would ever be much of a cook or seamstress. At least she could keep their new home tidy and warm. When she saw that Ciarán's leg was starting to bother him, she stopped Conall and climbed off his back, offering the saddle to Ciarán. He smiled at her regard and did not attempt to argue, knowing how stubborn she could be.

The first night they stopped with a couple near Finton who were happy to have them in exchange for a small bit of coin. The couple's three children were chucked out of their bed into their parent's, freeing a pallet for Ciarán and Fiona. Fiona realised she would have to implement a nit comb after the night's sleep, but they had shelter and a rich stew was shared among them all, including Farley.

The second night they were near Balleybofey but stayed in an inn as they were not welcome at Uncle William's home. Liam came to join them for a meal, and he and Ciarán chatted late into the evening over a few jars of porter. Fiona feigned exhaustion and went to her bed early to leave the young men to their own company. She was thankful to Liam for the help he had given them, but she was quite sure it was out of pity for Ciarán, not affection for herself. Farley was reluctant to leave the pub as food droppings were plentiful, so he had to be lifted and carried away, his head turned over Fiona's shoulder, looking sadly at a piece of gristle below the nearest table.

They arrived after dark at the Hayes estate. They went first to the stables, where the groom welcomed them and showed them to a stable for Conall. Together, they unpacked Conall's bags, wiped him down and offered him some hay and a few oats. Conall surveyed his new quarters and was not displeased. The stables were well built and kept fresh. He noted curiosity in some of the horses, a touch of awe, even fear in a few, and then picked up on one mare that was absolutely miserable. He would need to send Fiona to this beast in distress, but not tonight. All were tired and in need of a good meal and a bed.

After settling Conall, the couple went up to the manor house and knocked at the tradesmen's entrance. The housekeeper, Mrs McTavish, opened the door and invited them into the kitchen for a bowl of soup and some wheaten bread. They accepted gratefully and Farley followed along in happy anticipation. The housekeeper frowned momentarily at Farley and then remarked that as he was small, it would hardly matter so he was allowed into the kitchen without further ado.

"You'll find the cottage made up and ready for you," Mrs. McTavish informed them. Ciarán thanked her and was surprised at the generous welcome. Maybe this would all work out fine. Certainly, the staff were kind-hearted. When they had finished their meal, he took the key and a lantern from the housekeeper and he and Fiona walked down the gates to the cottage that they would call home.

After breakfast, Ciarán met Bennett in the library for the day's instructions. Fiona decided to spend the morning grooming and rubbing down Conall as he had worked hard over the past few days. She made her way to the stables, followed by Farley, and introduced herself to one of the stable boys. He was able to show her where the brushes and curry combs were and advised her that he would see to feeding Conall. Fiona replied that she would take care of Conall herself as the horse was not kindly disposed to most people. The boy looked immensely relieved, as he had already been told by the groom that the stallion was of a vicious nature.

Conall greeted Fiona with pleasure and touched noses with Farley. They had an extended communication and when Farley leaned into

376

Fiona, she learned that one of the horses in the stables was intensely unhappy as its rider was over fond of the riding crop and had a terrible hard hand on the reins. Fiona promised Conall she would look into the situation but didn't want to step out of bounds on her first day. She decided to concentrate on getting Conall perfectly groomed and comfortable in his new abode in the hope that he would be a bit less cantankerous than usual. She doubted that she would succeed, but it she enjoyed tending to the immense beast regardless.

While picking out Conall's hooves Fiona became aware of a disturbance in the stables. A young man swaggered in, tapping his crop against his newly shined riding boots. He shouted at one of the stable boys to get his horse tacked up, and then strode up and down the boxes, inspecting the horses, most of them backed up in their stalls away from him. When he came to Conall, Fiona warned him, without looking up to stay clear of the stall. The young man ignored her admonition and went up to the stall door, leaning over it to take a look at the girl and defiantly encroaching on Connell's territory. The elbow resting on the top of the door was promptly bitten by Conall who also kicked the door for good measure.

Leaping back, Wilfred Hayes Jr, cursed soundly and declared,

"This is a vicious creature. It should be shot at once."

Fiona stood up from her work, placed her hands on her hips and marched up to the aristocrat, eyes blazing.

"Did I not tell you to stay away? Are you deaf or stupid?"

There was a gasp from the stable boy who had just led up Willie Hayes' mount. Both boy and horse were ignored though.

"How dare you speak to me that way! Do you know who I am?"

"You could be the archangel Michael for all I care. If I tell you not to mess with my horse, then you better listen." With that, she went back to cleaning hooves, turning her back on Willie in obvious dismissal.

"You insolent slattern! Who are you and what are you doing in my father's stables? I'll have you sacked I will." As his voice rose, the horses about started to shift uneasily and roll their eyes. The stable lad backed up the mare he was leading and paced it down the stalls, away from the shouting.

Hearing the raised voice, the groom came into the stables from where he was inventorying supplies in the tack room.

"Can I help you sir? Is there some problem?"

Willie's face had gone nearly purple with rage.

"There certainly is! You have some sort of gypsy girl here in our stable and she has been grossly impertinent." The groom raised his eyebrows in question. Willie waved extravagantly towards Conall's box. "Over there, with that rabid beast, who should be shot I say. Look what he's done to my riding coat." With that he waved his elbow in the groom's face. Mr. Tierney, the groom, eyed the coat with disinterest.

"That would be the horse belonging to the new assistant. I was told he was a proper stallion and to keep the lads away. What? Is his wife in there grooming now?" Fiona popped her head over the stall door.

"Morning Mr. Tierney. Thank you for this lovely stall and the use of the brushes and all. I'm sure Conall will be very happy here," and she turned back to her horse, beginning to comb out the tangles in the mane. Mr. Tierney was impressed to see the horse dip his head for her so that she could reach up the length of the mane. Ciarán had mentioned that his wife had a way with animals and that was clear to see.

But Willie was furious that the attention had been taken from him and demanded it back. "I won't have her in here," he insisted.

"She's not properly trained to be around people of quality. She spoke to me as if I were no better than a common peasant." Tierney mused that Willie was likely much worse than a common peasant but kept his opinion to himself.

With a sigh, Tierney attempted to placate the irate youth.

"Begging your pardon sir, she's only here to groom her husband's horse and not to serve you. She doesn't work for the estate."

"Well, I want her off the estate!"

Tierney scratched the back of his neck, disturbing a fly that had settled there.

"You'll have to discuss that with Mr. Bennet, Sir. I imagine if the wife goes, so will the new assistant, and Mr. Bennet had trouble enough hiring this one."

"Why Mr. Bennet needs an assistant is beyond me! He's obviously getting too old and too lazy to do the job properly. I shall be writing to my father about this." As Willie made this threat at least once a day, Tierney took no notice of it. Instead, he took the reins from the stable boy and handed them to Willie.

"Your ride is ready sir." Willie whipped the reins from the groom's hand and walked his horse over to the block and mounted. With a ferocious kick to its sides, the mare bolted forward out of the yard. Tierney wandered over to Conall, being careful to not get too close.

"That was foolish lass. He'll make trouble for you."

Fiona acquiesced with a nod, then stroking Conall's muzzle fondly explained,

"He threatened to have Conall shot. I got a wee bit angry I'm afraid."

Tierney grimaced.

"The lad has very little power here but thinks he is lord of the manor while his father is away. It's not a good combination. Mind yourself around him."

"Aye, good advice I'm sure Mr. Tierney. I thank you." Satisfied that he had done what he could, Tierney ambled back to the relative peacefulness of the tack room. In his absence, the stable lad crept up to Conall's stall. Conall showed his teeth but refrained from further advances as he realised the boy meant no harm.

"Miss," the boy begged, "Could you teach me how you get the big horse to bow like that for you?"

Fiona smiled at the boy.

"It's Missus lad, and I don't know if I can teach you or not. Do you ever listen to the horses?" The boy looked at her and gave her a slow smile in return.

"I sleep here at night and hear them rustling and blowing in the dark. They do be talking to each other, I think. Sometimes, one will snort real loud like and another will stomp it's foot, as if the first one said something rude. And if I'm rubbing

380

them down and give one of 'em a good scratch, he'll blow his lips and chew on me hair like he's saying thanks."

"You are listening then. Well done lad. I'm sure you can learn lots of things from the horses. I'm happy to help you. Now come in here," she opened the stall door, but the boy hesitated. "It's alright. If I let you in Conall will be gentle as a lamb." She took the boy's arm and pulled him up to the stallion. "Here now, place your hand here on his side and close your eyes." Nervously, the boy shut his eyes. "Breathe lad! You're fine. He won't hurt you. Just breathe." After a time, the boy's posture relaxed, and his breathing aligned with the horse's. Softly, Fiona asked him to listen to Conall.

"Now, tell me what Conall had to say to you." The boy turned to her, with face shining.

"I saw him galloping with a man on his back and they jumped a fence together."

"That would be my husband. Conall is really his horse. You saw rightly. Conall loves to gallop and he's a great one for the fences. You just keep listening like that and after a bit, the horses will learn to listen to you. You understand now?" The boy nodded, proud of his own success. "Now tell me lad, who's the horse in these stables that is so unhappy. Conall is well worried about him."

"Oh, that would be Your Honour's mare. He whips that horse something terrible and it starts to tremble awfully whenever I get the saddle out. I can't hardly bear to tack her up, but Master Hayes must have his ride, and he'd beat me if I didn't get his horse ready." Fiona was not surprised. Of course, it would be Willie Haye's mount. Poor creature. She'd have to see what she could do. Yet, she mustn't lose this job for Ciarán. He did need a post and perhaps that eejit, Hayes would go back to England soon.

Having managed a trip to the town for supplies, Ciarán and Fiona had supper in their own home for the first time. Fiona had plans to plant a small garden so that she would not need to purchase vegetables or tatties but for the time being, they had some money from John to help them stay fed until Ciarán's first pay packet. Ciarán was full of the day he had spent with Bennett – they had toured the estate in Bennett's one horse carriole. Bennett had introduced Ciarán to the tenants and pointed out the arable and grazing lands. It would be Ciarán's duty to travel around the estate on a regular basis making sure all the fences were in good condition and that the tenants were working the land properly. He would report to Bennet at the beginning of each day for orders and at the end of each day to discuss any problems that had arisen. In that way, Bennett could spend more time close to the manor house, dealing with the clerical tasks and keeping an eye on the young Hayes.

Fiona mentioned that she had met Willie Hayes but did not elaborate. Ciarán put down the spoon he was eating with and looked at Fiona, waiting. She did her best to ignore him. Finally, Ciarán stated that he had heard all about Fiona's meeting with Hayes, as the young man had come storming into the library when Bennet and Ciarán had returned from their tour of the estate.

"Oh," Fiona said quietly.

"Could you not try to be a bit more respectful love?"

"I'm very happy to be respectful of someone who deserves it, but not some stuffed up lout who thinks he's king of the world because he inherits money instead of earns it."

Ciarán sighed and rubbed the space between his brows.

"We need this job Fi."

Fiona slammed down her spoon and jumped up from the table.

"You need this job. I don't work here, remember?" She grabbed his bowl, finished or not and cleared the rest of the table in a clatter. Ciarán muttered something about going to see Conall and left the cottage. When he returned later in the evening, after having chatted with Tierney and sharing a warming nip of whiskey, he found the cottage dark. Making his way to the small room at the back that served as a bedroom, he scraped his shin against a bench and swore audibly. Finally, making it to the bedroom he pushed open the door and sat heavily on the bed, only to be met by a low growl. He had disturbed Farley's nap and was being roundly told off. Cursing again, he threw off his clothes and tried to lift the blanket and warm himself, but the dog lay solidly in his way.

"For the love of God, Fiona, tell your bloody dog to make a bit of room for your husband!"

Part Four: Earth

Mother Earth, my home,
Wind me close in your loving coil.
To be reborn in your fertile soil.

THE HAYES ESTATE

The work on the Hayes estate was not dissimilar to what Ciarán had done with his uncle, though on a larger scale. Ciarán did miss the kennels and the nascent stables that were such an important part of the McGovern farm, but he recognized there would be much less activity on an estate that was only visited by the owner once a year. Presumably, Hayes Senior had horses and dogs aplenty on his holdings in England.

Fiona had no real work to do, other than cook and tend house, which she found rather boring. She and nan had never been fastidious housekeepers and were not particular about food (probably due to having a goat and a greedy dog as acolytes). As a result, Ciarán often found that he preferred to take meals in the kitchen at the manor with the rest of the staff. He was there working with Bennett, and it was convenient to sup nearby, rather than walk down the road to his cottage, never knowing if a meal would be prepared or not. He turned some soil over behind their cottage to encourage Fiona to plant a garden. She brightened at his suggestion and was quick to plant some herbs for healing. Rosemary and mugwort grew easily in the plot. She did dig some potatoes as well, remembering the price of them in the market in town. It wasn't like the home she had with Nan because there were no goats, but it was starting to feel more like a place where they could survive for the while.

Conall needed regular exercise and when Ciarán wasn't riding him around the estate, Fiona took him out around the countryside. She quickly gathered that the primarily Scots Presbyterian's of the area would not take kindly to a Listener or a cunning woman. On the other hand, they were on the parsimonious side and would not look askance at some free veterinary advice. She would nod in greeting at a farmer working with a sheep or a cow, and then ask in a vague manner what the problem was. The farmers were sometimes taciturn, sometimes garrulous in their responses. She would seem to listen, sitting as close to the poorly animal as possible, actually listening to the animal instead. Then, in an offhand manner, mention some cure she had heard of. If the farmer seemed interested, she would offer to find the remedy and bring it along the next day. In this way, she worked her way around the estate, sometimes in person, sometimes by word of mouth. Before long, Ciarán was getting hailed by farmers asking if his 'wee wife would drop by with that poultice she made for the sheep over on the next farm,' or would his wife see to a calf that wasn't thriving. Ciarán was satisfied that Fiona was thriving, in her own way.

It was a day that Ciarán was working in the office. Fiona had just returned from a ride out on Conall to look into a problem with foot rot in a herd of sheep. She finished rubbing down Conall kissing him goodbye on the soft spot on his muzzle. She stepped out of the stall and prepared to leave the stables. Farley alerted her with a growl, and she looked up to see Willie Hayes coming her way. She looked around for a stable lad, but they were all out exercising the few horses of the Hayes entourage, and the groom was at the manor house asking Bennett to order some new tack.

"Well, if it isn't the foul-mouthed bitch," he sneered as he approached Fiona. She thought about running but she knew he would outpace her, so she stood her ground. He was quick as he grabbed her and pushed her up against a stall door. Farley leapt up and bit one of his arms, which freed Fiona for the moment she needed to pull her knife from her apron pocket. She could hear Conall kicking his stable door and knew he'd have it down in a minute.

"Let go or I'll gut you. If I don't manage that, that stallion will be out of his stall soon and he'll trample you."

Willie dropped her other arm and took one step back, glared into her face and then spat in it.

"I'll get you and your vicious animals." He aimed a kick at Farley who dodged it with an offended yelp.

"You touch my animals and you'll be a dead man, titled or not." She slashed the knife in front of him, letting the sun catch its blade in the late morning light. She made no attempt to wipe the sputum from her face, ignoring it entirely.

Willie pulled himself up to his full height and waved his riding crop,

"I could have you arrested for threatening me."

Fiona cocked her head to look at him and let out a bark of laughter.

"Don't you know everyone on this estate wishes you gone? They'd probably have a knees-up if I got rid of you."

Furiously, Willie stomped over to his mare's stall, shouting for someone to tack up his horse. There was no answer.

"Both boys are out exercising the other horses. Would you like me to do it for you?" She smiled sweetly and spoke with exacting politeness.

"I could hardly trust your class of person to do it properly." Fiona shrugged and walked away, leaving the young patrician helplessly looking at his mare. He had never saddled a horse in his life, but he would be damned before he'd ask Fiona for help. Unfortunately, the poorly tacked horse suffered from a slipping saddle and was blamed when Willie fell off. But that was not unusual. A poor horseman, he always blamed his mount.

The young Hayes did not favour early mornings, choosing to drink late into the evening so he was never found in the stables before noon. This gave Fiona ample time to visit his horse, a long-suffering mare named Bella. Tierney had no objection to Fiona assisting with the workload by grooming the horse. Bella found Fiona's gentle attentions soothing and poured out her plight to Fiona. Willie had no seat, so overused his spurs and reins, sawing at poor Bella's mouth as if it were a tree. Fiona spread honey on the sore spots in the mare's mouth and massaged her back and applied a plantain poultice along her bruised ribs. The Viscount had purchased Bella for his son as the mount had been described as steady and placid. A previous owner had treated Bella with respect, so she had never had any reason to develop bad habits. However, under Willie's treatment, she had grown twitchy, and was prone to chewing on her stable door. She had become difficult to saddle and even the stable boys were losing their tempers with her, occasionally swatting her when she reared and shied away from the bridle. This, Fiona could solve. She pulled both boys aside and explained that Bella didn't want to be tacked up because that meant going out with Willie, who was an abusive rider. She informed them that their lack of patience was only

390

frightening Bella more and making their jobs more difficult. She instructed them in slow movement and soothing verbiage. Tierney, somewhat bemused, did not intervene. He rarely did the tacking up and was not bothered how the boys did it, so long as no one from the manor house complained.

Dealing with Willie was another matter. As she could not stand the sight of him and he would never listen to her, Fiona found herself at an impasse. The only solution that she could see was to make riding so unpleasant for him, that he sought another pastime. She discussed this with Bella, asking her if she could enhance her pace when moving through mud, and always stop directly when requested, especially when moving at speed. This would increase the likelihood of Willie being thrown. The possibility that he might injure himself and not be able to ride for an extended period also passed through Fiona's mind. It was also not impossible that he might break his neck. People died in riding accidents all the time.

It was not surprising when Willie came back from a ride covered in mud and swearing a stream of obscenities at Bella. The stable boy took the reins as Willie dismounted and proceeded to kick at the horse, who jumped away in alarm. The boy pleaded for Willie to stop, as the mare was becoming impossible to control. Fiona, watching from Conall's stable went forward to assist. She took Bella by the bridle and blew into her nose, calming her. She looked into Fiona's eyes and begged for help.

"Whatever is the matter Master Hayes?" she asked, deliberately dropping his title.

He glowered at her and hissed, "You must call me 'Your Honour!' I am the son of a Viscount!

391

You would think there would be a decent mount and a competent groom in my father's stables. Instead, there are unschooled horses and rude and incompetent children. It's just not good enough."

Fiona stroked Bella's muzzle. "Unschooled?"

"Unschooled and untrained! This horse is useless!"

Fiona raised her eyebrows but said nothing to Hayes. She tapped Bella, asking her to bow and then climbed into the saddle. She threw the stirrups over Bella's neck as they were much too long for her and of no use to her anyway. She tied the reins in a knot and left them on Bella's neck. Using the pressure of her seat and thighs she requested that Bella walk out into the yard and walk a figure of eight, then trot two circles and finish in a canter around the perimeter. She returned the horse to Hayes and as Bella bowed, swung her far leg over her neck and stepped to the ground. She shrugged and smiled up at Hayes, "She seems perfectly well trained to me, but I've only just learned to ride."

Hayes raised his riding crop, as if to hit her but noticed that both stable boys and Tierney were watching with interest. Instead, he turned on his heel and marched back to the house, flinging his crop down in the stable yard.

Tierney was shaking his head.

"You shouldn't have done that Missus. He's already taken a dislike to you and now you've made him look a fool."

"He is a fool!" Fiona retorted, "And cruel. This horse has suffered enough. Can you not discourage him from riding somehow? Tell him Bella is lame or something."

Tierney sighed.

"I need my job. We all do," he waved his hand at the two boys. "We haven't the privilege of being rude to his Honour and you shouldn't either or you'll find your husband out of work. He's only been kept on because Bennett insists but if you keep making trouble, you'll both be out on the road, and I know that's not what your husband wants. The Lord only knows what you want." He took in the boys gaping and shooed them away. "Off you go lads, you have work to do." Then he lifted Bella's reins over the horse's head and led the horse to her stall, quietly untacking her and rubbing her down thoroughly.

Over a quiet supper in their cottage, Fiona described her demonstration on Bella. Ciarán ran his fingers through his hair and shook his head at her.

"You will get me sacked you know," he admonished.

"I can't bear to see him destroy that lovely creature. Bella is a darling; she wouldn't hurt a fly and she's literally being beaten to death."

"I think that's a bit of stretch," Ciarán argued.

"Not so much physically, but her heart has gone out of her. She doesn't understand why she is being punished when she's only trying to do as she's told. It's not her fault that Master Hayes doesn't know not to kick and pull on the reins at the same time!"

"It's 'his Honour', Fiona. You have to give him his title. These people find their titles very important."

Fiona pushed away her plate and made to get up. Ciarán didn't know whether to chastise her or placate her. He decided to try the second approach. Reaching across the table, Ciarán took her hand.

"I know it's hard. Your vocation is to take care of animals and there's an animal suffering that you can't help. Why don't you stay away from the stables as much as possible? Come out with me when I ride the estate."

Fiona nodded.

"Maybe," she replied and looked down at their clasped hands. "Are you sorry you married me?" she asked, annoyed to find a quiver in her voice.

Ciarán pulled her round to his side of the table and took her in his lap.

"My silly wee *asthore*. What fun would there be in a docile, sweet wife? You are as wild and headstrong as my Conall, and I love you both the way you are." Fiona answered by throwing her arms around his neck and pulling herself as close as she could.

That night, Farley did have to move to the bottom of the bed, and his sleep was much disturbed.

And so, it became their habit to ride out on Conall in the morning, although sometimes Fiona rode an elderly pony to give it some exercise. It was the childhood pony of Willie and was distrustful of humans and irritated by the interruption of his grazing, but he found Fiona far less annoying than Willie, and was boastful about his outings with the impressive stallion. Fiona and Ciarán either brought their dinner with them in a napkin or were invited into a cottage to share a meal with the tenants. In this way, Ciarán got to know the tenants well, and they were quick to advise him of any damaged walls or poorly stock. He was more approachable than the manager

Bennett and certainly more understanding of their issues.

On the days when Fiona did not accompany Ciarán, she found time to practice her listening skills with a variety of animals. She had not done much work with cats, a fiendishly difficult species to communicate with as they could be aloof one moment and purring and rubbing against you the next. You had to catch them in the right mood. You also had to catch them awake. Fiona observed the stable cat for a long time, watching her bask in the brief moments of sunshine or stalk through the stables, offended by the noise of the groom and stable boys. Once she was privileged to watch the cat pounce on a mouse and delicately devour it.

Eventually, the cat condescended to come to Fiona and butted her head against Fiona's shins. Fiona crouched down and dutifully began scratching the cat behind the ears. Soon enough, a purr began to rumble forth. Fiona continued with her labours and was rewarded with a message. *You do this rather well*, remarked the cat, indicating that the other ear also needed to be scratched. After the second ear had been attended to the cat rolled on its back and exposed its belly for a rub. Fiona laughed, *I won't fall for that one*, she informed the cat. *I know full well you'll attack me.* The cat chirruped in amusement and then stood up, flicking her tail delicately and looking over her shoulder, '*Not as dumb as you look*,' she commented as she strode off.

The next time she was at the stables, Fiona brought with her a jug of milk and poured the cat a saucer full. After finishing her repast, the cat cleaned her whiskers, contemplating the human crouching before her. *So, you are a Listener*, she said, and Fiona answered in the affirmative. *You may be useful to me at some point*, and Fiona replied that she hoped she could be. The cat stared hard into Fiona's eyes, a glare that would make most humans uneasy, but Fiona understood it was a test. *Very well then*, said the cat, *I will call upon you in the future.*

And so, one evening when Fiona was preparing supper, the cat appeared at her doorstep, meowing an alarm. Fiona left the potatoes she was scrubbing and followed the cat as it led an urgent journey back towards the stables. She found Mr. Tierney and a stable boy holding three kittens and a bucket.

"What are you doing?" Fiona exclaimed.

The groom, annoyed at the interference tried to ignore her but the stable boy laughed and announced that they were drowning the kittens.

"Whatever for?"

The groom put the bucket down with a huff of impatience, he just wanted the unpleasant task over with.

"We don't need another cat. One is enough. Now leave us to do our work and get on your way Missus."

Fiona snatched the kitten he was holding and reached for the stable boy's two kittens.

"I'll have them. Give them here and I'll take them home with me."

"You can't be having the mother cat. I need her to keep the mice down in the stables. And I'll be locking her in the next few days, so she doesn't follow after her kits."

"That's fine," Fiona replied, "I just want the kittens." The groom nodded to the stable boy who reluctantly parted with the two kittens. He had really wanted to see them drown. It would have been good craic.

"As long as you keep them down there at the cottage, I don't care what you do with them. They'll die anyway without their mother." Fiona snatched the kittens to her breast and marched off with them. They wouldn't die if she could help it.

So it was that she fed the kittens every hour for the next three days. She dipped a cloth in warm milk and let them suck on it. One sickened with diarrhoea, not able to stomach the cow's milk. Fiona did all she could for it, but the little one was too weak and faded away. It was buried respectfully behind the cottage and St. Francis was asked to take the kitten home. The other two did manage to hang on, struggling to gain weight and strength. Fiona kept them wrapped up in a blanket in a box by the fire. She got up through the night to feed them, extending the breaks between feed times by an hour every third day. After the night feeds, she would hurry back to her warm bed and tuck her cold feet against Ciarán to warm herself. He would grunt in displeasure but never pulled away from her.

A mouse was left on the doorstep one morning. Fiona knew what it meant and smiled to herself. She had learned to speak cat. She would let the queen know that she would find the kittens decent homes with farmers that needed good mousers.

One morning, Fiona woke up feeling a bit lightheaded but assumed she just needed a cup of tea. She lifted the kettle left over the embers of the fire and decided it didn't need refilling. Bending down to blow on the kindling she had lit, she was overcome with nausea and had to run outdoors to retch up the bile churning in her stomach. Weakly, she dragged herself back indoors and crawled into bed. Ciarán, who had risen and was

397

getting dressed asked her what was the matter? Fiona groaned and said she must have eaten something off. She curled up into a ball and pulled the quilt over her head.

Ciarán walked up to the main house and poked his head into the kitchen, asking if it was too late to beg a bowl of porridge and a cup of tea. The cook, just tidying up after the staff had eaten was not best pleased but granted him a bowl and a cup.

"And what's the matter with your own wife that she can't feed you?" she demanded.

"She's poorly this morning," he shoved some porridge in his mouth and wiped it, the cook made it so much better than Fiona. "Says she must have eaten something off."

"Not surprising, from what I hear about her cooking," the cook muttered and then she laughed out loud. "Or maybe I should be congratulating you, young man!"

Ciarán glanced up from the meal he was devouring

"What?"

"Morning sickness boyo, your wife has morning sickness." Ciarán still looked confused. "She's maybe expecting a babby!"

Ciarán nearly choked and then stood up suddenly, spilling his tea across the table.

"No! She can't be!"

"Why ever not? You are married, aren't you?"

"Oh Jaysus!" Ciarán ran his hand through his hair, "I've got to go to the cottage. Can you give a message to Mr. Bennet that I have been detained?" Without waiting for an answer, he hurried out of the kitchen and ran down the path to the cottage, throwing open the door, he found

Fiona sitting at the table slowly nursing a cup of tea.

"Are you better then?" he gasped.

"What are you all out of breath for?" she asked with alarm. "Is something wrong?"

"Is there," he paused uncertainly, "Is there something you need to tell me?"

Fiona just stared at him, standing there, hair on end, face flushed from running and still panting. Then she burst out laughing.

He was offended.

"I don't find something this serious funny."

"I can't help it," now she was gasping for air. "It was just the way you looked, as if something truly dreadful had happened. I was only sick. I'm fine now."

"But aren't you, could you be," she leaned forward as if to pull the words from him, "Are you with child Fiona?" he sputtered.

It was her turn to be flummoxed. She and nan had never quite got around to discussing childbearing, as it wasn't a topic that needed addressing when she was a *wean*. But now - she stopped and tried to remember when she last had her courses. With the move to Strabane and all the change in her life, she hadn't been paying that much attention. Of course, there had been the blessed rush of blood a few weeks after the rape. She had told Kathleen, who had held her and assured her that she had been praying. And since then? They had only been married the few months. She could be with child though. She only cycled once every six months or so, but she must have passed her fertile period by now. It was so hard to know, with her slightly different biology. She was overcome by an overwhelming need to talk to Nan. Nan would know. Nan would have cycled at a goat's schedule and Eala would have only been able to breed in the early Spring. Had they been able to know when they were pregnant? Maybe the answer was in the book. Without replying to Ciarán, she ran to the cupboard beside their bed where she kept Nan's book and sitting on the side of the bed, began turning the pages rapidly, scanning the old script, looking for answers.

Ciarán came to sit beside her, watching her whip through the pages, while biting her lower lip in concentration.

"Why are you looking at the book *acushla*?"

She stopped suddenly and looked up at him, her face screwed up tight in anxiety and her breath coming fast.

"Because I don't know! I don't know anything!"

He sat with her, letting her finish her scrutiny and then waited when she slammed the book shut and pushed it away from her. She put her head in her hands and he stroked her back.

"I'm sure you could ask someone. I could take you to a doctor if you would want that."

Lifting her face from her hands but remaining hunched into herself, she turned to him with a look of disappointment on her face.

"Sure, I know how babies are born Ciarán. I helped Nan enough times with remedies for the mothers. But I don't know how I will have a baby – how I will know, how long it will take, what to look out for. Nan never told me and it's not in the book."

"Surely, it's just the same for you as always?" Yet her face let him know it was different.

"I'm a Listener," Ciarán. She spoke as if to a child, "We cycle as the animal we are bound to. I

400

know that much. My courses come every six months. I'm just not sure about the rest."

Ciarán swallowed hard. He managed to strangle out,

"I hadn't realised."

"Of course not," she snapped and then was immediately sorry for her tone. "I'm sorry. I'm sorry Ciarán. It's not your fault. It's mine."

He slipped his arm around her and pulled her into his lap.

"It's no one's fault my love. If it comes early, people will just think we were a bit eager. That happens often enough. As long as the baby is healthy, nothing else matters. It will be just the one baby, won't it?"

"Do you mean am I going to have a litter of whelps?" She laughed at the horror in his face, and then when he tried to apologize, she laughed again.

"One, Ciarán. We only ever have one and it's always a girl. Surely, you've figured that out by now." When he shook his head, she began to count on her fingers, "Me great granny with her blackbird, me nan and Billy, me mother and her swan. No men Ciarán, not one. I'm that sorry if you had your heart set on a boy and a big family, for you won't get either."

"One is enough." He took one of her hands and kissed the palm gently. "Now tell me *cailín*, are you with child?"

Fiona turned to Ciarán, brushing the hair off his forehead, she kissed him there and then walked to the window, leaving him behind her. She stood very still and placed her hands on her abdomen, breathing slowly and trying to listen. Deep within herself, she felt a faint pulse, not her own, but entwined with her own. She felt her heart

401

skip a beat and then ran to her husband, throwing her arms around him,

"Yes," she said, "Yes!"

Conall was aware something was different with Fiona and took to nuzzling her abdomen. She found this terribly ticklish and tried to push his head away, but he persisted. Neither would he gallop for her or take high jumps. She could hardly force the stallion to her will, though she insisted that she was well enough. It was early days, but he was almost more protective than Ciarán, who scolded her for carrying water, and once even tried to scrub the floor so she didn't have to do it. She watched him for a few minutes and then shoved him aside, assuring him that women had been doing housework and having babies since time began. Still, he watched her anxiously. If there was only to be the one child, God willing, it would be a fine, healthy *cailin*. He wasn't so sure about the listening bit though. He admired Fiona's abilities, but it set her apart, making her stand out as someone different than others and not able to make friends easily with other women. However, he had little choice in the matter, due to Conall's attentions, Fiona was fairly sure the child would bond with a horse. She instructed Ciarán that the child must be given a horse, not a pony, as she would grow out of a pony and yet be bound to it. Ciarán assured her that they would find their only child a marvellous steed though he wondered why Fiona was advising him now. Surely, she would be there at the time, to choose the animal and help her child bond appropriately.

Farley was less excited about the prospect of a new life. His bond was with Fiona and no mere child could interfere. It was bad enough that Fiona wasted so much time on Ciarán. She should remember who had been there first and always. One night, lying in bed, Farley was curled against Fiona's stomach as was his habit. It was then that the child quickened. Fiona woke up startled and lay her hand on her belly in wonder. The child moved again, pushing ever so slightly against Farley. Instinctively, he kicked out at it. Fiona grabbed his paw and admonished him. She wouldn't be having any of that sort of behaviour. He was incensed and got off the bed to stalk out into the kitchen and sleep by the stove. It wasn't as comfortable or as warm as the bed though, so he returned, plopped into his place, and grunted in displeasure. Fiona fondled his velvet ears and kissed the top of his head. "Never mind *storeen*, you will always be my prince."

ME AND MY DOG ARE ONE

Willie had asked the maid to meet him at the summer house, well behind the manor house. This was a convenient trysting place for him as it was dry, and far enough from the house that noise would be acceptable. He found the country girls could be rather loud when enjoying his favours. They obviously hadn't learned the more genteel ways of the London ladies. He sat and smoked a cigar while waiting for Emily, the rather lovely house maid he was currently consorting with. She had a round, plump ass, and a considerable bosom. Her cheeks were rosy and her hair a vivid black. She told him she loved him, which was amusing. She wasn't a brilliant conversationalist, but Willie didn't need her for that.

Emily came running down the lawn and looking once back over her shoulder towards the manor, rushed into the summer house. She threw her arms around Willie and kissed him with a smack on the lips.

"I'm sorry I'm late!" she squealed, "I'm so sorry. I know you hate waiting, but Mrs. McTavish told me I had to polish the dining room table before teatime. I had to do it, or she'd get ever so angry, and I didn't want her to be suspicious either." Willie cut her off by placing a hand over her mouth, grabbing her lush bottom, and pulling the girl towards him.

"I might have to punish you for being late," he leered and watched her eyes grow wide. He had enjoyed spanking her on several occasions. Once he must have gotten too enthusiastic as she had become somewhat frightened of him after that. Oh well, it was good for a woman to be frightened of men. It kept them obedient. He turned Emily around and had her bend over, resting her hands on the summer house bench. Then he pulled up her skirts and took her quickly, without preamble. She was not ready and whimpered in pain, but he ignored her.

While she cleaned herself with a cloth from her apron pocket, Willie did up his trousers and prepared to leave. He was astonished, and rather annoyed when she reached out for his arm and took hold of his sleeve.

"Master Hayes," she began.

He yanked his arm free,

"What is it?" he snapped.

"It's just, I need to tell you something Sir." She hesitated and he grew impatient, turning to go but she reached for his sleeve again.

"It's, well, Sir, I'm with child." Her face flushed red, and she looked down at the floor. "It's your child of course," she added quickly.

Willie snorted and considered Emily's belly while musing on her remarks. Did this girl honestly think he would believe her? He had only forced himself on her once before she had willingly conceded to his demands. She was clearly a slut and had probably been ridden by half the men on the estate, and now she was trying to palm a child off on him. She was just looking for money. Oldest trick in the book. He laughed then. These people were so simple. How he could endure it in this country much longer he did not know.

"My dear, it's no concern of mine if you are in the family way. That's your problem," he patted down his jacket, making sure she hadn't lifted his purse and then sauntered back to the house. Emily sank to her knees in the summer house and sobbed. She had never expected his Honour to marry her, but she thought he would have given her a cabin on the estate and left her some money for the child. Girls were always getting pregnant by their masters; her mother had warned her. But most masters were kind enough to supply a bit of money to ease the burden of shame.

Fiona was hanging lavender from the line Ciarán had put up for her in the cottage. She had several rows of herbs and plants hanging now and it made her feel as if she were home again with Nan. Although, the cottage she had now was so much more pleasant than the cabin she and Nan had existed in. The tidy rows of healing herbs made her feel like she too would someday be a wise woman, as Nan had been. At least she now had a home in which to dry and store her remedies. She was even starting to make a name for herself among some of the tenants, though she had mainly been offering healing for their livestock.

She was surprised out of her reverie when she heard a knock on the door. She was not accustomed to visitors and the day's weather wasn't the sort that encouraged people to go outdoors. She got down off the chair she had been standing on, thinking that Ciarán would be enraged to see her climbing about in her delicate state. She smiled, Ciarán was so excited about the baby. It was a relief to be able to give him something, after he had sacrificed so much for her. She was still smiling when she opened the door and saw one of the house maids standing on the step. Ever since her unpleasant experience at the McGovern's, she had steered clear of house staff, finding them full of airs, and far too grand for the likes of her. This girl did not look condescending though. She stood awkwardly, rubbing her palms against her apron. She tucked a stray strand of hair in her cap, looked once at the ground and then back at Fiona.

"I hear you can do cures," she blurted out. Fiona nodded but did not speak. She observed the girl, the agitation was obvious but something else - fear, she could smell it. Farley came to Fiona's side and pushed his head out the door to sniff the girl as well. Yes, the little maid was terrified.

"I mostly work with animals," Fiona offered. She watched the colour drain from the girl's face and thought she might faint. Instinctively, she reached out and took the girl's arm. "Come in and sit a bit." She settled the girl on a chair by the table and put some tea in a pot. Lifting the kettle from the stove, she poured the hot water and wet the tea. She placed a cup and the milk jug in front of the girl and then sat down opposite her. "You work up at the house?" The girl nodded and took a sip of her tea, but only after inspecting it carefully. "It's just tea," Fiona reassured her. "I haven't slipped anything in it yet as you haven't told me what ails you." The girl looked into her teacup and then spoke, so softly that even Fiona with her sharp hearing had to lean forward to gather the words.

"Do you know," Emily whispered. "Do you have a recipe to stop a child?" Fiona sat back in her chair and stared intently at the housemaid. The girl seemed to shrink under Fiona's scrutiny.

"I've never made the recipe," Fiona finally answered. "It's a dangerous thing, for the person taking the remedy and the person supplying it. I could be arrested." She folded her arms over her chest and decided she would turn the girl away. She couldn't risk her happy life now, not while she had Ciarán and with a baby on the way. Things had turned out so much better than she had ever expected. However, this poor maid would lose her position, and probably be beaten by her family, maybe even be shunned by the community, and made to live on her own outside of the village. That was what usually happened to unwed mothers.

Emily began to weep, not bothering to wipe the tears that ran down her face, dripping onto her starched white apron. Fiona was uncomfortable. She did not know how to comfort people. Animals were her natural patients. At the back of her mind, she remembered what had happened to her and the wash of relief when her courses had come. She too, could have been an unwed mother. But why couldn't the girl marry? What had happened to this *girseach*?

"Will he not marry you?" Fiona queried. Emily just shook her head, now beginning to move on from weeping to sobbing.

"I knew he wouldn't, him being so grand and all. He forced me at first, then I pretended to like it because I thought he'd give me a cabin and some means. That's what happens with lots of maids that get a child from their master."

"Your master?" Fiona could see Willie, leering at this girl across from her, fondling her breast and forcing his hand up her skirt. For a moment, Fiona felt her own nightmare and thought she would be ill. Her vision blurred and Farley rushed to her side, pawing at her lap, and trying to bring her back to the present. She gripped the table, closed her eyes, and took a deep breath. Then she looked Emily square in the face. "It was that wee gobshite, wasn't it? Master Hayes, may the divil take him."

"Yes," Emily sobbed. Then she threw her apron over her head and gave in entirely to her

408

hysteria. Fiona got up from the table and went to her cupboard in the bedroom, pulling out the book. She returned to the table and began leafing through the pages. Lovage was the only pertinent plant she would be able to get hold of easily. It wasn't the most reliable of remedies for pregnancy, but it was all she could lay her hands on quickly. Parsley would help as well. She would need to study the recipe carefully and make sure she dosed the girl adequately, while not poisoning her.

"If I give you a remedy, do you have someone you could go to? You'd be ill for a day or maybe several days afterwards." Fiona realised she was taking the risk. She hadn't meant to, but she knew how narrowly she had escaped the same fate as this girl was suffering. She had to help.

Emily reappeared from under her apron and blew her nose juicily into said apron. After wiping her eyes, she nodded and said her sister would look after her. She had a cabin not too far from the Hayes estate but far enough from Emily's mother. Fiona took the details of how far along Emily was and instructed the girl to come back to her in a week and the remedy would be ready.

"Oh, bless you! Bless you. You are saving my life," Emily threw her arms around Fiona, who tried to escape the embrace but was overcome by the housemaid's superior weight and size.

"You must keep this entirely between us," Fiona warned, and Emily could only agree, for she too would be at fault if they were found out. Promising her silence and thanking Fiona again, the girl agreed to come back on the same day next week. And then she was gone. Fiona sat with her hand on Farley's head and contemplated her choice. Was she doing the right thing? She hoped so. Too bad she couldn't get a remedy to his

Honour that would destroy his sex drive. With Emily out of the picture, he would only move on to another of the household staff. Well, he would stay well clear of Fiona. She had enough of men who abused women for amusement. She was prepared now. A gun was generally more effective than a knife. She reached into her apron pocket and fingered the small pistol Ciarán had given her. After her repeated altercations with Willie, Ciarán had realised that Fiona's boldness and disregard for convention seemed to infuriate men with power. He could not always be present to intervene, and Farley only seemed to fan the flames. A pistol did not need to be used. It was only a warning. He thought Fiona's familiarity with a knife made her too handy with it. A gun she did not know and would never use.

As Fiona's pregnancy developed, Ciarán became continuously more solicitous. He encouraged Fiona to take more meals at the big house, where the food was more substantial, and the cooking was done by someone else. She rarely took his advice though. She hated sitting crowded together along the long table, waiting to have things passed to her while some of the girls made faces and whispered behind their hands. They often gave reproving glances when she slipped large portions of meat to Farley. She knew some of them had siblings at home that didn't eat as well as her dog, but she couldn't apologise for feeding Farley. She felt his needs too keenly.

As she wouldn't come to the table, Ciarán took to pocketing a bit of his meals at the manor house and bringing back parcels to Fiona. They would sometimes take strolls in the afternoon, before he had to return to work, and he would share out the tidbits he had saved for her. If the

410

weather was clear, these walks became a pleasant reprieve from Ciarán's work on the estate and gave him more time with his wife, as she was no longer joining him regularly as he travelled the estate. Fiona would hold his hand and they would chat about their coming child. They decided she would be named Kathleen, after his sister, although, if she bonded with a horse, perhaps she would be better called Epona, the old Irish goddess of equines. Or perhaps, Epona could be a middle name Ciarán had suggested. They would save as much money as they could in Strabane and then move back to Donegal and maybe rent some land near Ciarán's family. Fiona thought they could start a herd of goats. She could make cheese (though she remembered hating the process, surely, she would have more patience now.) She could sell cheese and remedies as Nan had done and Ciarán could grow potatoes and maybe get a cow and some sheep. They would live simply but they would be happy. Their daughter would learn to read and write. She would go to school if she wanted to but if she didn't, they would teach her themselves. She would learn to read Dickens and recite poetry. She would be talented, beautiful, and safe. At the back of her mind Fiona compared her pleasure at the coming child with Emily's despair. At least she had saved the housemaid the disgrace of having to carry an unwanted child.

At the end of a walk, Ciarán would kiss Fiona goodbye and remind her to have a rest before preparing tea. He would go back to his duties: collecting rent, tending to repairs and keeping the stable of horses in good condition. Mr. Bennett handled any big problems, including Wilfred Hayes. It wasn't such a bad job really. It had been a good deal more fun working on his uncle's farm with his cousin, but he was managing here at the Hayes estate. He did miss Liam though. They had had some grand times together. But that was before Fiona. Ciarán wondered if maybe Liam was jealous. Would he have been jealous if Liam had fallen in love and made him second best? Perhaps so. Ah well, there was little he could do about it now.

Ciarán needed to visit the McGuiness holding as they hadn't paid their rent. He wasn't relishing the task because he knew the family was struggling due to an injury McGuiness has sustained when a pig knocked him over. The Viscount had always charged the maximum rent possible, but Hayes Senior was known to be forgiving with the long-term tenants. Some sort of arrangement had to be made, to prove to the landlord that he would receive his rent eventually. Interest would be added to the debt, further burdening the family but maybe a good harvest would sort them out. Last year, their barley had not done well. Ciarán wasn't sure why. In many ways, he didn't feel qualified for this job, knowing a great deal more about horseflesh than crops. Liam's glowing letter of reference had gotten him the job but also raised expectations. Still, Bennet had not complained yet.

Fiona was accompanying Ciarán on this visit as she had been told that the McGuiness sheepdog had a rare case of worms and had grown thin as a wraith. Although relieved that she hadn't killed young Emily, Fiona was determined to concentrate her efforts on animals. It had been too stressful to worry over the housemaid. She hadn't yet the knowledge for that kind of healing.

Fiona had packed some garlic and parsley but was worried that McGuiness had already tried these well know remedies for worms. Wormwood was harder to come by so likely he hadn't tried that. Fiona had a small bit left from Nan's stores. She tucked the dried leaves into a bit of paper, remembering Nan cackling at her as Fiona again made a mistake in identification. It seemed so long ago and yet, she almost felt as if she could reach out and touch those days. If only she could.

Ciarán had collected Conall from the stable and trotted up to their cottage. Farley came out first, having heard Conall, and Fiona waved from the door. She checked that she had all the herbs she might need as well as Nan's book. She never went to a healing without it. You couldn't hold everything in your head, at least Fiona couldn't. It seemed Nan had, but then she had a lot more years to practice than Fiona. She threw her bag over her shoulder and ran out the door to her husband waiting for her. Her husband! It still felt strange and wonderful to say that.

Conall bent down and with a hoist from Ciarán, Fiona was seated behind him, Farley trotting alongside. She turned when she heard another horse's hooves behind them. It was Willie Hayes. Fiona slumped in the saddle and then poked Ciarán in the back. He turned and saw the young master. With a quiet curse, Ciarán reined in and waited for Wilfred Hayes. As the young man drew up alongside them, Ciarán touched his cap, Fiona just glared. She hated the man and made no effort to hide her feelings. Fiona felt for her pistol; she had really enjoyed target practice, developing quite a skill with the little pistol, though Ciarán kept reminding her it was just for show, that she would never need to fire it. But she would never let herself be hurt by a man again.

Master Hayes ignored Fiona and addressed Ciarán,

"I thought I'd come along with you. I hear you are going to visit one of the tenants who can't bring himself to pay his rent."

Wondering who the feck had told Hayes where he was going Ciarán tried to put off the ignorant fool.

"You don't need to bother Sir; I can sort this. Sure, he's only a bit behind and his family has been on the land for years. He'll come good. No worries, Your Honour."

"Nevertheless, I will be joining you. I do need to make sure my father's estate is being run properly. I know you Irish, always scheming behind our backs on how to cheat us. I'm here to make sure that sort of thing doesn't happen."

Actually, that was not why young Hayes was here at all. His father had expressly forbidden his involvement in the management of the estate, probably quite aware that his son had the negotiating skills of a wild boar. This was not what Ciarán needed. He was already worried about how to approach McGuiness, a man at least twenty years his senior and whose family had been on the land for well over a hundred years. Ciarán had planned to get Fiona to see to the dog, chat with the cottier a bit and then gradually work around to the question of arrears. That would never happen with the pig-headed Willie about.

"Really, Sir, I have your best interests at heart," *the hell I do*, Ciarán thought. "I'd never dream of cheating your father who was kind enough to give me this job."

Wilfred Hayes thinned his lips and remarked,

414

"My father didn't hire you. The senior manager did, and you have yet to prove yourself, so I'm coming along."

Sighing deeply, Ciarán nodded and prompted Conall into a trot. As they progressed towards the McGuiness holding, Wilfred passed a variety of remarks regarding his father's tenants, all of which, were of a derogatory nature. "Of course, none of them can read or write and are as filthy as savages. It's no wonder so many of them fall ill and die. What can be expected when you live like an animal?" He had a point there, Ciarán had to agree. The mud and wattle cabins, often shared with livestock were hardly hygienic but when people were so worn with work and hunger, when did they clean? If you barely had the money to pay the rent on a humble cabin, how were you going to afford a stable for your livestock? Things had improved since the famine. More and more small holdings now had a cottage and a separate stable for the cow or donkey, but there were still families living on the far edge of poverty. God help them.

Barely listening to the litany of complaints, Ciarán was jarred into attention when Wilfred pointed his whip at Farley and asked,

"Does that mangey terrier go with you everywhere?"

Icily, Fiona interjected, "He goes with *me* everywhere."

"Your Honour," Wilfred reminded.

"*Pog mo thoin,*" Fiona answered, smiling sweetly. Ciarán coughed to cover his intake of breath.

Wilfred looked to Ciarán,

"What did she say? Can she not speak the Queen's English?"

"My wife prefers her native tongue. She just gave you an honorific title in Irish. It's a compliment, Sir." Ciarán dearly wanted to give Fiona a good shake, but at the same time had to smother a laugh.

Wilfred looked doubtful but could hardly argue as he had not bothered to learn a word of Irish. They continued down the road without further remark, Wilfred occasionally throwing a glance at Farley who ignored him entirely. Fiona was all too aware of the attention the young master was giving her dog and decided to keep a close eye on the eejit.

When they arrived at the holding, McGuiness himself came out into the yard. He took one glance at Wilfred Hayes and closed his face down like a slammed door. Ciarán decided to move quickly before young Hayes made matters worse.

"Morning, sir. How is your leg doing now?" Ciarán didn't wait for a reply but rushed right on, "I brought my wife to see to your farm dog. She said you were having problems with it. Is that right? Hopefully, she can sort the wee beast out. Here Fiona," he tapped Conall who bowed and Ciarán helped Fiona down from the saddle. "Why don't you go off and see to the dog right away? Can't run a farm properly without a good dog, can you?" Fiona looked up at him bemused, then understanding, began moving towards the house.

"Is he indoors or out in the fields? I'd like to see him right away. I've a couple different herbs to try. Have you tried carrots? They can work sometimes, you know." Ciarán almost had to laugh. He'd hardly ever heard Fiona speak that many words together to a stranger. McGuiness led Fiona around the back of the house, while discussing the benefits of parsley. Fiona asked him if he'd tried garlic and offered him the wormwood she had brought.

The two men dismounted at the front of the house. Ciarán knotted the reins at Connall's neck and left him free while Wilfred stood awkwardly, holding his own horse. "Why aren't you tying up your horse," he demanded of Ciarán. Ciarán shrugged and gestured towards Conall.

"He's not going anywhere. Do you want me to take your horse Sir?" Wilfred threw the reins at Ciarán and began to pace around the yard. A few chickens scratched in the dirt in front of the door and laundry hung over the bushes. The door cracked open, and a woman scuttled out, curtseying to the Master, and nodding at Ciarán. She was carrying a bucket and was obviously heading to a well for some water, she was followed by a young boy, about four years old.

Just then, Fiona returned with McGuiness and Farley shot out around the corner of the house, startling the chickens. One clucked loudly and scuttled away from the terrier, towards Wilfred's boot. As the chicken approached him, Wilfred kicked it away with undue force, disliking the thought of the mite ridden creature near his boot.

The little boy broke from his mother and ran towards the fallen hen. It lay stunned, or dead, on the ground. The child kneeled by it and gathered it into his chest, sobbing,

"Little Red Hen! Little Red Hen!" The mother put down her bucket and went to the boy, trying to quiet him but his sobs grew louder. McGuiness' face turned a shade of puce, but he held his tongue.

"Oh, for goodness' sake!" exclaimed Wilfred. "It's just a bloody chicken. They can get another."

"It was the child's pet," Ciarán explained, "And these people rely on their hens for the eggs. You will have to pay them compensation, Sir."

But Wilfred was fixed on Fiona, as she stood, arms across her chest, glaring at him, with not one ounce of respect or fear in her eyes. Suddenly, he leapt forward and grabbed Farley by the scruff.

"It's the dog's fault. How about if I broke his neck? Would I have to pay you compensation as well?"

Farley wriggled and snapped but could not break free from the man's grasp. The mother picked up her son and buried his face in her apron. Something wrong was about to happen. Both Ciarán and McGuiness stepped forward and tried to say something placating but Fiona cut across them.

"You hurt so much as one hair on that dog's head, and I'll kill you," Fiona had her small pistol pointed straight at Wilfred Hayes.

"You wouldn't dare," he gloated, giving Farley a violent shake.

The gunshot seemed to hang in the morning air for eternity. The little boy whimpered against his mother's skirts, but no one said anything. Fiona scooped up Farley into her arms, checking him for injury but terriers are tough creatures.

Ciarán and McGuiness looked at the body, collapsed in front of the house, the blood from the head wound seeping into the hard-packed earth. A chicken neared the dead man and gave an exploratory peck.

"I did it!" Ciarán exclaimed, "You have to say I did it. My wife is with child. She can't go to prison. I did it."

McGuiness said nothing for a moment, then walked up to Wilfred and eyed him carefully.

"I've got a terrible hungry sow down in the byre. She'd make short work of this."

"You can't," his wife gasped but McGuiness ignored her.

"Give us a hand here Mr. Gallagher and we'll just pop down to the pig's pen with this." Ciarán, frozen, needed to be prompted again, "Will you now? I can't be standing here all day."

Ciarán untied Wilfred's horse and slapped it on the rump, knowing it would find its way back to the stable. Then he took Fiona by the shoulders, gripping her hard enough to leave bruises.

"Do you realise what you've done?"

Her lip was trembling,

"I've ruined everything. But Farley ..."

"Yes, Farley," Ciarán said bitterly.

"I could feel everything. He was going to kill us," Fiona said slowly and evenly. She was staring off into space and Ciarán felt her slipping away into her listening trance, so Ciarán grabbed her chin and forced her to look at him.

"Get on Conall and go home and pack. Now. You can go back to Glenties and stay with John."

"I can't leave you!" she protested.

"You have to," Ciarán countered. "It's too dangerous for you to stay here. He was the son of a Viscount. There will be questions and a search. Just do as I say this one time. Please." Without waiting for a response, he hoisted her up onto Conall's back and handed her Farley. "Make haste," and with a forward tug on Conall's reins, he set them off towards their cottage.

McGuiness helped Ciarán drag the corpse to the pigsty. They stripped the body, burned the clothes, and then dismembered the landlord's son, tossing the body parts into the pen, where the sow and her offspring set into the meal with gusto. When the men had finished, they rinsed their bloody hands in a bucket and then poured the bucket into the pen.

Ciarán turned to McGuiness,

"Why are you helping me?"

"Because you'll be changing the books and erasing my little debt. You might lower the rent a bit while you're at it," McGuiness remarked, wiping his hands on his trousers, and rubbing his stiff leg.

"I don't have that kind of authority. I'm only an assistant to the manager."

McGuiness leaned heavily on the fence, resting his leg and watched the pigs at their work.

"Sure, you can work something out." Ciarán knew that he would have to try. "When the teeth turn up, I'll bury them," McGuiness added and Ciarán nodded his agreement.

On returning to the cottage, Ciarán found Fiona sitting on their bed, her bag by her side and her cloak on, ready to travel.

"You should be gone by now," he said more roughly than he had intended. She nodded in agreement but made no move to leave. "It will be dark soon and you need to be off and on the road by then. I'll put out that you were feeling poorly from the baby and have gone home to stay with your family. Has anyone been by to ask about the horse?"

"One of the stable lads. I told him the master's son had started out with us but found the McGuiness cabin too dirty for his liking and had gone along on his own. They're out looking to see if he had a fall," she answered.

"That's good. And did they want to know where I was?"

"I said you were helping McGuiness with some chore about the place, that I'd come back on me own as I felt poorly." That was believable as her morning sickness has been frequent and obvious to all.

"It's as if you'd read my mind," Ciarán said, and then took both her hands in his. "I'll miss you, Fiona. You're a right pain in the arse, but God help me, I love you." He pulled her up into his arms and held her tightly for as long as he dared. He lay his hand on her belly, willing the child within to give him one farewell kick but it sat silent. Then he kissed Fiona softly on the lips and pushed her towards the door. Farley licked his hand once and then his family left the cottage, leaving Ciarán on his own.

He had expected the constable sooner, but the estate staff had scoured the countryside before giving up the search and asking the law for help. The constable had gone first to the McGuiness place and questioned the cottier. He had explained that the young master had stopped by, killed one of the chickens and left when the child started crying. McGuiness' wife had stood by, listening to the tale, and wringing her hands in her apron. The pigs hadn't quite finished their feast and if the constable looked into the pigsty, he might have been able to recognize a bit of human anatomy. However, he had gone on his way, pitching up at Ciarán's cottage later in the day.

Ciarán agreed that Wilfred Hayes had accompanied him, uninvited, out to the McGuiness holding but that he had not stayed.

No, he didn't know where Hayes had gone onto as Ciarán had stayed at the holding for some time. Yes, Ciarán's wife had been with him but was suffering terribly with the morning sickness and had to go home. Yes, his wife was quite able to manage Ciarán's ferocious stallion. The constable looked doubtful but had heard queer things about the woman so let it be.

"Would you say the young master was not well liked?" the constable asked.

Ciarán shifted uneasily in his chair and offered the constable more tea. The constable refused.

"I wish I had some cake for you but with herself gone ..."

"Can you answer the question Mr. Gallagher?"

"Well, he was a young man and a bit hot-headed. People knew he just needed a bit of growing up to do."

"He was the same age as yourself," the constable remarked.

"True," Ciarán conceded. "But you don't grow up so quickly when you've never worked a day in your life." The constable laughed, added some milk to his tea and took a large mouthful.

"Is it true that McGuiness was behind in his rent?"

Ciarán saw which way this was going, the murder could be pinned on McGuiness, which could never happen. McGuiness had a family and was innocent.

"Ach, it was a small thing. In fact, we sorted something out when I was there. I've meant to put it by Mr. Bennet but what with the search and all, I haven't had the time. Sure, McGuiness is a good tenant, his family has been here for years. He broke his leg last winter so got a wee bit behind on the holding and things weren't so good for him but he's a grand man, so he is."

"I've visited him. He said Master Hayes killed one of his laying hens."

"That's right. He did so. It was a pet of the wee boy's and the *wean* let off an awful scream, like a banshee he was. I think that drove Master Hayes away. It was a terrible noise." The constable noted the corroboration of stories in his notebook. He stood up and reached across the table, shaking Ciarán's hand.

"I thank you for your time sir. I hope your wife is feeling better and can come back to you soon. Where are her people by the way?"

Ciarán blanched, wondering why the constable would want to know that. "Over towards the west coast, a wee place. You'd never have heard of it." The constable smiled but felt no need to put that note in his book.

Wilfred Hayes senior was not surprised when he got the message that his son had gone missing. The boy had been in more trouble in his short life than the Viscount cared to remember. This last business with bedding the wife of well-known member of parliament had been too much. Drink, gambling debts, expensive horses destroyed by poor handling – it had all come his way via his son and heir. Still, Wilfred Junior was his progeny, and the Irish were not handling the case well. They hadn't even a clue at this point, other than some vague nonsense about a tenant being in arrears. Tenants didn't murder their landlord's sons. It would be too obvious. The Irish may be uneducated, but they weren't stupid, sly was more like it.

He took the boat over, a beastly crossing as usual and arrived at his estate a good week after young Wilfred had disappeared, seemingly into thin air. Bennet met with the Viscount in the library, the morning after he arrived. The manager gave what information he had – Hayes Junior had gone out in the morning with the assistant, Gallagher, and his wife. They had stopped at the McGuiness place. Yes, they were in arrears, though Gallagher said he had it sorted – and then the young gentleman had left on his own. A thorough search had been done and both Gallagher and McGuiness questioned.

"What about the wife?" Lord Hayes asked.

"Which one sir?"

"Both of them, preferably," Lord Hayes replied.

"Well, Gallagher's wife has gone home as she is sick with her first child. We can have McGuiness' wife questioned today if you like."

"I would like that," the Viscount commanded, "And find out where Mrs. Gallagher has gone so we can send word to the local constable. She can be questioned at home if she is that ill." Bennet was not sure how ill Mrs. Gallagher was, having heard that she left the estate on a wild stallion that few men could control. He agreed to make the necessary arrangements right away and would get back to the Viscount as soon as possible.

It was Mrs. McGuiness that broke down. She had been anxious from day one and had not been at all pleased with her husband's decision to dispose of the body via the pigs' feeding trough. She didn't think that the new assistant Gallagher could get their debt erased and even if he could, what good would it do her if her husband was taken away? There was also the small question of mortal sin – surely this sort of lie would add years to her soul's stay in purgatory, if she even got that far. When taken into the cabin, to be questioned away from her husband, she broke down in tears and told all, though she did manage to blame the shooting on Ciarán as requested. This helped with the rest of her story where she explained that Ciarán had forced her husband, at gunpoint, no less, to feed Wilfred Hayes Junior to the pigs. When asked why Ciarán would kill his employer's son, Mrs. McGuiness had to fabricate a bit by explaining that the young master had been having an affair with Ciarán Gallagher's wife. It was a lovely tale, seamless even, and the constable was thrilled as he recorded it. He went to Bennet and the two of them arrested Ciarán, throwing him into the gaol at Strabane.

USING THE POWER

Fiona did not go to John's house. She knew she would find no sympathy there. She sought out the cabin where she had first met Ciarán, where she had nursed him back to health and come to love him. It was with surprise and alarm that she saw a ribbon of smoke reaching up from the chimney. She placed Farley on the ground and circled the cabin with Conall, picking up the scents with her dog. Kathleen! They both realised together. So, Kathleen had had enough of John's imperiousness and Maire's bossiness. It was brave of her to be living on her own, but then, Kathleen had already experienced the worst pain and lived through it. There was very little left to be afraid of.

Fiona slipped off Conall's back and knocked on the cabin door. Kathleen opened it, recognised her sister-in-law, and embraced her in a hug. Then standing back from Fiona she realised something was very wrong.

"Put the horse away and come to me indoors," she said. Fiona nodded, leading Conall to the stable which he remembered unkindly. She removed his tack and rubbed him down with a bit of grass that she pulled from the field outside. Apologising to Conall for his accommodation and meagre fare, she left the horse and went to consult with her sister-in-law.

Kathleen had prepared two cups of tea and some scones and butter on the table. There was a dish of bread and milk on the floor for Farley. She gestured for them to eat and sat at the table across from Fiona, taking the younger woman's hand when she had finished her first scone. Fiona told the story simply - Kathleen had heard of the difficulties of working with the landlord's son and was not surprised by the report of the young man's cruelty. When Fiona came to the part where Farley's life was threatened, Kathleen gasped and reached for the terrier, lifting him into her lap to reassure herself of his health. Farley leaned into her chest and licked her chin in thanks for her concern. There was no surprise on Kathleen's face when Fiona confessed that she had shot Wilfred Hayes. It was as if Kathleen had expected that as a natural outcome. She was concerned for Ciarán though. Of course, he had taken the blame to protect his wife and child, but would anyone actually pin the crime on him? Would he be safe? Fiona shook her head, unsure and frightened herself. Wearied from her journey and the anxiety of the day, Fiona put her head on the table and sobbed. Kathleen came around to sit beside her and stroke her hair. No words were said.

It was preferred that John not know Fiona was 'visiting,' as they put it, so Fiona kept close to the cabin, helping Kathleen with various chores. Kathleen had started her goat enterprise, but her primary income came from her dressmaking and crocheting skills. She still went up to her brother's house on an almost daily basis, to visit or share a meal. In this way, along with the odd visit to Glenties, she was able to keep up on any news and hear if a young assistant in Strabane had been apprehended of murder. At first, the news of Wilfred Hayes Junior's disappearance filled all the papers, with many theories abounding: he'd run off with a married woman (again), he'd been killed in a drunken brawl, he was being held hostage for ransom. Fiona and Kathleen read the news, taken a day old from John's house, with relief. Then came the day when the paper reported an arrest in connection with the disappearance. There was the story of Mrs. McGuiness pouring out the tale, and the grisly details of her taking the constable up to the pigsty to show him the satisfied pig who had fed on Wilfred Hayes Junior's corpse. It turned out a bit of his Honour was left over. They read that Ciarán would be taken for trial in Londonderry.

"I can't leave him to take the blame. Please God, I can get there in time." She stood up from the table where they had read the paper, Kathleen having run back from John's hugging it to her breast and now still breathless from her journey. She tried to stop Fiona, even taking her arm while Fiona picked up her bag and began collecting her belongings.

"Are you sure Fiona? What about the baby? Ciarán wanted his child born safe. How can you ever get him free and not endanger yourself and the baby?"

"Do you mind if I take the loaf Kathleen?" Fiona pulled herself free from the woman, who shook her head and handed the bread to Fiona.

"Take whatever you need. Do you want me to come with you?"

Fiona declined, then put down her bag abruptly and hugged Kathleen with all her might.

"I'll get him free for you Kathleen. You don't need to lose anyone else. And I'll make sure the babby is born free as well. Farley and I will work something out. I promise." Tight-lipped, Kathleen nodded. She couldn't stop Fiona; all she could do was pray at this point.

Conall had been idle for a few days and was eager to move. There was no need to urge him into a gallop and he maintained a rapid pace throughout the journey, knowing he was going to be reunited with his rider. The journey took two days, one night spent curled by a stone wall at the side of the road, Fiona too tired and worried to seek alternative shelter. Curled up with Farley under the night sky, she feared she might arrive too late. She could not let her husband die for her. He had already given up too much for her as it was.

Derry was the largest town Fiona and Farley had ever been in. They were overwhelmed by the noise and the traffic but at least there were plenty of people to ask the way to the gaol. When they reached the edifice, she tied up Conall outside and entered the forbidding building, stopping at the front desk to ask for the officer in charge. The man at the desk looked down at the muddy, pregnant woman and laughed out of the side of his mouth. As if the officer would speak to the likes of her!

"I have important information regarding the death of Wilfred Hayes," Fiona insisted.

"That trial is over and done with Ma'am," he looked Fiona up and down lecherously, "Or is it, Miss? Anyway, the murderer is caught and convicted. Due to be hung tomorrow."

Fiona clutched as the child in her abdomen kicked her rib. She wouldn't stand down. She couldn't. She had come, just in time but she was here to confess.

"That's nonsense," she said, lifting her chin. "First of all, he wasn't murdered, he was shot in self-defence, and I know who did do it, because I was there. It certainly isn't the man who was tried. Someone is telling a pack of lies. Now I know the Viscount Hayes, I work for him as a matter of fact, and he won't take mistakes kindly. I suggest you let me see the officer in charge right away."

"You work for the Viscount?" the officer smirked in disbelief.

Fiona took a deep breath, closing her eyes for a moment. Then speaking very slowly, as if to an imbecile.

"Of course, I do. And as you've never been within a mile of the master's property, you have no reason to doubt me. I will remember to tell him that the receiving officer at Londonderry gaol treats the Viscount's servants with rudeness and impudence and I'm sure he'll see it fit to have you replaced."

The officer glowered at her but couldn't take the chance. She was filthy but could have just been travelling. Her accent was common, but she strung her words together well enough. Nah, it wasn't worth the risk. Without actually speaking to Fiona, he left the room and walked down the hall to the prison officer's office. He informed Lieutenant Birch that there was additional information on the Hayes case. Birch was not best pleased, but when the gentry are involved, it is always best to be particularly thorough.

Fiona was not so much ushered as shoved into Lieutenant Birch's office. He was a surprisingly young man that sat hunched over a desk piled high with paperwork. He pushed the pile in front of him aside as Fiona entered and he stared at the woman before him. She was small but stood with a confidence not usually seen in women of her rank, for she was clearly a common labourer. She had a small terrier with her, which immediately began sniffing around the baseboards of the room.

"Well?" he said, hoping to finish this interview as quickly as possible and get back to the requisition order he was working on.

"Ciarán Gallagher is innocent of the crime of murder. In fact, no murder was committed. Wilfred

Hayes Junior, attempted to take my life so I shot him. As you can see, I am with child and my husband preferred to take the blame rather than risk that his unborn child come to any harm."

"I see," Lieutenant Birch sighed. Obviously, the young woman had concocted this ridiculous tale to try to save her husband. No woman wanted to be a widow.

"You don't believe me," Fiona said. She looked down at the floor and Birch followed her gaze. Good God! The floor was crawling with mice! Birch wanted to scream and could almost feel the horrid creatures running up his trouser legs. He wondered at the terrier, who sat amid the melee, quivering with the effort of self-control. Fiona bent down and a mouse crawled into her hand. She held it up to her face for a moment and murmured something to the vermin and then placed it on the floor. "Perhaps you've heard of Lieutenant Distaff?" she enquired of the Lieutenant. "He had me put in gaol. Then he was killed by a pack of dogs." This was said coolly, as if it were a mention of the weather. There was another soldier too, Lennox, I believe, he used his horsewhip on me. He got killed as well. You see, Lieutenant, I have no problem disposing of people that hurt me or mine."

"Are you threatening me?"

"No, of course not, just explaining to you that we are quite capable of protecting ourselves. My husband is the dearest person in the world to me and I will protect him. Besides, he is completely innocent and surely, you don't want the death of an innocent man on your conscience?" She made a motion with her hand and the mice returned to their holes in the wall. "Would you like to visit with the rats next Sir?"

431

Lieutenant Birch was relieved that his desk was full fronted, and the young woman had not seen him draw his feet away from the swarm of mice. His abhorrence of vermin was near pathological. How had this girl known that? He definitely did not want to see any rats and was appalled that so many mice lived within spitting distance of his desk. He had to grip the edge of his desk till his finger joints hurt. This Mrs. Gallagher obviously had some sort of gift but he, for one, had no inclination to see anymore of her performance. It was highly irregular, but he had to do something to get rid of the bloody woman before she called a plague upon his prison.

"As it happens, we have Mr. McGuiness in custody as well," Fiona gave him a sharp look.

"Aiding and abetting a criminal."

"Feeding his pig," Fiona murmured. "I guess his wife turning traitor didn't protect her family after all. It wasn't as if she even saw anything. She had her hands full with her desperate lad. You know Hayes killed the child's wee chook before he made an attempt on my life?"

Birch made a sort of choking sound deep in his throat. The woman was clearly mad.

"I did not know that. However, as McGuiness is in custody, I can question him again regarding the incident. Perhaps he will tell a different story now."

"Ciarán will have made Mr. McGuiness promise not to involve me. You'll have to tell him that I have told you what really happened and it's quite alright for him to tell the story properly. And you should release him as well. Mr. McGuiness was not aiding a criminal since my husband is not a criminal."

"But you are," Birch's head was beginning to hurt.

"Are you not listening?" Fiona leaned forward, both hands slapping onto her knees. Birch gave a little start in case the gesture was another signal to the animal world. "I told you that Hayes tried to kill me, and I shot him in self-defence. Since when is that a crime?"

"A gentleman, of breeding and high standing in the community would never attack a woman and certainly not in broad daylight with witnesses present."

Fiona looked up at the ceiling and gave out a sigh of exasperation.

"Just because someone is rich doesn't make him a gentleman and Wilfred Hayes were as far from a gentleman as could be imagined. As for breeding, I certainly wouldn't repeat that mating in my kennel if something like Wilfred was whelped. Finally, he was not of high standing in the community. He was feared and despised. Quite frankly, culling him was a kindly service I did for the Strabane."

Birch spoke slowly and carefully. Yes, it was clear. She was raving.

"I will interview Mr. McGuiness. If there is any change in his story, a judge will be sent for. However, there is the issue of your husband's confession."

Fiona rubbed her swollen belly.

"Obviously given under duress."

"Yes, so," Birch agreed, thinking of the horrifying child this insane woman would spawn. "I will send word to you. Where are you staying?"

"With my horse. I will find a livery nearby and let your officer at the front desk know where I am." With that she stood and went to the door,

433

pausing with her hand on the knob, "I will hear from you shortly Lieutenant. If you can't find me, one of my friends will find you." She glanced meaningfully at the skirting board and Birch felt his stomach turn. He nodded and breathed out when Fiona finally left the room.

If a dog could laugh, Farley would have done so. As it was, he trotted gaily up to Conall, tail vibrating and communicated the whole interview. Conall was nervous for Ciarán though, and not nearly so amused as Farley. He also felt the exhaustion as Fiona leaned against him. Listening and speaking to an entire mischief of mice had taxed her abilities. At least the happy accident of Birch being terrified of small furries had magnified the display. Conall bowed for her, and she dragged herself into the saddle. She asked the horse and dog to lead her to the nearest stable. Once there, she offered the few coins she had to the proprietor and then fell into the straw to rest. The owner made some remark about it being a stable and not an inn, but Farley growled and Conall made to bite him, so the man desisted. Fiona fell into a fitful sleep and Farley ate the bread she had carried with her from Kathleen's, although he did save Fiona a small bit. Then he too, curled up for a short nap.

The gaol was only around the corner, so Fiona was able to walk back and leave her current address. The officer on the desk still curled his lip at her but she had no time to confront him. She needed to start collecting the dogs of Derry. Freeing Ciarán and keeping herself out of the clutches of the law was going to take more than an altered confession.

Meanwhile, Birch had first McGuiness and then Ciarán brought to his office, both in chains of course as they were felons. McGuiness was happy to recant and give the honest recollection of the event if that is what the 'little lady' wanted. She was a grand lass, and he would do whatever she asked. She was very clever and well handy with that wee pistol of hers. When asked if the shooting had been in self-defence, McGuiness had looked confused. Well, that Hayes boy was going to kill Fiona's dog, and everyone knew that dog was the world to her. She and that dog were never seen apart. Ciarán, poor man, was second place to that dog. It was likely the baby would be too. Never seen such a powerful love for a dog before. So, well, maybe that is what she meant. She'd sure die of grief if any harm came to that dog.

"Certainly, you can see, Mr. McGuiness, that a man's life is worth more than a dog's?" Birch reprimanded. There was a long pause while McGuiness pondered this and then he shook his head slowly.

"The ways I look at it, Sir, is it depends on the dog, and it depends on the man. Now my wee bitch at home, she's a right good sheepdog and she's whelped some grand pups, she has. Well, I'd say, she's worth more than a fair few men that I've met."

Birch thought he might want to be hanged himself. How could he deal with these people? He saw Ciarán next. The husband put his face in his hands and sobbed briefly when he heard that his wife had confessed. When asked what had really happened, he gave a story similar to that of McGuiness, but then added some nonsense about the dog and the woman being bonded and the death of the dog would lead to the death of the woman. It sounded like something out of a fairy story. Maybe these men had drunk too much of the local poteen and turned their brains. How could he go to a superior and spout this foolishness? There had to be a conviction. A Viscount's son had died. Someone must swing in repayment.

What could happen really? He had to let the verdict stand and deal with the consequences afterwards. There wasn't much one young woman could do. He sent no word to her accommodation. He would have to proceed as planned.

Birch had his dinner at his regular pub and stayed for a few drinks with a fellow officer. Stepping out into the dark street, he was surprised to find it was so late. The streets were mostly empty now and there was an icy wind blowing in from off the bay. He would march back to his rooms as quickly as possible, maybe have a quiet brandy and do his best to sleep.

As he walked, he imagined he heard a low growling sound, then the rat-a-tat of toenails on cobbles. There were a lot of stray dogs in Londonderry. He looked over his shoulder but couldn't see anything. He had probably had too much drink taken and was still spooked by the queer interview with Mrs. Gallagher. Only the noise got louder, and there seemed to be more than one set of paws behind him. No, not just behind him, in front of him too. He went to lean on the side of a building and stepped on a small form that leapt up and bit him in the ankle. He stepped away, only to find more creatures under his feet. He shouted and kicked out. Then a voice:

"I wouldn't hurt them. I can't let anyone hurt my friends."

That woman! "Y, y, you." he stuttered.

"If you hurt us, we tend to get a wee bit out of control. I didn't mean for them to kill that second fellow in Glenties, but he did whip me with his riding crop and the creatures, they don't like it when a Listener is hurt."

"What do you mean by this?" Birch tried to speak with authority, but his voice only seemed to increase the decibel of the growling.

"I want me husband freed. You never even sent me a message, so I know you intend to do nothing and see him hanged in the morning. That just won't do Sir. They've changed their confessions, haven't they?"

"Yes, but a crime has been committed and someone must be punished!"

"What crime?"

"You shot a man dead for no reason at all!"

A large breed dog leapt up growling and pinned Birch to the wall. He slavered at the lieutenant's throat.

"Call him off!" the lieutenant shrieked.

"We're angry that you consider Farley's life to have no meaning." Her words dripped with venom, but he stupidly persisted.

"He's just a dog!" Birch heard his voice rise with hysteria. The hound at his throat nipped at his ear, pulling the lobe clean away.

"That was a ridiculous thing to say," Fiona remarked. "'Just' these dogs can rip you to pieces. Or 'just' these dogs could work your sheep, protect your property, keep the rats off your children, and be your soul's companion. These dogs have as much value as you and me self. Maybe more, I'd say more. Now lieutenant, you have a choice here. Arrange an escape for me husband, and you can sort Mr. McGuiness as well while you are at it. His wife is a useless ninny but that is not his fault. He loves his dog at any rate."

"Or what?" he was clutching at his bleeding ear and was fairly sure what the alternative would be.

"Well, we won't kill you now. That would be pointless if we want you to go back to the gaol and open a few doors. I think I would put a marker out on you. Every horse you try to ride will toss you off. Every dog you pass will urinate on you. Every gull overhead will dump his innards on you and every rat, Sir, every rat will wait till you are asleep and then chew on what's left of your ear. It will be a slow death, a tortuous, terrifying, slow death. Just what you would deserve for letting justice be unjust."

"I will lose my rank. I may even be court martialled!" he wailed.

Fiona screeched back at him,

"I do not care. You and your fellows have taken everything from me – me mam, me nan, me maidenhood and now me husband. You have to give him back. I will not let you have him!" The lane vibrated with the growling, deep guttural, and menacing. Certainly, the people of the houses could hear it, but they would be too afraid to venture out. Birch realised he had soiled himself. He was not a brave man. He was a glorified clerk. He could not fight her.

"I will do it," he whispered. He wondered could she hear him above the din.

"Good man," she said. "I will be waiting outside the gaol."

And so, it was that the cell containing the two accused men was unlocked and the men were escorted out the back door of the prison. Birch later told his superiors that he had been attacked and held at gunpoint by Mrs. Gallagher, that she had a mob of Fenians with her and they had forced their way into the gaol, accomplishing the release of her husband. Mrs. Gallagher, he kept repeating, was the ringleader, a real monster of a woman and it was she who should be hunted down and destroyed. She was a public menace; he reiterated the previous murders she had committed but did add that he thought the husband was ignorant of his wife's ill doing. Birch had kept his part of the bargain – Gallagher and McGuiness were free, but he would be damned if that bitch would go unmolested.

Fiona stood in the quiet of the night, holding Conall's reins. She heard the creak of a door on its hinges and then two figures came towards her, one broke away and ran to her, encompassing her in his arms. "You bloody eejit," Ciarán breathed into her ear and then held her close again, pausing to kiss her fervently.

She handed him the reins.

"You must go. Kathleen is expecting you."

"But we are both going," he insisted, clinging to her.

"No, not after what I have done this day. They will look for me. I will put you in danger."

"You can't go off on your own Fiona! What about the baby?"

She placed her hand on his cheek and smiled into the darkness. He had never completely understood.

"I'm not alone love. I would that I could be with you, but I will never be alone. Please go now, before they change their minds. I will come to you when I can, I promise."

He held the hand pressed against his cheek,

"This isn't right Fiona, please come with me," he pleaded but she had already pulled away and slipped into the night, a small terrier at her heel. Conall stamped worriedly and tossed his head. Ciarán didn't know what to do. He couldn't chase her or shout. McGuiness came up to him then and touched his elbow.

"She's right, you best be going. I'm off me self now. If you ever see your missus again, tell her I'm that grateful," and he too ran off through the unlit streets.

Conall pushed his muzzle against Ciarán, urging him. With no other option the man mounted his horse and headed towards Donegal. Fiona would go home. He was sure of it. She had spoken so fondly of the cabin she had grown up in near Maghera. He knew there were caves there – a good enough place to hide as any. He would search for her there. He would find her, and they would be a family together, they would.

Heavy with child, Fiona soon found walking painful. Her back ached something terrible and her feet felt like hot bricks. She had to rest so much more often than she would have normally. There were few hedgerows to hide from the elements with mostly the stone fences dividing the fields. She tried to find stables, warm from the animals and lined sometimes with straw. Often though, the floor was bare excepting piles of dung and sitting in the slick, damp enclosures gave little respite to her weary body. She longed for Ciarán and dreamed of going home to him in Glenties but knew that was impossible. She had threatened and frightened an officer and probably got him demoted. She knew Birch would seek out revenge.

In towns, she kept her head down and moved quickly. In Glendowan, she found a newspaper that someone had used to block up a hole between the slats of wood in a stable. There was an article about her and a rough sketch; it included Farley. People were warned to look out for a pregnant young woman accompanied by a rough terrier. There was a warning that she was dangerous and a known murderer. There was also a bounty offered for her capture. She sighed heavily and the horse she was sharing accommodation with turned to her with concern. She thanked him for his bother, and he reached his muzzle to nuzzle the top of her head. At least the animals would not betray her. Indeed, they had all been as helpful as could be – cows and goats offering what little milk they might have left and horses proffering oats, if they had them.

There was one horrid wet night where she had been lucky enough to find a stall with hay. She crumpled into the bedding and the inhabitants had been happy enough to let her rest on their fodder. A cow and a draught horse promised to look out for her and warn her of the farmer's visit in the morning. Farley, also feeling the drain of the baby and the anxious journey, fell into a deep sleep.

Unfortunately, the farm animals had not fully comprehended the seriousness of Fiona's case and let her sleep when the farmer's wife approached. The wife was a quiet woman, not gentle, with a stern line crossing her face as her lips pressed into what could never be a smile. She was lean and wiry, pushing the cow aside as she placed the stool and bucket next to the bovine. It was then that she spied Fiona and that Fiona and Farley both woke up, startled and terrified.

Eithne Carlin examined the young woman with the dog. She knew well who they were. There had been soldiers by the town asking people to look out for the fugitive and her terrier. She could see that Fiona was heavily pregnant and very much worse for wear. The mother to be, was smeared with muck, wan and hollow eyed. She probably hadn't eaten a proper meal in weeks and what little nourishment she had taken in was being sequestered for the baby. Even the dog looked tired and old. Eithne nodded at Fiona but said nothing.

Fiona stood slowly, stopping to lean against the wall of the stable to overcome a wave of dizziness.

"I'll just be on my way. I'm sorry I took advantage of your hospitality without your consent." She lurched for the door.

"Sit yourself down again. There's no hurry. Me husband won't be coming for the horse till long after his breakfast." Fiona paused but made no move to settle herself.

"I've no interest in reporting you," Eithne continued, "But sure, I live a quiet life. Tell me your story if you're able. It will pass the time." Fiona observed the woman closely and then lay her hand on the cow and asked her if the woman had a good heart. The cow was equivocal. Eithne always milked her on time and never left her painful. She cleaned the stall and certainly took care that the cow stayed healthy, but affection or friendship had never been offered. Fiona pondered. She could hardly run off in her state. She would have to take a chance. She slipped again to the floor and leaned against the wall of the stable.

"It's not a pretty tale," she began.

"The good ones never are," Eithne began to milk the cow and waited for Fiona to begin. Fiona felt an overwhelming need to unburden herself. She wasn't a murderer and didn't deserve to be chased through the countryside. Maybe this woman could understand. So, she told Eithne Carlin of how she was only just married a year. That her husband had been working for an English landlord. Then she described Wilfred Hayes Junior – how he had put a house maid in trouble, how cruel he was to animals and then how he had tried to kill Farley. All through her tale she sat crouched over, her head hanging. How happy they had been when they married and how dreadful it had all turned out. Finally, she lifted her head and looked Eithne in the face.

"I couldn't let him kill Farley. He's my soul. I know you can't understand, no one can, but it was self-defence. I am no murderer."

Eithne continued to milk, making no comment for some time. When the cow was stripped dry, she wiped her hands on her skirt and moved the bucket out of the way of hooves. She sat on the stool, her hands resting on her thighs, looking out of the stable across the fields and the dark clouds resting thickly above.

"I had a younger sister. She was as unlike me as could be. Eyes as blue as the sea and lovely, curling yellow hair. Her cheeks were pink, and we liked to feed her treats to see her plump up all cream and roses. She was our little pet. We spoiled her rotten, but her laughter was such a joy to us."

Eithne paused.

"I married a man well my elder, but it was what I could get. At least he had a bit of land. But Rosie, that was her name, she was so bonny and lively, she was able to get a good job in service. She was working at a manor house outside Letterkenny, very posh. She'd write home to us of the fine linens she laid on the table and the silver she polished. There were great meals, that she had as well in the servant's kitchen. She got on well with the other girls too. They all shared a room and would giggle together at night. She was so happy, and she sent home money every month."

Another pause. Eithne swallowed hard.

"The master noticed Rosie. She wrote of that too – she saw no harm in it as he spoke kind words to her and smiled at her. I was worried though. And I was right to be worried. He apparently told her he loved her, his wife was cold and distant, the whole tale so ridiculous but Rosie wasn't the suspicious type. I would have put my knee where it hurts but Rosie didn't want to anger him, he had been so kind to her and given her little gifts. She let him have his way and of course she got with child. As soon as she began to show, she was sacked and came home to the cabin. Daddy was beside himself. He beat her and called her a slut and a whore. She wanted to come to me then, but my husband wouldn't have it. The priest denounced her at church. She was all alone and went to live in a deserted cabin by herself. I used to bring her food. One day when I got there, I heard an awful buzzing. I opened the door and there she was, hanging from a ceiling beam, the flies all about her."

Eithne stood up abruptly and lifted the pail of milk.

"You can shoot all the landlords you like young lady. I've no forgiveness left in my heart for them. Wait there a bit and I'll bring you some food and then you best be going. My husband would surely like the bounty that comes with turning you in."

A CHOICE MUST BE MADE.

Was it a dream or a memory? Sitting on her Nan's lap with a puppy in her arms – Fiona was crooning to it and cuddling the pup as if it were a baby. Nan nodded and said, "Aye, this is the one." She laid one hand on the Fiona's head and one on the pup and began to chant. It was Gaelic but not in a dialect Fiona had ever heard. The words were old. The chanting went on and both Fiona and the pup grew sleepy. She let her head rest on her Nan's bosom and closed her eyes. Gently Nan took Fiona's hand and lifted a knife with the other hand. With a quick movement, she slashed Fiona's palm, blooding flowing over the edge of the cut; Fiona sat up sharply. Nan then nicked the pup's pad and pressed it to Fiona's wound. The pup yelped and Fiona found herself yelping with it, both of them squirming to get out of Nan's iron grip.

"Now dear," Nan said. "You have your helper, your own wee acolyte. Please God, he will serve you better than your mother with that bloody swan."

Fiona eased the child off her breast and watched Farley carefully. Of course, he knew what she was thinking. This was the one thing she never wanted to do. She had hated her mother for changing and leaving her. Changing to be as your acolyte was denying your purpose as a Listener. If she became an animal herself, how could she help any other creatures? Yet, she knew if she stayed human, Ciarán would never give up looking for her and if he found her, they could both end up in gaol, or dead. It was too much of a risk for him, and what of the child? What sort of life could she

446

offer her perfect, darling daughter always hiding and running? Always looking over her shoulder and dreading the worst? Never having enough to eat or a warm place to sleep? No, it was for the best. She would leave her baby with Kathleen, that quiet, sad woman who had had her hopes of a family taken away from her at the same time that Fiona had been given the gift of meeting Ciarán. Kathleen would love the child as her own and maybe, Ciarán would have some hand in the raising of the baby girl. Maybe the girl would have her own father, if not her own mother. It was the best Fiona could do.

She needed to find her way back towards Glenties, to the cabin where Kathleen lived, the cabin where she had first met and fallen in love with her child's father. It would be easier to travel now that she had survived the birth. She shivered in memory of the night she crouched screaming into her fist, as the labour pains had wrenched her body. Farley had paced frantically beside her, panting with her pain. When the child slipped from her womb, Farley had licked its face clean while Fiona had cut the cord. Together they had marvelled at the baby's first cry and then worried that someone would hear her. Farley had hastily eaten the after birth while Fiona, wrapping the infant in her shawl, struggled to her feet. They had to move on.

On her earlier journeys through the country, she had travelled the roads with Conall and Ciarán, but now she would have to cut through fields and keep well hidden. She hadn't been sighted in several weeks, but Fiona knew there were constables out looking for her. She should have let the dogs kill that officer after he had freed Ciarán. Instead, she had left Birch, insulted and angry, very angry. Of course, he wanted revenge. She had become too soft-hearted living with people this long.

Travelling West from Londonderry since Ciarán's release, Fiona knew she shouldn't go back to her old home that she had shared with Nan and the goats, but those days called her. Life had been a struggle and there had been the pain of her mother's absence, but it had been the place where Fiona had grown and stood at Nan's elbow, absorbing her years of listening and healing. She had never felt as safe as she had then. And now she was a fugitive, she would never know who she could trust and who would turn her in. With a bounty on her head and poverty so overwhelming, the temptation would be overwhelming for most. It wasn't as if she could blend in with other girls. With her huge brown irises and red grizzle hair, she was not commonplace. Even just the description, 'the girl with a dog' was enough for some people to recognize her. Food, if not found, had to be stolen and the rest snatched in stables and abandoned cabins with little, or no warmth. She was always damp and after her little one was born, there was also the issue of having clean clouts. Many, she stole drying on a hedge. Washing and drying wasn't a task she had time for as she moved through the country. Was she eating enough to nourish the child? Fiona looked at the ribs coming through Farley's coat and knew that she was not. Yesterday, a blessed woman had left a pie on the window to cool, and Farley had leapt up and snatched it as they passed. He had burned his mouth, but they had eaten well that night. Today, there had been nothing. Fiona felt her stomach reaching around and grabbing her backbone. She had never felt hunger like this before. The baby seemed to be sucking all the goodness out of her and Farley. Her child was a parasite, but how she loved it.

She stroked the wee *girseach's* soft cheek and peered into the face. Fiona vaguely remembered Nan saying all babies had blue eyes. This child meant to keep her blue eyes though. She would look like her father, crystal blue eyes and forest brown hair. She would be a beauty. Unless she bonded with some creature that changed her looks. If she bonded - could it happen Fiona wondered if there was no one there to teach the child and do the ritual? Was this the end of the Listeners line? Fiona didn't know. It wasn't something Nan had time to teach her. This was another repercussion to her decision to give the child up, yet she was determined to continue towards Kathleen. Fiona could not care for the baby, and she could not bear to see it wither and die, like the famine babies in their shallow graves. Ireland had seen enough starvation. Her child would not be one more dead innocent.

It was growing light so Fiona would need to make haste and leave the stable she was sheltering in. It was long abandoned, with only the faintest whiff of cattle about it, but some other drifter might be aware of it and seek it as a place of shelter. That had happened to her before and the traveller, a friendly widow on her way to Londonderry had shared food with Fiona and exclaimed over the baby, only to report Fiona in the next town. Farley had heard the horses long before the constables had arrived, giving them just enough time to run through the fields and lay flat amid the grasses, praying that the men did not ride in their direction and that the baby would stay silent. Fiona had wanted to curse the woman who had betrayed her but had heard the sad tale of her husband's death and how she had left her two sons in service to a farmer. The woman herself was on her way to work in one of the factories in the city, a fate Fiona could not even begin to imagine. Fiona had heard that the factory workers were shut in with the heat and the noise for ten hours per day. Starving would be preferable to that. However, the woman had children and no one else to turn to so what choice did she have? Fiona had a choice, just not a very pleasant one.

Continuing walking, her bare feet tracing paths made by cattle and sheep, Fiona tried to figure out how her life had come to this. She had set out to be a helper to animals; their voice in a world where the needs of the helpless were ignored. How had things turned so violent? Had she let Farley's defensive nature take dominance? Or far worse still, had she infected the dog with her own frustration and rage? Nan had never killed anyone, nor had any of the goats, except for Billy on that last day. But Nan had kept herself to herself. Fiona had tried to be a part of the world. She should never have agreed to care for Ciarán, then she never would have fallen in love with him. She had ruined his life. He could have had a sweet and comely wife with a bit of land. Gráinne would never have murdered anyone. Fiona had killed four men – admittedly, on her own, she had only killed the one, but she hadn't prevented the others. Yes, the men had all deserved their fate, but it was a life of turbulence that she had drawn Ciarán into. And who was she to judge who should live or die?

If she had been able to stay with Nan, in their shabby cabin on the cliffs above the sea, would she and Farley have become such a force of destruction? If Nan had lived, Fiona could have had more training and possibly have learned to control her power and use it more wisely. So, it was really all the fault of the man who had killed Nan. But this was a silly argument. It made no difference now. All that mattered was that she stop. She would bring no more harm to Ciarán, and she would save her child from this fierce life.

The cabin where Fiona had nursed Ciarán stood at the edge of John's holding, well away from other dwellings. Fiona wanted to run to it and open the door, build up the fire and pretend that Ciarán would soon be there; that he would read to her of an evening, and they would sit, Farley between them, staring into the flames, talking about their plans for their daughter. She even started up the path to the door but, no, it would be too cruel to see that home again and know it was gone forever. She would wait until Kathleen came out. Kathleen, she knew she could trust, if only because of the gift she was giving her. John, or his missus, would be sure to turn Fiona in, but not Kathleen. She cared for her brother and wanted a child too much.

It was hard to pick out Kathleen's scent over the smell of goat - she had more goats now! Fiona remembered how Kathleen and she had chatted about goats, how they were easy keepers compared to sheep. Goat cheese and milk were a bit stronger than that from a cow but liked well enough. Kathleen had wanted some way of earning that was her own, not wanting to be beholden to a brother who still silently blamed her for marrying a Fenian. Fiona watched Kathleen step out of the byre, a bucket in each hand. Her head was down, and she was concentrating on her steps so as not to spill the milk. Fiona didn't want to disturb her, but the baby chose this moment to grizzle. Kathleen nearly tripped, losing some of the milk. Fiona stepped out from behind the goat's shelter and walked towards Kathleen, shaking her head firmly. Kathleen understood the need for silence, put down the buckets, and looked towards the road to the big house. There was no one coming.

"Fiona," Kathleen whispered, "Where have you been? Ciarán is tearing the country apart looking for you. Oh! And the baby's been born!"

Fiona motioned with her head, and they moved to hide behind the byre completely.

"You know he mustn't find me. If he finds me, he'll either have to turn me in or be hunted himself. I want him to be free. I want my child to be free." She looked down at the furrowed brow of her infant as it fussed, reaching for her breast and food that Fiona really could no longer offer. How she loved her daughter and what a short time they had had together. How could she ever let her go? "Please," Fiona choked, "Please take her and care for her as your own. I know you will be a good mother to her." She handed the child to Kathleen, who clasped it in her arms with a joy and wonder that eased Fiona's agony slightly. "You can tell Ciarán to come home now. He'll never find me. Tell him," she gulped, "I've decided to join Farley."

"I don't understand Fiona," Kathleen tried to tear her eyes away from the baby she had just been given but only succeeded for a moment.

"Ciarán will understand. He'll know to stop looking. Maybe if he can, maybe he'll want to help you raise the *wean*?"

This time Kathleen was able to look at Fiona,

"Of course, he will. His own child! He'll worship the ground she walks on, all the more so

452

if she's all he has left," her tone was accusing but Fiona couldn't explain. It would take too long and be too painful. She reached out and touched the child's waving fist. The baby grasped her finger and squeezed with surprising strength.

"If you can't find a wet nurse, the goat's milk will do fine." With that, Fiona turned, and following her dog, ran off through the fields and on towards the coast. There would be caves there, privacy and time for Fiona to change and start a new life.

Crouched in an overhang where the sea crashed beneath them, Fiona made a fire and attempted to roast some fish she had caught, rotating it periodically over the flame. A pot would have been useful, she could have boiled up some seaweed and mussels, but she fled with next to nothing. It hardly mattered. This would be the last cooked meal she ate.

She let her arm wrap around Farley, and they sat snug together, sharing the flesh of the fish as she tore it off the bones.

"I've given away or lost everything I've ever loved, except you. There is always you Farley." The dog licked her fingers in reassurance. "I'm not even sure how this is done. I read the ritual in Nan's book, but I have never seen it done, obviously." The book had been left tucked into the shawl wrapped around Fiona's child. Fiona was not sure if Kathleen would burn the book or save it for the little girl, as an only memory of the mother she would never know. If Ciarán saw the book, he would recognize its use, but also its danger. Maybe it would be him that would burn it. It was another thing Fiona had been forced to leave behind her. Her home and Nan had been the loss that started this path, then her husband, her daughter, and now she would have to give up her human life.

Kathleen stood for a long time holding the infant. Should she run after Fiona, beg her to return? Should she rush up to John's house and insist on a search party? Surely, that would lead to Fiona's death though, hardly an appropriate return for the marvellous gift Kathleen had just been given. A child, to raise as her own, an answer to a dream, a reason to plod on through life. Ciarán would be thrilled as well – he had worried that both mother and baby had died, Fiona alone giving birth, God knows where. How had she managed?

The child mewled hungrily and shook a tiny fist at Kathleen. Its miniature face screwed up in a red wrinkle and began to bawl. Goat's milk would be needed immediately, even the novice mother could see that, and a name. She couldn't think of this darling creature as 'it.' Tucking the baby firmly into her arm, Kathleen decided to go straight to John's house. Maire would have clouts and clothing for the child and maybe give Kathleen some advice. She managed to lift one of the buckets in her free hand and began the walk up to the big house, stopping often, to check the baby's positioning in her arms. This gave her time to decide what she would say to John and Maire.

At the door, Kathleen put down the milk bucket and lifted the latch, entering the warmth and bustle of the kitchen. The baby, now hollering, managed to make all movement and noise stop. She sang solo to a room of women, entrancing them.

"Lord in heaven, what have you there?" the kitchen maid was at Kathleen's elbow,

"Is it a foundling? Are you sure it's not a fairy child?"

Of course, it was Maire, direct and purposeful who stepped forward and took the child from Kathleen's arms.

"Betty, warm up some of that goat's milk and then go find a clean clout. Go on! Don't stand there staring." She settled herself in the rocking chair by the fire and began to unwrap the vaguely familiar shawl the infant was wrapped in. A worn and tattered volume fell to the floor with a smack. Kathleen darted in and picked up the book, pocketing it before Maire could ask to see it. Maire eyed Kathleen suspiciously.

"Who's is it?"

"Ciarán's," Kathleen lifted her chin defiantly. Whatever Maire and John thought, this baby was home. It would not be sent away, regardless of who had birthed it.

"And Fiona's, I assume?".

"She gave it me, and no, I don't know where she went, and I wouldn't speak of it anyway. She gave me her child for safekeeping, and I won't break that trust." Suddenly with tears in her throat, "She gave me this gift."

Maire nodded, she had expertly stuck a finger in the child's mouth, and it was sucking vigorously, though this appeasement would not last long. "Does she intend to return and claim the child?"

Kathleen could not speak. She shook her head and let the tears run down her cheeks.

"That is wise." She stood up and placed the infant in Kathleen's arms. "I'll fetch the milk. Sit in the chair and rock her. When she is done feeding, make sure you get her to burp. She won't like the goat's milk at first as it will be different to what

455

she's used to, but she is hungry and will take it soon enough." She paused, watching Kathleen envelop that baby with all her being. "I'll speak to John about sending someone to find Ciarán. He should come home to greet his daughter."

Through her tears, Kathleen smiled, "Her name is Brigid, after our mother. Ciarán will like that." Maire agreed and went off to organise a cradle and some clothing for the new member of the family. It would be introduced to the family as Ciarán's daughter, cousin to Maire's own children. Little would be said of Aunt Fiona, after all, she was gone.

In a cave in Maghera, Fiona sat holding Farley to her. She felt such a failure, but there was no other way for her now. What harm could two stray dogs do roaming the countryside? They might steal the odd chicken but could be forgiven that. Dogs follow their instinct. There are no moral questions to debate. Leave that to the humans with their constantly changing values and their emotions warring with their intellect. A dog's way was easier. Holding Farley, she slowed her breath and let his thoughts become her thoughts, his senses became her own. The chant finally came to her:

Take my form and make of me,
A creature that I long to be.
No more in human body bound,
The girl I was will not be found.
A new life in a dog I seek,
Another language I will speak.

Any human considerations she had dissolved. She let herself and her acolyte become as litter mates. She was dog.

GOODNIGHT SWEET PUP

Kathleen looked out across the fields. There were those two small dogs again. They were both a sort of reddish-brown and blended in well with the grasses, but she had been looking for them. She had seen them every evening now for a week. They reminded her of Fiona's wee dog Farley. What a clever little thing he had been. She wondered what had happened to him. Surely, he must be long dead. Would he have lived long on his own without Fiona? She didn't know why, but she had the sense that Fiona was no longer of this world. Certainly then, her dog was gone as well.

The two dogs had gone over the hill now and were heading towards another farm. They would have to be careful, or a farmer would shoot them for worrying the sheep. There were lambs at foot and farmers were extra vigilant when they first let the lambs out from the sheds.

She went back indoors to add some onions to the stew and check if the potatoes were soft yet. Ciarán and Brigid would be home soon. He took that child with him everywhere. Fair enough, after losing his wife he was that much more attached to his daughter. Kathleen remembered Fiona thrusting the child into her arms and saying, "tell him I'm gone. Tell him to stop looking. And care for her, Kathleen. Care for her as much as I would," and then she had ran off with that dog of hers. Kathleen calling after her, but not following. The child was hungry, and the wind had been fierce that day. She had taken the infant indoors and sat in Maire's cosy kitchen feeding the baby warm goat's milk Eventually, the child had stopped crying and gave herself over to sleep, in Kathleen's arms.

But that was years ago. Brigid was a strapping lass of six now, out with her father helping on the farm and with the horses. Kathleen had asked if Brigid had 'the touch,' with the horses but Ciarán had nearly bit her head off.

"Let's bloody well hope not!" The girl was tall and slim, with dark hair like Ciarán – maybe she was only her father's child and had nothing from her unfortunate mother.

It had worked out well for Kathleen. She had her brother running her small piece of land that had been her husband's and she had a child to care for. It was as cosy a home as she could hope for. Of course, she missed a husband, but one couldn't have everything, and Brigid was such a joy.

Then there was the bustle at the door and Ciarán came in, depositing his daughter on the threshold after removing her from his shoulders. They were full of the fresh air and boisterous with their achievements.

"Good day?" Kathleen asked, stirring the stew, and starting to pull out three bowls.

"Good enough. We've been out with John and the sheep, checking on the lambs. I've heard tell that there's two curs about worrying the flocks, but we didn't see any sign of them."

Kathleen nodded,

"I've heard the same but haven't seen them about either." She didn't want to tell him she'd been watching the dogs and thinking of another dog from years ago. It would only upset him. He was doing well now, concentrating on raising his daughter and leaving the past behind him.

"I'd hate to have to shoot a dog, but no one around here can spare a lamb," pulling out a chair he settled at the table.

"I hope you both washed outside."

"Aye, we did Aunty Kathleen. Look at my lovely clean hands," Brigid flourished her fingers at her aunt.

"Well sit down then and I'll serve the stew." Hot and full of potatoes, carrots and onions and a bit of mutton, the meal warmed and filled them.

"Is there any bread left?" Ciarán queried, knowing full well that Kathleen always had a loaf by, but he had no intention of getting up and looking.

"I'll get it Daddy," Brigid sprang from the chair with the unending energy of the young. She carried the loaf to the table and then took the butter and knife from the window where it was left to stay cool and lay it all in front of him. "Can I have a piece too?"

"Course you can darling. And I suppose you'd like some honey on it?" Kathleen went to the press and pulled out a jar of honey that she had gathered from her bees. Sighing, she thought of Fiona, what a terrible thing to have to miss out on, the raising of your own child. How odd that she was thinking so much of Fiona today. She had been close to the girl but had only known her for that brief time, yet she was forever indebted to Fiona for giving her Brigid. Of course, a baby would never survive with a mother on the run but all the same, it had been a sacrifice. Kathleen doubted that she could have done it. Well, it was done, and the child was well cared for and loved. It was all for the best.

When Brigid had finished her bread and honey, Kathleen leaned over and wiped the sticky face and hands.

"A great girl like you still as messy as a babby, now get on and start cleaning the dishes." Kathleen poured herself and Ciarán another cup of tea and asked him how the lambs were getting on.

"Oh, well enough. The twins are a bit weak though. I'll keep checking on them regularly. But we'll have enough to sell and then the money from the shearing at the end of summer."

There was a barking outside and they both looked up. Unlike most farmers, they kept no dogs. Ciarán had flatly refused; despite the extra work it had caused him. Dogs were too painful a memory. They both went to the door and looked out. Brigid dropped her dishcloth and ran to the door.

"Look Daddy, it's the two doggies there's been talk of. Do you think they're wild? Will they take the lambs?" Ciarán shrugged but went for his gun.

"I'll just follow them a bit."

"Can I come too?"

Kathleen interjected,

"Of course, not love! You could get hurt. Stay here home safe with your Auntie, your Daddy will take care of them."

The dogs had come quite close to the cottage now and stood staring at the gathering in the doorway.

"How strangely they look at us!" Kathleen suddenly felt a cold trickle of sweat down her back. "Lord, Ciarán, they must be mad. Don't let them come near!"

"Don't shoot them Daddy," Brigid rushed forward, "Maybe they are just hungry."

But then one of the dogs sprinted towards the girl, straight for her. Without thinking, Ciarán raised the rifle and shot it, just before it could leap on Brigid. The dog now lay before them, bleeding into the hard-packed ground in front of the doorway. And still, it looked at them. The second dog walked up and sniffed his fallen companion. Then he sat and stared at Ciarán. Ciarán stared back.

"Farley," he choked. The dog licked his hand and then turned and walked away.

"NOOOOOO!" Ciarán fell to his knees, pulling the dog he had shot to his chest. "NO, NO!" He held the dog to him, rocking back and forth, tears springing from his eyes as he howled. Both Brigid and Kathleen stood back in shock.

Kathleen touched his shoulder,

"Ciarán ..." but he shook her off.

"Daddy, Daddy, why are you crying??" The girl tried to grab hold of her father, but he pulled himself away in agony.

"What have I done?" he roared.

"What have you done Daddy?" Now the child was crying as well.

"I've killed your mother, *cailín*. I've killed your own mother."

In a deserted cabin, on a cliff overlooking the sea, an old dog found a heap of straw that may have once been a bed. He turned three times in the straw and curled into himself, his tail resting over his nose. He was tired. It was time now. In the distance there was the sound of goats bleating and then he heard, "Farley, where have you got yourself to now?" and so, he went to meet his mistress.

The End

Frances Gaudiano was born in Los Angeles, California but has lived in England, Ireland and Indonesia. Wherever she was, it was always with dogs. After obtaining a master's degree in Dramatic Literature, Frances began a career teaching and working in the theatre. However, she felt her dogs were not happy with this choice, so Frances re-trained as a veterinary nurse to better tend to the needs of her canine companions. She has been a registered veterinary nurse for many years, supplementing her income with the writing of veterinary articles and a textbook on Veterinary Dermatology. The Listener is her first published novel.

Printed in the UK
by
clocbookprint.co.uk

CPSIA information can be obtained
at www.ICGtesting.com
Printed in the USA
LVHW080751040122
707747LV00004B/112

9 781914 071423